P9-CMF-391

ALLEN
LEWIS

The New JUNIOR CLASSICS

VOLUME SIX • STORIES ABOUT BOYS AND GIRLS

The New JUNIOR CLASSICS

Edited by MABEL WILLIAMS *and* MARCIA DALPHIN

With Introduction by WILLIAM ALLAN NEILSON, *Former President of Smith College; Introduction to First Edition by* CHARLES W. ELIOT, *Former President of Harvard University*

DE LUXE EDITION

With Over One Thousand Illustrations in Color

VOLUME SIX

STORIES ABOUT BOYS AND GIRLS

P. F. COLLIER & SON CORPORATION

Acknowledgments of permissions given by authors and publishers for the use of copyright material appear in Volume X.

CR

MANUFACTURED IN THE UNITED STATES OF AMERICA

CONTENTS

(The sources of the stories in this volume will be found listed on page 488.)

SUSANNA'S AUCTION

FROM THE FRENCH

With Illustrations by

BOUTET DE MONVEL

I

SUSANNA

SUSANNA is no longer a little girl. She is now three years old. That is not so very old, but even at that age a girl may be headstrong and like to have her own way in everything.

And such is the case with Susanna. When she has made up her mind to do a thing she is not willing to give it up. She wishes to do just as she pleases. Susanna is very, very obstinate.

And Susanna has another fault. She will climb up on the furniture. Nobody can tell how many times she has fallen and pulled over the table and chair upon which she was climbing, and broken things.

And this very story is written to tell you the sad things that happened to Susanna through these two faults of hers—her obstinacy and her love of climbing.

Susanna tips the vase.

One day when she and her mamma were in the parlor together Susanna climbed upon a seat, as usual.

Now if she had been content to sit down upon the seat like a well-behaved little girl and look over the picture book which lay on the table beside her, nobody would have said a word.

But Susanna never looks at a picture book long at a time, no matter how pretty the pictures are. So she soon shut it up and pushed it one side.

Then she got up on her knees upon the seat and began to tip a vase of flowers that stood upon the table first over one side and then the other with both hands.

"Take care, Susanna!" said her mother. "You will break the vase."

But Susanna kept right on tipping the vase and smelling the flowers, without minding at all what her mother said.

"Susanna, do you not hear me?" said her mother, speaking again. "I tell you you will break the vase."

Then Susanna, without turning her head, or even looking at her mother, replied:

"If I break it I can pay for it."

II

PAPA APPEARS

"If I break it I can pay for it!" That was the rude and saucy thing that Susanna said; and just at that moment the door opened and in walked papa!

There stood Susanna looking sullenly down at the broken vase.

"What is the matter?" he asked. "Has Susanna been naughty? Has my little daughter been disobedient?"

But Susanna did not answer. She shut her lips tightly, and did not lift her eyes. So mamma had to tell the story.

Papa listened. When mamma had finished he spoke, and his voice sounded very harsh and cold, not a bit like the gentle tones in which he usually spoke to his little daughter.

"Very well," he said, "it is all very simple; Susanna said if she broke the vase she could pay for it. She has broken it, and now let her pay for it."

"Unless," he added, "she is really sorry for her disobedience, and will ask pardon, and will try to do better in the future."

He stopped and looked at Susanna. But she only shut her lips together tightly, and it was plain that she was not one bit sorry, and that she did not mean to speak.

Susanna is not sorry.

The precious purse.

Then mamma came up, oh, the poor mamma! who was grieved to see her little daughter so naughty, and so unhappy—for we all know we are never happy when we are naughty.

"Come, Susanna," she said gently. "Ask pardon of papa and mamma."

But Susanna was mute.

"Will you not ask pardon?" she said.

Not a word from Susanna.

"Ah, very well," said papa. "It seems that Susanna prefers to pay for the vase. Then let her go for her money."

Now Susanna kept her money in a pretty little velvet purse that her Uncle Felix had given her on her very last birthday. And in this purse was a gold piece, and some silver coins, all bright and new. She was fond of the purse and the money, too. And when papa said "Let her fetch the money," she could have cried right out loud had she not been so "stuffy."

But though she kept her lips pressed tightly together, when she went to get it, she could not help hugging it and talking to it and kissing it all the way back. But there was something worse than that loss in store for her.

III

THEY MAKE READY FOR THE AUCTION

Susanna came back, opened the purse, took out the gold piece and the silver coins, and handed them to mamma—in all, two dollars and fifty cents.

"But," said papa, "the vase cost much more than that. That vase is not worth less than twenty dollars! Did you know that, Susanna?"

Susanna did not answer.

"My dear," said papa gravely, turning to mamma, "what do you think about it all?"

"I think that Susanna is sorry for what she has done, and that she is all ready to say so, and to go to papa and kiss him. Is it not so, Susanna?"

Susanna dropped her head.

"Come, my little daughter," said mamma, "be a good girl; give me your hand, and we will go and ask pardon of papa."

Susanna put both her hands behind her back.

"Susanna!" said mamma.

"Let her alone, my dear," said papa. "Since she is determined not to ask pardon, and her two dollars and a half is not enough to pay for the vase, we must sell what things belong to her. Let us see! What has she got?"

The money.

"There are her gowns, her pretty hat, her"—Mamma was going to say more, but papa interrupted her.

"I beg your pardon," he said, "but a little girl's clothes belong to her parents. They only provide them for her so that she will not have to go without."

Here Susanna made up a face. But papa went on. "She has really nothing of her own except her toys and her dolls. We must sell those. We will sell them at auction," he added.

"But where?" asked mamma.

"Right here, tomorrow," said papa. "We will invite all the cousins, boys and girls, to come and pass tomorrow afternoon with us. Then we shall have plenty of buyers."

The next day at two o'clock they arrived — all the boy and girl cousins, and all the uncles and aunts. There were a great many, for the family was a large one. Some little friends were also invited. The parlor where the auction was to be held was crowded. All the heavy pieces of furniture were taken out, and five rows of chairs were set for the children. The elder people stood behind them, and in the dining room.

With hands behind her.

And Susanna? What did she say to all this preparation? Not a word! She remained sullen. Once during the night mamma thought she heard a stifled sob or two from the little bed which stood near her own; and she asked Susanna if she were crying.

"No, mamma," said Susanna. "I am wiping my nose."

There was nothing then but to go on with the auction. And this was done.

IV

THE AUCTION BEGINS

All Susanna's dolls and toys were brought out and arranged upon the table, and the auction began.

Uncle George was the auctioneer. Now Uncle George is usually the jolliest of uncles. He knows how to play all sorts of games and can tell the most delightful stories. But on this occasion he was grave. He did not even smile. He walked slowly up the steps and in behind the table. He had a small ivory hammer in his hand. He looked around upon the boys and girls with a sad and gloomy air.

Uncle Julius, who has a loud voice, took his place beside Uncle George to help him. "Gentlemen," he said—an auctioneer never addresses the ladies—"gentlemen, we will open the sale with this doll. It is dressed and has joints; its hair is frizzed and it has a china head and blue enamel eyes. Pass it on, please," and he handed it down to the buyers to examine. There was a murmur of delight among the girls as they passed it from one to another.

"Oh! what a sweet china head," whispered Marie to Helen.

"What am I offered for it?" asked Uncle Julius.

No one answered.

"Such dolls are certainly worth five cents," said Uncle George.

There was a stir among the buyers.

"Why don't you bid?" asked Andrew of his little sister Marie. "Call out three cents."

"Three cents!" said little Marie.

"I beg your pardon!" interrupted Uncle George. "But this is a real sale. I must warn you that I can have no joking. I said that such dolls were worth five cents. At auctions all articles bring more than in the shops. The only way to do is to make a higher bid—say six cents, seven cents, eight cents."

"Eight cents!" shouted Eliza very loud.

"That's right," said Uncle George. "I see that you understand, Eliza. Go on!"

"Ten cents!" shouted Helen, making a bid for Marie.

The auction.

Eliza stood up, trembling with eagerness, and cried: "Eleven cents!"

Helen, too, sprang up from her chair, and the struggle began.

"Twelve cents!" "Thirteen cents!" "Fourteen!" "Fifteen!"

Then there was a dead silence. Eliza sat down; she had to give up. She had got to the end of her money.

"Sixteen cents! I am offered sixteen cents for this fine china-headed doll. Shall I not have another bid? Shall I not have seventeen cents?" asked Uncle George.

He waited an instant, but no one spoke. Then he brought his ivory hammer down upon the table. "The doll belongs to Miss Helen, that is—I believe—to the little Marie," he said. And it was handed to Marie.

After that the rest of the dolls were sold, and then came toys of all kinds. For Susanna had had many presents from her uncles and aunts as well as from the friends of her papa and mamma. And those kind friends had never suspected that some day their gifts would have to be sold at public auction, just on account of Susanna's obstinacy.

V

THE SALE CONTINUES

It would take too much space to tell how toy after toy was sold, in order that Susanna's possessions might pay for the broken vase.

But some things must not be passed by.

You remember the struggle between Eliza and little Marie over the fine doll with a china head and blue enamel eyes? Before the sale of the dolls was over they had another.

This time it was a sleeping doll that they both wanted, that is, a doll that shuts its eyes and goes to sleep when laid in the bed. But Marie outbid Eliza a second time and the sleeping doll was knocked off to her.

But when it was handed to her by Uncle Julius she found that it would not go to sleep. It was out of order, and it lay flat with its eyes wide open. Then Marie, being a small girl only three years old, began to cry.

Eugene was also very young, and when he saw his dear little cousin crying he, too, began to cry out of sympathy. And the two made such a disturbance the auction had to stop till Marie was comforted.

When the animals were put up for sale the boys began to bid, and soon a battle was raging between Andrew and Leopold over an elephant with big ears. They bid very fast, one over the other, and the elephant seemed likely to be sold at a high price, when Leopold suddenly thought to remark that his left ear was torn. He said this so loud that Andrew heard him. He was going to outbid Leopold, but when he heard him say that, he stopped an instant to examine the elephant. While he was looking, Uncle Julius, hearing no one bid, knocked it off to the crafty Leopold.

Mention must be made, too, of a lovely sheep, which had real wool. It wore a blue ribbon around its neck, and went on wheels and could bleat. There was much lively bidding for this, and great excitement, as Uncle Julius caused it to bleat after every bid, and Leopold paid the last cent in his purse to secure it.

Susanna is indifferent.

There was a cow which had a great success and brought a good price. She gave milk and could bellow. A general scrimmage took place over this cow, for everybody wanted her. She was finally knocked off to Helen for forty cents. Leopold, who had farming tastes, was quite wretched because he could not even bid upon her, and resolved to make a private trade with Helen, and exchange his elephant for her.

"But where was Susanna during all this time?" "How did she appear while her auction was going on?" "Was she sorry to see her dolls and cows and sheep and elephants sold?" "Did she not run to papa and ask pardon and beg him to stop it?" I hear these questions from the readers.

Alas, no!

She looked on, at first, with an air of indifference.

She did not seem to care even when Uncle Julius milked her cow to show that it really did give milk. During the battle between Andrew and Leopold over the big-eared elephant, she showed no interest. Soon after that she became sullen and put her chin down into her collar and set the toe of one boot over the other and was "the very picture of obstinacy."

But the story is not yet finished.

VI

SUSANNA YIELDS

Everything was sold. Uncle Eugene had just bought the last—a whole lot of toys for three cents, to give to the poor children in that part of the city—when Susanna's nurse discovered another doll tucked away in a corner of the closet where Susanna's playthings were kept. She brought her out and gave her to Uncle Julius.

It must be owned that she was a very shabby doll. She had, however, seen better days. She had been given to Susanna by her friend Joseph. And Susanna had been so much pleased with her—for she was then a beautiful creature—that she had named her Josephine as a compliment to the giver.

But of late Susanna had been so taken up with her other children that she had allowed poor Josephine to be knocked about, until she had lost first an arm, then a leg, then an eye, and at last more than half her hair. Yes, she was a very shabby child—a poor useless invalid. But, shabby as she was, she must be sold with the rest of the family.

Uncle Julius held her up that all might see her, and said, "We will now sell a sick doll, which"—

"Pardon, Papa! Pardon, Mamma!"

But his sentence was never finished. Susanna, struck with shame and sorrow at the thought of having her sick child sold, threw herself upon Uncle Julius and tried to seize hold of Josephine, crying out:

"No! no! it is Josephine! I can't have Josephine sold!"

Then came a great flood of tears. As her papa and mamma hastened to her, she cried again: "Pardon, papa! Pardon, mamma! It is Josephine! I can't have Josephine sold. Pardon! pardon!"

The auctioneer arose from his chair with dignity. "Do you ask pardon, Miss?" he said.

"Yes. I want Josephine," was the answer.

"That is sufficient," said Uncle George. "The auction is over. Uncle Julius, return Josephine to her mother."

Uncle Julius did so, and Susanna hugged her and covered her with kisses. And at the same time her papa and mamma kissed Susanna, who promised to be a good child in the future.

"And so I suppose they gave back to her all her playthings," somebody says. By no means. You forget that Uncle George said the sale was a real one. So, of course, the things were really sold, and could not be taken back.

But to keep Susanna in mind of her promise to be a good child, her papa and mamma bought a set of bedroom furniture for Josephine. Still, although her little mother now loves her dearly, and with constancy, Josephine can never regain the leg and arm and eye which she has lost. But Susanna tells her that if she is obedient her hair will grow again.

POLLY PATCHWORK

By RACHEL FIELD

With Illustrations by the Author

THIS happened a long time ago when your great-grandmothers were little girls, and you can believe it or not, as you think best. After all, it is only a story with no feelings to get hurt if people don't happen to like it.

• • •

Well, there was once a little girl named Polly who lived with her grandmother in a cottage on the edge of Cranberry Common, which lies in a hollow between Tumbledown Mountain and the sea. It was the smallest house for miles about and rather queer as to chimney and shutters, but it had a twisted thorn tree growing beside it and a lilac bush by the door, and that is far more important, especially in spring. It had a garden, too, so full of orange marigolds that there was never room for anything else to come up. For years the neighbors had urged Polly's grandmother to grow more useful things, like potatoes and carrots and cabbages, to put by for the winter. She agreed with them perfectly and planted all the seeds they brought her, and still nothing but the orange marigolds ever came up. It seemed as if the soil just wouldn't have anything to do with useful seeds. So after a while the neighbors gave up advising, and Polly and her grandmother were delighted, for they much preferred marigolds.

But now marigold time was past and even the thorn tree was losing its red berries. Every morning when Polly went out to pick up fir cones for their fire the ground would be white with hoar frost, and wild geese honking overhead as they flew south in great triangular-shaped companies.

"That means winter is nearly here," said the grandmother as she measured out their johnnycake meal in a big yellow bowl, "and you will need a new dress to keep you warm."

She sighed as she said it, for she was thinking how soon snow would be all round the doorstep and the wind blowing up like a cracking whip from the sea, and that when they had bought enough molasses and johnnycake meal to last all winter there would be very few coppers left in the old china pitcher on the mantelpiece—not nearly enough to buy a new dress for Polly, though, to be sure, it did n't take so many yards to go round her.

Now, Polly knew why her grandmother had sighed, and when the sun was warm overhead and all the crickets making a great to-do in the brown grass at her feet she gathered the roundest and reddest thornberries she could find under the old tree. Then she begged a needle and thread of her grandmother and strung them into a necklace for herself. They looked so shiny and scarlet that she felt sure they would keep her warm all winter, but her grandmother knew better, and she shook her head when Polly set off for school in her cotton dress.

"Red beads are all very fine," said she, "but they won't keep the wind out like woolen. We must see what we can find in the attic."

So she climbed up under the eaves to rummage in an old pine chest filled with the queerest odds and ends you ever saw. There were an old guitar with faded yellow ribbons and only one string; a high silk hat with a crumple in the middle; a parasol without any handle; one tarnished silver shoe buckle; a pair of lace mitts, and at the very bottom a patchwork quilt made out of gay squares sewed together in a colored jumble of red and green and blue and yellow, with figures and flowers and plaids and stripes of every sort besides.

"The very thing!" said the grandmother, holding it up to the light. "Not a hole in it, and we have two comforters to sleep under, so this will do nicely for Polly!"

She carried it down by the fire and set to work with scissors and thimble and needle and thread. First she spread the quilt out smooth and flat, and then she laid one of Polly's old dresses down on it and cut all round the edges, being careful to allow for growing—both sideways and endways. Then she sat down to work with all her might. She sewed so hard that her cheeks grew almost as red as the thornberries outside the window, and her needle went click, click, click against her thimble like a little clock ticking very fast. All the time she sewed she rocked back and forth and sang a snatch of tune over and over. Her own grandmother had taught it to her long ago, and it went something like this:

Fold and snip, and snip and fold,
Some are young and some are old.

In and out, and out and in,
Some will dance and some will spin.

Sew and stitch, and stitch and sew,
Some will come and some will go.

Knot and twist, and twist and knot,
Some will wed and some will not.

Polly could hear her grandmother singing this when she turned in at the gate after school, and she knew something important must be going on for her grandmother sang it only on special occasions. But when Polly opened the door and saw the reason she felt like singing a very different sort of tune. Still, her grandmother seemed so pleased with the patchwork dress that Polly hadn't the heart to tell her she would rather be cold than wear it.

"The very thing!" said the grandmother.

"It's a mercy I found it," her grandmother told her. "They call it the crazy-quilt pattern, and all the bits are real silk and as good as when my Great-aunt Mehitabel pieced it together. I can remember seeing her make it when I was a little girl no bigger than you. Come here and let me try it on."

Now, Polly did not like the sound of the name any more than she liked the looks of it, but she stood as still as she could to have it fitted. This was not so easy to do. Her grandmother might as well have tried to fit the sails of a little ship about her, so stiff and billowing did it stand out in every direction.

"Well, I give up!" said she at last when she saw that she could not make it fall in soft folds, "but it will flatten down after you've worn it awhile. The colors are so nice and bright it won't matter if it does balloon out a little."

Polly thought it would matter very much to her, and she wished the colors would all fade, for even the dingiest brown would be better than a dress made out of a patchwork quilt.

But presently she went out to bring in another basketful of cones and there was a little thread of a new moon just showing above the fir tops, and the sky still pink with sunset, and all the crickets singing and the tree-toads ringing their little bells to keep the frost away, so she could not help feeling better about it. And she looked over her left shoulder and wished a wish on the little new moon.

"If you please, Moon," she said, "I should like to win the spelling match on Friday."

Now that was asking a good deal of the Moon, and Polly knew it. Almost any of the other boys and girls at school were better at spelling than she. Still, she thought it would do no harm to have the Moon on her side, too!

"I mean to finish this dress for you to wear to school Friday afternoon," her grandmother told her as they sat over their supper. "It's the last day of the fall term and I hear they are having a spelling match, with all the school committee coming."

"Yes," said Polly, "and a solid silver medal for the one who wins it."

"Well, well," said her grandmother, "then we must certainly have this done in time. I wouldn't want you to stand up there before them all in your old one."

And she began to stitch faster than ever. Her needle flashed in and out like a firefly.

"She may not be able to get it done by day after tomorrow,"

thought Polly. "There are a great many stitches still to sew."

So she comforted herself with that thought all the evening, and her grandmother had no idea what was going on inside her head as they sat side by side with the fire snapping and the wind in the old thorn tree just outside. Every now and again her grandmother would point out some special patch that she remembered.

There was a red one with figures of little black boys dancing horn-pipes on it. That had been a silk handkerchief once, her grandmother told her, and had belonged to a Sea Captain who had given it to her Great-aunt Mehitabel when she was a little girl. Polly's grandmother could remember hearing how he kept a parrot who could whistle "Yankee Doodle" and say: "Trim your sails and face the music," as plain as could be.

Then there was another—a yellow one, as bright as a buttercup—that her grandmother said Great-aunt Mehitabel had worn herself the time she danced with General Lafayette.

"Yes," the grandmother told her, "she danced the minuet with him right before the Governor and all the rest, and she never missed a step or forgot to keep her toes turned out."

But the prettiest patch of all was a very small white one with forget-me-nots and moss rosebuds scattered over it. And that, Polly's grand-mother told her, had come all the way from Paris and was a bit from the best party sash of cousin Mariana Gay who lived long ago down South.

"They say she was as pretty as her name," the grandmother said, smoothing the flowers with her finger. "She had eyes as blue as these forget-me-nots and cheeks as pink as the roses. That's her guitar in the chest up attic. She used to sit on her balcony, watching the boats go up and down the Mississippi River, and play and sing 'Listen to the Mock-ing Bird.' "

But Polly's mind was all on next Friday and what she should do if she had to wear a patchwork dress to the spelling match, so that she paid little attention to all this. However, she had queer dreams that night—very queer ones indeed. She dreamed that cousin Mariana Gay was saying "Trim your sails and face the music" to General Lafayette, and that Great-aunt Mehitabel was doing a hornpipe with the Sea Captain. It was all mixed up.

Friday came along at last, and a snapping cold day it was, with the wind blowing the last of the thornberries off the old tree. Polly's grandmother was still sewing away on the patchwork dress when Polly started off for school, but when she came back at noon there it was finished—buttons and all.

"I said I'd have it ready for you to wear this afternoon if my thimble finger dropped right off doing it!" her grandmother said, and her eyes were as bright as could be behind their spectacles.

And Polly saw how pleased she was and how many hundreds of stitches she had sewed into it, so there was nothing for her to do but put it on and set off for school again.

She walked very slowly between the spindly fir trees on the old wood road, for she had no wish to reach the yellow schoolhouse that stood at the crossroads. Every step of the way her feet dragged more and more.

Clang! clang! went the schoolhouse bell. That meant it was nearly time for them all to gather. Polly heard it, and never had it sounded so loud and fearsome to her before. She stood still at the edge of the wood road and listened. Just for a minute she thought she would turn back. She could stay on the Common all the afternoon, and her grandmother would never know she hadn't been at school. But she happened to look down and see the red patch, halfway up her skirt, with the black boys dancing their hornpipe on it as cheerfully as could be. And it seemed to her she could hear the Sea Captain's parrot saying to her quite distinctly: "Trim your sails and face the music." So she right-about-faced and walked straight up the steps and into the schoolroom. But she had hardly set one foot over the threshold before one of the boys spied her and piped up:

> "Polly Patchwork, now it's cool,
> Wears a crazy quilt to school.
> Thinks she'll win the spelling match
> In her dress of patch, patch, patch!"

And all the rest joined in as she went to her seat in the front row. It was rather hard to remember the advice of the Sea Captain's parrot, but she did the best she could.

Polly put on the patchwork dress.

They did not dare to go on singing the song after the teacher came with the school committee, who sat, along with several mothers, in chairs against the wall. The oldest of the school committee, the one with a gray beard and spectacles, made a speech and showed them the silver medal in its little box all lined with pink cotton, and Polly thought it looked as round and shining as the full moon, and the pink cotton that wrapped it like sunset clouds as she had often seen them, and she wished with all her heart it might belong to her.

Now it was time for all the scholars to line up on the platform—a girl and a boy, a girl and a boy, with the oldest ones at the head and the middle-sized ones in the middle and the smallest ones at the foot. Polly was quite near the bottom, but it would not have made any particular difference where she happened to be: everyone would have stared at her just as hard, for such a queer, gay kind of a dress as hers had never been seen before and probably never will be again. She could hear the laughter and whisperings and nudgings about her on every side, and even the visitors in their chairs at the back of the room leaned forward to peer and ask each other what child it was who cut such a strange figure. Polly saw and heard all this, and her cheeks grew very red as she stood hanging her head and keeping her eyes on a crack in the floor. The little boys on either side of her snickered because her skirts billowed out so stiffly about her. She tried to press them closer with both hands, and as she did so she looked right down on the yellow patch. Then suddenly she remembered all about Great-aunt Mehitabel and how her grandmother had said she was n't afraid when she danced the minuet with General Lafayette, or, at any rate, if she had been, she had n't missed a single step or forgotten to keep her toes turned out. Polly did n't know one step of the minuet, but she did know how to turn out her toes as well as anybody. So she did, right then and there, and she folded her hands in front of her and held her head up instead of down. It was n't nearly so bad after that, for it makes a great difference in people's feelings if only they have their toes and their heads fixed right!

And then the spelling match began, and all the scholars were too busy trying to get the right number of letters in the right places, and the school committee and the visitors too busy listening to make sure that they did, to pay so much attention to Polly and the patchwork dress. First they began with little easy words like *"such"* and *"sure"* and *"school"* where there would only be one letter to make trouble. Then they began to grow harder and harder till it was *"receive"* and *"believe"* and *"neighbor,"* and it seemed as if the *ie's* and *ei's* got mixed up in the strangest ways.

Now the line on the platform was not nearly so long as it had been. Every time a boy or girl spelled a word wrong, the teacher would shake her head and someone would go to a seat with all hopes of the medal gone, and the one next in line would move up to fill the empty place. Polly had been very lucky so far. All the words that came her way had been those she knew how to spell—even *"scissors,"* which is not such an easy one after all with *c's* and *s's* what they are. She gave a deep sigh when that was past, but she took no chances with her toes and the tilt of her head, for she had learned from Great-aunt Mehitabel what a difference they can make.

The spelling match began.

Only six were left standing on the platform now—four girls and two boys. And Polly was still in the line. It went like a flight of steps leading from tall Mary Jane Peters with her pigtails and plaid dress and Jimmie Willis in his square-toed boots down to Polly at the foot looking very small and solemn, at least as much of her as showed above and below the patchwork dress which stood out more stiffly than ever about her.

There was a long pause as the man with the gray beard who gave out the words turned over a new page in the speller and cleared his throat. Everyone knew from the silence and the way he looked that something out of the ordinary was coming.

"Spell 'Mississippi'," he said, and he fixed his eyes on Mary Jane Peters.

"M," began Mary Jane, and she twisted the top button of her dress nearly off while she tried to remember the way all the *s's* and *i's* and *p's* ought to go, *"i——"* then she looked up at the ceiling but that did n't seem to help any; *"ss—i-s."* She stopped short, and anybody could see she had n't an idea what came next.

"You try, Jimmie," the teacher said.

Mary Jane Peters was going down to her seat, looking as if she wanted to cry.

Jimmie went very carefully and slowly. He got past the first and second *s's* and most of the *i's,* but when it came to the *p's* he was all at sea.

Now the girl next to him was trying it, but she was no better. It began to seem as if the whole schoolroom were full of *i's* and *s's* and *p's* that had got out of their right places.

Now there were two ahead of Polly; now just one; now she was standing on the platform all alone. She clasped her hands tight in front of her and tried to think how the letters ought to go, but she had n't an idea, really. Just then a wonderful thing happened. She looked down and there between her fingers she could see the white square with the forget-me-nots and moss rosebuds, and she pressed her hands tight together and said under her breath:

"Oh, please, cousin Mariana Gay, please help me to spell it right!"

And whether you believe it or not, Polly could see her as plain as plain sitting on the balcony playing her guitar, and the boats going up and down the river with the name that was so hard to spell. It was perfectly still in the schoolroom, so still that Polly could hear the wind in the fir trees outside, but she could also hear cousin Mariana Gay saying quite clearly and pleasantly:

"M-I-double S-I-double S-I-double P-I."

Polly repeated every letter after her as she said them, while all the scholars leaned forward on their benches, holding their breath to make sure she had every one right.

"Thank you, cousin Mariana Gay," she said softly when she got to the end.

But no one heard her, there was such a clapping of hands and stamping of feet all over the schoolroom.

Then the school committee all shook hands with her, and the teacher took the medal out of its pink cotton and hung it on a ribbon round Polly's neck, with all the boys and girls crowding round to see.

And the teacher said she had never suspected that Polly was such a good speller and the school committee said how surprised they were that such a little girl could spell such a long word.

But Polly's grandmother didn't seem surprised at all when Polly came home with the medal and told her all that had happened. She only nodded her head and said:

"What did I tell you? It isn't everybody can have an experienced dress like yours to give them advice when they need it! Run out, now, and bring in another basketful of cones to start the fire for supper."

THE MISS BANNISTERS' BROTHER

By E. V. LUCAS

Illustrations by WARREN CHAPPELL

I

CHRISTINA'S father was as good as his word—the doll came, by post, in a long wooden box, only three days after he had left for Paris. All the best dolls come from Paris, but you have to call them "poupées" there when you ask the young ladies in the shops for them.

Christina had been in the garden ever since she got up, waiting for the postman—there was a little gap in the trees where you could see him coming up the road—and she and Roy had run to meet him across the hay-field directly they spied him in the distance. Running across the hay-field was forbidden until after hay-making; but when a doll is expected from Paris . . . !

Christina's father was better than his word, for it was the most beautiful doll ever made, with a whole wardrobe of clothes, too.

Also a tiny tortoise-shell comb and a powder puff. Also an extra pair of bronzed boots. Her eyes opened and shut, and even her eyebrows were real hair. This, as you know, is unusual in dolls, their hair, as a rule, being made of other materials, and far too yellow, and their eyebrows being just paint. "She shall be called Diana," said Christina, who had always loved the name from afar.

Christina took Diana to her mother at once, Roy running behind her with the box and the brown paper and the string and the wardrobe, and Chrissie calling back every minute, "Don't drop the powder puff, whatever you do!" "Hold tight to the hand-glass!" and such things.

"But it's splendid!" Mrs. Tiverton said. "There isn't a better doll in the world; only, Chrissie dear, be very careful with it. I don't know but that father would have done better to have got something stronger —this is so very fragile. I think, perhaps you had better have it only indoors. Yes, that's the best way; after today you must play with Diana only indoors."

It was thus that Diana came to Mapleton.

How Christina loved her that first day! She carried her everywhere and showed her everything—all over the house, right into the attic; all over the garden, right into the little black stove-place under the greenhouse where Pedder, the gardener, read last Sunday's paper over his lunch; into the village, to the general shop, to introduce her to the postmistress, who lived behind a brass railing in the odor of bacon and calico; into the stables, to kiss Lord Roberts, the old white horse. Jim, who groomed the General, was the only person who did not admire the doll properly, but how could you expect a nice feeling from a boy who sets dogs on rats?

II

It was two or three days after this that Roy went down to the river to fish. He had to go alone, because Christina wanted to play with Diana in the nursery; but not more than half an hour had passed when he heard feet swishing through the long grass behind him, and, looking up, there was Christina. Now, as Christina had refused so bluntly to have anything to do with his fishing, Roy was surprised to see her, but more surprised still to see that Diana had come, too.

"Why, did mother say you might bring Diana?" he asked.

"No," said Christina, rather sulkily, "but I didn't think she'd mind. Besides, she's gone to the village, and I couldn't ask her."

Roy looked troubled: his mother did not often make rules to interfere with their play, and when she did she liked to be obeyed. She had certainly forbidden Christina to take Diana out of the house. He did not say anything. Christina sat down and began to play. She was not really at all happy, because she knew it was wrong of her to have disobeyed, and she was really a very good girl. Roy went on fishing.

"Oh, do do something else," Christina cried pettishly, after a few minutes. "It's so cold sitting here waiting for you to catch stupid fish that never come. Let's go to the cave." The cave was an old disused lime-kiln, where robbers might easily have lived.

"All right," Roy said.

"I'll get there first," Christina called out, beginning to run.

"Bah!" said Roy and ran after. They had raced for a hundred yards, when, with a cry, Christina fell. Roy, who was still some distance behind, having had to pack up his rod, hastened to Christina's side. He found that she had scrambled to her knees, and was looking anxiously into Diana's face.

"Oh, Roy," she wailed, "her eyes have gone!"

It was too true. Diana, lately so radiantly observant, now turned to the world the blankest of empty sockets. Roy took her poor head in his hand and shook it. A melancholy rattle told that a pair of once serviceable blue eyes were now at large. Christina sank on the grass in an agony of grief—due partly, also, to the knowledge that if she had not been naughty this would never have happened. Roy stood by, feeling hardly less unhappy. After a while he took her arm. "Come along," he said, "let's see if Jim can mend her."

"Jim!" Christina cried in a fury, shaking off his hand.

"But come along, anyway," Roy said.

Christina continued sobbing. After a while she moved to rise, but suddenly fell back again. Her sobbing as suddenly ceased. "Roy!" she exclaimed fearfully, "I can't walk."

Christina had sprained her ankle.

Roy ran to the house as fast as he could to find help, and very soon old Pedder, the gardener, and Jim were carrying Christina between them, with mother, who had just come back, and nurse walking by her side. Christina was put to bed at once and her foot wrapped in bandages, but she cried almost incessantly, no matter how often she was assured that she was forgiven. "Her sobs," the cook said, coming downstairs after her twentieth visit to the nursery, "her sobs are that heart-rending I could n't stand it; and all the while she asks for that blessed doll, which its eyes is rattling in its head like marbles through falling on the ground, and Master Roy and Jim's trying to catch them with a skewer."

Cook was quite right. Roy and Jim, with Diana between them, were seated in the harness-room, probing tenderly the depths of that poor Parisienne's skull. A housemaid was looking on without enthusiasm. "You won't do it," she said every now and then; "you can't mend dolls' eyes with skewers. No one can. It's impossible. The King himself could n't. The Primest Minister could n't. No," she went on, "no one could do it. No one but the Miss Bannisters' Brother near where I live at Dormstaple. He could. You ought to take it to him. He'd mend it in a jiffy—there's nothing he can't do in that way."

Roy said nothing, but went on prodding and probing. At last he gave up in despair. "All right, I'll take it to the Miss Bannisters'

Brother," he said. "Dormstaple's only six miles." But a sudden swoop from a figure in the doorway interrupted his bold plan.

"You'll do nothing of the kind," cried nurse, seizing the doll, "with that angel upstairs crying for it every minute, and the doctor saying she's in a high fever with lying on the wet grass"; and with a swirl of white skirts and apron, nurse and Diana were gone.

Roy put his hands in his pockets and wandered moodily into the garden. The world seemed to have no sun in it any more.

III

The next day Christina was really ill. It was not only the ankle, but she had caught a chill, the doctor said, and they must be very careful with her. Roy went about with a sad and sadder face, for Christina was his only playmate, and he loved her more than anything else; besides, there was now no one to bowl to him, and, also, it seemed so silly not to be able to mend a doll's eyes. He moped in and out of the house all the morning, and was continually being sent away from Christina's door, because she was too ill to bear anyone in the room except nurse. She was wandering in her mind, nurse said, and kept on saying that she had blinded her doll, and crying to have its eyes made right again; but she would not let a hand be laid upon her, so that to have Diana mended seemed impossible. Nurse cried too as she said it, and Roy joined with her. He could not remember ever having been so miserable.

The doctor looked very grave when he was going away. "That doll ought to be put right," he said to Mrs. Tiverton. "She 's a sensitive little thing, evidently, and this feeling of disobeying you and treating her father's present lightly is doing her a lot of harm, apart altogether from the chill and the sprain. If we could get those eyes in again she'd be better in no time, I believe."

Roy and his mother heard this with a sinking heart, for they knew that Christina's arms locked Diana to her side almost as if they were bars of iron.

"Anyway," the doctor said, "I've left some medicine that ought to give her some sleep, and I shall come again this afternoon." So saying, the doctor touched up his horse, and Mrs. Tiverton walked into the house again.

Roy stood still pondering.

Suddenly his mind was made up, and he set off for the high road at a good swinging pace. At the gate he passed Jim. "If they want to know where I am," he called, "say I've gone to Dormstaple, to the Miss Bannisters' Brother."

IV

Miss Sarah Bannister and Miss Selina Bannister had lived in Dormstaple as long almost as anyone could remember, although they were by no means old. They had the red house with white windows, the kind of house which one can see only in old English market towns. There was a gravel drive before it, in the shape of a banana, the carriages going in at one end and out at the other, stopping at the front doorsteps in the middle. A china cockatoo hung in the window. The door knocker was of the brightest brass; it was a pleasure to knock it.

Behind the house was a very large garden, with a cedar in the midst; and a very soft lawn on which the same birds settled every morning in the winter for the breakfast that the Miss Bannisters provided. The cedar and the other trees had cigar boxes nailed to them, for tits or wrens to build in, and half cocoanuts and lumps of fat were always hung just outside the windows. In September, button mushrooms grew on the lawn—enough for breakfast every morning. At one side of the house was the stable and coach-house, on the other side a billiard room, now used as a workshop. And his workshop brings us to the Miss Bannisters' Brother.

The Miss Bannisters' Brother was an invalid, and he was also what is called an eccentric. "Eccentric, that's what he is," Mr. Stallabrass, who kept the King's Arms, had said, and there could be no doubt of it after that. This meant that he wore rather shabby clothes, and took no interest in the town, and was rarely seen outside the house or the garden.

Rumor said, however, that he was very clever with his hands, and could make anything. What was the matter with the Miss Bannisters' Brother no one seemed to know, but it gradually kept him more and more indoors.

No one ever spoke of him as Mr. Bannister; they always said the Miss Bannisters' Brother. If you could see the Miss Bannisters, especially Miss Selina, you would understand this; but although they had deep, gruff voices, they were really very kind.

As time went on, and the Miss Bannisters' Brother did not seem to grow any better, or to be likely to take up his gardening and his pigeons, again, the Miss Bannisters had racked their brains to think of some employment for him other than reading, which is not good for anyone all day long. One evening, some years before this story, while the three were at tea, Miss Selina cried suddenly, "I have it!"—so suddenly, indeed, that Miss Sarah spilt her cup, and her brother took three lumps of sugar instead of two.

"Have what?" they both exclaimed.

"Why," she said, "I was talking today with Mrs. Boniface, and she was saying how nice it would be if there were someone in the town who could mend toys—poor Miss Piper at the Bazaar being so useless, and all the carpenters understanding nothing but making bookshelves and cucumber frames, and London being so far away—and I said 'Yes,' never thinking of Theodore here. And, of course, it's the very thing for him."

"Of course," said Miss Sarah. "He could take the old billiard room."

"And have a gas stove put in it," said Miss Selina.

"An oil stove," said Miss Sarah; "it's more economical."

"A gas stove," said Miss Selina; "it's more trustworthy."

"And put up a bench," said Miss Sarah.

"And some cocoanut matting on the floor," said Miss Selina.

"Linoleum," said Miss Sarah; "it's cheaper."

"Cocoanut matting," said Miss Selina; "it's better and warmer for his feet."

"And we could call it the Dolls' Hospital," said Miss Sarah.

"Infirmary," said Miss Selina.

"I prefer Hospital," said Miss Sarah.

"Infirmary," said Miss Selina. "Dr. Bannister, house surgeon, attends daily from ten till one."

"It would be the prettiest and kindliest occupation," said Miss Sarah, "as well as a useful one."

"That's the whole point of it," said Miss Selina.

And that is how—five or six years ago—the Miss Bannisters' Brother came to open the Dolls' Infirmary. But he did not stop short at mending dolls. He mended all kinds of other things, too; he advised on the length of tails for kites; he built ships; he had even made fireworks.

V

Roy walked into Dormstaple at about one o'clock, very tired and hot and dusty and hungry. With the exception of a lift for a mile and a half in the baker's cart, he had had to walk or run all the way. A little later, after asking his way more than once, he stood on the doorstep of the Miss Bannisters' house. The door was opened by old Eliza, and as the flavor of roast fowl rushed out, Roy knew how hungry he was. "I want to see the Miss Bannisters' Brother," he said, "please."

"You're too late," was the answer, "and it's the wrong door. Come tomorrow morning, and go to the Hinfirmary. Mr. Theodore never sees children in the afternoon."

"Oh, but I must," Roy almost sobbed.

"Chut, chut!" said old Eliza, "little boys should n't say must."

"But when they must, what else is there for them to say?" Roy asked.

"Chut, chut!" said old Eliza again. "That's himperent! Now run away, and come tomorrow morning."

This was too much for Roy. He covered his face with his hands, and really and truly cried—a thing he would scorn to do on his own account.

While he stood there in this distress a hand was placed on his arm, and he was drawn gently into the house. He heard the door shut behind him. The hand then guided him along passages into a great room, and there he was liberated. Roy looked round; it was the most fascinating room he had ever seen. There was a long bench at the window with a comfortable chair before it, and on the bench were hammers and chisels and all kinds of tools. A ship nearly finished lay in one place, a clock-work steamer in another, a pair of rails wound about the floor on the cocoanut matting—in and out like a snake—on which a toy train probably ran, and here and there were signals. On the shelves were colored papers, bottles, boxes, and wire. In one corner was a huge kite, as high as a man, with a great face painted on it. Several dolls, more or less broken, lay on the table.

All this he saw in a moment. Then he looked at the owner of the

Roy told him everything, right from the first.

hand, who had been standing beside him all the while with an amused expression on his delicate, kind face. Roy knew in an instant it was the Miss Bannisters' Brother.

"Well," said the Miss Bannisters' Brother, "so when one must, one must?"

"Yes," Roy said, half timidly.

"Quite right, too," said the Miss Bannisters' Brother. " 'Must' is a very good word, if one has the character to back it up. And now tell me, quickly, what is the trouble. Something very small, I should think, or you wouldn't be able to carry it in your pocket."

"It's not in my pocket," Roy said, "it's not here at all. I want—I want a lesson."

"A lesson?" the Miss Bannisters' Brother asked in surprise.

"Yes, in eye-mending. When eyes fall inside and rattle, you know."

The Miss Bannisters' Brother sat down and took Roy between his knees. There was something about this little dusty, nervous boy that his clients (often tearful enough) had never displayed before, and he wished to understand it. "Now tell me all about it," he said.

Roy told him everything, right from the first.

"And what is your father's name?" was the only question that had to be asked. When he heard this, the Miss Bannisters' Brother rose. "You must stay here a minute," he said.

"But—but the lesson?" Roy exclaimed. "You know I ought to be getting back again. Christina—"

"All right, just a minute," the Miss Bannisters' Brother replied.

When the Miss Bannisters' Brother came back, Miss Selina came with him. "Come and get tidy. You are just in time for dinner," she said, "and afterwards we are going to drive home with you."

"Oh, but I can't stop for dinner!" Roy cried. "It's much too important to stop for dinner; I'm not really hungry either."

"Dinner will only take a little while," said Miss Selina, "and the horse can be getting ready at the same time; and if you were to walk you would n't be home nearly so soon as you will if you drive, dinner time included."

"Besides," said the Miss Bannisters' Brother, "I'm much too hungry to give lessons. I need heaps of food—chicken and things—before I can give a lesson."

"But Christina—" Roy gasped again.

"And, as a matter of fact, we've thought of a better way than the lesson," Miss Selina said. "Mr. Bannister is going with you; but he must eat first, must n't he?"

It took a moment for Roy to appreciate this, but when he did he was the happiest boy in Dormstaple.

He never tasted a nicer chicken, he said afterwards.

VI

Certainly not more than three-quarters of an hour had passed before the carriage was on its way to Mapleton—with the Miss Bannisters' Brother propped up with cushions (for he could not bear the jolting of carriages) on the back seat, and Miss Selina and Miss Sarah, who had come to look after their brother, on the other. Roy was on the box. You never saw such puzzled faces as the Dormstaple people had when the party went by, for the Miss Bannisters' Brother had not driven out these twenty years; but their surprise was nothing to that of old Eliza, who wandered about the rooms all the rest of the day muttering, "Little himperent boy!"

At the Mapleton gates Roy jumped down and rushed up to the house. His mother came to the door as he reached it. "Oh, Mother, Mother," he cried, "he's come himself!"

"Who has come?" she asked, forgetting to say anything about Roy's long absence. "I hoped it was the doctor. Christina is worse, I'm afraid; she won't sleep."

"It's all right," Roy assured her. "I've brought the Miss Bannisters' Brother, who mends dolls and everything, and he'll put the eyes right in no time, and then Chrissie'll be well again. Here they are!"

At this moment the carriage reached the door; but Mrs. Tiverton's perplexities were not removed by it. On the contrary, they were increased, for she saw before her three total strangers. Miss Selina, however, hastily stepped out and took Mrs. Tiverton's hand and explained the whole story, adding, "We are not coming in; my sister and I have a call to pay a little farther on. We shall come back in less than an hour for our brother, carry him off, and be no trouble at all. I know how little you must want just now even people that you know." In spite of Mrs. Tiverton's protest, Miss Selina had her way, and the sisters drove off.

While this conversation had been in progress, Roy had been speaking to the Miss Bannisters' Brother. He had been preparing the speech ever since they had started, for it was very important. "Please," he said, "please how much will this visit be, because I want to pay for it myself?"

The Miss Bannisters' Brother smiled. "But suppose you haven't enough," he said.

"Oh, but I think I have," Roy told him. "I've got seven-and-six, and when the vet. came to see Lord Roberts it was only five shillings."

The Miss Bannisters' Brother smiled again. "Our infirmary is rather peculiar," he said. "We don't take money at all; we take promises; different kinds of promises from different people, according to their means. We ask rich patients' friends to promise to give away old toys or story books, or scrapbooks, or something of that kind, to real hospitals—children's hospitals. We find that much better than money. Money's such a nuisance. One is always losing the key to the money box."

Roy was a little disappointed. "Oh, yes," he said, however, "I'll do that. Won't I just? But, you know," he added, "you can always break open a money box if it comes to the worst. Pokers are n't bad. And there's a way of getting the money out with a table knife."

It was just then that the Miss Bannisters drove off, and Mrs. Tiverton asked their brother to come to Christina's room with her. Roy would have given anything to have been allowed upstairs; but as it was forbidden he went to see Jim and tell him the news. He found, however, that the housemaid had already told not only Jim but everyone else.

"Now it will be all right," she was saying. "The Miss Bannisters' Brother will do it! Why, he made a wooden leg for a tame jackdaw once!"

VII

Christina was moaning in the bed with Diana in her arms as the Miss Bannisters' Brother sat down beside her. "Come," he said gently, "let me feel your pulse."

Christina pushed her wrist toward him wearily.

"Oh, no, not yours," he said, with a little laugh. "Yours does n't matter. I meant this little lady's. I'm not your doctor. I'm a doll's doctor."

Christina turned her poor flushed face toward him for the first time. A doll's doctor—it was a new idea. And he really seemed to be all right—not anyone dressed up to make her feel foolish or coax her into taking horrid medicine. "Was it your carriage I heard?" she asked.

"Yes," he said. "I have come on purpose. But so many dolls are ill just now that I must be getting away soon. It's quite a bad time for dolls, especially French ones. They are very delicate."

"Mine is French," Christina said, growing really interested.

"How very curious!" he answered. "I had a French patient the other day—a Parisian, too—whose sight had become so very weak that she had to wear glasses. And now for the pulse," he went on, and he drew out a large gold watch.

Mrs. Tiverton was looking on with tears in her eyes. Christina had not taken this quiet interest in anything or kept so still in bed for many hours. Not even the sleeping draught had had any effect.

The Miss Bannisters' Brother held Diana's tiny wrist and looked very grave. "Dear, dear!" he said. "I ought to have been sent for before, and then I could have cured her here in your arms. As it is, I must take her to the light. Won't you have that nice jelly while I am treating Miss ——? Let me see, what was the name?"

"Diana," Christina said.

"Ah, yes—Miss Diana. By the time you have finished the jelly I ought to have finished my visit." So saying he rose and carried Diana to the window seat behind the curtains, while Mrs. Tiverton gave Christina the jelly. Christina took it, nurse said afterwards, like a lamb—though I never saw a lamb take jelly.

Meanwhile, the Miss Bannisters' Brother had taken some tools and a tube of seccotine from his pocket, and he had lifted up Diana's hair, cut a hole in her head, and was busily readjusting the machinery of her eyes. It was all done in five minutes, just as Christina was eating the last mouthful. "There," he said, returning to the bedside, "that's all right. It was a very simple operation, and didn't hurt at all. I think our patient can see now as well as ever."

Christina peered into Diana's face with a cry of joy, and sank back on the pillow in an ecstasy of content.

Neither Mrs. Tiverton nor the Miss Bannisters' Brother dared to move for some minutes. While they sat there the doctor tiptoed in. He crossed to the bed and looked at Christina. "She's asleep," he said. "Splendid! She's all right now. It was sleep she wanted more than anything. Don't let her hear a sound, nurse, for hours."

They found Roy waiting for the news. When he heard it he jumped for joy. His mother caught him up and hugged him. "You thoughtful little imp!" she cried—and, turning to the doctor, told him the story. He went off, laughing. "I shall take my door-plate down when I get home," he called out as he drove off, "and send it round to you, Bannister. You're the real doctor."

When the Miss Bannisters drove back they found tea all ready, and Mrs. Tiverton would not hear of their leaving without it. And when they did leave, an hour later, they were all fast friends.

VIII

Roy and Christina never think of going to Dormstaple now without calling at the red house.

WHEN MOLLY WAS SIX

By ELIZA ORNE WHITE

Illustrations by KATHERINE PYLE
Decorations by WARREN CHAPPELL

January

MOLLY'S BIRTHDAY

MOLLY'S birthday came on the first of January with that of the year. It was so near to Christmas that she always felt a little uncertain as to whether she should have any presents.

"Now that you are getting to be such a big girl," her father said the night before her birthday, "I think that Christmas presents are enough."

"Don't tease the poor child, Henry," said her mother.

"I shall expect to see a very different looking person tomorrow," her brother Turner observed. "The human body changes entirely once in seven years, and as this is your seventh birthday, the change will undoubtedly begin in the morning."

"But I am only going to be six," Molly objected.

"That is true; but all the same it is your seventh birthday."

Molly was never sure when Turner was joking and when he was in earnest, so she looked at him somewhat doubtfully as she put up her face to be kissed. She then bade her grown-up sister Ruth and her ten-year-old sister Flora good night, and went upstairs with her mamma.

Molly awoke early the next morning, so early that the daylight was only just beginning to come in at the windows. Her Aunt Mary whose room she shared, was still fast asleep, for she had been to a New Year's party the night before. Molly crept stealthily out of bed and ran to the long looking-glass that stood near one of the windows. It was light enough for her to see that she was not in the least changed. She was still a very small girl, and her curly hair was as tangled as it always was in the morning. She had never really expected to be different, but she had had a faint hope that she might be a little taller, and that her hair would have straightened in the night. She went back to bed and stayed there quietly for some minutes, hoping that her aunt would wake of her own accord, for Molly had learned by sad experience that she did not like to be disturbed in the morning. It was growing lighter every moment, and Molly was so anxious to go downstairs to see her presents that at last she could stay still no longer. She sprang out of bed and began to dress in haste. She got on pretty well until she tried to fasten the waist of her gown, which seemed to have altogether too many buttons. She wondered why it was that grown people, who had long arms, had gowns that buttoned in front, while the gowns of little children, who had such short arms, always buttoned behind.

At this moment her aunt opened her eyes. "Molly Benson, what are you doing?" she cried.

"I'm dressing myself," said Molly proudly, "for I am in a hurry to see my presents."

"Dressing yourself! I should think so!" and Miss Benson began to undo the little girl's unevenly buttoned gown.

When Molly was at last made tidy, she went downstairs to the dining room, where the family had assembled for breakfast. At her plate there were five mysterious-looking paper parcels. One was irregular in shape and had a knob on top.

"It is a doll! I know it is a doll!" she exclaimed in excitement. On the outside of the bundle was written: "For Molly, from her loving mother." She undid the string with trembling fingers. "It is a boy. I am *so* glad," she said, "because I have so many daughters."

"I told mother that the girls needed a brother to keep them in order," said Turner.

The new-comer was dressed in a dark blue sailor suit, trimmed with white braid. A sailor cap of dark blue was on top of his flaxen curls, and his blue eyes were full of beauty and intelligence.

"He is lovely," said Molly enthusiastically, "and I know he is going to be the best of all my children, except Jane. I shall call him George Washington, because he is so good."

"Boys are always good," said Turner.

The next package she opened was small and hard. On it was written: "For Molly, from her papa." It contained a napkin-ring of plain silver with a beaded edge. On the outside was engraved, "Molly"; and inside were her initials and her papa's, and the date.

Molly could not like the napkin-ring so well as the doll, but she kissed her father and thanked him for his present.

"Twenty years from now," said Turner, "you will prefer the napkin-ring to George Washington. I can foretell that he will be a total wreck by that time in spite of his name."

The next present which Molly undid was a family of paper dolls from Flora. Ruth had painted them, but Flora had planned their clothes and named them. Molly was much pleased with these new friends. There were two more presents: one was a little paint box from Ruth; the other a Testament, bound in red morocco, from Molly's Aunt Mary.

She was not in the least changed.

"Turner did not give me anything," the little girl thought, feeling somewhat aggrieved. At that moment she chanced to look under the table, and there she saw—oh, joyful sight!—a sled! a large sled, large enough for her and Turner and Flora all to coast on together. It was low, wide, and long, and it was painted black.

"Oh, how lovely!" said Molly. "Is that your present, Turner?"

He nodded.

"You are the nicest boy I ever saw."

"Even nicer than George Washington?"

"Even nicer."

"And handsomer, of course?"

Molly glanced from her brother's freckled face to the blue-eyed, flaxen-haired doll, and felt a little doubtful; so she said nothing, but dived under the table and dragged out her sled.

"If you will only tell me that I am handsome as well as good, I will take you and Flora coasting on Brown's hill this afternoon," said Turner.

"Truly! How perfectly splendid!" and Molly clapped her hands.

"But if you don't tell me that I am handsome, my feelings will be so deeply hurt that I shall be obliged to leave you at home," he added.

"Of course you are handsome," said Molly, "only not the same kind of handsome that George Washington is."

Molly had been too busy, so far, to give any thought to the weather, but now she ran to the window and saw a beautiful sight. The sun was just rising and sending rays of light over the trees and shrubs in the garden. When she had gone to bed the night before, there had been only commonplace snow on the ground, but it had rained all night, and the rain had frozen as it fell. Each twig was outlined in ice, and the garden looked like a fairy wood full of trees and shrubs made of glass. Even the summer-house had turned to glass in the night.

"The year has changed on its birthday," said Molly, "even if I am the same on mine."

It was so cold all day that the snow did not melt, and when Molly started with Turner and Flora, after dinner, the sun was shining so brightly that the trees and shrubs took on an added splendor, and it seemed as if they were not made of common glass, but hung with sparkling diamonds. Molly felt as if she were a young princess wandering in an enchanted wood.

"How lovely it is!" she said with a deep-drawn sigh of delight.

"It's awfully slippery," said Flora.

When they reached the pasture that led to Brown's hill, Turner let down the bars and his little sisters ran through joyously.

The hill was a long one; it was quite steep in the beginning, and then sloped away more gradually until it reached the level meadow below. Here there was a little pond which was covered with ice.

Turner put Flora in front, on the big black sled, and Molly in the middle, and then he got on behind so that he could steer.

Away they went, so fast that Molly was frightened, and clung to Flora with both hands. It seemed as if they were flying down the hill, and Molly felt as if they were running a race with the wind. At last they reached the little pond and skimmed over that too, and then they began to go slower and slower until at length the sled stopped, as if it were worn out and needed rest.

"Oh, dear!" said Molly as they began to walk up the long hill, "I wish that hills were all down without any up."

"And yet if they were all upside down you would n't like it," said Turner. "Get on, and I will drag you up the rest of the way."

"I wish I were only six years old," said Flora, as Molly took her place on the sled.

"You are a lazy thing," said Turner.

The next time they went down the hill Molly was less afraid, and after they had gone down three or four times she thought there was nothing in the world so delightful as coasting on a big sled with a big brother. Did birds feel so free and joyful when they spread their wings and flew away? Were fairies any happier? On the whole, she thought that she would rather take her chances as Molly Benson, for birds and fairies could not have a sled for a birthday present, or a silver napkin-ring, or a George Washington.

They coasted all the afternoon, until the sun went down, and the diamonds faded into common glass. But the world still seemed like an enchanted place to the little girl, for something of the glory of the day was in her heart.

"Mamma," she said, as her mother was putting her to bed that night, "how many more days shall I be six?"

"There are three hundred and sixty-four days left, Molly."

"Will they all be as happy as this, do you suppose, mamma?"

"Not all, darling; but there will be something beautiful in each day for my little girl if she has the eyes to see it."

"Yes, there will always be George Washington," said Molly.

February

A SUNDAY VALENTINE

Molly was sitting in the square old-fashioned pew at church. As she was a very little person, her view was somewhat limited. It was chiefly confined to the row of heads that appeared above the back of the seat in front of her. Today there was only one head there. It was a shiny bald head belonging to a very old gentleman. Molly wondered as she looked at him whether he was thankful enough that he did not have long curly hair to be pulled by his Aunt Mary when she combed it. But perhaps he did not have an Aunt Mary. Her Aunt Mary was sitting in the pew by her side, tall, straight, and handsome. If she had not been there, Molly would have ventured to climb upon the seat, and enlarge her view by looking over the back of the pew; for directly behind her there often sat a very beautiful young lady who looked just like a fairy princess. Molly was sure of this; because she had often seen pictures of fairy princesses, and they always had curly yellow hair and blue eyes, like Miss Sylvia.

It was Valentine's Day; and Molly wondered whether there would be an especial service, as there had been at Thanksgiving and Christmas.

That morning she had heard her sister Flora say, "It's Valentine's Day! I think it's a mean shame to have it come on Sunday."

"What is Valentine's Day?" Molly had asked her father.

"It is a day when people tell their friends how much they love them," he had said, stooping to kiss her upturned face.

Molly was thinking about this now, while she sat very still on the faded damask pew-cushion, with her legs dangling down in a most uncomfortable fashion. She thought: "How nice it would be to write a valentine all my own self to Miss Sylvia, and tell her how much I love her; and I can give it to her when church is over."

Molly had a pencil in her pocket, and she knew that her mamma kept some paper under the pew-cushion, so that her little daughter could amuse herself during the sermon. Molly looked up furtively at her Aunt Mary, and saw that her face was fixed with apparent absorption upon the minister; so she ventured to put one of her hands under the pew-cushion to try and find the paper. First she found a palm-leaf fan, all torn on the edge, and looking so shabby that she felt quite ashamed of it and hastily put it back; and then she moved softly along to the other end of the pew toward her father, that she might see if the paper was under the cushion where she had been sitting. She found it; but she could not help making it rustle as she pulled it out. Her Aunt Mary shook her head at her with decision. Her father looked at her aunt appealingly. "Let her write; it is a harmless amusement," he seemed to say.

Molly glanced doubtfully from one to the other, and then cautiously slid down and seated herself on the cricket. She looked up with shy apprehension at her aunt, but gained confidence when she saw that she was merely looking at her father with an expression with which the little girl was familiar. It was half resigned, half protesting. It said as plainly as words:—

"If that were my child, I would make her behave herself."

It was a whole year since Molly had had any valentines, and she could only dimly remember what they were like. Should she write on her paper, "I love you, Miss Sylvia.—Molly Benson"? No, that was not enough; and besides it was Sunday, and it would be better to make it a Sunday valentine. She could find something about loving one another, in the Bible, and she could copy it. She took down her little Testament, which happened to open toward the end of the volume, and turned the leaves diligently. Her Aunt Mary looked at her, and was beginning to shake her head again; but Molly held her book up triumphantly. Even her Aunt Mary could not object to her reading in church if the book that she read was the Bible.

Molly looked through the pages slowly, for she found it hard to read the long words. At first she could not find anything at all appropriate, and she began to be afraid that they did not have any Valentine's Day when the New Testament was first written. She felt discouraged, and was just going to shut her book, when she came to a whole chapter that seemed to be all about loving one another. Molly thought it must be the "Valentine Chapter." She was glad now that her Aunt Mary had persevered and taught her to read, in spite of the fact that her father and mother had thought her too young to learn.

Molly did not know how to write; but she could print very neatly, although it took her a long time to do it. She printed: "Beloved, let us love one another." Then she found something so much to the point that it seemed as if it must have been written on purpose: "I beseech thee, lady, not as though I wrote a new commandment unto thee, but that which we had from the beginning, that we love one another."

Molly thought that the words "commandment" and "beginning" were too long to write, so she left out that part of the sentence, and printed the rest of it as carefully as she could: "I beseech thee, lady, that we love one another." Then some more words on the page caught her eye: "I would not write with paper and ink."

Molly wondered why the person who had written this letter would not write with ink. Could it be for the same reason that she was not allowed to write with ink? No, that was not possible; because if his letter was in the Bible, he must have been a grown-up person, and there would have been no danger of his upsetting the inkstand. She could think of no way of explaining this little sentence; but it gave her a very friendly feeling for the man who had been writing his letter without ink such a long, long time ago.

Molly was so absorbed in her occupation that she forgot to get up with the others when they stood up to sing. She rose hastily in the middle of the second verse. She did not know what they were singing; but she liked the music, and so she joined in and sang the tune softly, as well as she could, to words of her own.

"I am very happy," Molly sang; "I love everybody. I love papa, and mamma, and Ruth, and Turner, and Flora, and Aunt Mary, and dear Miss Sylvia; and I love the gentleman who could n't write with ink and paper. I love everybody, everybody, everybody! I love God, too. He has made me very happy. I hope he won't mind because I did n't find the place in the hymn-book, and so have to sing my own words, which are n't as pretty as the music. This is my valentine-hymn, and this my special service."

When church was over, and the people began to leave their pews with the rustle and buzz that always follows, Molly clasped her paper tightly in her hand, and shyly opened the door of Miss Sylvia's pew. Molly wished that all doors were as small as pew-doors, they would be so much easier to open. A pew-door seemed made on purpose for little children.

Alas! there was no pretty golden-haired fairy princess there; the pew was empty. Molly felt bitterly disappointed; but then she remembered that she could copy her valentine on pink paper, and carry it that afternoon her own self to Miss Sylvia. Her papa said that she might; and Flora gave her some pink paper.

Molly felt some misgivings as she walked up the driveway that led to the house where Miss Sylvia lived with her uncle.

"Suppose she should n't like the valentine," she thought. "Suppose she should say, as Aunt Mary did, 'You silly child' "—

Just then a big black dog came out from behind a tree, and jumped up on Molly, putting two of his big paws on her shoulders. Poor Molly was now thoroughly frightened. She ran up to the door very fast, and pulled the bell; and then she turned to look at the dog, who raised his eyes to hers reproachfully.

"Poor thing, you did n't mean to hurt me, did you?" she said doubtfully. "That was your way of hugging. I suppose you wanted to tell me that you loved me. It is your kind of valentine. Oh, please, don't do it again! *Please* don't; for you are so big, and I'm so very little."

At that moment the maid came to the door.

"Down, Ponto! Down!" she said. "Don't touch the little lady. Whom do you want to see, miss?"

"Miss Sylvia. Please tell her it's Molly Benson."

The maid looked doubtful.

"I don't think Miss Sylvia can see anyone today."

Molly's heart sank. She felt like crying. Presently, however, Miss Sylvia, who had heard the voices below, came to the head of the stairs.

"My dear little Molly," she said, "I am so very glad to see you."

Molly watched her come down the stairway, and she thought her more lovely than ever. She made up her mind that if she ever grew up into a young lady, she would have a blue gown with ribbon and lace down the front of it, just like Miss Sylvia's.

"What do you want, dear?" asked Miss Sylvia. Her face looked sad; and if she had not been a grown-up person, Molly would have thought that she had been crying.

The little girl did not answer. A sudden fit of shyness had seized her. She held out her valentine mutely.

"For me?" asked Miss Sylvia.

Molly nodded.

"Oh, how pretty!" Miss Sylvia said, as she took it. "Pink is my favorite color."

She seated herself on the lowest step of the staircase, and motioned to Molly to come and sit beside her.

"What is it?" she asked.

"It is a Sunday valentine, all out of the Bible," said Molly, who had found her tongue.

Miss Sylvia opened it and read it.

"Beloved, let us love one another. I beseech thee, lady, that we love one another. I love you.—Molly Benson."

Miss Sylvia turned and put her arms around the little girl.

"You dear child, how lovely of you to write this for me all yourself!" she said.

"It would have been much nicer," said Molly, "only Flora would n't let me have the ink, and so I had to print it in pencil."

"It could n't have been nicer," said Miss Sylvia; "I like it best just as it is. How did you ever think of anything so sweet?"

"Aunt Mary said you would n't care for it at all," observed Molly. "She"—

"Mary knows nothing about it," said Miss Sylvia, with decision.

She kissed Molly again and again. "I can't tell you how much good you have done me," she said. "Something has happened which has made me very unhappy today, and I was feeling as if nobody cared very much about me; and just then you came in at the door, like a little good fairy."

• • •

"She liked it ever so much, papa," said Molly, that evening. "She said she had never had such a lovely valentine. Do you suppose it was because it was a Sunday valentine, or because it was on pink paper?"

March

AFTERNOON TEA

Miss Sylvia Russell was to be "At Home" on a certain afternoon, and she asked Mr. and Mrs. Henry Turner Benson and family, among other people, to come and see her. Poor little Molly was heartbroken, when the day arrived, because she was not allowed to go with the others.

" 'Family' means Flora and me, mamma, just as much as it means Turner and Ruth, and Aunt Mary," she suggested.

"My dear," said her Aunt Mary, "little girls do not go to teas given by grown-up young ladies."

Molly thought this very hard, for she knew that Miss Sylvia was fond of her, and she cried a little when she saw Ruth and Turner start for the tea with the older members of the family. Her Aunt Mary told her not to be such a baby, but her mamma comforted her by promising to bring her home a macaroon and a cocoanut cake, and perhaps a piece of candy.

Molly sent a message by her mamma to Miss Sylvia, who, she was quite sure, was expecting to see her. Molly was afraid Miss Sylvia would be very much disappointed when she did not come; indeed she felt almost sorrier for Miss Sylvia than for herself.

Bridget was putting Molly to bed when the family came home, but Molly slipped out of the door and ran along the passage with her little bare feet.

"Did you give my message to Miss Sylvia, mamma?" she asked, as she buried her curly head in her mamma's black silk gown.

"Yes, darling; and she said she was very sorry, but that she could not have seen anything of her little Molly if she had come, because there were so many, many people; and she sent you these roses and this candy, and she says some day soon she will have a very small afternoon tea on purpose for you."

Molly took the pretty pink roses, and her mamma kept the candy for another day. The little girl felt very happy as she crept back to bed.

A few days later, when the postman came to the door bringing big envelopes with big letters in them for big people, he also brought a little envelope with a little card in it for a little person. The direction was printed, so that Molly could read it herself. It ran:—

MISS MOLLY BENSON AND TWO OF HER FAMILY,
KNIGHTSBRIDGE, MASS.

There was a rough little picture of a doll in the right-hand corner next the word "family," so that Molly should make no mistake.

Molly opened the envelope neatly with a pair of scissors, as she had seen her Aunt Mary do, and on the card inside she read:—

> *Miss Sylvia Russell,*
> *At Home,*
> *Friday, March nineteenth,*
> *From three to five o'clock.*
> *To meet Miss Julia Esterhazy.*

Molly clapped her hands and danced with delight, for Julia Esterhazy was her dearest friend, who lived in the big white house just across the way.

Molly ranged her dolls in a row, and tried to decide which were the most deserving. Some had been so naughty that there was no question of taking them, and others were too small to go out to tea with a grown-up lady; but there were four about whom she was uncertain, and she finally took them into the library, that Turner and Flora, who were studying their lessons, might help her decide.

In the first place, there was Jenny, named for Molly's mamma, and usually called Jane to avoid confusion. She was the oldest of all the dolls, and did not look so fresh as in her early youth, but she was the most unselfish of the family.

"Jane's complexion seems to have gone off," Turner remarked. "Too many late hours, I suppose."

"I think I ought to take her to Miss Sylvia's," Molly said, "she is so good; and then I ought to do more for her than for the rest, because she is so ugly."

Next came Sylvia Russell Benson, who, Molly felt, must surely have the honor of drinking tea with Miss Sylvia, because she was her namesake. She was a fair-haired, blue-eyed doll, with a sweet disposition, and a blue cashmere gown.

Then came George Washington Benson, who was dressed in his neat sailor suit; Molly wished him to go because he was her only son.

"Don't take George Washington," Turner advised; "for if he is the only fellow there he'll be awfully bored."

Lastly there was the Princess, a very grand personage, in a red velvet gown. She was so distinguished that Molly felt in awe of her and afraid to leave her behind; at which Turner said that she did not show proper spirit. Molly, therefore, left it uncertain whether the Princess or Jane should have the pleasure.

The day before the tea, Molly caught cold; it was not a bad cold, but as her Aunt Mary was putting her to bed she said carelessly, "If it isn't pleasant tomorrow, you won't be able to go to Miss Sylvia's."

Molly felt that she should surely die if she could not go to the tea.

The next morning she crept out of bed at an early hour, and ran to the window. She pulled back the blue-and-white chintz curtains softly, that she might not wake her Aunt Mary, and peered out into the gray dawn. The night before everything was brown, for there had been a thaw which had melted all the pretty white snow from the fields and the hills, but now, in the places where everything had been dark, there was a soft white powder. The ground was all white, and the hills were white, too, and even the trees were bending under the weight of a white burden; while from the sky, as far up as Molly could see, floated down myriads of feathery, starlike little snowflakes. It was all so beautiful that she clasped her hands together, and looked at it in silence. She was brought back to the actual world at last by her Aunt Mary.

"Molly Benson!" she exclaimed, "come back into bed this minute, unless you want to have pneumonia."

"You won't be able to go out of the house today," her aunt observed as she was dressing Molly, a little later.

Molly said nothing; she had learned by experience that it was best not to dispute her aunt's decisions.

"I *think* mamma will let me go. I *think* mamma will let me go," she kept murmuring to herself.

At breakfast everybody was delighted with the snowstorm, for different reasons.

"We shall have some good coasting," said Turner.

"And tobogganing," added Ruth.

"I can take my dinner to school and stay over the noon recess," said Flora.

They all had forgotten about Molly's afternoon tea. She sat quite silent for a time, but at last she plucked up her courage.

"Papa," she asked, "don't you think we may have a thaw by afternoon?"

"Not the least chance of it," her father replied, with a laugh.

There was another silence.

"Papa," said Molly at last, "don't you think it will stop snowing pretty soon?"

"Oh, no; we are in for a solid snowstorm this time."

"Papa," said Molly wistfully, "don't you think I can go to Miss Sylvia's, even if it does snow?"

"Indeed, she can't, Henry," interposed Molly's Aunt Mary; "she has too much of a cold. It would be a ridiculous idea, and besides, Sylvia won't expect the children to come in such a storm."

Molly's spirits sank lower and lower. Two tears trembled on the lids of her blue eyes doubtfully for a minute; then she bravely forced them back. Her mamma looked up just in time to catch the pleading, eager expression of her face.

"Do you want to go very much, my little girl?" she asked.

"Very, *very* much," said Molly.

"But if you were to take cold and be ill, and make yourself and all of us very unhappy, you would wish you had stayed at home."

Molly was not sure about this, so she kept silent. She thought she would be willing to be sick if only she could be sure of the afternoon tea first.

When breakfast was over she went up to the playroom, and, taking in her arms Jane, who was always her comfort in sorrow, she wept bitterly.

"We are not to go to the tea, Jenny," she said, "none of us; none of us. So you need n't feel badly, dear, because you might have had to stay at home. The Princess can't go, and Sylvia can't go, and I am not to go myself."

She was still sobbing when Turner came in to get his French grammar. "Hullo!" he said. "What's the matter?"

Molly continued to sob.

It always made Turner feel sorry to see people cry, even if they were very small people like Molly.

"I guess I would n't cry," he said slowly. "Would n't you like a popcorn ball if I can get one down street?" he added.

She shook her head.

"Perhaps Miss Sylvia will ask you another day," he suggested.

"She's going away for a visit pretty soon," Molly said in a subdued voice.

"Well, if I were the clerk of the weather, I'd tell the snow to hold up this afternoon," said Turner. "I'd say, 'Winds to the north, colder weather, a thundering big snowstorm all through New England, and especially on the hills and toboggan-slide in Knightsbridge; but in the village itself, between Main and Chatham streets, pleasant weather, fair, southerly winds, and a flood of sunshine.' "

Molly began to laugh, and Turner felt as if the sunshine were coming. "I wish you were the weather man," she said.

Everybody went out that morning except Molly and her mamma. Molly's papa went to his law office; her Aunt Mary went to teach the Literature class at the high school, as she did every Friday, while Ruth and Turner took their dinners to the high school, and Flora carried hers to the grammar school.

Molly's mamma told her to get her work and come and sew with her while she mended the stockings. The little girl felt as if she could never be happy any more, but she did not wish to trouble her dear mamma, and so she said nothing about the afternoon tea. By and by they heard the telephone-bell ring, and Mrs. Benson went to see what was wanted. Presently Molly heard her say, "It's such a storm and she has a little cold, so her father is afraid to let her go."

Molly listened eagerly; she wished she could hear the voice at the other end of the telephone, which she was sure was Miss Sylvia's. What could she be saying?

"You are very kind," said Mrs. Benson, "but that will be a great deal of trouble, and do you want to send the horse out on such a day?"

Molly could hardly wait for the next words.

"Very well, then," said her mamma; "she will be ready at three o'clock."

Molly ran and flung her arms around her mother and pressed her cheek against her hand; she was too happy to speak. Then she caught up Jenny and hugged her, too. "Jane, you shall go to the party instead of the Princess," she said, "because you are the best of all my children. Mamma, what did Miss Sylvia say?"

"She said she would send the covered sleigh for you and Julia this afternoon, and that she is sure you won't take cold if you are well wrapped up."

Julia was already in the sleigh when it came, and she laughed because Molly had on so many wraps, and called her "Mother Bunch." Julia was six months older than Molly, and an inch taller. Her hair was much darker, and her eyes were a very dark brown.

"Why did you bring that hideous old Jane?" Julia asked, as she caressed her two pretty Paris dolls, Lily and Maud.

"I love her the best of all my children," Molly said sturdily.

"I should get her a new head if she belonged to me."

"But she would n't be the same person then," Molly objected.

When they reached Miss Sylvia's house, John, the man, helped them out of the sleigh, and then he handed out the four dolls very respectfully, as if they had been live ladies.

Miss Sylvia was waiting in the hall to receive them; she had on her pretty blue gown with ribbon and lace down the front of it. She kissed both the children, and then she shook hands gravely with the four dolls, but she evidently preferred Jane, who, she said, looked as if she had force of character and reserve strength. Presently she led the way into the dining room. At one end, in the bow window, there was a small table about as high as a kindergarten table, covered with a white cloth. On it were two very small silver candlesticks, with a white candle in one and a blue one in the other. Some forget-me-nots and lilies of the valley were in a blue bowl on the middle of the table. There were seven places laid, with three small plates for Miss Sylvia and the little girls, and four very tiny plates for the four dolls. There were, besides, three small white-and-gilt cups and saucers for Miss Sylvia and the little girls, and four tiny white cups and saucers for the four dolls. At Miss Sylvia's end of the table were a small silver cream-pitcher and a white china teapot with a wreath of roses painted on it. The teapot contained tea made of molasses and water which was very delicious. In front of Molly was a little china dish full of animal crackers, and in front of Julia a silver dish filled with cocoanut cakes and macaroons. Each doll had an oyster cracker on her plate, and Miss Sylvia hoped they would not find these too large to eat; she said they were their pilot biscuit. Molly and Julia each had a little card with verses at her plate, and a barley-sugar animal. Julia's was a cat, and her verse said:

> Here's a sweet cat for a sweet child.
> She ne'er will scratch nor bite.
> E'en if you bite her, she's so mild
> She'll think you wholly right.

Molly's animal was a rabbit, and her rhymes said:—

> I hope you will welcome this rabbit, my dear,
> I hope you will welcome this rabbit.
> He puts back his ear, for he wishes to hear,
> But indeed 't is a curious habit, my dear,
> Indeed 't is a curious habit.
>
> He rushes and skips through the snowstorm, my dear,
> He rushes and skips, though 't is snowing,
> And I can't keep him back
> But he makes a quick track,
> And he says, "To my Molly I'm going, my dear,"
> He says, "To my Molly I'm going."

Molly wondered why grown people did not have molasses and water instead of tea, it was so much nicer. Miss Sylvia seemed to think so too, for she said a little went a great way, and she took only very small sips, so as to make it last a long time.

They had a merry time playing games and telling stories after they finished their tea, and five o'clock came only too soon. Miss Sylvia then put on their things, and she bade her two young friends good-bye for a whole month, for she was going away on her visit the next week.

"What a lovely time we had!" said Molly to Julia, as they were driving home. "I never had such a good time. I don't suppose we shall ever have such a good time again."

"Of course we shall," said Julia, "lots of better times."

Julia had already begun upon her candy, and said that it was very nice, and she advised Molly to eat hers; but Molly saved her rabbit and put him away tenderly in her drawer in the bureau, to remind her thenceforth of the blissful day when she had taken afternoon tea with Miss Sylvia.

April

NONESUCH

Poor little Molly was heartbroken because Tartar, her pussycat was dead. As her name suggests, she was not an amiable pussy, but this made no difference in Molly's feelings, even although there were unhealed scratches on her little hands.

Strange to say, it was her Aunt Mary who gave her the most comfort,—her Aunt Mary, who never was sympathetic over small griefs, but who had a heart for pussycats, and could therefore understand the great sorrow of a pussycat's death.

"Only yesterday she was *so* well, and she gave me such long, strong scratches," sobbed Molly, "and now she is dead; run over by that dreadful cart."

"It is a great pity, and I am almost as sorry about it as you are," said her aunt. "But, after all, it isn't as if she were a young pussy. You see she is a grandmother, and might not have lived very long, and her sight was a little dim, or it would not have happened."

"She always seemed young to me," said Molly with another sob.

"I was very fond of her, too," said her aunt, who was more demonstrative with pussies than she was with people, "but it does n't do any good to cry, Molly; it will only make you ill."

"One of the hardest things," said Molly, "is that nobody understands how I feel. Turner says she was a cross old thing,"—here she gave another sob,—"and papa says he will get me another; and even mamma,—even mamma says she hopes we can have one now who won't claw the furniture. Oh, dear! I don't want any other! They all talk as if a new pussycat could be better than the old one. Oh, what pretty fur she had!"

"She was very pretty," assented her aunt.

"Yes, she was"; and Molly buried her face once more in her small handkerchief.

"Molly, you must control yourself. Think how much better it is than if it were one of the family. You could hardly show any more feeling if I or your mother were to die."

"Oh, I should feel lots worser if it were you, Aunt Mary; and if it were mamma I should die myself. I am glad I have *something* left," she said, as she grasped her aunt's hand. She always admired her handsome young aunt, even when she was severe; but she loved her dearly when she was kind.

"It is so nice that you understand just how I feel," Molly went on. "Aunt Mary, somehow it seems as if this—this great sorrow made us love each other more."

It was almost a week before Molly was ready to consider the idea of having another cat, and six days is a long time when one is only six years old. At the end of the sixth day her aunt proposed that she should write to Miss Sylvia Russell, who was staying with a family who were fond of cats, and ask if she could not get her a kitten.

Molly printed the note "all her own self" to Miss Sylvia. She asked her aunt at first how to spell some of the words. "How do you spell that kind of *dear,* Aunt Mary?" she began.

"D-e-a-r, of course."

"And how do you spell *Sylvia,* please?"

Her aunt, who was writing a letter herself, glanced up impatiently, but spelled the word for her. They went on in this way for some time; then Miss Benson said, "Molly, are you writing that note, or am I?"

"I am."

"Then please don't ask me how to spell any more words until I have finished my letter."

This was why the first part of the note to Miss Sylvia was spelled better than the last part. Molly said:—

> DEAR MISS SYLVIA,—Aunt Mary says you know a lady who has cats. My dear cat is dead. I cried a grate deel. Plese I like a torter-shel best. Plese send one with out sharpe clors if you can.
>
> Your loveing, MOLLY.

Three days later there came a letter for Molly from Miss Sylvia, who wrote as follows:—

> DEAR MOLLY,—I am very, very sorry for you. I remember the time when my pussycat died. It was long, long ago, when your Aunt Mary and I were little girls. I have had greater sorrows since, such as grown-up people have, but they have never crowded out the memory of those days.
>
> Fortunately for you the friends with whom I am staying are going to Europe in a few weeks, and they want to find a good home for their cat, so I send her to you by express. Her name is Nonesuch, and she is well named, for I know none

such as she is. I suppose she has claws, like other cats, but I have never seen them. In fact she is so gentle and good that if you were not very fond of cats and very good to them I should not send her to you.

No new friend can ever quite take the place of an old one, but Nonesuch can make a place of her own. I am glad that you and I are such old, old friends, Molly.

Your loving, SYLVIA RUSSELL.

"Miss Sylvia does not say whether she is a torter-shell or not," Molly said, as her mother finished reading the letter.

"She is probably a lank, cadaverous thing, with a lame leg and rough fur," said Turner; "one of those brownish cats that look as if they had been black once, and were sent to the dye-house to be done over, and came back rusty-looking."

"Oh, Turner!" said Molly reproachfully, "why do you think she will be like that?"

"Because if she had been a good and beautiful tortoise-shell, of course the Grays would have taken her to Europe with them."

"Well, anyways, she will be a cat," said Molly contentedly; "and if she is lame, and cross, and ugly, she will need to be loved all the more."

It seemed to Molly that she could not wait for the hour that was to bring Nonesuch. All day, whenever the bell rang, she hung over the balusters to see if the expressman had come. She wished that the cat had been sent by mail, for she knew just when to look for the postman, and she was sure he would have had room for her in his brown leather bag. The day passed, however, and no pussy appeared. Molly began to be afraid that she was lost. When the expressman came at night, she ran eagerly into the kitchen. She saw that he was bringing in a barrel.

"Oh, please, have you got her there?" she asked. "Did it take all that room just for one small pussycat?"

"I'll be blasted if I know what the young one is talking about," the man said with a good-humored laugh. "There's potatoes in that barrel, little lady."

"Potatoes!" Molly's face fell.

She looked at the man doubtfully for a moment before she made up her mind to pursue the subject, for she was shy with strangers; but the occasion was so serious that she could not give way to fear. She clasped her hands behind her and looked beseechingly into his face.

"Please, sir," she said, "will you look out very carefully in the express house for a pussycat? You see if she got left over, by mistake, the way our box from grandmamma did at Christmas, she might starve."

"I guess we'd hear her quick enough before she starved," said the man. "Cats mostly don't keep their feelings to themselves."

The next night, when Molly was sitting in the parlor after tea, playing jackstraws with Ruth and Flora, Bridget came to the door.

"There is an express package in the kitchen for you, Miss Molly," she said with a solemn face.

"An express package!" Molly slipped down from her chair and darted into the kitchen. There, in the middle of the room, stood the expressman, smiling broadly, and at his feet was a wooden box with slats across the top.

"She's come in, in her own Saratogy," he said. "I wonder the ladies don't take to traveling in their own trunks, too, now that they make 'em so large."

Molly was already bending over the box. She saw two bright yellow eyes, and a sweet little face partly yellow and partly white, with a large black spot just over the nose.

"She is a torter-shell! She is a torter-shell!" she exclaimed in delight.

The rest of the family had assembled in the kitchen by this time, and Turner began to take the slats off the box, while Ruth went to get some milk for the little traveler. As soon as the bars were removed from her prison, Nonesuch stepped daintily out and walked directly up to Molly's Aunt Mary and rubbed against her feet. She seemed delighted to have found friends. Molly caught her up and held her close in her arms. "You dear thing. You dear, dear, *dear* little thing!" she said.

"The king is dead, long live the king," murmured Turner.

"Stop, Turner," said his mother, "you shall not spoil the child's pleasure."

But Molly knew and cared nothing about kings. All she thought of was a dear, fluffy creature curled up in her arms, with bright eyes and four sound legs and a beautiful tail.

"What a sweet purr she has," she said. "Come, Aunt Mary, and listen to her sweet purr."

"She must be very hungry," said Ruth, who came in just then with the milk.

"And thirsty," added her father.

Molly put her down on the floor reluctantly, and she found her way at once to the saucer and drank up all the milk.

"I don't see why Miss Sylvia's friends did n't take her to Europe with them," said Molly. "She is so beautiful and so good."

"It must have been because they were afraid she would not be satisfied with the European mice," Turner answered.

When Turner put her down cellar for the night, she gave a series of shrill and heart-breaking mews.

"What a sweet mew she has," said Turner. "Come, Molly, and listen to her sweet mew."

"You are a bad boy," said Molly gravely.

She and her Aunt Mary followed Turner downstairs to inspect the quarters of the new-comer.

"Poor little pussy, she does n't like the great, dark cellar," said Molly. "She will be very lonely if we leave her here all by herself this first night. Aunt Mary, *dear* Aunt Mary, don't you think she might sleep with us just this one night?"

"My dear child! What an idea!"

At that moment Nonesuch came and rubbed against Molly's aunt in the most human way, as if to plead her cause.

"She is telling you that she will be very good, Aunt Mary."

Miss Benson stooped to pick up the cat.

Molly waited in suspense.

Pussy put her paws around the neck of Molly's aunt, and began to purr softly.

"Good pussy," said Miss Benson; "good little Nonesuch. She will stay down cellar, won't she, like a good little cat?" As she spoke, she put her down on the floor.

"Miauw, miauw," said Nonesuch in a sad and surprised voice.

"Aunt Mary! Aunt Mary! she is *so* unhappy."

"Miauw, miauw," said Nonesuch again.

"Molly," said her aunt, "I think we shall have to keep her with us this first night."

When Molly was put to bed, dear little Nonesuch nestled down by her, and when Miss Benson came upstairs, later in the evening, they were both fast asleep; and pussy's little face was pressed close to Molly's face, and her soft paws were around Molly's neck.

May

A MOVABLE FEAST

"I think we ought to have some kind of a party for Miss Sylvia, now she has come home," said Molly to Julia one spring morning. "She had such a lovely afternoon tea for us."

The two little girls were playing in the garden behind Molly's house. They were making mud cakes and frosting them with the snow that still lingered in what had been the great drift on the north side of the house. It was very valuable now, because there was so little of it left.

"She would n't care for our kind of party," said Julia, as she made a large P on the frosting of the cake that was especially designed for the Princess.

"Yes, she would," said Molly. "I wish we knew when her birthday is. It ought to come when the flowers have their birthdays, for papa says she is like a flower."

"People are never like flowers," said Julia, "and just as likely as not her birthday is in December or January."

Miss Sylvia happened to come to see Molly's Aunt Mary that very morning, and the two children ran into the house to ask her about her birthday.

"I did not have any birthday this year," she said.

"No birthday!" they exclaimed, feeling very sorry for her.

"I only have a birthday once in four years," said Miss Sylvia; "can you guess when it is?"

"On the 29th of February," said Flora, who had just come home from school.

"Yes, and there was n't any 29th of February this year, and so I am left high and dry without any birthday."

"Poor Miss Sylvia," said Molly.

"Can't you choose some other day for your birthday?" suggested the practical Julia.

"It would be a good plan. I could make a movable feast of my birthday and have it in June, one year, and in August, at the seashore, another year, or in September, in the mountains."

"Oh, have it in May this year," cried the children.

"Have it next Saturday," said Molly eagerly, "and take us to the woods, and let us have a birthday feast for you."

"My dear, Miss Sylvia does not want to be bothered with you children," said Molly's Aunt Mary.

"Indeed I do. My birthday shall be next Saturday, which is May day, and Flora and Julia and Molly and I will have a birthday feast; and we won't invite you, Mary. We don't want any tiresome, grown-up people."

"Can't Elizabeth come, too?" asked Flora. "She is only eleven and a half, and although she is almost a year older than I am, she is very young for her age."

Elizabeth Dennison was Flora's most intimate friend.

"Yes, Elizabeth can come, too, if she will try to be very good, and very, very young."

Early Saturday morning Molly heard some heart-rending mews outside of her window, before she opened her eyes. This was nothing new, for almost every morning, as soon as Nonesuch was let out of the cellar-door, she climbed the trellis that led to the balcony, and then ran up the roof to Molly's window.

"Oh, I hope it is a pleasant day!" she said, as she went to open the window and let in the pussycat. Alas! when she pulled back the blue-and-white chintz curtains, she saw that the wind was blowing in great gusts and the raindrops were chasing each other down the window-pane.

"Oh, Nonesuch, how wet your feet are!" said Molly, as she tried to dry the pussy with a towel. "And isn't it too bad, dear Nonesuch, that it is raining? But probably it will clear before eleven o'clock," she added hopefully.

"Even if it does you can't go to the woods today," said her Aunt Mary, "because it would be so wet that you would all take colds."

When she heard this, Molly could not help shedding a few tears.

"Don't cry, Molly," said her aunt. "You have the whole summer before you; one rainy day does n't matter."

"But the whole summer won't be Miss Sylvia's birthday," said poor Molly, "and mamma had made us such cunning little cakes to take to the woods."

"I am very sorry for you, but it can't be helped."

That morning, soon after breakfast, while Molly was telling Jane, and George Washington, about her great disappointment, she saw John, Miss Sylvia's coachman, come up the steps with a note. She went to the door herself. "Is it for me?" she asked.

"Yes, miss."

Molly ran with her note to her mamma, who read it aloud.

> MY DEAR LITTLE MOLLY AND JULIA (and my larger but not quite grown-up Flora and Elizabeth),—I am so sorry that I chose the wrong birthday. But isn't it lucky that I have n't any birthday this year? Because if it had really been the 1st of May we could n't have postponed it, but as it really isn't, we can have the feast just as well next Saturday, on the 8th, and if it turns out that I have made another mistake, and the weather still thinks it too early to go to the woods, why we'll have my birthday the next Saturday; so if your mamma does n't get tired making little cakes, I won't get tired planning for my birthday. Your loving friend,
>
> SYLVIA RUSSELL.

The next Saturday morning, when Molly went to the window to let in Nonesuch, the sun was gayly shining on a world that was fresh with the beauty of early spring.

At eleven o'clock Miss Sylvia's carriage came for the little girls.

Julia and Molly sat on the front seat with John, and Flora and Elizabeth sat behind with Miss Sylvia.

When they reached the woods, Miss Sylvia found a mossy rock under a tree which she said they would have for their dinner-table by and by, and they left their lunch-baskets and shawls there while they went to look for mayflowers.

"It is rather late for them," she said. "But I hope a few of them knew about my movable birthday, and were kind enough to put off blossoming until today."

It was very beautiful in the woods. The leaves were only beginning to open, and so a great deal of sunshine came in and lighted up the green grass and the soft green moss and the red checkerberries. Molly began pulling at the mayflower leaves as she saw the others do. At first nobody found any blossoms.

"They are shy little things," said Miss Sylvia, "and they have hidden under the moss and the evergreen."

"I'm afraid they thought your birthday was last Saturday," said Elizabeth.

"No, they didn't," Molly cried excitedly. "They remembered!" She had found a spray well hidden under the moss that was full of beautiful pink blossoms and half-opened buds, and they were so fragrant that the little girl thought she had never smelled anything half so sweet.

"Take it Miss Sylvia," and Molly held up the long spray shyly.

"It is the pinkest that I have ever seen," said Miss Sylvia, as she touched it caressingly. "It is almost as pink as my Sunday valentine."

"And ever so much sweeter," said Molly.

A great many mayflowers had remembered Miss Sylvia's birthday. The children liked to hunt for them among the dead leaves and the evergreens. Sometimes a rabbit or a squirrel would look at them with his bright eyes, as he frisked past them, and sometimes a bird would sing to them. Molly thought that she had never seen so beautiful a place as this wood full of flowers and wild creatures.

After they had picked all the mayflowers that they could find, Miss Sylvia said she thought they might like to make a wood and a lake just as she used to do when she was a little girl.

"Shall we make a wild lake in the Adirondacks, where there aren't any people?" she asked.

"How can you make a lake when there isn't any water here?" Julia protested.

Miss Sylvia took an irregular piece of glass out of one of the baskets, and said, "When my mirror fell and broke the other day, I thought, 'Now we can have a lake on Saturday when we go to the woods.' "

She put the glass down on the ground as she spoke. The children pulled the moss up around the edge so that nobody could see that it was only a broken piece of glass. It looked like a tiny, tiny lake for very small people.

"I think we ought to have some trees," said Elizabeth.

"Isn't the moss their trees?" asked Molly.

"No, it is only their bushes. What kind of trees shall we have?"

"Birch trees," said Molly, "for they have the smallest leaves."

They had almost no leaves, for they were just beginning to open. The children picked some little branches, and stuck a great many of them into the ground close together near the lake, so that they might look like a wood.

"We ought to have some pine trees, too, if it is a lake in the Adirondacks," said Miss Sylvia. "We must certainly have some 'first growths'; that means the very oldest trees that have been growing for years and years."

The children ran off much pleased to look for pine balsam trees. Julia was the first to find one. They all broke off small branches and stuck them into the ground in among the birches. They looked very tall and majestic, and Miss Sylvia said it was evidently a "primeval forest."

"Let us have some apple trees, too," she said, "full of ripe, red apples."

"It isn't the season for apples," said Julia.

"I am sure that apple trees would n't grow where there were n't any people," added Flora.

"Oh, you terribly practical children! When I was a little girl it was the season for apples all the year round, and they always grew in a primeval forest."

"I think it is the season for apples in the Adirondacks," said Elizabeth.

"And I am sure that somebody lived there once," said Miss Sylvia. "A kind of Robinson Crusoe. He lived there a long time and he planted the apple trees, and after a while he went back to his old home, but the apple trees lived and flourished."

As she spoke she picked some sprays of checkerberry with their green leaves and bright red berries.

Molly clapped her hands. "Oh, Miss Sylvia, how dear they are They are little baby apples!"

"I think we will have only a few apple trees," Miss Sylvia decided. "One for each of us."

Molly and Julia planted five little apple trees full of red apples close to the edge of the lake."

"They are Fameuses," said Molly.

"No, they are Baldwins," said Julia.

"I am sure they are Astrachans," said Elizabeth, "because they come very early before the leaves turn."

The little forest was reflected in the placid lake, and so were the five apple trees. Molly counted five more apple trees, only these were upside down.

"This is the loveliest place I ever saw; it is like the Garden of Eden," said Molly, who had just learned about the Garden of Eden at Sunday school.

"Where are Adam and Eve?" asked Julia.

Molly looked perplexed. "They have been turned out," she said at last, brightening, "because they ate one of those dear little apples."

It was time for luncheon now, and Miss Sylvia and the older children went to prepare for the feast, while Molly and Julia had a tea-party on the edge of the lake, with twigs for people and acorn cups for dishes.

Miss Sylvia called them when lunch was ready, and they were sure that they had never seen any table look so pretty. There was a garland of mayflowers around the edge of the white table-cloth on the rock, and on this table-cloth were the little cakes that Molly's mamma had made, and some very small biscuits that Bridget had baked on purpose for the feast, while Miss Sylvia had brought tiny sandwiches, crackers with jelly between them, olives and candy. Everything tasted very delicious, because they were all so hungry.

"What fun we are having!" said Molly. "I am glad it rained last Saturday, for if we had come then we should n't be here now. Did you use to have such a nice time when you were a little girl, Miss Sylvia?"

"Yes, your Aunt Mary and I used to have lakes and forests and crotched-stick people."

"But you seem ever so much younger than Aunt Mary," said Molly.

"That is because I have had only six birthdays."

June

PRISCILLA

In June, Molly and her mamma went to spend a week with Mrs. Benson's mother, who lived, in summer, in an old-fashioned farm-house on a New Hampshire hillside. Molly was very fond of her grandmother, and of her Aunt Ruth, and this year her Aunt Flora, whom she had never seen, was to be there too, with her little daughter Priscilla. Priscilla was just Molly's age, and Molly was delighted to make the acquaintance of a new cousin.

When Molly and her mamma reached the farm-house, they saw Priscilla standing in the doorway with a very short black gown on and very long slim legs in black stockings.

"She's lots taller than I am," said Molly, in a disappointed tone, "and I wish I had such short dresses; but why does she have on a black dress, mamma?"

"Because her papa has died, Molly."

Molly looked very sober. "Poor Priscilla," she said. She had known that she should like her cousin, but now she felt as if she could not love her enough.

She ran up the steps and flung her arms around her Aunt Ruth.

"Priscilla," said her aunt, "this is your little cousin Molly; shake hands with her." Priscilla put out a small brown hand awkwardly.

"I am very glad to see you," said Molly; "and I am so sorry that I could n't have brought Nonesuch. She is my pussycat, but papa said he would be too lonely if mamma and Nonesuch and I all came away together."

Priscilla looked hard at Molly with her black eyes. She was shy with children of her own age, for she had no brothers or sisters, and it seemed to her as if she could not say one word.

"I think if we leave these children together they will get acquainted faster," said their Aunt Ruth. "I will show you to your room, Jenny."

As her aunt went out of the room, poor Priscilla cast a beseeching glance at her. She wriggled about on her chair, and looked down at the pattern on the rug.

"Do you like candy?" she asked at last, in despair.

"Very much," said Molly, brightening. "Have you got some?"

"No," said Priscilla, growing very red. "My mamma generally does not let me eat it."

"Oh," said Molly, trying to hide her disappointment. "I never can have much," she added.

There was another long pause.

"Don't you think it would be nice to go out to the barn and see the cows?" Molly asked, sliding down from her chair. "Last year there were such pretty cows and lovely bossies."

"There is a bossy out there now," said Priscilla. "It's quite small. Its name is Daisy; it's quite yellow."

"How perfectly lovely," said Molly. "Let's go to see it right off."

The ice was broken, and when the little girls came in from the barn their arms were around each other's waists, and they were chattering as fast as if they had known each other all their lives. A bossy is a very enlivening mutual friend.

The next morning Molly could hardly wait until breakfast was over, she was so eager to go to the barn with her Aunt Ruth and Priscilla when they fed the chickens.

After breakfast the two little girls followed their aunt into the kitchen, where she put some Indian meal in a large yellow bowl, and turned some water on it and stirred it with a spoon. Then she carried the bowl out to the hencoop, which was close by the barn. In the coop was a brown hen, who had twelve dear, downy, fluffy little yellow chickens.

Molly feeding the chickens.

"Let me feed them," Molly begged.

The little chickens were afraid to come to her, and the old hen scolded away in an angry fashion.

"Give the hen a little to try, Molly," said her aunt, "and when she sees how good it is she will tell all the little chickens that they may have some."

Molly took the spoon and dropped a little of the meal inside the coop. The old hen tasted it and thought it very delicious.

"Cluck! Cluck! Cluck!" she said, and all the little chickens ran as fast as they could to the meal which Molly held in her hand, almost tumbling over each other in their eagerness to get a taste.

"I suppose it is like ice cream to them," said Molly. "They are such dear, soft little things," she added, as she stroked them.

After the chickens were fed, Molly and Priscilla went into the garden with their aunt. Molly thought that she had never seen such a beautiful garden. The rosebushes were covered with blossoms and half-opened buds, and the air was full of their fragrance and of the odor of mignonette; and there were pink-and-white bleeding-hearts, and blue larkspurs, and so many yellow butterflies flitting from flower to flower that Molly could not count them. She and Priscilla helped their Aunt Ruth cut long sprays of pink roses, and white roses, and red ones, and they carried them into the house for her in a large basket. She gave them each a small bowl to fill with roses, because they were little girls, and she arranged some in a large bowl, because she was a grown-up person. When the house was fragrant with roses, the children went out-of-doors again.

"Let's play a game," said Molly. "Let's play 'Follow Your Leader,' and you will have to do every single thing that I do."

"All right," said Priscilla, "only I will be leader, and you must do just what I do."

She led Molly a race all over the barn, and then through the garden and back to the barn, sometimes hopping on one foot, and sometimes waving both hands wildly in the air, while Molly tried hard to keep in view a pair of slim black legs which whisked very fast around corners. At last Priscilla climbed the ladder that led to the hayloft and sank down on the hay. Molly scrambled up the ladder quite out of breath, only to see Priscilla slip over the edge of the loft and land on the hay below. She looked up with laughing eyes at Molly.

"You've got to do it; you promised to follow me!"

Molly went to the edge of the loft and leaned over dubiously. "I'm afraid."

"Coward!"

"It might hurt me."

"It's only soft hay; and it's great fun; it's just like flying."

"But I'm not a bird."

"I would n't be a 'fraid cat," said Priscilla, "besides, you promised."

Molly hung her feet over the edge of what appeared to her a frightful precipice and looked down at her smiling cousin.

"Come on," said Priscilla. "One, two, three."

"Oh, I can't do it," said Molly, drawing back.

"I hate people who are afraid," observed Priscilla, "and you promised, you know."

Molly slipped part way over the edge. It seemed to the poor little girl as if she could never land safely on the hay below.

"One, two, three."

She had let go and was flying through the air, and—here she was at the bottom, quite safe and sound, only a little out of breath.

"Isn't it fun?" asked Priscilla.

"I don't know," said Molly doubtfully. But before the morning was over she liked it just as much as Priscilla did.

While they were sitting together in the hayloft, Priscilla accidentally ran her head into a large cobweb, and got her hair and dress covered with it. "You must do it too, Molly," she said. "I am the leader."

"But you did not do it on purpose," Molly protested, "and it is so horrid."

"Never mind; you must do it."

"But there may be spiders in it."

"*There are,* but you have got to do it."

"I would rather go into the house to see Aunt Ruth."

"You don't play fairly; you must run your head into the cobweb; it's part of the game, and then I will tell you a lovely story about a fairy princess."

So Molly ran her curly head into the cobweb and was well covered with dust and dirt; and when the two little girls went in to dinner Priscilla's mamma said, "Priscilla Drayton, what a looking child! What have you been doing?"

And Molly's mamma said, "My dear little girl, did n't you remember that I put a clean gingham on you this morning?"

Molly hung her head.

"It was all my fault, Aunt Jenny," said Priscilla.

"Priscilla is generally very good," said Priscilla's mamma, "but she isn't used to playing with other children, and it excites her."

"Molly is the best little thing at home," said Molly's mamma.

"They seemed so quiet and demure yesterday afternoon," said their grandmother.

Quiet and demure they might be when they were apart, but they were never quiet and demure again when they were together. The long summer days were not long enough for Molly and Priscilla, and the week sped by altogether too fast.

Poor Priscilla was inconsolable when the last day came. She had never seen so much of any little girl before, and she loved Molly with all the passionate affection of a lonely child.

"Oh, dear, oh, dear," she sobbed. "It seems as if I should truly die if you go home, Molly."

"But you are coming to stay with us at Christmas," said Molly cheerfully.

"Christmas is years and years away. Wouldn't you like to stay here all summer and be my sister?"

Molly did not want to hurt the feelings of her dear Priscilla whom she loved so much, but she loved so many people at home that she was not sorry to be going there.

"I should like it if you could be my sister and live with me," she said; "but I have Flora, and Turner, and Ruth, and papa, and Aunt Mary, and my dear Nonesuch, and then there is Julia Esterhazy and Miss Sylvia Russell, so you see I couldn't live with you."

When it was time for Molly and her mamma to be driven to the station, Molly's hat was nowhere to be found. They looked for it high and low, in the hayloft and in the garden, as well as all over the house.

"Molly, you must not be so careless," said her mamma. "I am afraid we shall lose the train."

Priscilla, red-eyed and very sober, sat silently in a corner of the room.

"If you expect to catch the train, you must start at once," said Mrs. Benson's mother.

"We shall have to lend Molly one of Priscilla's hats," said Mrs. Drayton. "Priscilla, run upstairs and bring me down your best hat."

Priscilla was gone a long time. and when she came back she had Molly's brown hat in her hand. "I found it," she said. "I hid it, for I thought if she didn't have a hat she couldn't go home; but if she's got to go, I'd rather she would go in her old hat than in my best one."

They did lose the train, and came back to spend one more night. Priscilla was much pleased at first, but as the evening wore on she felt that it would have been better if Molly had gone in the afternoon, for now they must have the sad parting all over again.

The next day, just before Molly was to go home, Priscilla came into her room with a ten-cent piece in her hand.

"Molly," she said, "I love you very much, and I want to give you something to remember me by, and I haven't anything but common money."

"I don't want to take your ten-cent piece," said Molly, for she knew that her cousin had very little money.

"Molly, money is nothing to me," said Priscilla loftily; "I only care for it for what it will buy."

"It will buy such lovely things," said Molly, looking wistfully at the dime, "paper-doll furniture and dear little china dolls."

"And tissue paper for paper dolls' dresses," added Priscilla, "pink and blue and yellow."

Poor Priscilla was already half sorry that she had been so generous, as visions of the enchanting things she had meant to buy with that ten-cent piece floated before her eyes.

"Take it!" she cried heroically, as she thrust it into Molly's hands.

Molly hesitated.

"Take it!" Priscilla repeated.

Molly got her little purse, which had just a dime in it, and looked doubtfully at Priscilla's money. "Fourth of July is coming," she observed; "perhaps you might want your ten cents."

Priscilla caught a glimpse of that other dime in Molly's purse. The sight of it and the idea of the Fourth of July were too much for her strength of mind.

"Molly," she suggested, "suppose we exchange. Suppose I give you my dime and you give me yours? Then we shall each have something that belongs to the other."

July

HOW MOLLY SPENT HER TEN CENTS

Molly meant to keep Priscilla's ten cents always, but she had not been at home many days before she received a letter from her cousin that changed her plans. It was a long letter because Priscilla had dictated it to her mamma. Molly's mamma read it aloud.

> "DEAR MOLLY,—I miss you very, very much. I cried the day you went, for it was so lonely. I have spent your ten cents. I meant to get pink and blue and yellow tissue paper, but the Fourth of July came and I got fire-crackers instead. They are all gone now, but it was fun while they lasted. They made a splendid noise. I like fire-crackers.
>
> "We have a new bossy. She is an Alderney, and she is mine. I have named her for the person I love the best next to mamma. She has a very pretty name. Can you guess what it is?"

Molly's mamma paused when she came to this part of the letter.

"Ruth, for Aunt Ruth?" Molly suggested.

"No."

"Rebecca, for grandmamma?"

"No."

"What has she named it?"

"I have named her Molly for you," Mrs. Benson read.

Molly looked very much pleased at the idea of having such a charming namesake.

"Please get something to remember me by on my birthday," the letter proceeded. "As I have spent your ten cents, I want you to spend mine, and then we shall be even. My birthday is the 8th of July. I wish you were my sister.

"Your loving cousin,

"PRISCILLA DRAYTON."

"It is the 8th of July today, Molly dear," said Mrs. Benson.

"Then I think I had better go and look around in the shops."

"You will find a great variety of things at Fletcher's," said her mamma; "and if you like, you may go there all by yourself like a grown-up person."

This pleased Molly, and she put on her brown hat and started out with a little shopping-bag that her Aunt Ruth had given her at Christmas, with her small purse in the bottom holding her ten-cent piece. Just as she reached the gate, she saw Julia Esterhazy coming out of the big white house across the way.

"Where are you going, Molly?" Julia asked. "I was coming over to play with you."

"I am going downtown shopping," said Molly, feeling that she was a very important person.

"What are you going to buy?"

"I don't know."

"You don't know what you are going to buy?"

"It may be tissue paper, or it may be paper dolls' furniture, or it may be a new dress for Sylvia or Jane, but whatever it is, it must cost just ten cents"; and Molly told Julia the story of the exchange of the dimes.

"I should get candy if it were mine," said Julia, "and then you could give me some."

"But I don't want to eat up my lovely present," said Molly.

It was a warm day, and the two little girls were glad to get under shelter away from the hot sun.

Fletcher's was a very delightful shop. It had almost everything in it that anyone could want. In fact, it was so full of charming things that it was hard to make a choice. Molly's eyes were first fascinated by a card full of paper-doll children, and their pretty blue, red, and white dresses. There was a back and a front view of each little girl that were to be cut out and pasted together to make a complete person, and there were besides a tennis racket and a hoop and a dear little doll in a doll's carriage for the paper-doll children to play with, and a shopping-bag and a green watering-pot. Molly was afraid these children and their outfit cost a great deal of money, and that she could not afford to buy them.

"How much are they?" she shyly asked the man behind the counter.

"Twelve cents and a half a card. They are cheap for that, for they came from Germany. Do you want one of these cards?"

Molly shook her head. "I only have ten cents," she answered, with a sigh.

"I would call it ten cents, seeing that it is you," he said.

He was a pleasant man, with kind gray eyes. "Ten cents is dirt cheap for two children and their entire wardrobe, not to mention play-things," he added.

"Yes, it is very cheap," said Molly.

Julia, meanwhile, had discovered some paper-doll furniture. One card was full of kitchen things, and another was devoted to parlor furniture, while a third displayed a bedroom set.

"How perfectly beautiful!" Molly said, as she looked at the little brown bureau, with its white-and-red bureau cover and the red pin-cushion full of pins.

"What a dear little rug!" said Julia, pointing to a charming brown coon-skin rug.

"And look at the towels and the little towel-rack," said Molly.

"And the bed and washstand and the pretty blue screen," added Julia.

"See the brown chairs and the dear little brown clock. What fun it would be to cut them out, Julia."

"Look at the parlor set," said Julia. "See the piano, and the red sofa and chairs, and the tall piano-lamp with its red shade."

"The kitchen is a dear place," said Molly. "See the table with a lobster on it in a dish, and the sweet little cooking-stove, and the pretty blue dishes in the cupboard; they all look so real."

"See the spice-box," said Julia. "Pepper, nutmeg, c-i-n-n-a-m-o-n, cinnamon."

"Oh, look at that dear pussycat in the kitchen!" said Molly. "How much are these cards?" she asked.

"Ten cents apiece."

"Only ten cents! I don't know which I want the most."

"*I* should choose the parlor set." said Julia.

"I like the kitchen and the bedroom set best, because we could have the most fun with them."

"The same things come at five cents a card in a smaller size," the man behind the counter stated.

"At five cents a card! Then I can have two of them, Julia; and I can send one of them to Priscilla, for poor Priscilla has spent all her money on fire-crackers, and has n't anything to remember me by."

"I should keep them both," said Julia. "If she chose to spend her money on fire-crackers, that is her lookout. We could have lots more fun with the kitchen and parlor furniture, too."

"Yes, we could," said Molly: "I must look around a little more before I decide," she added prudently. "Oh, Julia! See that pretty pink gingham with white spots on it! How becoming that would be to Sylvia! It takes only half a yard for her clothes. How much is it for half a yard?"

"It is twenty-five cents a yard," the clerk replied.

"How much would that be for half a yard, Julia?"

"I don't know."

"We don't know how much it would be for half a yard," said Molly appealingly.

"Well, I'll call it ten cents."

"Ten cents!" said Molly. She was almost sorry, for if it had cost more she could not have bought it, and it would have been a little easier to choose.

"Look at this sweet doll, Molly," said Julia, from the other end of the shop. "A tiny doll and yet so prettily dressed. How much is it?"

"Ten cents."

"Everything is ten cents in this store," said Molly, in despair. "I can't ever decide; but I have so many dolls that I don't really need any more."

"Oh, Molly, see this!" and Julia paused before a tall, round basket. A white card hung above it, and on this card was printed in large black letters:

CHILDREN'S GRAB BASKET

5 CENTS A GRAB

EACH ARTICLE FULLY WORTH 7 CENTS

Julia pushed up the cover of the basket, and she and Molly peeped in over the top. There were flat parcels to be seen and three-cornered parcels, and long ones and square ones, and they were all done up in tissue paper. There was something very interesting and mysterious about the grab basket. Those paper packages might have something in them even rarer and more beautiful than the paper dolls, or the furniture, or the pink gingham.

"You could have two grabs for ten cents," Julia suggested. "You could grab and I could grab, and I could give you my thing."

She was longing to know the contents of a certain interesting irregular parcel.

"The furniture is so sweet," said Molly; "and I am sure I want it."

"The paper dolls are sweet, too," said Julia.

"Yes, and so is the pink gingham. I shall *have* to grab to decide it."

Meanwhile a more important customer had come in with whom the clerk was absorbed, so Molly went over to him and handed him her ten cents.

"We have decided to take two grabs, and here is the money," she said.

"All right. Did you say you would have silesia or percaline, madam?" he asked, turning to the other customer.

"You grab first," said Julia.

Molly looked from the flat parcels to the three-cornered ones, and could not decide which to choose.

"I think I will shut up my eyes," she said, and she put in her hand at random and pulled out a small, flat parcel. She opened it eagerly, and took out a block of black paper, to be used as a slate, and a pencil with which to write on it. She was sadly disappointed, and felt very much like crying.

"It is a horrid thing," said Julia. "We don't want a paper slate when you have got that nice blackboard. You were very silly to shut your eyes. I shall choose with my eyes open. I am going to take that queer thing that looks as if it might be a doll."

She took out the enticing-looking package, and began to untie the string, and presently drew forth a pink-and-green-and-white china vase of a hideous shape. It was too large for dolls and too small for people, and too ugly to please either.

"That grab bag is perfectly horrid," said Julia.

Molly was sure that she had never been so unhappy. She knew, now that it was too late, that she wanted the paper-doll furniture more than anything in the whole world. The two little girls were very sober all the way home. When they reached Molly's gate, Julia handed over the vase.

"Take the old thing," she said. "You have got something to remember Priscilla by always now, and you can send the paper slate to her."

"Well, what did you buy, dear?" her mamma asked cheerfully, as Molly came into the parlor.

The little girl found it hard to keep back her tears. Her Aunt Mary and Turner were sitting there too. She felt that it would have been easier to confess her folly to her mamma alone.

She held up the vase and the paper block silently.

"The block was a sensible choice," said her mamma, "but I don't see why you chose the vase."

"I did n't choose either of them," Molly burst out. "We grabbed and we got them."

"In short, they chose you," said Turner.

Then the little girl told the whole sad story. "I *did* want the paper-doll furniture so much," she ended.

"Why did n't you buy it, then?" asked her aunt.

"Because we thought it would be more fun to grab."

"This will be a very good lesson for you, Molly," said her aunt. "It is never well to spend money unless you are sure what you are spending it for. I am sorry for you, but you will never be so foolish again."

"There will be time to go to Fletcher's before tea," said Turner. "I will go with you, and we will pretend that the dime I have was Priscilla's, and you shall choose what you want all over again."

Miss Benson raised her eyebrows in disapproval, but Turner added quickly, "She can't learn a lesson, Aunt Mary, unless she has some more money to spend."

Molly danced up and down with pleasure, and she and Turner went to Fletcher's together. This time she made her choice very quickly, for she knew just what she wanted. She bought the bedroom set and the kitchen furniture. She remembered Julia's words: "I should keep them both. If Priscilla chose to spend her money on fire-crackers, that is her lookout."

But now she herself had spent her money foolishly, and if Turner had thought, as Julia did, that nobody who had made an unwise investment ought to have anything given her, she would never have had the dear paper-doll furniture. So she kept the kitchen set, and sent the bedroom set to Priscilla.

August

LITTLE MISS ROBINSON CRUSOE

In August, Molly went to the seashore with her Aunt Mary and Ruth and Turner. The Bensons had taken a cottage there for six weeks. As it was a very small cottage, and they were not a very small family, they could not all be there at once; and besides, somebody had to stay at home with Molly's papa until his vacation.

The cottage was close by the sea, and there was a beach where Molly could dig with her shovel, and where she could go in bathing with the others, in her little red bathing-dress. It was all pleasant enough, but there were times when she was very lonely, for all her life she had had a child to play with, and now there was nobody, not even Flora. She used to look wistfully at the children on the beach, and tell her Aunt Mary about them.

"None of them are the right size," she would say. "They are either too big or too little; but there was a sweet one in the water today. She was very young, not more than four; but she would be better than nothing. Can't you ask her mamma if I may play with her?"

"I don't know her mamma, Molly."

"Can't you find some little girl the right age, Aunt Mary?"

"I can't go about like the town crier, asking if anybody has a little girl six years old who could play with my niece Molly."

Molly laughed.

"There are a great many little girls who don't have any child to play with. Think of poor Priscilla," said Miss Benson. "Suppose you and I go to the beach and try to find some of those pretty shells. Don't you think that I am almost as nice as a little girl, Molly?"

"You are different. I love you best, but you don't dig wells and play house. You just read your book and say, 'Don't get your feet wet, Molly Benson.' "

Molly and her aunt went over to the long beach beyond the bathing beach, and they were soon so busy picking up shells that Molly forgot to wish for a child. It was such a beautiful day that one could not but be happy. The sky was blue, and the sea was bluer still, and there was enough wind to make little waves, just the right size for a little girl, and there was a great deal of brown seaweed on the beach, and there were so many shells that Molly began to dance with delight. They were all of one variety, but some were pale cream color, and others were a brighter yellow. The most remarkable thing about them was that each shell had a small hole at one end. They seemed made on purpose for a little girl to string together. On the whole, Molly had a pleasant afternoon, although her aunt grew tired of looking for shells after a time, and sat down on the sand and put up her red sunshade and took out her book. Molly hated that book, for it was always appearing just as she was beginning to have a nice time. Today she had not seen it, for it had been concealed in her aunt's brown shopping-bag. Molly could not understand how any one could want to read when it was possible to pick up shells and dig deep wells in the sand. She had never been away from her mamma so long before, and she missed her sadly, for she was one of those grown people who seem exactly like a little girl, and so did Ruth when she had any time to give to Molly, but at present she and Turner were very busy, for they had a great many friends who invited them to take long sails or to play tennis. Molly could not go on sails because it made her seasick, and nobody seemed to remember how much she liked to play tennis in her own way.

One afternoon, Ruth found her crying, "Why, you poor little dear, what is the matter?" she asked.

"Turner does n't want me to play tennis with him and Frank," she sobbed. "But I would have picked up the balls for them so nicely; and Aunt Mary says you won't want to be bothered with me, and that I may go to the post-office with her when she finishes her letters. I don't want to go to the post-office! It isn't a pretty walk! She told me I ought to be thankful I was at the seashore, for so many children can't go there, but I'm not glad one bit. The seashore isn't any use if you have n't anybody to play with, and your brother is cross, and you can't go to the beach, but have to take a walk in the dusty, hot road to the horrid post-office. She says I am a naughty girl. Oh, dear, I want to go home to papa and mamma and Flora."

"I will go to the beach with you, Molly," said Ruth, "if Aunt Mary does n't mind."

Molly stopped crying and her face brightened.

Digging down to China.

"Run and tell her that I will take care of you until tea-time, and that she can have an 'afternoon out.' "

Molly ran off, and came back presently. "She says I may go! She says I may go!" she cried, clapping her hands.

"I suppose I may as well take a book," Ruth suggested.

"Oh, please don't; you might lose it, you know."

Ruth laughed. "I am afraid you are getting spoiled," she said; but she did not take her book. It was not so many years since she had been a little girl herself, and she could remember how unhappy she was when Turner went away and she had n't anybody to play with. She and Molly walked to the long beach, and dug such deep wells that Ruth expected every moment to reach China; and they made a fort, and watched the tide rise and wash it away.

"Suppose we walk to the little desert island at the end of the beach," said Ruth at last. "I have never been there, and it looks as if Robinson Crusoe lived there."

"It isn't really an island," Molly declared.

"I know it, and I don't suppose we shall really find Robinson Crusoe; but we may as well imagine something interesting while we are about it."

The water went almost around the point that they called Robinson Crusoe's island, and when the tide was high, as it was now, only a narrow, rocky path led to it. Ruth and Molly picked their way over the stones. The white sand dune and the long, coarse green grass looked very picturesque against the blue sky.

"We ought to find a deserted hut on the other side of that sand dune," Ruth observed impressively.

When they reached the "desert island," Molly ran on ahead. "Now we will find Robinson Crusoe's house," she cried. She stopped suddenly on the other side of the sand dune. "It is here! A real little house!"

There, in very truth, was a little shelter something like their summer-house in the garden at home, with a roof and a seat. On this seat there was a red parasol.

"It must be that Mrs. Robinson Crusoe lives here," said Molly, much pleased.

"Look on the floor," said Ruth.

Under the seat was a small pail, just the size of Molly's pail, and painted blue like hers, and in it was a small shovel, just the size of Molly's shovel; while in a corner of the summer-house sat a doll, a charming Paris doll, with flaxen hair and brown eyes. She wore a pink gingham gown and a broad-brimmed white hat.

"Oh," said Molly, with a sigh of delight, "there is a little Miss Robinson Crusoe!"

"We will sit on this seat to rest," said Ruth; "I don't believe the Robinson Crusoes will mind."

Presently they saw two sail-boats coming into view, and also two tiny sail-boats, the right size for a family of dolls.

"Look, Ruth," said Molly eagerly; "see the big sail-boats and their children. Did you ever see anything so sweet as those little young, small sail-boats, exactly like the big ones! They look as if they were just hatched out."

In each of the large boats was a grave, elderly gentleman.

"I know who they are," said Ruth; "one of them is Esther Dana's father, and the other must be Mr. Townsend. They are great yachtsmen, and the little boats must be models that they are trying."

It was so exciting to watch the boats that Molly forgot all about little Miss Robinson Crusoe until the fleet went around the promontory and was lost to sight.

"I suppose we may as well go home," Ruth said, after the last sail had disappeared.

"Please can't we wait to see if Mrs. Robinson Crusoe and her little girl won't come back?" Molly begged.

A moment later, a lady and a child came into view.

"They are coming," said Molly. "They have been down to the beach to watch the boats. There *is* a little Miss Robinson Crusoe! There truly is! And she's just about as large as I am."

Ruth stepped forward to explain to the lady how they happened to be where they were. Mrs. Robinson Crusoe had a pleasant face, and she looked at the sisters with interest. Little Miss Robinson Crusoe clung to her mamma, and whispered something Molly could not hear.

"Yes," said Mrs. Robinson Crusoe, "I will ask her."

"Are not you one of Mrs. Benson's daughters?" she inquired of Ruth, presently.

"Yes, I am Ruth, and this is Molly."

"I used to go to school with your mother. I have been trying to get to see her ever since she has been down here."

"Mamma will be delighted to see you," said Ruth, "but she will not be here until next week."

The little girl pulled her mamma's gown impatiently again and whispered something, looking hard at Molly.

"Lucy is very anxious to know if Molly cannot come to play with her sometimes," said Lucy's mother.

"Molly will be very glad to play with Lucy," Ruth replied.

The children immediately made friends over the Paris doll.

"What is her name?" Molly asked.

"Grace."

"That is a pretty name. I have a Sylvia at home who looks something like her, except she has blue eyes. I only brought Jane down here, for there was n't room for my whole family, and she needed the change most. Your little pail and shovel are just like mine."

"Do you like to dig wells?" Lucy asked.

"I love it. Do you like to play house?"

"Of course I do."

"Whose little boats are those that were sailing around the point just now?" was the next question.

"One of them is my papa's, and he will sail it for us tomorrow if we like."

"Do you play house every day in this dear place?"

"Yes, with mamma. I have n't any little girl to play with, but now you have come we can keep house together."

"Molly," said Ruth, "it is getting late, we must go home."

"But I can come again tomorrow, can't I, Ruth?" Molly pleaded.

"Do let her," said Mrs. Robinson Crusoe.

"Yes, she can come if Aunt Mary does not object."

"Be sure to bring Jane tomorrow," said Lucy, as she bade Molly good-bye.

The next day, Ruth took Molly to the point early in the morning. Lucy was waiting for her with Grace in her arms, and Mrs. Robinson Crusoe was sitting in the shelter reading a book. Now that Molly had a little girl to play with, it did not trouble her to have people read books.

Lucy and Molly became great friends before the morning was over, and so did Grace and Jane.

After a time, Lucy's papa came to say that he would sail his little boat if they wished.

"How lovely!" said Molly.

"Would you like to have your daughter go on a sail?" he asked Molly.

"Is there room for her?"

"Yes, there is just room; she isn't so large as Grace."

The children walked down to the beach, carrying their dolls. Mr.

Robinson Crusoe put a shingle in the sand for Grace to lean against, for he said she looked delicate. He seated Jane in the little boat, and he got into a rowboat himself. There was a strong breeze, and the little boat flapped its sails as a bird might flap its wings, and started to go out to sea. The children looked on eagerly. Jane seemed to enjoy her sail immensely at first, but all at once there came a strong gust of wind, and the little boat dipped far down in the water.

"It's going to upset," said Lucy.

"Oh, dear! Jane will drown," cried Molly.

Alas! before Mr. Robinson Crusoe could reach the boat it had capsized, and poor Jane had sunk.

"Papa, you must get her," Lucy said eagerly, "she's Molly's favorite child. She's there, right there, under your oar."

"Of course I will get her," he called back cheerfully; "I am not going to be responsible for the death of a favorite child."

Fortunately, the accident happened so near the shore that Mr. Robinson Crusoe was able to fish Jane out. Her clothes were all bedraggled, and her complexion, which had been poor for a long time, was ruined, but these are trifles to a mother, and Molly clasped her in her arms with great joy.

When Mrs. Robinson Crusoe saw what had happened, she said that Jane was so pale she must have fainted, and that they ought to send for the doctor. Mrs. Robinson Crusoe played that she was the doctor, and she ordered a wash to be put on Jane's face. She had her painting materials with her, for she was going to make a sketch later in the morning, so she touched Jane's complexion with the wash the doctor recommended, and she looked as beautiful as she had ever looked in her early youth.

When Turner came for Molly at noon and was shown Jane, he said that the sea air had evidently made her over.

Henceforth, every pleasant day Molly went to play with Lucy, and Miss Benson and Ruth heard no more about the lonely seashore; for a desert island is a charming spot, if the joys of the sea and the sand can be shared with a little Miss Robinson Crusoe.

September

A FAMILY FLIGHT

Molly and her Aunt Mary came home from the seashore before the rest of the family, to take care of Molly's papa, whose vacation was over early in September.

The morning after their return, her aunt said, "There is something that I think you will like to see down cellar, Molly."

"Down cellar!" said Molly. "What can it be?"

"Guess."

"Apples?"

"No."

"Rats?"

"No, not rats."

"Something alive?"

"Something very much alive."

"Mice?"

"No."

"I can't guess," said Molly, "you will have to tell me."

"I won't tell you, but I will show you."

Miss Benson went down the steep, dark cellar stairs and Molly followed her. There was only a gray light in the cellar, although the sun was shining, for the windows were very small and high up. It was cold and damp, and Molly was glad that she did not have to live there. Her aunt went into the coal-cellar, where a barrel was standing near the window. Molly peeped over the edge, but the light was so dim that at first she merely saw something moving.

"Feel of them," said her aunt.

Molly put her hand into the barrel, but before she had touched anything, Nonesuch, who had just come running down the cellar stairs, jumped into the barrel. Molly's eyes were getting used to the light, and she cried in excitement, "They are little baby Nonesuches."

"Yes, little kittens," said her aunt.

"How many, Aunt Mary?"

"Count them and see."

"Nonesuch won't let me."

Miss Benson put Nonesuch on the cellar floor, and made her stay there while Molly counted the kittens.

"There are three of them! Oh, Aunt Mary, how lovely! A white one with a little black spot on its chin and a cunning black tail, and a yellow one, and—oh, Aunt Mary! there is a little tortoise-shell one just like its mamma! Oh, oh, Aunt Mary, it is too sweet! There will be one for Flora, when she comes home, and one for me, and one for Julia Esterhazy. May I go and get Julia now?"

"Yes, if you like."

Molly ran across the street to tell the good news to Julia.

"Guess what has happened over at our house?" she cried. "We have ever so many new people in the family."

"Do you mean that your Aunt Flora and your Cousin Priscilla have come to make you a visit?" Julia inquired.

"No, it isn't big people, it's little people: a new family. Nonesuch has three baby children, and you are to have one."

Julia was almost as excited as Molly, and she ran eagerly after her across the street and down the cellar stairs.

Miss Benson followed the children, and took one kitten after another out of the barrel that Julia might get a good view of them.

"You can choose which you will have, Julia," said Molly.

"The tortoise-shell," Julia decided promptly.

Poor Molly wanted that one herself, but they were all very sweet, and she could be contented with any of them.

"They have n't got their eyes open," said Julia.

"They are very, very young," Miss Benson explained, "and it will be almost a week longer before their eyes open."

The next morning, Molly went down cellar "all by her own self" to see the kittens. She put her hand eagerly into the barrel, but to her great surprise she could feel nothing but hay; and when she looked into the barrel there was not one kitten to be seen. She put her hand as far down in the hay as she could reach, for she thought the kittens might be hidden in it, but she could not find them. She ran upstairs with the tears in her eyes and her lips trembling.

"Aunt Mary! Aunt Mary!" she said, "the kittens are lost, all of them; somebody has taken them away."

Her aunt went downstairs and looked in the barrel herself. It was too true, the kittens had vanished.

Molly sat down on a box in the cellar and began to cry.

"They were all *so* lovely," she sobbed, "but especially the dear tortoise-shell one. And now they are lost, quite lost."

"Don't cry, Molly, we shall be sure to find them," said her aunt. "Nonesuch probably did not like to have us meddle with the kittens, and it is she who has hidden them."

"Oh, I wish she would tell us where they are."

Molly ran upstairs to find Nonesuch, and taking her in her arms said, "Dear Nonesuch, won't you please show us what you have done with your children? The white one and the yellow one, but especially the dear tortoise-shell? I would n't hurt them for anything in the world.

I love them, Nonesuch; I *love* them just as much as if I were their grandmother. Won't you please run and show me where they are?"

But Nonesuch only shut her eyes and began to purr.

"I think if we watch her we shall soon find the kittens," Molly's aunt suggested.

A few minutes later, Nonesuch went to the door at the top of the cellar stairs and began to mew.

"She wants us to let her down cellar," said Molly, who ran to open the door. Molly and her aunt walked softly downstairs behind the pussy, and waited to see where she would go, but Nonesuch heard them coming, and as she did not want them to find her family, she stayed quietly in a corner of the cellar.

"I expect we shall have to spend the day down cellar," Molly observed gravely.

"You run upstairs and play with your dolls," said her aunt. "It is too damp for you here; and I will pretend to go away, too, but really I will watch Nonesuch."

Molly ran off, but she was too excited to play with her dolls, although she told Jane and George Washington all about the dear kittens who were found yesterday only to be lost today. It seemed a long time before she heard her aunt come upstairs.

"Have you found them, Aunt Mary?" she asked eagerly.

"No, I can't get any clue to them; I don't believe they are in the cellar. I think Nonesuch has been playing a game of bluff with us, and I can't spend any more time looking for them."

Molly's face fell. "I wish Turner were at home," she said, "for he would find them."

"Turner is coming home this afternoon for a day or two; but I have no doubt the kittens will turn up before he does."

Miss Benson was very busy that morning, helping Bridget preserve peaches, and so she did not think again of the kittens.

Julia came over to play with Molly, as usual, but although the two little girls hunted in every corner of the cellar and all over the shed, and although they watched Nonesuch carefully, they could find no trace of the missing family.

When Turner came home in the middle of the afternoon, Molly ran up to him and flung her arms around him.

"Dear Turner," she said, "I am so glad to get you back, for you will find my lovely family."

"I left your lovely family in a blooming condition at the seashore."

"I mean kittens, not people. Nonesuch has carried away her three dear babies, and we can't find them anywhere."

"I suppose she thinks that one cat is enough for one family. Why try to find them? Why"—but as he saw Molly's face change he added hastily, "I was only joking. I am as hungry as a wolf, for I have n't had any dinner; but after I have foraged for something to eat, I will find the kittens."

"But they may starve first," Molly objected.

"Would you rather have a starved brother, or starved kittens? Do you love them better than you love me?"

"No," Molly said, with some hesitation, "only they might die, you know, and it would n't hurt you to be a little hungry."

Turner, however, insisted upon satisfying his appetite at once; but after he had disposed of some cold beef and bread and butter and half a pie, he and Molly started on what he called "a life-saving expedition."

They went through the shed in vain, and they even explored the summer-house and looked under the piazza, but not a trace of a kitten could be found.

"It is a regular 'Family Flight,' " said Turner. "Nonesuch evidently believes with Miss Hale in change of scene for a young family. We have had our outing, and she does not want to be behind the fashion and so is taking hers."

Turner and Molly next directed their attention to the cellar, but the kittens were nowhere to be seen.

"I think they may be in the coal," Molly said, diving into it for the fifth time that day and coming out with very black hands. "If we could only find one of them it would be some comfort; the tortoise-shell is such a darling, and besides, she belongs to Julia."

"My poor sister Molly
Is quite melancholy
Just because a small kit
Has decided to flit,"

said Turner.

Molly began to laugh. "Did you make that up your own self?" she asked.

"No; it is a translation from Ovid."

Nonesuch meanwhile had walked down the cellar stairs, for the door was open. Turner and Molly were so far away that she thought it safe to go to her starving family, so she climbed up on an old blind at the other end of the cellar. Molly happened to turn her head just in time.

"Look, Turner! Look! Where is she going? She was over there this morning, but Julia and I could n't find anything in that corner."

Molly and Turner quickly crossed the cellar. "It is almost as exciting as a game of 'Hunt the thimble,' " he remarked.

When they reached the spot where Nonesuch had been, she had jumped down on the floor and was demurely licking her paws.

"We're warm, we're very, very warm," said Turner.

"I'm cold."

"I mean we are very near finding them. Look here; here is a hole where the pipe used to go. Perhaps she has hidden them there. We'll go back into the other cellar, Molly, and watch her."

It was not long before they saw Nonesuch climb up on the blind again. Molly held her breath. Yes, it was really so; she was climbing into the hole. Her head was lost to sight; presently there was nothing to be seen but her tail, and then even that had disappeared.

"Now, Molly, we must find how far in she has carried the kittens. It will be very hard to get them out."

"But you *must* get them out."

"They are in between the cellar ceiling and the kitchen floor." Turner put his arm as far into the hole as he could, but he did not reach Nonesuch.

Molly's face fell. "We shall have to get a plumber to take up the kitchen floor," she stated.

"I shall have to take up some boards myself, I suppose; but are you sure you care enough about the kittens to make me take all that trouble?"

"Oh, Turner! Of course I do."

"Do you love them as well as you love George Washington?"

"Yes."

"Better?"

"You are a bad boy, and I shall ask papa to take the floor up when he comes home."

"I suppose I may as well save father the trouble."

Molly followed Turner upstairs, and she and her Aunt Mary and Bridget all watched him take up a board under the sink, where he expected to find the kittens. After it was up they listened, and could hear a very faint mew.

"Oh, they are there! They are there!" Molly cried.

Turner had to take up two more boards before he could reach the kittens. At last he put his arm under the floor and fished out a soft little ball of fur.

"It's the white one," said Molly, "my own dear white one! And it's alive, quite alive."

"Very much so," said Turner. "It is mewing for all it is worth."

He put in his hand once more and pulled out, not a plum, but another kitten.

"It's Flora's! It's the darling yellow one," said Molly. "Oh, Turner, you must find the tortoise-shell, too."

"Here she is," and he successfully landed the third member of the family.

"They are all three alive," said Molly. "How sweet they are! I am almost glad they were lost, are n't you, Aunt Mary? For it is so nice to find them. Turner, you are just as good as a plumber."

October

PRISCILLA THE SECOND

When a cousin has done one the great honor of naming her bossy Molly, the least one can do is to give the dear cousin the lesser glory of a kitten for a namesake. So Molly's kitten was called Priscilla. At first this caused some confusion.

"Priscilla has her eyes open at last," Molly announced one day.

"At last!" said Turner. "I should think from your description of that young woman she had always had her eyes open."

"I mean Priscilla the kitten, of course," Molly explained impatiently.

Another day she said, "Oh, mamma! Priscilla was carried upstairs today by her mamma."

"Is the poor child ill?" Molly's mother asked.

"How funny you are, mamma! I mean Priscilla the kitten"; and Molly began to laugh.

"We shall have to call the kitten Priscilla the Second, to avoid mistakes," said her mother. And Priscilla the Second she always remained after that. It was rather a long name for a small kitten, but Turner said he had no doubt that she would grow up to it, if she lived long enough.

The first day that Nonesuch brought her babies upstairs was a very exciting time. Molly and Julia were having school with Miss Benson, as they always did now in the morning. The door was partly open, and in walked Nonesuch carrying Priscilla the Second by the nape of her neck.

"Aunt Mary! Aunt Mary!" Molly cried. "See Nonesuch walk into school just as if she were a person, except she carries her baby in her mouth instead of her arms."

Nonesuch left the kitten at Miss Benson's feet, and then went down cellar and brought up the tortoise-shell kitten. She evidently thought that her children needed the advantages of school. She tried hard to bring up the third kitten, but it was a little too heavy for her. It was distracting to the lessons to have so many pupils, and so, to the children's great regret, Miss Benson would not let Nonesuch and her daughters stay.

When Molly told Turner what had happened, he made a rhyme to celebrate the occasion:—

"Nonesuch had a little kit
Whose coat was beauteous reckoned,
And everywhere that Nonesuch went
She took Priscilla Second.

"She carried her to school one day
To get an education;
The stern Miss Benson turned her out
Because she caused elation."

The next day, something still more wonderful happened. When Molly awoke in the morning, she heard Nonesuch mewing, as usual, outside her window. She ran to open it, and in jumped pussy. She did not seem satisfied, however, but kept on mewing, and went back to the window.

"What is the matter with you?" said Miss Benson. "She wants us to see something, Molly."

Molly and her Aunt Mary followed Nonesuch to the window, and looking down to the balcony below, they saw Priscilla the Second, who seemed very lonely all by her small self on the large balcony. Nonesuch had successfully carried her up the trellis, but she could not get her up the long slant of the roof to the second story.

"Aunt Mary! Aunt Mary! Please, please run down and get Priscilla the Second before she tumbles through the railings," Molly cried.

Happily, Miss Benson arrived just in time to save the little creature from an accident.

All this was in Priscilla the Second's babyhood, so to speak. She was a lovable little kitten from the first, and more like her mother in disposition than the "dear tortoise-shell," who was a small copy of her parent in looks, but who was selfish and self-willed. The yellow kitten, whom Flora named Buffy, was the largest and most enterprising of the three. He was the first to leave his mother. A comfortable home was found for him, when he was a few weeks old, with the kind expressman who had brought Nonesuch to Molly.

As soon as Nancy, the tortoise-shell kitten, was old enough to be happy away from her mamma, she went across the road to live in the big white house with Julia and her mother.

After the departure of her brother and sister, Priscilla the Second became still more intimate with her mother. Nonesuch was gradually teaching her all the things she knew herself. She showed her how to keep her pretty coat clean, and she taught her how to play, and one morning she gave her a lesson in climbing.

Julia and Molly were having their lesson in spelling in the schoolroom by the window which overlooked the garden where the other lesson was taking place. Nonesuch was sitting in the shed watching Priscilla the Second feebly climb into the lilac bush. A tub full of water stood just below the bush. It was sunk into the ground, and was used for watering the plants by Molly's mother, and for a lake by Molly and Julia. The little kitten was so small that she found it hard to climb.

"There she goes," Molly said under her breath; "she is really beginning to climb."

"How do you spell 'tongue,' Molly?" her aunt asked for the second time. "I shall not let you children sit near the window, if you can't attend to your lessons."

Molly darted out of her seat and ran swiftly toward the door.

"Sit still, Molly Benson," her aunt commanded.

"Priscilla the Second is drowning," Molly explained, in tragic tones; and without waiting for permission, she rushed to the rescue. The poor little kitten had lost her balance, and had fallen from the bush into the tub of water. Miss Benson and Julia eagerly watched to see what would happen. Would Molly be in time? The little creature had sunk, and could not be seen. Nonesuch, however, had hastened to help her child. She braced herself against the edge of the tub, and waited until her daughter rose to the surface of the water; then she leaned over and grasped Priscilla the Second's neck with her teeth and landed her safely on the grass. When Molly reached them, she found the kitten was quite well, only very wet, and thoroughly frightened. Molly took Priscilla the Second into the house, and there was a very long recess in school that morning.

When October began to draw to its chilly close, and it was no longer pleasant for kittens to live out-of-doors, Mrs. Benson tried to find a new home for Priscilla the Second. She heard that Patrick Riley, the man who worked for the Esterhazys, wanted a kitten for his children, and she told Molly the fact.

"But I don't want to give away my dear kitten," said Molly, "I want to keep her forever."

"Darling, we shall only have room for one cat this winter. Would you rather give up Nonesuch and keep Priscilla the Second?"

"I would rather keep both of them. It's pretty hard if we haven't room for one cat and a small kitten in our large house."

"The poor little Rileys haven't any kitten. They had one, just as you used to have Tartar, but it died."

"They must get another of some little girl who has five or six kittens."

Mrs. Benson said no more about the departure of Priscilla the Second for a day or two, but she told Patrick that he might ask his children to come and look at her. Molly was very unhappy when she heard this. "They will want her, if they see her, mamma," she said. "They will never be contented with any other kitten."

When the three little girls arrived at the kitchen door, Bridget summoned Molly. Poor Molly held Priscilla the Second very tight in her arms, as if she were afraid that the Rileys would carry her away by main force. They were pleasant-looking children. One of them was about Molly's age—she was the quietest and shyest of the three; another was older; and there was a younger one. The little one had on a blue coat that had once belonged to Julia.

"What is the kitten's name?" asked the oldest child.

"Priscilla the Second."

"That's a funny name; it's too long."

"That is her name, and if I ever give her away she has always got to be called by the whole of it, *Priscilla the Second*."

"It's a very pretty name," the youngest child hastened to say.

"What is your name?" inquired Molly.

"Her name is Katie," said the oldest girl, "and this is Lizzie, and I am Annie."

"Do you like cats, Katie?"

"We love them," Annie replied.

The little Katie meanwhile was stroking Priscilla the Second's fur in an ecstasy of delight. "What a beauty she is," she murmured. "Dear, darling kitty"; and she put her cheek down to the pussy's soft fur.

Molly's heart sank.

"What bright eyes she has," said Annie. "And look, Katie, at her dear little black tail, and the rest of her as white as a snowdrift."

"Except for the black spot on her chin," said Katie.

Molly felt still more unhappy when she saw that every beauty of her pet was being discovered by the sharp eyes of the little Rileys.

"I should think it would be very easy to get kittens where you live," she hazarded, "there are so many children."

"We've moved up to a house all by itself, where there are n't any neighbors," Annie explained. "And where we used to live there are n't any pretty kittens, they are mostly black or gray."

"Oh."

"I never saw such a pretty kitten," said Katie.

"There never was such a pretty kitten," said Lizzie, speaking for the first time.

"Would n't you rather have a doll than the kitten?" Molly asked desperately. "I could n't give up Jane, or George Washington, or Sylvia, or the Princess, but I would give each of you one of my dear smaller dolls."

Lizzie evidently wavered, and Molly grew hopeful, but Annie and Katie remained firm. "We'd rather have the kitten, for it's alive," Annie decided.

"Come, Molly; your tea is ready," said Mrs. Benson. "Say good-bye to the children."

"Good-bye," said Molly, hugging Priscilla the Second tighter than ever, and trying to forget the longing glances that the Rileys cast upon her.

That night, after her mamma had put Molly to bed, the little girl called to her as she was leaving the room. She had been very sober all the evening, and it was evident that something weighed on her mind.

"Do you suppose that Annie and Lizzie and Katie would give Priscilla the Second enough to eat, mamma?" she inquired.

"I am sure they would, dear."

"But if they are quite poor, they may not have enough for people and a kitten, too."

"They always have enough to eat, and it takes very little to feed a cat."

"Mamma."

"Yes, darling."

"I wish those children had n't come here."

"Why, dear?"

"Because they seem to want Priscilla the Second so very, very much, and I can't give her up, I can't, I can't!"

"Suppose your cat had died, and you had very few playthings; and suppose you lived in a lonely place away from other children; don't you think you would care more for Priscilla the Second than a little girl could who had a great many playthings, and ever so many neighbors, and one cat already?"

"No, I don't," Molly said stoutly.

"Good night, Molly."

"Good night, mamma."

For three days Molly looked very serious indeed. Julia wondered what could be the matter, and Miss Benson was afraid that she was going to be ill. Toward the end of the third day she said to her mamma, "I suppose those children have got to have Priscilla the Second. Annie and Katie came to see her again yesterday, and Patrick told Julia that they were 'clean gone' over her. If she must go, I'd rather have her go right off. Can Julia and I take her there this afternoon in a basket? It will be *some* comfort if I can carry her there myself."

"Yes, dear, if your Aunt Mary or Ruth will go with you."

Miss Benson and the two little girls set forth with Priscilla the Second that afternoon. Molly carried the basket all the way. It was a long walk to the Rileys' house, for they lived at the other end of the town. On the way they met Miss Sylvia, who had just come back from the mountains.

"Where are you all going?" she asked.

When they told her, she said she would like to join the procession. She and Miss Benson walked on ahead, for they had a great deal to talk about, as they had not seen each other since June.

There was a large field opposite the Rileys' house that was used as a cow pasture in summer. Molly thought that it must be even more fun to play there than in the garden at home, for it was so much bigger, and besides, a little brook ran through it, which would make a delightful river to sail boats in or span with bridges. The Rileys' house was very small, but this made it all the more sociable. The kitchen seemed to be the parlor and the dining room too, and Molly thought it was a very nice arrangement, because the little girls would never have to be careful of the furniture. Annie and Lizzie and Katie were running about the room barefooted.

"Why don't you wear your shoes and stockings?" Julia asked.

"Sure, miss, I want to save their shoes and stockings for school," Mrs. Riley replied.

"I wish mamma would let me take off my shoes and stockings every afternoon," Molly said.

The three little girls and two older boys and a toddling baby boy all looked with interest at Molly and her basket.

"Guess what I've got here?" she asked.

"Is it—is it the kitten?" Katie demanded breathlessly.

Before Molly could reply, Priscilla the Second answered the question herself by giving a long, wailing "Miauw."

The faces of the children were so radiant that Molly felt somewhat comforted.

"It *is* the kitten," said Katie rapturously. "It is Priscilla the Second."

November

A THANKSGIVING DINNER

The Bensons were to dine with Mrs. Benson's mother, in Boston, on Thanksgiving Day. She always left New Hampshire just before Thanksgiving. This year Priscilla and her mamma were to be there, too.

Molly took cold a few days before Thanksgiving, and so she could not go to Boston with the others. Her mother stayed at home with her, but in spite of this, the little girl could not help crying when she saw the rest of the family going out of the door.

"Poor Molly," said Flora, "I would stay with you, if it would make you feel any better."

"I will bring you home a nice, large orange," said her father.

"And I will bring you some candy," Ruth promised.

"I will eat enough turkey for both you and myself," said Turner generously.

"Oh, dear!" said Molly, after she and her mother were left alone, "why should I have such a dreadful cold just at Thanksgiving time, when I wanted to go to grandmamma's *so* much?"

"We must try to have a nice little Thanksgiving all by ourselves, Molly. Suppose we stop and count up all the things we have to be thankful about."

"There is George Washington," said Molly, brightening, "and there is dear Nonesuch."

"Suppose we let Nonesuch eat her Thanksgiving dinner with us?" suggested Molly's mamma.

"Can we truly have her? What fun!"

Nonesuch was not usually allowed to come into the dining room, but Mrs. Benson thought that it would do no harm to give her her dinner there just this once. Nonesuch rubbed against Molly, and began to purr in a pleased way, when she found herself in the room.

Molly and her mother had their dinner of tomato soup, turkey, and cranberry sauce and mashed potato, on top of the table; and dear little Nonesuch had her dinner of tomato soup, turkey bones, and potato and bread, under the table.

As they were finishing their turkey, the doorbell rang, and Bridget brought in something wrapped in white paper, which she put on the table in front of Molly.

"Miss Sylvia Russell has sent you this, Miss Molly," she announced.

"Oh, then it is something very nice, I know."

On the outside of the paper was written:

"For my dear Molly, from Miss Sylvia, who is so sorry that her little friend has to stay at home on Thanksgiving Day."

Molly undid the bundle eagerly, and saw a tin dish.

"What is it?" she asked blankly.

"It is a mould of ice cream, and Bridget can take it into the kitchen and turn it out."

"Ice cream! How perfectly lovely! How do you suppose Miss Sylvia knew that ice cream is my favorite dessert?"

Presently Bridget brought the ice cream in on a platter.

"It is a lion, mamma! It is almost too pretty to eat!"

"It will melt, if you don't eat it. But here are some verses. We will read them, and see what Miss Sylvia says about it"; and Mrs. Benson read:

> "I hope you will welcome this lion, my dear,
> I hope you will welcome this lion;
> He is gentle and kind,
> And soft-hearted, you'll find.
> Pray eat him, and see if you like him, my dear.
> Pray eat him; his name is Orion.
>
> "They tell us that lions will eat us, my dear,
> They talk of the danger of lions;
> But those who speak so
> Have no knowledge, I know,
> Of the singular breed of Orions, my dear,
> Of the singular breed of Orions.
>
> "So eat him and grow like Orion, my dear,
> As strong and as brave as Orion;
> And if he should seem
> Naught but common ice cream,
> Remember he 's *really* a lion, my dear,
> Remember he 's really a lion."

"Orion is a very funny name for him, I think," said Molly. "I wonder why Miss Sylvia called him Orion?"

"Orion was a mighty giant. I suppose she called him that because he was such a strong lion. You may help to him, Molly."

"Which part do you like best, mamma, his head or his tail?"

"I will take a small slice of his mane, thank you."

"I am going to take a leg and the wishbone," said Molly. "But perhaps lions don't have wishbones? Oh! It is vanilla! My favorite kind! How lovely Miss Sylvia was to send me such nice ice cream! Such a nice lion, I mean."

After Molly and her mother had finished their ice cream, they had some nuts and raisins, and while they were eating them, the little girl looked out of the window and saw a gray squirrel scamper up a tree.

"Mamma," she said, "don't you suppose that dear squirrel would like to have some Thanksgiving dinner, too? Would n't he eat some of our nuts?"

"I am sure he would, Molly. I think if I were to put some nuts in a basket outside the window on the window-sill, he would be very glad to come and eat his Thanksgiving dinner."

Molly clapped her hands with delight, and Mrs. Benson filled a small basket with nuts. Then she threw a shawl over her head and went out into the woodshed. Molly watched, and presently saw her come to the outside of the window with a plank, which she placed so that one end of it rested on the window-sill and the other end on the ground.

"That's the squirrel's road, isn't it?" she called with glee. "Now he can walk right up to the basket, can't he?"

Mrs. Benson came back into the house presently, and she and Molly waited eagerly to see what would happen. Pretty soon the squirrel ran down the tree, and once more they saw something gray with a bushy tail whisk across the lawn.

"He is coming here! He is! He is!" cried Molly, running to the window.

"Be careful. Stand back, Molly, you have frightened him."

The little squirrel had paused to look up at the house with his bright eyes, while his sharp ears were on the alert for any sound. He saw Molly come toward the window, and being a prudent and timid little squirrel, he scampered across the lawn and ran up the oak tree in the garden.

"Oh, dear!" said Molly. "I am afraid he won't come back any more. Who would have thought that *anything* could be afraid of a small girl like me?"

"Have patience, and keep still. If you do, I am pretty sure he will come back, for he has seen the nuts."

So Molly retreated to the sofa in the corner, and kept very, very still, scarcely daring to breathe. By and by the squirrel came down from the tree and advanced cautiously to the window. He cocked his head to one side, and looked and listened. He heard no sound, and he did not see Molly and her mamma, so he came up the plank to the window-sill. Finally he took a nut in his two little paws. Mrs. Benson and Molly were so much interested that they had forgotten that somebody else was watching the squirrel, and before they could stop her, Nonesuch had climbed up in a chair by the window and dashed one of her paws wildly against the window-pane.

"She wants to catch the squirrel," said Molly. "Naughty Nonesuch!"

The squirrel had scurried away in great haste, and Nonesuch looked very much surprised when she found she could not catch him, for she had forgotten that the window was shut.

"Naugty, naughty Nonesuch!" Molly said again. "Or perhaps she isn't naughty. Perhaps she thinks squirrels are rats with furs on, because it is cold weather."

Molly and her mother and Nonesuch watched a long time before the squirrel came again. Nonesuch was in the chair that was close to the window. She had learned that it was shut, and so had the squirrel, or he would never have ventured back, as he did after a time. He ran up the board and stood on the window-sill, looking in triumph at Nonesuch.

"Don't you wish you could catch me?" he seemed to say; "but you can't, on account of that window."

He came again and again for a nut, taking one at a time, and then scampering up into the oak tree to eat it, and Nonesuch watched him patiently. He always cocked his head on one side and looked at her saucily. He came so many times that at last they began to suspect that he was not always the same squirrel.

"I can't tell whether he is many, or whether he is only one," said Molly, "but I think he is at least two, because sometimes he is very fat, and sometimes he is quite thin."

"He *is* two," she exclaimed presently, in excitement. "The fat one and the thin one are coming together."

"Look at Nonesuch, Molly."

It was altogether too much for the self-control of poor Nonesuch to see two squirrels together on the window-sill. She made a frantic dash with her paw against the glass, and looked very unhappy when she did not succeed in catching one, for she had forgotten again about the window.

"Look at the fat one. He is a greedy thing! He won't let the thin one have a single nut. You mean thing! Look quick, mamma! He is so greedy that he has upset the basket."

It was too true, the basket had been overturned, and a shower of nuts descended upon the snow. A few moments later, to Molly's intense delight, four squirrels appeared, as if by magic.

"The thin one has told all his friends about the nuts, I am sure he has," said Molly. "See how angry the fat one is to find that so many squirrels have found out his secret! He is trying to drive them away! There are nuts enough for them all, so why does he mind? How they whisk their tails! It seems as if they were all tail, mamma."

When the last nut was gone, Molly and her mother and Nonesuch regretfully left the window.

"It has been a very nice Thanksgiving," said Molly. "Lions and squirrels are almost as interesting as Priscilla and grandmamma."

December

THE RILEYS' CHRISTMAS TREE

The day before Christmas, something very pleasant happened: Priscilla and her mother came to make the Bensons a long visit.

When Molly saw her dear cousin once more, she flung her arms around her, and hugged and kissed her as if she could never leave off.

"You have got on a pretty blue dress," Priscilla observed, looking at her critically, "and you are taller, but I shall love you just the same."

"I must show you Nonesuch," Molly said, running to find her favorite. She picked her up and held out her right front paw, that Priscilla might shake hands with her.

"This is your cousin Priscilla, Nonesuch," she said gravely.

Priscilla and Nonesuch shook hands, and became fast friends at once.

Priscilla was then shown all Molly's dolls. She thought that George

Washington had rather a conceited look, but she supposed it was natural, as he was the only brother among so many sisters. This made Molly very unhappy, but she was pleased to have Priscilla take a great fancy to Jane. She said she put one at ease. She was rather in awe of the Princess and Sylvia.

Later, at dinner, she was very much afraid of Molly's Aunt Mary and of her papa, and of Turner and Flora; but she liked Ruth, because, as she expressed it, she was a "grown-up Molly."

After dinner, Julia came over, and although Priscilla did not have a word to say to her at first, the three little girls grew very sociable before many minutes passed.

"Something nice is going to happen this afternoon," Molly confided to Priscilla. "Miss Sylvia is going with Flora, and Julia, and me, to take some Christmas presents to Patrick's children."

"He is the man who makes our fires," Julia explained.

"We went to his house," Molly proceeded, "to take Priscilla the Second."

"That 's the kitten."

"She knows it 's the kitten, Julia. They did n't seem to have anything to play with (not that it matters much, for one can always pretend); so Aunt Mary suggested that we should dress some dolls for them. She and Miss Sylvia and Ruth dressed them mostly, but we children helped, and we sewed up some muslin bags this morning in school, and filled them with candy. Turner gave us the candy."

"And we are going to take some stockings, and mittens, and picture books," Julia added.

"Flora and Julia and I bought the picture books with our own money," Molly went on; "and you can come with us, Priscilla, and carry one of the dolls. Aunt Mary and Ruth have to stay at home to get our Christmas tree ready. I must show you the dolls," and she opened the closet door with pride. "We have n't done them up yet. Here they are, all in a row. Are n't they sweet?"

The three dolls, like the Riley children, were of different sizes, making one think of a flight of steps. There was a strong family resemblance between them, for they all had flaxen hair and blue eyes. The oldest was dressed in red, and wore a red hood, which Molly's mamma had crocheted; the middle one was in blue, and had on a blue crocheted hood; and the youngest was in pink, and wore a pink hood.

"I wish they were all three mine," Priscilla said enviously.

"We have an engine and some cars for the little boy," said Molly, "and Miss Sylvia is going to give the big boys some jackknives. Here she comes now."

"So this is Priscilla," Miss Sylvia said cordially. "I feel as if we ought to be old friends, because I have heard so much about you from Molly."

Priscilla looked hard at Miss Sylvia, and she did not wonder that Molly thought her like a fairy princess.

"We will do the dolls up in tissue paper," said Miss Sylvia. "Can't you find some, Molly, without troubling your Aunt Mary? The other things are all ready, I see."

After the dolls were equipped for their journey, Miss Sylvia said:

"You can carry the largest doll, Julia, because you are the oldest; and Priscilla can carry the middle-sized doll, and Molly can take the smallest."

Miss Sylvia carried the other presents in a basket, and Flora took some oranges and the bags of candy in another basket.

When they reached the Rileys' house, Miss Sylvia knocked on the door, and Mrs. Riley opened it.

"Oh, and is it you, Miss Sylvia?" she exclaimed. "Sure and you look like the blessed Saint Elizabeth."

"We have come to see the children," Miss Sylvia explained.

"They are all out in the field making believe have a Christmas tree. I told them it was foolishness, for they have n't nothing to speak of to put on it."

Molly's eyes shone, and she ran off very fast in the direction of the field. How charming it would be to put real presents on a make-believe Christmas tree! For if it is always pleasant to "pretend," there is a certain satisfaction that comes from real things.

At first Molly could not see the Rileys, but at last she discovered them in the farther corner of the vacant lot, behind some hemlock trees.

The snow had come early that year, and the sleet had fallen afterwards. There was a hard crust everywhere in the meadows, so that little people and big people, too, could walk on it as if it were ice.

When Molly and her friends reached the spot where the Rileys were playing, they became speechless with admiration, for before their astonished eyes was a whole miniature village. The buildings were all white, but so they often are in New England villages. Each house was made of blocks quarried out of the snow. There were open spaces for the doors and windows, as there are in blockhouses, and the children had put branches of hemlock inside, to look like green blinds and green doors. The roofs were all flat; they were made of pieces of wood about as large as the cover of a starch-box, put across the tops of the houses, and then covered with a thin layer of crust. Some diminutive snow chimneys crowned these structures. As for the church, it was very imposing, for it had a high tower and two wide doors. It stood near the common, a charming little round inclosure, fenced in by a hedge of tiny hemlock branches. The schoolhouse stood on one side of it and the village store on the other.

"I have never seen anything so beautiful," said Molly. "Did you make it yourselves?"

"Tom and Pat helped us."

"They were your architects, I suppose," said Miss Sylvia.

Tom and Pat, meanwhile, had retreated to the other end of the field.

The children were so entranced by the snow village that at first they did not notice the Christmas tree, but at length Priscilla pointed it out.

"Isn't it beautiful?" she asked.

"A real, live, out-of-doors Christmas tree, growing in the fields. How perfectly lovely!" cried Molly.

"It is n't half so pretty as the house ones," cried Annie. "We did n't have any of them glistening balls, and we had to put on real snow instead of the make-believe kind."

"I think real snow is a great deal prettier," said Miss Sylvia.

It was a touching little Christmas tree, for it had tried so hard to copy its drawing-room sisters. The Rileys did not realize how pretty it looked out-of-doors, under the blue sky, with the real snow on its branches. There was n't much else on them, to be sure, but there was a little of the crinkly barley candy that comes at Christmas time, tied on with some bits of bright ribbon; and there was a toy watch for the little boy; while some kindergarten mats that Katie had made at school, and some Christmas cards that had been given to the children the year before, helped to brighten up the somber green branches. To add to the gayety of the scene, Priscilla the Second was frisking about, looking as white as the snow, and wearing a pretty blue ribbon around her neck.

"Suppose you children run off to the other end of the field for a few minutes," said Miss Sylvia to the little Rileys, "and we will call you when we want you."

After they had gone, Miss Sylvia and the children decorated the Christmas tree.

"I wish we had known that they were going to have a Christmas tree, and we would have brought some glistening balls," said Miss Sylvia.

"The candy bags and the other things will make it look very pretty," said Flora.

They tied the bags of candy to the branches of the tree.

"What shall we do with the oranges?" asked Molly.

"We'll put them in a ring around the bottom of the trunk of the tree," Julia decided.

So they arranged them in what Miss Sylvia called a fairy ring around the trunk, and then they hung the picture books over the branches.

"What shall we do with the mittens and stockings?" Flora asked in despair.

"We'll put them on the ends of the branches as if they were hands and feet," Miss Sylvia replied.

They left the train of cars just outside the village, and they seated the three dolls in front of three houses in the village.

"What can we do with the jackknives?" Molly inquired.

"We will put one jackknife in the lap of the doll in red, and the other in the lap of the doll in blue," said Julia.

When everything was ready, Julia and Molly ran to call the children.

"Ask the boys to come, too," said Miss Sylvia.

Tom and Pat, however, had disappeared.

The little girls and the small Harry were very glad to follow Julia and Molly. When they saw the Christmas tree, they were as much overwhelmed with admiration as Molly had been when she saw the snow village. They did not say anything at first, but their eyes danced. At last Katie discovered the dolls. She gave a little cry of delight.

"There are three of them."

"Yes," said Molly. "A big one, and a middle-sized one, and a little one. The youngest is for you."

"We made some of the clothes ourselves," Julia added proudly.

"The jackknives are for Tom and Pat," said Flora.

Katie, meanwhile, had seized the doll in pink, and clasped her in her arms as tenderly as if she had been alive. "What pretty hair she has," she said, "and such blue eyes. Sure and they shut up! Look, Annie, when you hold her this way they shut up."

"She's asleep," said Molly.

Annie was rapturously examining the doll in red, and Lizzie had taken blissful possession of the one in blue. The little boy had discovered the train of cars, and was already beginning to play with them.

"It will soon be dark," said Miss Sylvia, "and we must be going home, for we have a long walk."

Molly looked wistfully behind her. "I never saw anything so beautiful as this snow village," she said.

"Oh, that is nothing," Annie replied. "Any one can have a snow village. Snow is plenty."

Molly meant to try to make one in the garden at home, but she was sure that it would not be so beautiful.

"We thank you very much for all the things," said Annie shyly.

"We must really go now, Molly," Miss Sylvia insisted.

"Yes," added Flora, "we must get home in time for our own Christmas tree."

"It won't be like this one," said Molly regretfully "Nothing can be as beautiful as this." She wished that their Christmas tree was to be out-of-doors under the blue sky, with real snow on the branches, and that they could arrange it themselves, while Annie wished that she could have a Christmas tree in the house like Molly.

"We 've had a lovely time," said Molly. "I never had such a lovely time before."

"Neither did we," Annie returned. "Good-bye and I wish you all a Merry Christmas."

NELLY'S HOSPITAL

By *LOUISA M. ALCOTT*

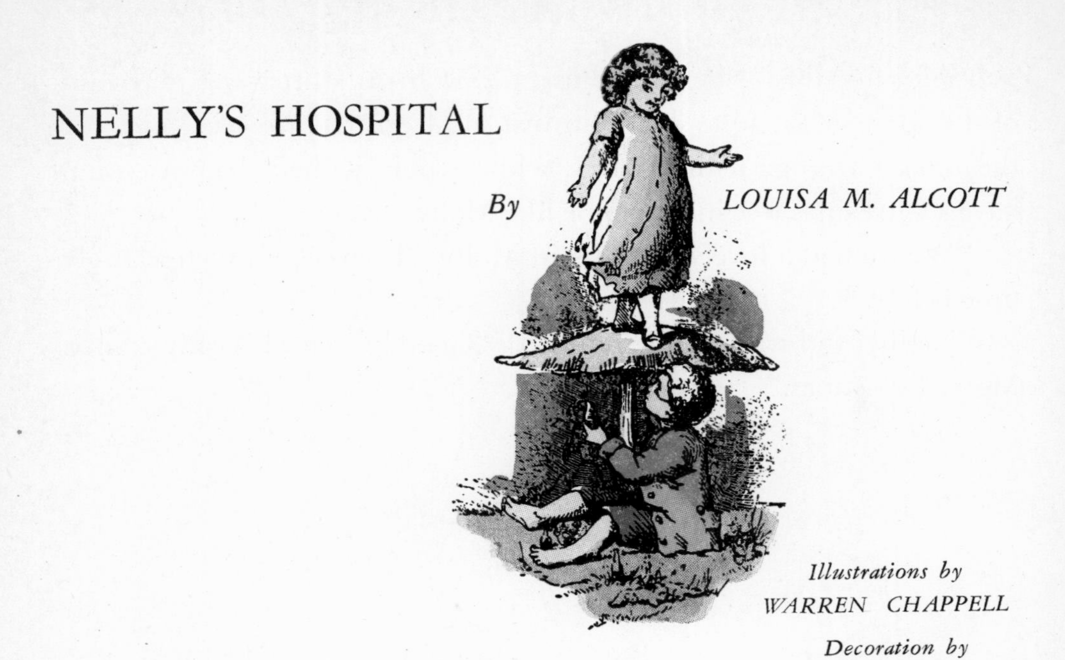

Illustrations by
WARREN CHAPPELL
Decoration by
A. LEDGARD

NELLY sat beside her mother picking lint; but while her fingers flew, her eyes often looked wistfully out into the meadow, golden with buttercups, and bright with sunshine. Presently she said, rather bashfully, but very earnestly, "Mamma, I want to tell you a little plan I've made, if you'll please not laugh."

"I think I can safely promise that, my dear," said her mother, putting down her work that she might listen quite respectfully.

Nelly looked pleased, and went on confidingly. "Since brother Will came home with his lame foot, and I've helped you tend him, I've heard a great deal about hospitals, and liked it very much. Today I said I wanted to go and be a nurse, like Aunt Mercy; but Will laughed, and told me I'd better begin by nursing sick birds and butterflies and pussies before I tried to take care of men. I did not like to be made fun of, but I've been thinking that it would be very pleasant to have a little hospital all my own, and be a nurse in it, because, if I took pains, so many pretty creatures might be made well, perhaps. Could I, mamma?"

Her mother wanted to smile at the idea, but did not, for Nelly looked up with her heart and eyes so full of tender compassion, both for the unknown men for whom her little hands had done their best and for the smaller sufferers nearer home, that she stroked the shining head, and answered readily:

"Yes, Nelly, it will be a proper charity for such a young Samaritan, and you may learn much if you are in earnest. You must study how to feed and nurse your little patients, else your pity will do no good and your hospital become a prison. I will help you, and Tony shall be your surgeon."

"Oh, mamma, how good you are to me! Indeed, I am in truly earnest; I will learn, I will be kind; and may I go now and begin?"

"You may, but tell me first where will you have your hospital?"

"In my room, mamma; it is so snug and sunny, and I never should forget it there," said Nelly.

"You must not forget it anywhere. I think that plan will not do. How would you like to find caterpillars walking in your bed, to hear sick pussies mewing in the night, to have beetles clinging to your clothes, or see mice, bugs, and birds tumbling downstairs whenever the door was open?" said her mother.

Nelly laughed at that, thought a minute, then clapped her hands, and cried: "Let us have the old summerhouse! My doves only use the upper part, and it would be so like Frank in the story book. Please say yes again, mamma."

Her mother did say yes, and, snatching up her hat, Nelly ran to find Tony, the gardener's son, a pleasant lad of twelve, who was Nelly's favorite playmate. Tony pronounced the plan a "jolly" one and, leaving his work, followed his young mistress to the summerhouse, for she could not wait one minute.

"What must we do first?" she asked, as they stood looking in at

Clearing out the summerhouse.

the dim, dusty room, full of garden tools, bags of seeds, old flowerpots, and watering cans.

"Clear out the rubbish, miss," answered Tony.

"Here it goes, then," and Nelly began bundling everything out in such haste that she broke two flowerpots, scattered all the squash seeds, and brought a pile of rakes and hoes clattering down about her ears.

"Just wait a bit, and let me take the lead, miss. You hand me things; I'll pile 'em in the barrow and wheel 'em off to the barn; then it will save time and be finished up tidy."

Nelly did as he advised, and very soon nothing but dust remained.

"What next?" she asked, not knowing in the least.

"I'll sweep up while you see if Polly can come and scrub the room out. It ought to be done before you stay here, let alone the patients."

"So it had," said Nelly, looking very wise all of a sudden. "Will says the wards—that means the rooms, Tony—are scrubbed every day or two, and kept very clean, and well venti—something—I can't say it; but it means having plenty of air come in. I can clean windows while Polly mops, and then we shall soon be done."

Away she ran, feeling very busy and important. Polly came, and very soon the room looked like another place. The four latticed windows were set wide open, so the sunshine came dancing through the vines that grew outside, and curious roses peeped in to see what frolic was afoot. The walls shone white again, for not a spider dared to stay; the wide seat which encircled the room was dustless now, the floor as nice as willing hands could make it, and the south wind blew away all musty odors with its fragrant breath.

"How fine it looks!" cried Nelly, dancing on the doorstep, lest a footprint should mar the still damp floor.

"I'd almost like to fall sick for the sake of staying here," said Tony, admiringly. "Now, what sort of beds are you going to have, miss?"

"I suppose it won't do to put butterflies and toads and worms into beds like the real soldiers where Will was?" answered Nelly anxiously.

Tony could hardly help shouting at the idea; but, rather than trouble his little mistress, he said very soberly: "I'm afraid they wouldn't lie easy, not being used to it. Tucking up a butterfly would about kill him; the worms would be apt to get lost among the bed-clothes; and the toads would tumble out the first thing."

"I shall have to ask mamma about it. What will you do while I'm gone?" said Nelly, unwilling that a moment should be lost.

"I'll make frames for nettings to the windows, else the doves will come in and eat up the sick people."

"I think they will know that it is a hospital and be too kind to hurt or frighten their neighbors," began Nelly; but as she spoke, a plump white dove walked in, looked about with its red-ringed eyes, and quietly pecked up a tiny bug that had just ventured out from the crack where it had taken refuge when the deluge came.

"Yes, we must have the nettings. I'll ask mamma for some lace," said Nelly, when she saw that; and taking her pet dove on her shoulder, told it about her hospital as she went toward the house; for, loving all little creatures as she did, it grieved her to have any harm befall even the least or plainest of them. She had a sweet child fancy that her playmates understood her language as she did theirs, and that birds, flowers, animals, and insects felt for her the same affection which she felt for them. Love always makes friends, and nothing seemed to fear the gentle child, but welcomed her like a little sun who shone alike on all and never suffered an eclipse.

She was gone some time, and when she came back her mind was full of new plans, one hand full of rushes, the other of books, while over her head floated the lace, and a bright green ribbon hung across her arm.

"Mamma says that the best beds will be little baskets, boxes, cages, and any sort of thing that suits the patients; for each will need different care and food and medicine. I have not baskets enough; so, as I cannot have pretty white beds, I am going to braid pretty green nests for my patients, and, while I do it, mamma thought you'd read to me the pages she has marked, so that we may begin right."

"Yes, miss; I like that. But what is the ribbon for?" asked Tony.

"Oh, that's for you. Will says that, if you are to be an army surgeon, you must have a green band on your arm; so I got this to tie on when we play hospital."

Tony let her decorate the sleeve of his gray jacket, and when the nettings were done, the welcome books were opened and enjoyed. It was a happy time, sitting in the sunshine, with leaves pleasantly astir all about them, doves cooing overhead, and flowers sweetly gossiping together through the summer afternoon. Nelly wove her smooth, green rushes; Tony pored over his pages; and both found something better than fairy legends in the family histories of insects, birds, and beasts. All manner of wonders appeared, and were explained to them, till Nelly felt as if a new world had been given her, so full of beauty, interest, and pleasure that she never could be tired of studying it. Many of these things were not strange to Tony, because, born among plants, he had grown up with them as if they were brothers and sisters, and the sturdy, brown-faced boy had learned many lessons which no poet or philosopher could have taught him, unless he had become as child-like as himself, and studied from the same great book.

When the baskets were done, the marked pages all read, and the sun had begun to draw his rosy curtains round him before smiling "Good night," Nelly ranged the green beds round the room; Tony put in the screens; and the hospital was ready. The little nurse was so excited that she could hardly eat her supper and directly afterwards ran up to tell Will how well she had succeeded with the first part of her enterprise. Now brother Will was a brave young officer who had fought stoutly and done his duty like a man. But, when lying weak and wounded at home, the cheerful courage which had led him safely through many dangers seemed to have deserted him, and he was often gloomy, sad, or fretful, because he longed to be at his post again, and time passed very slowly. This troubled his mother, and made Nelly wonder why he found lying in a pleasant room so much harder than fighting battles or making weary marches. Anything that interested and amused him was very welcome, and when Nelly, climbing on the arm of his sofa, told her plans, mishaps, and successes, he laughed out more heartily than he had done for many a day, and his thin face began to twinkle with fun as it used to do so long ago. That pleased Nelly, and she chatted like any affectionate little magpie, till Will was really interested; for when one is ill, small things amuse.

"Do you expect your patients to come to you, Nelly?" he asked.

"No, I shall go and look for them. I often see poor things suffering in the garden and the woods, and always feel as if they ought to be taken care of, as people are."

"You won't like to carry insane bugs, lame toads, and convulsive kittens in your hands, and they would not stay on a stretcher if you had one. You should have an ambulance and be a branch of the Sanitary Commission," said Will.

Nelly had often heard the words, but did not quite understand what

Nelly, climbing on the arm of his sofa, told her plans.

they meant. So Will told her of that great never-failing charity, to which thousands owe their lives; and the child listened with lips apart, eyes often full, and so much love and admiration in her heart that she could find no words in which to tell it. When her brother paused, she said earnestly:

"Yes, I will be a Sanitary. This little cart of mine shall be my ambulance, and I'll never let my water-barrels go empty, never drive too fast, or be rough with my poor passengers, like some of the men you tell about. Does this look like an ambulance, Will?"

"Not a bit, but it will, if you and mamma like to help me. I want four long bits of cane, a square of white cloth, some pieces of thin wood, and the gum pot," said Will, sitting up to examine the little cart, feeling like a boy again as he took out his knife and began to whittle.

Upstairs and downstairs ran Nelly till all necessary materials were collected, and almost breathlessly she watched her brother arch the canes over the cart, cover them with the cloth, and fit an upper shelf of small compartments, each lined with cotton wool to serve as beds for wounded insects, lest they should hurt one another or jostle out. The lower part was left free for any larger creatures which Nellie might find. Among her toys she had a tiny cask which only needed a peg to be water-tight; this was filled and fitted in front, because, as the small sufferers needed no seats, there was no place for it behind, and, as Nelly was both horse and driver, it was more convenient there. On each side of it stood a box of stores. In one were minute rollers, as bandages are called, a few bottles not yet filled, and a wee doll's jar of cold cream, because Nelly could not feel that her outfit was complete without a medicine-chest. The other box was full of crumbs, bits of sugar, bird seed, and grains of wheat and corn, lest any famished stranger should die for want of food before she got it home. Then mamma painted "U. S. San. Com." in bright letters on the cover, and Nelly received her charitable plaything with a long sigh of satisfaction.

"Nine o'clock already. Bless me, what a short evening this has been!" exclaimed Will, as Nelly came to give him her good-night kiss.

"And such a happy one," she answered. "Thank you very, very

Nelly's ambulance.

much, dear Will. I only wish my little ambulance was big enough for you to go in. I'd so like to give you the first ride."

"Nothing I should like better, if it were possible, though I 've a prejudice against ambulances in general. But as I cannot ride, I'll try and hop out to your hospital tomorrow, and see how you get on"—which was a great deal for Captain Will to say, because he had been too listless to leave his sofa for several days.

That promise sent Nelly happily away to bed, only stopping to pop her head out of the window to see if it was likely to be a fair day tomorrow, and to tell Tony about the new plan as he passed below.

"Where shall you go to look for your first load of sick people, miss?" he asked.

"All round the garden first, then through the grove, and home across the brook. Do you think I can find any patients that way?" said Nelly.

"I know you will. Good night, miss," and Tony walked away with a merry look on his face, that Nelly would not have understood if she had seen it.

Up rose the sun bright and early, and up rose Nurse Nelly almost as early and as bright. Breakfast was taken in a great hurry, and before the dew was off the grass, this branch of the S. C. was all astir. Papa, mamma, big brother and baby sister, men and maids, all looked out to see the funny little ambulance depart, and nowhere in all the summer fields was there a happier child than Nelly, as she went smiling down the garden path, where tall flowers kissed her as she passed and every blithe bird seemed singing a Godspeed.

"How I wonder what I shall find first," she thought, looking sharply on all sides as she went. Crickets chirped, grasshoppers leaped, ants worked busily at their subterranean houses, spiders spun shining webs from twig to twig, bees were coming for their bags of gold, and butterflies had just begun their holiday. A large white one alighted on the top of the ambulance, walked over the inscription as if spelling it letter by letter, then floated away from flower to flower, like one carrying the good news far and wide.

"Now everyone will know about the hospital and be glad to see me coming," thought Nelly. And indeed it seemed so, for just then a blackbird, sitting on the garden wall, burst out with a song full of musical joy; Nelly's kitten came running after to stare at the wagon and rub her soft side against it; a bright-eyed toad looked out from his cool bower among the lily-leaves; and at that minute Nelly found her first patient. In one of the dewy cobwebs hanging from a shrub near by sat a fat black and yellow spider, watching a fly whose delicate wings were just caught in the net. The poor fly buzzed pitifully, and struggled so hard that the whole web shook; but the more he struggled, the more he entangled himself, and the fierce spider was preparing to descend that it might weave a shroud about its prey, when a little finger broke the threads and lifted the fly safely into the palm of a hand, where he lay faintly humming his thanks.

Nelly had heard much about contrabands, knew who they were, and was very much interested in them; so, when she freed the poor black fly, she played he was her contraband and felt glad that her first patient was one that needed help so much. Carefully brushing away as much of the web as she could, she left small Pompey, as she named him, to free his own legs, lest her clumsy fingers should hurt him; then she laid him in one of the soft beds with a grain or two of sugar if he needed refreshment, and bade him rest and recover from his fright, remembering that he was at liberty to fly away whenever he liked, because she had no wish to make a slave of him.

Feeling very happy over this new friend, Nelly went on singing softly as she walked, and presently she found a pretty caterpillar dressed in brown fur, although the day was warm. He lay so still she thought him dead, until he rolled himself into a ball as she touched him.

"I think you are either faint from the heat of this thick coat of yours, or that you are going to make a cocoon of yourself, Mr. Fuzz," said Nelly. "Now I want to see you turn into a butterfly, so I shall take you, and if you get lively again I will let you go. I shall play that you have given out on a march, as the soldiers sometimes do, and been left behind for the Sanitary people to see to."

In went sulky Mr. Fuzz, and on trundled the ambulance until a golden green rose-beetle was discovered, lying on his back kicking as if in a fit.

"Dear me, what shall I do for him?" thought Nelly. "He acts as baby did when she was so ill and mamma put her in a warm bath. I have n't got my little tub here, or any hot water, and I'm afraid the beetle would not like it if I had. Perhaps he has pain in his stomach;

I'll turn him over, and pat his back, as nurse does baby's when she cries for pain like that."

She set the beetle on his legs, and did her best to comfort him; but he was evidently in great distress, for he could not walk, and instead of lifting his emerald overcoat, and spreading the wings that lay underneath, he turned over again, and kicked more violently than before. Not knowing what to do, Nelly put him into one of her soft nests for Tony to cure if possible. She found no more patients in the garden except a dead bee, which she wrapped in a leaf and took home to bury. When she came to the grove, it was so green and cool she longed to sit and listen to the whisper of the pines, and watch the larch tassels wave in the wind. But, recollecting her charitable errand, she went rustling along the pleasant path till she came to another patient, over which she stood considering several minutes before she could decide whether it was best to take it to her hospital, because it was a little gray snake with a bruised tail. She knew it would not hurt her, yet she was afraid of it; she thought it pretty, yet could not like it; she pitied its pain, yet shrunk from helping it, for it had a fiery eye, and a keen quivering tongue, that looked as if it wanted to sting.

"He is a rebel. I wonder if I ought to be good to him," thought Nelly, watching the reptile writhe with pain. "Will said there were sick rebels in his hospital, and one was very kind to him. It says, too, in my little book, 'Love your enemies.' I think snakes are mine, but I guess I'll try and love him because God made him. Some boy will kill him if I leave him here, and then perhaps his mother will be very sad about it. Come, poor worm, I wish to help you, so be patient and don't frighten me."

Then Nelly laid her little handkerchief on the ground; with a stick gently lifted the wounded snake upon it, and, folding it together, laid it in the ambulance. She was thoughtful after that, and so busy puzzling her young head about the duty of loving those who hate us, and being kind to those who are disagreeable or unkind, that she went through the rest of the wood quite forgetful of her work. A soft "queek, queek!" made her look up and listen. The sound came from the long meadow-grass, and, bending it carefully back, she found a half-fledged bird, with one wing trailing on the ground and its eyes dim with pain or hunger.

"You darling thing, did you fall out of your nest and hurt your wing?" cried Nelly, looking up into the single tree that stood near by. No nest was to be seen, no parent birds hovered overhead, and little Robin could only tell its troubles in that mournful "queek, queek, queek!"

Nelly ran to get both her chests, and, sitting down beside the bird, tried to feed it. To her great joy it ate crumb after crumb, as if it were half starved, and soon fluttered nearer with a confiding fearlessness that made her very proud. Soon baby Robin seemed quite comfortable; his eye brightened; he "queeked" no more, and but for the drooping wing would have been himself again. With one of her bandages Nelly bound both wings closely to his sides for fear he should hurt himself by trying to fly; and, though he seemed amazed at her proceedings, he behaved very well, only staring at her, and ruffling up his few feathers in a funny way that made her laugh. Then she had to discover some way of accommodating her two larger patients so that neither should hurt nor alarm the other. A bright thought came to her after much pondering. Carefully lifting the handkerchief, she pinned the two ends to the roof of the cart, and there swung little Forked-tongue, while Rob lay easily below.

By this time Nelly began to wonder how it happened that she found so many more injured things than ever before. But it never entered her innocent head that Tony had searched the wood and meadow before she was up, and laid most of these creatures ready to her hands, that she might not be disappointed. She had not yet lost her faith in fairies, so she fancied they, too, belonged to her small sisterhood, and presently it did really seem impossible to doubt that the good folk had been at work.

Coming to the bridge that crossed the brook, she stopped a moment to watch the water ripple over the bright pebbles, the ferns bend down to drink, and the funny tadpoles frolic in quieter nooks where the sun shone; and the dragon-flies swing among the rushes. When Nelly turned to go on, her blue eyes opened wide, and the handle of the ambulance dropped with a noise that caused a stout frog to skip into the water heels over head.

Directly in the middle of the bridge was a pretty green tent, made of two tall burdock leaves. The stems were stuck into cracks between the boards; the tips were pinned together with a thorn; and one great buttercup nodded in the doorway like a sleepy sentinel. Nelly stared and smiled, listened, and looked about on every side. Nothing was seen but the quiet meadow and the shady grove; nothing was heard but the babble of the brook and the cheery music of the bobolinks.

"Yes," said Nelly softly to herself, "that is a fairy tent, and in it I may find a baby elf sick with whooping cough or scarlet fever. How splendid it would be. Only I could never nurse such a dainty thing."

Stooping eagerly, she peeped over the buttercup's drowsy head, and saw what seemed a tiny cock of hay. She had no time to feel disappointed, for the haycock began to stir, and, looking nearer, she beheld two silvery-gray mites, who wagged wee tails, and stretched themselves as if they had just waked up. Nelly knew that they were young field-mice and rejoiced over them, feeling rather relieved that no fairy had appeared, though she still believed them to have had a hand in the matter.

"I shall call the mice my Babes in the Wood, because they are lost and covered up with leaves," said Nelly, as she laid them in her snuggest bed, where they nestled close together and fell fast asleep again.

Being very anxious to get home, that she might tell her adventures, and show how great was the need of a Sanitary Commission in that region, Nelly marched proudly up the avenue, and, having displayed her load, hurried to the hospital, where another applicant was waiting for her. On the step of the door lay a large turtle, with one claw gone, and on his back was pasted a bit of paper, with his name,

"Babes in the wood."

"Commodore Waddle, U.S.N." Nelly knew this was a joke of Will's, but welcomed the ancient mariner, and called Tony to help her get him in.

All that morning they were very busy settling the newcomers, for both people and books had to be consulted before they could decide what diet and treatment was best for each. The winged contraband had taken Nelly at her word and flown away on the journey home. Little Rob was put in a large cage, where he could use his legs, yet not injure his lame wing. Forked-tongue lay under a wire cover, on sprigs of fennel, for the gardener said that snakes were fond of it. The

Babes in the Wood were put to bed in one of the rush baskets, under a cotton-wool coverlet. Greenback, the beetle, found ease for his unknown aches in the warm heart of a rose, where he sunned himself all day. The Commodore was made happy in a tub of water, grass, and stones, and Mr. Fuzz was put in a well-ventilated glass box to decide whether he would be a cocoon or not.

Tony had not been idle while his mistress was away, and he showed her the hospital garden he had made close by, in which were cabbage, nettle, and mignonette plants for the butterflies, flowering herbs for the bees, chickweed and hemp for the birds, catnip for the pussies, and plenty of room left for whatever other patients might need. In the afternoon, while Nelly did her task at lint picking, talking busily to Will as she worked, and interesting him in her affairs, Tony cleared a pretty spot in the grove for the burying-ground and made ready some small bits of slate on which to write the names of those who died. He did not have it ready an hour too soon, for at sunset two little graves were needed, and Nurse Nelly shed tender tears for her first losses as she laid the motherless mice in one smooth hollow, and the gray-coated rebel in the other. She had learned to care for him already and, when she found him dead, was very glad she had been kind to him, hoping that he knew it and died happier in her hospital than all alone in the shadowy wood.

The rest of Nelly's patients prospered, and of the many added afterwards few died, because of Tony's skillful treatment and her own faithful care. Every morning when the day proved fair, the little ambulance went out upon its charitable errand; every afternoon Nelly worked for the human sufferers whom she loved; and every evening brother Will read aloud to her from useful books, showed her wonders with his microscope, or prescribed remedies for the patients, whom he soon knew by name and took much interest in. It was Nelly's holiday;

but, though she studied no lessons, she learned much and unconsciously made her pretty play both an example and a rebuke for others.

At first it seemed a childish pastime, and people laughed. But there was something in the familiar words "Sanitary," "hospital," and "ambulance" that made them pleasant sounds to many ears. As reports of Nelly's work went through the neighborhood, other children came to see and copy her design. Rough lads looked ashamed when in her wards they found harmless creatures hurt by them, and going out they said among themselves, "We won't stone birds, chase butterflies, and drown the girls' little cats any more, though we won't tell them so." And most of the lads kept their word so well that people said there never had been so many birds before as all that summer haunted wood and field. Tender-hearted playmates brought their pets to be cured; even busy farmers had a friendly word for the small charity, which reminded them so sweetly of the great one which should never be forgotten; lonely mothers sometimes looked out with wet eyes as the little ambulance went by, recalling thoughts of absent sons who might be journeying painfully to some far-off hospital, where brave women waited to tend them with hands as willing, hearts as tender, as those the gentle child gave to her self-appointed task.

At home the charm worked also. No more idle days for Nelly or fretful ones for Will, because the little sister would not neglect the helpless creatures so dependent upon her, and the big brother was ashamed to complain, after watching the patience of these lesser sufferers, and merrily said he would try to bear his own wound as quietly and bravely as the "Commodore" bore his. Nelly never knew how much good she had done Captain Will until he went away again in the early autumn. Then he thanked her for it, and though she cried for joy and sorrow, she never forgot it, because he left something behind him which always pleasantly reminded her of the double success her little hospital had won.

When Will was gone and she had prayed softly in her heart that God would keep him safe and bring him home again, she dried her tears and went away to find comfort in the place where he had spent so many happy hours with her. She had not been there before that day, and when she reached the door, she stood quite still and wanted very much to cry again, for something beautiful had happened. She had often asked Will for a motto for her hospital, and he had promised to find her one. She thought he had forgotten it; but even in the hurry of that busy day he had found time to do more than keep his word, while Nelly sat indoors, lovingly brightening the tarnished buttons on the blue coat that had seen so many battles.

Above the roof, where the doves cooed in the sun, now rustled a white flag with the golden "S. C." shining on it as the wind tossed it to and fro. Below, on the smooth panel of the door, a skillful pencil had drawn two arching ferns, in whose soft shadow, poised upon a mushroom, stood a little figure of Nurse Nelly and underneath it another of Dr. Tony bottling medicine, with spectacles upon his nose. Both hands of the miniature Nelly were outstretched, as if beckoning to a train of insects, birds and beasts, which was so long that it not only circled round the lower rim of this fine sketch, but dwindled in the distance to mere dots and lines. Such merry conceits as one found there! A mouse bringing the tail it had lost in some cruel trap, a dor bug with a shade over its eyes, an invalid butterfly carried in a tiny litter by long-legged spiders, a fat frog with gouty feet hopping upon crutches, Jenny Wren sobbing in a nice handkerchief, as she brought dear dead Cock Robin to be restored to life. Rabbits, lambs, cats, calves, and turtles, all came trooping up to be healed by the benevolent little maid who welcomed them so heartily.

Nelly laughed at these comical mites till the tears ran down her cheeks; and thought she never could be tired of looking at them. But presently she saw four lines clearly printed underneath her picture, and her childish face grew sweetly serious as she read the words of the great poet, which Will had made both compliment and motto:—

"He prayeth best who loveth best
  All things, both great and small;
For the dear God who loveth us,
  He made and loveth all."

THE BAKER'S DAUGHTER

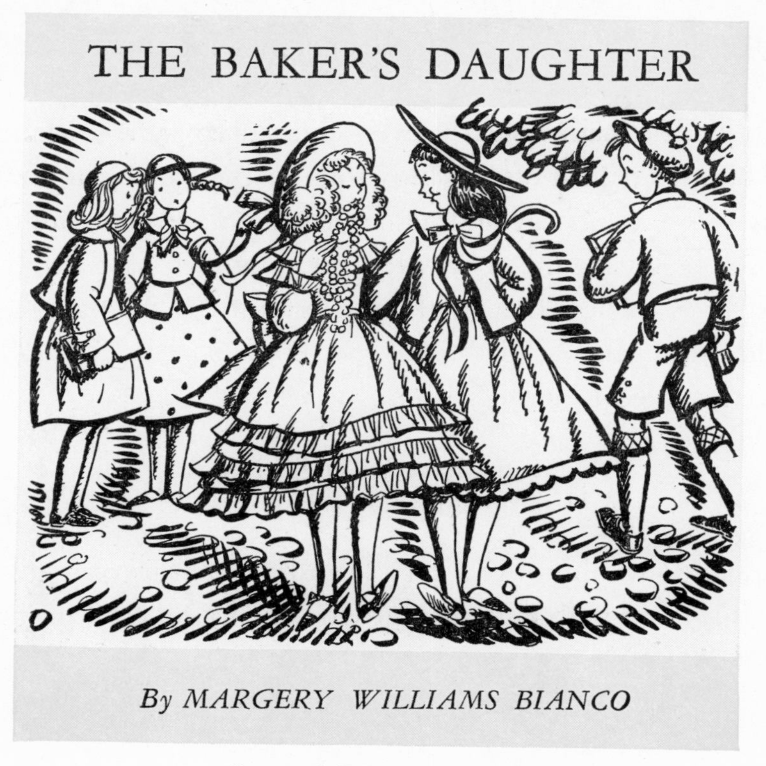

By MARGERY WILLIAMS BIANCO

Illustrated by GRACE PAULL

OH, BUT the Baker's Daughter is beautiful!

The Baker's Daughter has yellow hair, and every night it is curled with rags, and every morning it stands out in a frizzy fluff round her head. The Baker's Daughter has blue dresses and pink dresses and spotted dresses with flounces and flounces on them; she has beads around her neck and jingly bracelets and a ring with a real stone. All the girls in class sigh with envy of the Baker's Daughter.

But the Baker's Daughter is proud. She points her chin and she turns up her nose, and she is very, very superior. You never see her in the Baker's shop. She strolls up and down the sidewalk, sucking her beads.

You all know the Baker's shop, two steps down. It is warm in there, and busy. It smells of hot bread, and every few minutes the Baker, a hot, untidy little man in shirt sleeves, comes up from the basement carrying a big tray of crullers, or shiny rolls, or twisted currant buns. The Baker works hard all day and he never has time to do more than just poke his nose outside the doorway, every hour or so, for a sniff of cool air. It is hard to believe that anything so beautiful as the Baker's Daughter could ever come out of the Baker's shop!

Once I started to write a poem. It began:

> Oh, it is the Baker's Daughter,
> And she is grown so fair, so fair...

I thought I would make a very splendid valentine of it, all written out in a fine hand, with pink roses around and lots of crinkly paper lace, and send it to her, secretly. But unfortunately I found out that it was too much like a poem that someone else wrote a long time ago, and so I have never finished it. But still it always comes into my mind whenever I see the Baker's Daughter sucking her beads.

There was only one thing in the Baker's shop that at all came up in magnificence to the Baker's Daughter herself, and that was the big round cake that sat in the place of honor, right in the middle of the Baker's window. It was a chocolate cake, with all sorts of twirls and twiddles of lovely icing on it, and the word BIRTHDAY written in pink sugar letters. For some reason or other the Baker would never sell that cake. Perhaps he was afraid he would never be able to make another one quite so beautiful. He would sell you any other cake from his window but that one, and even if you went there very early of a Friday morning, which is cruller day, when there are no cakes at all, and asked him for a nice party cake, he would say:

"I can let you have one by three o'clock!"

And if you then asked: "But how about the cake in the window?" he would reply:

"That's not for sale. You can have one by three o'clock!"

For though you should offer him dollars and dollars, he would never sell that cake!

I seldom dare to speak to the Baker's Daughter. I am much too humble. But still she has friends. Never little boys; these she points her chin at, from across the street. But there are little girls with whom she is on friendly terms for as much as a week at a time. Naturally they are very proud. If you can't be a princess or a movie star perhaps the next best thing is to be seen walking up to the drug store soda fountain with the Baker's Daughter, and sitting there beside her on a tall stool eating pineapple sundae.

Now there was one little girl with whom the Baker's Daughter condescended at one time to be friends. Perhaps her name had something to do with it. She was called Carmelita Miggs, and Carmelita is a very romantic and superior name. She had black hair and a pair of bronze slippers, and she was the only little girl ever seen to stroll publicly with the Baker's Daughter, arm in arm. What they talked about no one knew. But Carmelita sometimes wore the Baker's Daughter's beads, and the Baker's Daughter would wear Carmelita's beads, and altogether they were very, very special friends while it lasted.

And it lasted until Carmelita had a birthday party.

The Baker's Daughter of course was invited, and several other of Carmelita's school friends. It was to be a real party, at four in the afternoon, with ice cream. And the Baker's Daughter said, very grandly, that she would bring a cake.

"I will bake you a nice one," said her father, "with orange icing on it. Now let me see... how many of you will there be?"

But that wasn't at all what the Baker's Daughter wanted. Anyone at all could bring a cake with orange icing. "I will choose my own cake!" thought the Baker's Daughter.

But all she said was: "That will be very nice!"

And in the afternoon, while her father was down in the bake-shop kitchen putting the last twiddle on the orange cake (for he wanted to make it something very special), and while her mother was taking forty winks in the back parlor, and the bakery cat was sound asleep, with her four paws curled under her, behind the counter, the Baker's Daughter crept into the shop on tiptoe, in all her finery, and stole—yes, *stole*—that big magnificent cake from the very middle of the shop window!

You see, she had had her eye on it, all along!

She lifted it up—and a nice, light cake it seemed—wooden platter and all, and she covered it over with sheets of waxy paper and carried it round to Carmelita's house.

Oh, but she looked proud, walking down the street with that big cake in her arms! Everyone turned to look at her.

"What a lovely cake!" cried all the little boys and girls when she arrived at Carmelita's house.

And the wrappings were taken off, very carefully, and it was set right in the middle of the table, with candles all around it.

"*What* a nice light cake!" said Carmelita's mother.

"All good cakes are light!" said the Baker's Daughter.

"It was very, very kind of your father to make such a splendid cake," said Carmelita's mother.

"I chose it myself!" said the Baker's Daughter, tossing her head.

They talked a little, very politely, and Carmelita Miggs showed all her birthday presents. And at last came the moment for the ice cream to be handed round on little glass plates.

You could have heard a pin drop.

"And now," said Carmelita's mother, "we'll all have some of that delicious cake!"

Carmelita had to cut it, because it was her birthday. She stood there feeling very shy, for there was a great silence all round; everyone's eyes were fixed on the cake, and all one could hear was Tommy Bates busily sucking his ice cream spoon, so as to get through first.

Only the Baker's Daughter sat there proudly, with her skirts spread out, looking indifferent, as though cakes like this were quite an everyday affair with her!

Carmelita took the knife and stuck it into the very middle of the pink icing, and pushed. You could have heard a pin drop.

But the knife did n't go in. Carmelita turned very red, and took a long breath and tried again.

Still the knife would n't go in.

"You must try harder, dear," said Carmelita's mother, smiling pleasantly. "I expect the top icing is a little bit stiff! Do you want me to help you?"

Now Carmelita knew that she had been pushing just as hard as she could. It came upon her, all at once, that there must be something very, very queer about that cake! But she took another long breath, again, and this time her mother put *her* hand on the knife, too.

You could have heard *two* pins drop!

And then, suddenly, there was a funny "plop," and the knife went in. And as it went in the cake slipped and turned a sort of somersault, and there it was, upside down, sticking on the tip of the knife that Carmelita's mother was still holding, and everyone looking most surprised. And that was n't the worst of it!

It was all hollow inside!

In fact, it was just a big pasteboard shell covered over with icing, and *that* was why the Baker would never sell it to anyone!

Can you imagine how the party felt? How the little boys and girls whispered and giggled, how Carmelita wept and the Baker's Daughter grew redder and redder, and snifflier and snifflier, and how Carmelita's mother tried to smooth everything over and pretend that it was really all very funny, and quite the nicest thing that could happen at any birthday party? And how, at the very last minute, while the ice cream was all melting away, they had to send out and buy a real cake, *somewhere else!*

But Carmelita Miggs did n't think it was a joke. She never, never forgave the Baker's Daughter for spoiling her party. For quite a long time she would n't speak to her at all. As for the other boys and girls, whenever they met Carmelita or the Baker's Daughter they would say:

"Now we'll all have some cake!"

You would think, after this, that the Baker's Daughter would have changed her ways. But not a bit of it! I saw her, only the other day, strolling up and down the sidewalk and sucking her beads just as proud as ever.

As I went past her I whispered very softly: "Now we'll all have some cake!"

And do you know what the Baker's Daughter did? I hate to tell you.

She stuck—out—her—her—tongue!

There, in the middle of the Baker's window, is another cake. This time it has green icing and pink roses, and two little sugar doves on top. It is even grander than the old one, and will probably last twice as long.

Unless, of course, someone else should have a birthday party!

TAKTUK

AN ARCTIC BOY

By HELEN LOMEN
AND MARJORIE FLACK

With Illustrations by
MARJORIE FLACK

I

HUNTERS IN THE ICE

TAKTUK sat quiet on the soft reindeer skins spread on the floor of the one room of his home. Taktuk did not like to sit quiet very often, neither did he like to sit at home. Just this very minute he was wishing that he were far out on the ice of Kotzebue Sound, where his father, uncle, and two cousins were on a seal hunt.

It was nearly two weeks since Taktuk had helped them start off. What fun he had had tussling with the dogs as he brought them out of their winter shelters and helped Pannigaluk, his father, hitch them in place to the sled! The big huskies were so wild to be off, they had fairly dragged Taktuk over the snow in their eagerness. Taktuk had been eager to go, too.

"Take me with you," he had begged. "See, I can help. I'll take care of the dogs for you! I am big, I am ten years old!"

But Pannigaluk had only shaken his head and said, "Not this year, we'll have enough of a load for the dogs to pull home, but some day when your legs are as long as your cousins', and you can run fast on snowshoes, then you can go with us."

With a bound they had started off like a streak across the blue-white snow; the dogs yipping and yapping and the men waving a good-bye. Taktuk had watched them with a little frown on his face. His Uncle Ned on snowshoes was running ahead; after him came the dogs, pulling the sled. Pannigaluk stood on the runners behind, holding tight to the long handle bars. George and Tom, Taktuk's cousins, off for their first seal hunt, were in the sled with the few provisions. Up the distant divide Taktuk had seen them go, showing dark against the sky, then disappearing on their way to the sea.

Since then, time had passed very slowly for Taktuk. Today he had found a willow stick shaped somewhat like a gun.

"If I learn how to hunt seal perhaps they'll take me next year," he thought to himself.

He ran to his grandfather, old Kuvnapuk, who was famous as a hunter, and asked, "How do you catch seal? Do you suppose I could learn?"

Old Kuvnapuk liked nothing better than to teach someone how to hunt. Seating himself on a box near the doorway he began:

"First you must learn how to get near enough to the seal to shoot him. Now, let's make believe Natsirk, your puppy, is a seal. He has just come up on the ice to nap in the sun."

Kuvnapuk told him how the seal, in the warm days of the spring, drags his cumbersome body from the sea to find a cozy spot on the green ice which for many months has roofed him in. He naps in the warm sun, but every few minutes he wakes, stretches his head high, and slowly turns it from side to side, scanning the ice about him. If all is well, he naps again. But at the slightest sign of danger, he wriggles his sleek body and like a flash flips down his hole.

Kuvnapuk told Taktuk how, in spite of all this watchfulness, the seal can be fooled into believing that a hunter crawling on the ice is only another seal like himself. That is because the seal is very near-sighted.

Then Taktuk himself "played seal" very cautiously, creeping flatly along the floor toward his sleeping puppy, which had no idea he was supposed to be a seal at that moment. Kuvnapuk called out directions:

"No, not that way, don't let him see your face; he'll know it isn't a seal's face!" or, "Now he sees you, lie still!" and then he showed Taktuk how to lift up his head and look about as the seal does.

But Kuvnapuk, who looked worried, was glad when the boy tired of the game. Now the old man sat very still on the little packing case, which served as a chair, and watched out of the one tiny four-paned window. The hunters should have been back long before this!

The sun lighted his white hair and made his wrinkled brown face look even browner. For nearly three days he had sat like this, silently watching, hardly stopping to eat or sleep. Though no word had been spoken, Taktuk knew why his grandfather looked worried. Kuvnapuk was old and wise in the ways of his country. All his life he had lived by hunting and fishing, and well knew the danger the spring "break-up" brings to the hunter on the ice.

Kuvnapuk did not like to see the last lingering patches of snow melt into the brown tundra, which is the name for moss ground in Alaska. He knew it meant that out at sea the winter ice would be breaking up. He knew the men had only their sled and dogs with them. He knew that with no boat they might be unable to reach land.

Softly Kuvnapuk began to mutter to himself as he swayed slowly and chanted a prayer of his forefathers:

> "Only come, only come,
> Only come, only come.
> I stretch out my hands to them thus—
> Only come—only come.

Taktuk looked down a little on the old-fashioned Eskimo prayers, for he had gone to the Mission school. He felt happier somehow as he looked at Navaluk, his mother, and saw her lips move in the "Bring back safe home" prayer to the "white-man's God."

Navaluk had seemed strangely quiet these last few days. Usually she sang little songs to herself as she went about her work. Taktuk looked at little Raisins, his baby sister, snuggled against her mother's back, under her warm dress. Her little head peered over her mother's shoulder. She whimpered and fretted as if she knew something was wrong. Navaluk quieted the child by shrugging her shoulders up and down, up and down, as she busied herself clearing away the remains of the last meal.

Taktuk wondered what his father was doing now off there on the ice. He was probably having some exciting adventure. How much nicer if he were out there with them instead of here with those who sat at home and waited and worried. Some day his mother and grandfather would be watching for him to return from a hunt. How important he would be then!

"Only come, only come"—Old Kuvnapuk's monotonous chant went on. It made Taktuk feel uncomfortable. He went quietly into the low vestibule of the house, which they call a cache. He took down his soft fawnskin coat and slipped into it. He would get water from the river for his mother.

Outdoors the fresh smell of grassy earth filled his nostrils. Things had changed since the men left. Summer was here in a day, it seemed, and the thick brown tundra was now exposed over the whole hillside, steaming in the fierce sunshine of spring. The heat of the long day had played magic with the fields of snow. The brown was giving way to a faint tinge of green along the edge of the tiny pool near the house.

Taktuk untied his two dogs, housed snugly under a wee burlap tent, and harnessed them to his sled of spruce boughs. One dog, Kopak, was too old now for the hunt, and Natsirk, the four-month-old puppy, was still too young. As he patted them, he felt more cheerful. On the sled he tied two buckets, and with a word to his dogs, they jogged off down the bank of the Buckland River, the boy clinging on to the handle bars.

Taktuk reached the water hole with some difficulty. The river ice had split here and there, and was dotted over with bright blue patches that were ponds of melted snow.

Coming back with his buckets filled, Taktuk was halfway up the bank when—what was that? Kopak and Natsirk stopped suddenly. They lifted their ears, listening; for what a barking resounded from the village! Every dog there was at it. They had caught some scent—yes, now Taktuk could hear other dogs far off in the distance answering the dogs in the village, until the echoing clamor filled the air.

Taktuk, in his excitement, left his dogs and water buckets to find their own way home. He darted straight to the house shouting to his mother: "They are coming, they are coming!"

As by magic every house in the village poured out its contents of furry Eskimos. There they stood chattering with excitement and pointing to the north. They knew what the racket meant. The four hunters were returning at last! Nearer and nearer came the sound of the homecoming dogs, then over the divide the men began to appear, looming black for an instant as they came into sight: one—two—three—but where was the fourth?

Taktuk watched them come nearer and nearer, the sled pulling heavily over the rough tundra. Who was missing? At last Taktuk could see their faces. There was Pannigaluk, his father. He at least had come back; he was safe; Taktuk was so happy he did not stop to look at the others. He just ran forward to meet his father as fast as his little legs could carry him. The dogs tugged harder on the heavy sled, smelling the familiar things of home.

In a few seconds more Pannigaluk was shaking hands, first with Navaluk—for Eskimos shake hands with their wives, too—then with old Kuvnapuk, and finally with every village friend, one by one. Eskimos love to shake hands on every possible occasion, and what a joyful occasion this was! Taktuk remembered the day he and his family had moved to this village from Shungnak, and how everyone at Buckland had shaken their hands in welcome. Even the tiny tots of children had greeted him that way and made him feel like one of them. So now, with the others, he put his little brown paw in the hands of the hunters who were back home from their dangerous hunt.

He was so happy over his father that he forgot that four men had started off but only three had returned.

II

THE COMING OF FAIRY

"The dogs are hungry; get some fish for them, Taktuk," commanded Pannigaluk. Taktuk felt proud as he helped unhitch the dogs and climbed up the thong-tied ladder to the fish cache, perched on long spruce poles high out of reach of stealing animals. He selected with special care some fine dried salmon for the dogs. They barked up at him as he threw them each a fish. But as Taktuk jumped down he noticed a little group about his father, anxiously asking questions. Little Fairy, his cousin, was standing near. She looked so unhappy; what could it mean?

Taktuk's Aunt Noaluk, who was Fairy's mother, was asking over and over again:

"Where do you think he is? Where do you think he is? Where do you think he is?" Then Taktuk suddenly remembered that only three men had come up over the divide; it was his Uncle Ned, Fairy's father, who was missing!

Taktuk started to run over to hear what had happened, when he heard his mother calling him, "Taktuk, Taktuk, come help me carry in this meat. Your father is hungry; I must cook him some warm food!" She was already busy skinning one of the big fat seals which had been unloaded from the sled.

Taktuk hesitated. He wanted to hear what the men were saying. "See, here is a nice flipper for you," said Navaluk. Candy is not more tempting to an Eskimo child than a raw flipper from a fresh-caught seal. And it was nearly a whole year since Taktuk had tasted one. So he decided to help his mother carry the meat into the house, and Navaluk gave him two flippers, one for his cousin, Fairy, too.

"Where is Fairy's father?" he asked.

His mother answered calmly: "We don't know; he was left on the ice and could not reach shore, but he may get back some day."

Taktuk thought it would be great fun to go drifting away on the ice. He had heard many stories of such adventures; and rather envied his uncle. He ran over to give Fairy the seal flipper. He had always liked her. Now she was extra interesting because she had a father floating off somewhere out in the middle of the Arctic Ocean. Also, she might need his protection.

Taktuk threw each dog a fish.

"Oh, Taktuk, how nice!" Fairy exclaimed, for a flipper was a treat to her, and she loved any attention from Taktuk.

The three returned hunters, Pannigaluk and George and Tom, were tired and hungry.

"After a little rest and some food I will tell you about it," Pannigaluk promised the eager, questioning neighbors. Buckland Village was twenty miles from the mouth of the Buckland River, which empties into the Arctic Ocean at Escholtz Bay. The village was very small, only a group of seventeen little log huts and the government schoolhouse. It was just like one big family, and anyone's good or bad fortune affected all alike.

Just as many people as could get in, crowded after Pannigaluk into his little house. Taktuk took his father's heavy hooded coat made of reindeer skin, "parka" in the white man's language. He hung it up on the peg in the cache, crowded with family provisions and clothing. Then he and Fairy squatted on the floor to hear the story of the seal hunt.

There was a feeling of warmth and peace inside the little house. The spruce fire filled the room with a pleasant glow and the boiling pot gave promise of a good supper. At last, after enjoying a good meal, Pannigaluk was ready to tell his story.

"After we left Buckland Village we traveled fifty miles to the shore of Kotzebue Sound; then on the white sea ice we started northwest over great ridges and hummocks.

"At last we found seal—and we had great fun watching the boys, George and Tom, on their first hunt. First they would crawl too fast over the ice and the seal would slip into the water and disappear, but they soon learned how to approach more cautiously, and then what good shots they made! They found out that a fat seal will always float, but a thin one must be shot in the head; if his hide is punctured he will sink.

"We worked hard for several days and had good luck, but the ice had begun to split, so we knew we had to hurry. Then on the seventh day Tom and George and I were getting supper ready in the shelter of the overturned sled, where we had staked out the dogs for the night. Ned was hunting alone and had not yet come back.

"A gentle wind had been blowing off shore, but suddenly it grew stronger, and now and then we heard a dull boom—boom!

"Closer and closer came the noise, and then a strange grinding sound. We knew the ice had split somewhere between us and the shore. There was open water between us and land. We were adrift on a shifting ice field. The wind and current were carrying us away from the land.

"I ran to the highest ridge. 'Ned! Ned!' I called. I could see him nowhere. I shouted and shouted, but the terrifying noise of the breaking ice, grinding and booming, drowned my voice. George and Tom had packed the sled and had the dogs harnessed ready to start for home—we dared wait no longer. There to the southeast, barring us, was open water, black and angry.

"Along the edge of the water we picked our way over the rough ice, until at last we found the open water narrow, and there was a small ice cake floating near us. Our luck was with us, for it was as good as a boat. Carefully we put the dogs on it, a few at a time, and paddled the ice cake across the narrow channel. Then we returned and took a load of seal and things, and on a third trip the sled itself! Then it was a straight run over solid ice to shore.

"We were wet and tired and hungry. The shore was sandy and bare of snow so we made a fire of drift logs and cooked some food; then we slept, and waited, hoping Ned would come. The next morning, when we woke up, the ice had broken completely away from shore and the sea lay before us, blue and calm with a pale gray mist over everything! Overnight winter and ice had vanished together.

"Ned was somewhere far out at sea on the moving ice field. We could do nothing to help him, so we came home. It is good to be home again. We still hope Ned will somehow reach shore. Other men have come back when lost at sea on the ice!"

Before the tale was done, Taktuk was drowsy listening to the drone of his father's voice and the crackling of the fire. He shut his eyes—the heavy smell of fresh meat in the warm room made him sleepy—soon he was lost in the land of dreams.

Taktuk stretched himself as he awoke, and touched Fairy, curled up asleep beside him under a soft fawnskin. She was still there, although it must be morning! Everyone was gone but Taktuk's family; even Noaluk, Fairy's mother, had left. It must be another day.

Seeing Taktuk awake, Navaluk came and whispered to him. "Fairy will live with us now. Uncle Ned has gone away, Noaluk will have enough to do to take care of herself and George and Tom. So Fairy will be like your little sister. You must play with her, Taktuk, and make her happy to be with us."

III

THE PROMISE

The entire village was rejoicing at the coming of spring. All earth was expanding and swelling after so long and solid a sleep; the grasses were reaching up to meet the sun, the flowers were bursting their buds into soft blooms of lavender, yellow, and blue. Willow twigs, long frozen and crisp, swayed ever so gracefully in the warm breeze, airing the new green shoots. The river, fairly gay in its freedom, flowed high along the banks and bathed the roots of the bluegrass, beach pea, and lupine.

The gulls had come over from their rookeries on Chamisso Island and screamed overhead, frightening the baby ducks and ptarmigan and geese hidden away so carefully in the tall grasses.

Taktuk felt restless and longed for many things. He longed to be a gull or a reindeer, and in his daydreams he imagined himself an ice cake, and drifted on and on, always north, seeing new and strange things along the coast.

Then a day came when all these dreams were forgotten and Taktuk was glad to be just the happy Eskimo boy he was.

"Soon we will all be going to Choris," Pannigaluk had told him. "You are getting to be a big boy, Taktuk, you can help at the reindeer round-up!"

Choris was on the Arctic Ocean, a peninsula on which they had built the corrals for the annual reindeer round-up and marking.

Taktuk never had been so excited before. It was even more exciting than last year, when, just before the freeze-up of winter, his family had moved down to Buckland Village from Shungnak on the upper Kobuk River. His family all his life had been moving about. His father, until this time, had been a trapper, so Taktuk had never seen a reindeer round-up. The other boys of the village had seen the reindeer round-up and worked every year of their lives and Taktuk had been listening all winter to their stories. Now, soon, he was not only to go, but also to help at the marking. Reindeer are not branded like cattle, but earmarked. "Will I be a herder, too?" he eagerly asked. "Am I going to have some reindeer all my own?"

Pannigaluk hesitated. "That is not what I meant, Taktuk. I said just to help the men, but if you work hard——"

"Oh, I'll work hard," said the boy. "I'll work like a man, I'll not sleep at all, I'll work day and night, day and night and——"

"Then if you do the work well and do just as you are told, you will be given a baby reindeer, a little fawn, for your very own."

"I'll bring it home and make a little house for it and feed it fish!"

Pannigaluk laughed.

"No, no, Taktuk, your poor little fawn would die if you fed it fish. We will give it your earmark and let it go back to the herd to eat lichens and moss and mushrooms, and then, next year, when you see it again, it will be big and strong."

"What's an earmark?" Taktuk asked.

"It is made by cutting little notches in the reindeer's ears—each reindeer owner has a different number of notches and a different kind of notch, so he can always tell which reindeer belong to him."

Still Taktuk did not quite understand. "But how do they know how not to make the notches alike—how will I know what mine will be?"

"The white man's company has a big book, and in this book are all the names and earmarks of the Eskimos who own reindeer. This year they will put your name in the book and a picture of your earmark. Your reindeer next May will have a fawn and so your deer will grow so that when you are a big boy—sixteen or eighteen years old—why, you will have a whole herd of reindeer all your own."

Taktuk was so filled with the wonder of all this that he had to go out and think it all over—"talk inside," as he called it. He sat down on the bank of the river—the river that led to the sea. Soon he would be going down it—and on across the big bay to Choris and the round-up.

He would be an owner, he would have a business! He had

always wished to be a famous hunter before he had come to Buckland Village—a great hunter like old Kuvnapuk, whom his family had always lived with. He had always imagined himself traveling over great distances in search of the Polar bear, walrus, whale, and caribou.

Now it was different—his whole idea of life was changing. He would be an owner instead of a hunter of animals, he would learn to care for and protect them instead of hunting and killing them!

Later Taktuk was to learn from his teacher just why the United States government had brought reindeer into Alaska from Siberia.

When the Eskimos were just hunters and fishers, they led a very dangerous and uncertain life. Seal were the principal food of those on the coast, and every time a man went hunting on the Arctic ice he risked his life; the ice might break and carry him out into the ocean. We have just read of that very thing happening to Ned.

The Eskimos in the interior used to live on wild game and birds, and the big Arctic hare. Some years there would be "drouth" of caribou and ptarmigan and hare—they simply would not appear. That meant starvation for the natives.

Then the government bought reindeer in Siberia and taught the natives how to take care of them. Reindeer are domesticated animals like cows. It costs nothing to keep them. They gather their own food and need no shelter, summer or winter. They assure their owners an unfailing supply of food. Their skins provide clothing, robes, carpets, boots, and gloves. They supply bone for their needles and sinew for thread. They can haul sleds in the winter faster than the dogs, though not so tireless.

So when Taktuk turned his thoughts from hunting and fishing to herding, he was doing just what the government was teaching all his people to do.

The next day he and Fairy watched Pannigaluk and a dozen young men set off for the Buckland Hills, where the reindeer herds were grazing. Now, for days at a time, the men would tramp the hills; working through the Arctic summer night, which is as light as day; never stopping to sleep; gathering the scattered reindeer together and driving the great herd down to the sea at Choris.

In a few days, Taktuk, with all the children, women, and old men of the village, would set off for the marking at Choris. Now, as Taktuk watched the men disappear, he felt the need of someone to discuss his new business project with. He felt very grown-up and important.

Turning, he critically looked Fairy over. Little Fairy, although her name came from the government teacher's book, looked very unlike a real fairy. Her solid little body was clothed in funny little trousers and hooded coat. Clumsy skin boots were on her feet. Her round face was framed in the soft wolverine that trimmed her hood. She looked up at Taktuk with faithful and devoted eyes.

Solemnly he shook her hand.

"You shall be my company," he declared, and slapped her on the back, the way he had seen the young men of the village do, white-man fashion.

"What's 'company'?"

"Well, I am going to be an owner, like the white men. Every owner has to have a company. You will be mine!"

Fairy giggled at this honor. Fairy was apt to giggle a great deal. This was her way of showing appreciation, happiness, or just contentment. All the women of the village giggled.

Now that he had a company, Taktuk was eager to impress her with his knowledge. From the men and older boys he had gleaned a fairly good idea of the round-up and what it meant.

Squinting at the sky and sniffing the warm spring air, he said:

"The summer comes quick, there will be lots of mosquitoes, the men will be glad!"

Fairy looked at him scornfully.

"Be glad! Who ever heard of anyone being glad because of lots of mosquitoes!"

"That just shows how much you don't know! The mosquitoes will help the men drive the reindeer down away from the hills to the sea!"

"That just shows how much *you* don't know—someone has been fooling you. How could a little tiny mosquito drive a great big reindeer anywhere?"

Taktuk was delighted; it is always a pleasant feeling to know more than someone else.

"Well, if you can't guess, I won't tell you; I don't believe you know enough about reindeer to be a company!"

Fairy was deeply hurt at this. She thought desperately—what could a mosquito do?

"I know," she cried, "they'd bite—they'd bite the reindeer and that would make them run!"

"You're right, they would run—and they will run to the sea. The sea breeze blows the mosquitoes away and the reindeer like to stand in the cool salt water."

Taktuk and Fairy were soon playing "Round-up" in the soft mud near the river bank. A peninsula was made and a miniature corral built on it with tiny willow twigs.

"See," said Taktuk, pointing with a stick to where the last gate should be, "when my little fawn comes through here, they will snip little notches in its ears, which will be my mark, and always afterwards they will know it belongs to me. I will be an owner and take care of my animals. Then soon I can sell them for meat to the white man's company. With the money I'll buy sugar and tea and raisins and a talking machine, and I will give you a sewing machine and calico and pretty beads and——" By this time Taktuk was quite out of breath. He had never talked so long in his life before, and Fairy was so amazed that her eyes grew rounder.

"And a doll?" she asked. "Like the teacher let me play with?"

"But you'll be my company—who ever heard of a company playing dolls!" Taktuk replied in a disgusted tone of voice.

Taktuk did not exactly know what the white man's word "company" meant himself. He had been busy gathering white men's words and names all winter. There was the school where children were taught to read and say white men's words and count. And there was the small store which sold calico for the women's dresses, and tea, and sometimes dried fruits and sugar, and also ammunition for the rifles that the men prized so highly.

Taktuk's Uncle Ned had come from Nome to marry and settle in Buckland; that is why his children were named Tom, George, and Fairy. Some children of the village were even named from canned goods, often from the labels on the packing cases. Taktuk's own name meant "Fog."

There was one boy he played with named Prunes. Taktuk thought this a splendid name. Prunes had a sister named Peaches. Taktuk's own little sister, who was born just a few months after they had arrived at Buckland Village, was named Raisins because that was the name on the packing case which was used as a chair in their home.

There was one sewing machine in the village. Taktuk felt that this must be magic of some sort; he used to watch Navaluk as she turned its little handle and made it whir the stitches out. The machine was used in turn by the women of the village. They had been very busy the last few weeks sewing new pink and blue calico dresses to wear to the round-up. These were made exactly on the same pattern as their fur parkas, with hoods to carry the babies in. Some were even banded with a bit of fur, but mostly they were finished at the bottom with a wide red band of calico. The colors of all of them were very gay.

The talking machine at the store was wonderful to Taktuk, too—there were three different songs it could sing, very hesitatingly. Taktuk secretly thought sometimes that the white man's magic in it must be slowly leaving it.

IV

THE TRIP TO CHORIS

The day to start for Choris had come. The last utensils had been stowed securely away in the bottom of the umiak, the family boat of walrus skin. It carried all the worldly possessions of the family: the tent, the cooking pots blackened from hard usage, odds and ends of clothing, the few garments not worn at the moment, and the staunch "seal poke," the Eskimo container for everything from water to fish and oil.

They were to paddle down the river twenty miles to Escholtz Bay and across it to the round-up station on Choris Peninsula.

Taktuk and Fairy were busy helping their mother in many ways. At last everything was ready and Kopak and Natsirk, with the other dogs, were put on top of all the rest of the possessions of the Pannigaluk family. It included now not only old Kuvnapuk and Fairy, but Noaluk and also George and Tom, who were well known for their good paddling. The umiak could carry everything and everybody. It was built with a frame of spruce lashed with thongs and covered with strong walrus hide.

Each family was now in its own boat, and everyone glowed in anticipation of the coming trip. The river was high from many streams of snow water, making paddling down stream easy. One by one the umiaks and skiffs set off, gliding down the river. How calm and still, after the hustle and bustle of packing, when the dogs had barked incessantly. Now they were quiet. Taktuk sat beside Fairy with his arms around Kopak and Natsirk; George and Tom were paddling, while old Kuvnapuk steered in the stern. Noaluk was placed in the middle, and Navaluk beside her, crooning a lullaby, held Raisins asleep on her lap. Her voice rose and fell in time to the dipping of the paddles:

"What do I see down there?
On the river—in the bend of the river,
A man jigging for a fish,
A man who is jigging!
A man who is jigging!"

Now and again the swish of the paddles frightened a fish. Taktuk wondered if the fish enjoyed the warm sun and bright flecks of light when a breeze ruffled the calm surface. He thought it must seem so much jollier than the winter days, when all the fish world was roofed over by thick, dull ice!

Racing by them at great speed went two of the young men, each in his new sealhide kayak which he had made during the winter. The summer before they had fashioned their boat frames of spruce, and now the kayaks, finished and in active use, glided like living things on the water.

Taktuk watched the little village, which for the last eight months had been his home, as it grew smaller and smaller in the distance. The houses seemed very wonderful to him, for they were much more like white men's houses than those of Shungnak, built of driftwood covered with sod. These of Buckland were made of logs chinked with moss and with only the roof covered with sod. The schoolhouse stood up higher than any of the others, with its flagpole the highest point for miles. What fun he had had at school last winter, the very first school he had ever been to! He and Fairy counted the houses in white-man numbers—seventeen in all. What a big village it seemed!

On and down the river they went. At last they came to a clutter of buildings, mound like, with sloping walls.

"See, Fairy, it is another village. It looks like Shungnak—our house was built like those," he exclaimed.

Then, as they came nearer, he asked Navaluk, "Where are all the people? Where have they all gone? There are no dogs about, no things by the doors. Where do you suppose they went?"

Navaluk shifted Raisins to a more comfortable position.

"That is the old Buckland Village. See, there is the house where I lived with your Aunt Noaluk when we were little girls."

"It looks like a sod house," remarked Fairy.

"Yes, it is covered with sod, but its frame is of driftwood—it was a nice warm house, too."

"But why did everyone leave their houses and move up the river?" Taktuk was eager to know.

"They had no more willow wood left to make fires to keep them warm—it was easier to move to a fresh place, where there would be plenty."

"Where did they get the logs to build the new houses with?" asked Taktuk of Noaluk.

Swiftly they glided along.

"The men floated logs down from the spruce woods, miles up the river. We were all so proud of those new houses!"

Taktuk watched the old deserted village disappear in the distance. It seemed bare and strange. Swiftly they glided along. Taktuk felt contented and happy. He liked the gentle motion of the boat. It was getting near night when a strange sound in the distance ahead made him sit up, alert—a strange honking and clatter.

Old Kuvnapuk's quick ears had heard it, too.

"Geese and ducks!" he cried. "We must be near the mouth of the river!"

A turn of the river, and hundreds of birds were in the air about them. Taktuk heard the noise of wings flapping madly, and the "honk-honk" of the geese resounding to the chorus of "quack-quack-quack" from the ducks. Beyond them Taktuk could see the big open space of the deep blue sea. They were at Igloo Point, on Escholtz Bay, at the mouth of the Buckland River, where the birds gathered every spring.

Quickly the umiak was beached. Old Kuvnapuk, Tom, and George had their rifles ready, and the sounds of shots echoed soon in a din of noise. Taktuk was just behind them. He was all excitement, picking up the birds until he could carry no more.

"Take them to Navaluk," old Kuvnapuk told him, "so she can fix them for supper."

Then a marvelous meal they had. Taktuk ate so much he felt very sleepy, but Tom and George were starting off to hunt again. Taktuk trailed on behind.

"Why do you shoot any more?" he asked. "We can't eat all you have already."

"We'll leave them here until we come back, after the round-up," Tom answered.

"But will they be good to eat by then?" asked Taktuk.

"Oh, yes, we have a place to keep them; we'll show you in the morning. You had better run along and go to sleep now. When you wake up you can help us."

Taktuk did not mind this suggestion—he was very sleepy. He curled up with warm reindeer rugs under and over him. Just as he was dozing off he heard a strange bird call. He opened his eyes and watched the crane. High over his head it flew, showing dark against the sky, which was golden red with the glow of the midnight sun.

The next morning Taktuk eagerly picked up the ducks and geese shot during the night. When he had a big load of them he called to Tom.

"Show me where to put them so they will keep fresh, and we will have them to eat when we come back from the round-up in the fall."

He followed Tom to a small hole in the ground, covered with a rough shelter. He looked down it—a ladder led down into the darkness below.

"Go down there and hang them up in the little room at the bottom of the ladder," Tom told him. Taktuk did not like this idea very much—it looked very dark and strange below—but he did not want Tom to think him afraid.

"Are you coming with me?" he hopefully asked.

"There isn't room for me, too," said Tom, who did not notice that the boy was afraid.

Taktuk slung the birds over his shoulder, gingerly placed his foot on the top rung of the thong-tied ladder, and started down. As soon as he was below the level of the ground he felt chilly. He wanted to go back, but he didn't want Tom to laugh at him. He did not dare look below into the darkness. About fifteen feet down his feet touched solid ground. It was frightfully cold; he shivered. In the dim light from the opening above he could see that he was in a little room, the walls of which were of solid ice. It was terribly still. The dim light, the cold, and the silence made Taktuk feel as if he had climbed back into winter. Above was the bright sunshine. Quickly he dropped the birds and clambered up the ladder. What a relief to come out in the hot summer sunlight!

Tom was still there. He grinned, for he admired Taktuk's pluck.

"How did you like it?" he asked.

"All right," said Taktuk, for now that he was above ground it was all right. "What makes it all ice? Doesn't it melt in the summer?"

"No, it never melts. The ground on top thaws, but the ice below is so solid and cold it never melts. You remember how the banks of the river near home still showed solid ice after the snow had melted?"

Taktuk did remember them only too well; he had slipped many a time on them the last few weeks.

"Who made the little room?" he asked.

"The white man's company; they use it to keep reindeer meat in."

As they came up to where the umiaks and kayaks of the village were ready to leave, Taktuk heard a strange noise. "Put-put-put-put——"

"It's the 'engine boat'!" exclaimed Tom. Taktuk had heard the boys tell of this wonderful boat of the white man's company. It had come to tow the skin boats across the bay to Choris on the icy waters of the Arctic Ocean.

There it came around the point, snorting and puffing like a huge animal.

Fairy ran up.

"See, Taktuk, a medicine man must make it go—I hear the drum!"

Taktuk was scornful at this display of ignorance.

"It's not a medicine man at all, it's the white man's magic called 'engine' that makes it go."

Then such a shouting and scurrying about! Soon all the eleven boats from Buckland Village were fastened in a line, one behind the other, and with a jerk they were off, as the engine boat towed them. How strange it seemed to Taktuk to go swishing and sliding on through the water with neither paddle nor sail!

Grandfather Kuvnapuk, who could not speak the white man's tongue, asked Tom to call to the white men, "Have you seen Ned, lost sealing on Kotzebue Sound three weeks ago?" But Hatta, the Lapp, who was steering the engine boat, only shook his head.

Kuvnapuk took some tobacco and stuffed it in his pipe, then, topping it with a few hairs from the outside of the little pouch made of squirrel skin, he puffed away his worries.

The hours came and went; day and evening passed; but the summer sun still remained high in the heavens. The winter was gone with its cold, snow, and dark days, and now the long summer day of three months was here, when day and night were one. Taktuk lay on his back until, lulled by the gentle motion of the boat and awed into silence by the glory of the flaming midnight sky, he slept.

The "chug-chug" of the engine boat ahead gave a pleasant sound, which waked him from his nap; the dogs barked from boat to boat. Taktuk called to his friends, and his voice echoed back clearly from the rolling green hills across the bay. What a strange spirit must live there, he thought, to answer him with his own words!

They glided on and on. Taktuk helped his mother start a fire in the little sheet-iron stove on a packing case in the middle of the umiak, and there, skimming over the water under a red sun, they ate many good things—hot seal soup and tea and dried reindeer meat of last spring.

As they turned west, it seemed to Taktuk that water continued to the ends of the earth. But finally, along the horizon, old Kuvnapuk showed him what appeared to be islands. It was Choris Peninsula, where the big reindeer corrals were.

V

CAMP ON CHORIS

Here, on the bay side of the peninsula, they decided to make camp. One by one the skin boats were dragged up on the beach, the umiaks were unloaded, tipped up, and propped securely by poles, to make a waterproof shelter for the family. Reindeer and hair-seal skins were used for the floor, where they sat and slept, having no use for beds and chairs. In almost less time than it takes to tell, a village was built.

Taktuk and the other boys staked out the dogs. Each dog was tied to a very short rope, and the short stakes pounded deep in the ground. This was to prevent the dogs from winding and tangling their ropes.

The old men and Tom and George immediately set out to fish for salmon. The boys and women gathered driftwood for the fires. The fishing party were lucky, returning with a good catch. Soon the hour-old camp gave forth the familiar sounds and smells of home.

As they were finishing their meal of the delicious salmon, a sudden silence fell over the camp. Taktuk wondered what it meant. Everyone was looking toward something in the distance. He saw slowly approaching the figure of a man—a man who was evidently either very old or weary, for he came slowly, dragging his feet heavily through the deep sand. Taktuk knew that no one lived anywhere near here; where could he have come from? George jumped up and started on a trot to meet the man. Taktuk followed at his heels, doing his best to keep up with him. The stranger was shouting:

"George—George—*ḳuyana* (good)—*ḳuyana!*"

Taktuk with wide eyes saw that this man was Ned—his uncle who had been missing so many days! The boy threw his arms around him and felt happy and relieved and triumphant as he walked back at his side. As they neared the waiting group great shouts of rejoicing rose from it. Ned seemed to regain new strength and shook hands with everyone; then, as he sat down to rest, Taktuk proudly brought him a large tin cup of warm food—the first warm food Ned had had for weeks.

Fairy was overwhelmed with joy—shyly and silently hanging about, worshiping her father. Everyone talked at once. It seemed as if this must be a miracle, but old Kuvnapuk smiled as he smoked his pipe—it seemed only natural to him—he had seen so many strange things in his day. The women giggled incessantly in their excitement; they were all eager and on edge to hear how Ned got here.

Ned, forgetting his weariness, was only too glad to recite his adventures to them.

"I heard you call," he told Pannigaluk, "but the roar of the ice and the wind carried my answers away. I could not reach you, for a great crack had widened almost into a river, so I could not cross it. By good luck I had just caught a large seal and had it on the same ice cake with me. I also had some cartridges left in my gun.

"The current caught the ice and carried it on away from you, and the wind helped it along. Then the fog came. I could see nothing or do nothing for days. I cut up the seal so I could carry some of it if I got a chance to reach land. On and on I went, when at last I saw land in the distance—I did not know where it was. Then I was lucky, for the tide carried my little ice island near shore, and watching my chance I skipped from cake to cake and reached the land.

"I guessed I was somewhere between Point Hope and Choris Peninsula, so I walked south for many, many days and nights, until at last I saw Choris. I knew you would be here for the reindeer round-up."

There was much rejoicing and merrymaking. Ned was invited to rest in the most comfortable of the umiak houses.

It was long before the camp had quieted to the silence of the night. It was night in name only, as the hours which were morning, noon, and night were easily forgotten where daylight continued all around the white man's clock.

VI

"REINDEER COME!"

The sun was high overhead when the camp stirred to life again. Taktuk was eager to explore the peninsula. In the excitement of making camp and the return of Ned, he hardly had noticed his surroundings. The camp had been pitched on the narrow sandy neck of low land which was all that prevented the hilly peninsula, jutting into the sea toward the south, from being an island.

Here was the huge corral Taktuk had heard so much about.

From the camp he could see part of it as it lay on the sandy neck. Tom and George set off soon after breakfast to inspect the corral. Taktuk followed along, his short legs trotting to keep up with their long strides.

The corral was built of spruce logs standing upright and close enough together to make almost a solid wall.

"Where did all those logs come from?" Taktuk asked Tom in amazement. He had never seen so many before at one time. Trees are very rare in the Arctic.

"We rafted them down the Buckland River from the timberland, and then across the bay."

"The same timberland where they got the logs to build our house with?"

"Yes, that is the only timberland we know anything about."

Tom was always patient with Taktuk's many questions—perhaps it also gave him a chance to display his own knowledge, but, in any case, he was very fond of his little cousin, to whom these things were all so new.

There were four enclosures to the corral groups. Tom called them "pails." There was a huge "outer corral," with a gate leading to a smaller one called the "pen." From the "pen" there was a gate leading into an even smaller "pocket," which in turn opened into the "chute" through which the deer are let out on to the narrow neck of land leading back to the mainland again.

Taktuk inspected the gates leading from one pail to another, and Tom showed him how they slid open to let the right number of reindeer through and how they were quickly closed again. Taktuk's interest was very keen, spurred on by his father's promise that he could help in the work later. He practised opening and shutting a gate, as Tom had hinted he might be allowed to do it in the round-up.

"I'd like to learn to 'throw' a deer, too," he insisted.

Tom laughed. "I am afraid the deer would throw you first."

The day grew hotter and hotter. Taktuk joined the younger boys on the beach. They had stripped off their clothes, and their sleek, shining little bodies splashed madly and gayly in the water. "Come on in!" they called to Taktuk. He jerked off his clothing and ran down to the edge of the water. He had never been in bathing before. He hesitated, but only for a moment, for he would not have them think him afraid. With a shout he splashed in. The shallow water had been warmed by the continual sunshine. Taktuk forgot everything about reindeer or round-up—forgot everything but the glorious feeling of the refreshing water.

They spent the rest of the day in and out of the bay, chasing each other over the warm sand, burying each other in it, then splashing in the water to get it off.

Taktuk wondered why the grown people did not join their sport. Later he was to learn that adult Eskimos never go in the water. None of the men can swim. They always drown when an accident happens to their frail skin fishing boats. The men did nothing but sit and watch for the coming of the reindeer herd; the women puttered about the camp. Taktuk hated to have to put his clothes on again toward night, but he was very hungry, and the smell of fish cooking soon drew all the boys back to camp like the hungry big mosquitoes which buzzed constantly about.

When he had eaten, Taktuk lay contentedly resting after his day of romping. He lazily watched the dogs, who slept heavily after the too warm day. They were shedding their coats of coarse winter hair that hung in bunches on them, or matted flat. You could pull it out in handfuls. Now and then a dog gave a quick, nervous snap at a swarm of mosquitoes, singing ever so close to his face, or struck them off his nose with a killing blow of his furry paw. The men, tired of sitting and looking, had gone to their tents for the evening meal and rest.

The air was filled with dull or quiet little sounds—a mother in one tent making pleasing mother tones to her wee child—the rattle of clearing away pots and pans from another tent—and from a third, two or three boys and girls singing a piece of a dance song, to the dull "tum-tum" of a seal drum. One energetic man chopped wood, willow and alder bows, into lengths to fit the little iron stoves, and with each stroke of the ax there came back an echoing thud from the hills to the north.

As Taktuk looked over to the hills where the mainland was he saw a strange sight. Could the hill be moving—was the soft brown brush sliding slowly down the hillside? He "spoke these things inside"—he thought them—but knew all the time that he was seeing the great sight for which he had come. The great reindeer herd!

The white man had said there would be eighteen thousand of them. Taktuk did n't know how many that would be, but now he saw them coming, a mile or two away, the mass of brown bodies dotted here and there with a pure white deer, and the branching antlers looking like willow boughs at the crest of the hill.

"Reindeer come!" he cried out in his excitement, and the camp was awake in a second. Taktuk had never seen all his people so excited before. "Reindeer come!"—"Reindeer come!" was called from every "boat tent." The dogs, catching the excitement and the scent of the deer, howled or barked according to their kind, and tugged and strained on their short-tether lines, too short to give them any freedom of movement.

"Keep them quiet," shouted Ned. "They must not frighten the deer." He ordered all the old people, women, and children to stand guard over the dogs and hold their attention from the reindeer as they came. Willow branches were waved over the dogs' heads to keep away molesting mosquitoes, soft words whispered in their ears; and they wondered at this unaccustomed kindness.

Taktuk was holding his dogs, Kopak and Natsirk. He liked nothing better than to play with his pets, but now he was impatient to give all his attention to the magnificent show before him. But he kept them quiet.

"There, Natsirk—hush, Kopak—shoo away mosquito—hush, Kopak," for Taktuk knew that one bark from a dog when the deer came close would mean a stampede, and the work of days and days of herding in the hills might be for nothing, and the gathering have to be done all over again. He had heard how this once had happened.

Now the reindeer were nearing almost to the narrow neck of land linking Choris to the mainland.

There were snorting and heavy and nervous breathing, and above all the "click, click, click" of the reindeer tendon at the "heel."

"Quiet, everybody," whispered Ned.

The slightest motion and a few deer might be frightened and carry the whole herd with them in their rush for open country. But Taktuk did not care to move—he stood spellbound, his head peering over the top of an umiak.

Here they came, close at hand, slowly and cautiously—snorting and searching from side to side for any trouble that might be in their path. Taktuk had never dreamed there could be so many animals; and yet here they were, now only a few feet in front of him, their antlers like a moving sea of brown brush, continuing on back to the hills.

Pannigaluk and the men who had gone out from Buckland Village before Taktuk had left, were slowly walking on behind the herd, guiding them, rather than driving them—because they move willingly enough ahead, but if frightened move off at an angle, and a stampede follows.

Taktuk dared not move, but there, almost within reach of the umiak, was the edge of the herd. The little umiak village was in the way of their straight march on to the peninsula, and the obstruction started the outer deer to running around in an enormous circle, "milling," the inner mass always working toward the outer edge—and around and around!

Taktuk had never dreamed there could be so many animals.

Now and then a fawn came in sight. Taktuk remembered what his father had told him about the fawns. Even the very youngest ones, only a few days old, are seldom harmed by the great surging mass of these milling animals. Each baby fawn runs close to its mother's side and, being swift and sure of foot, is not trampled on by the herd.

Here was a fawn coming right toward Taktuk. He could hardly believe his eyes as it came up to him and with a little sigh lay down at his feet. He leaned over to pat its soft little head, and it lifted up its pink nose to lick his hand! Frightened and lost from its mother in the great milling, whirling mass, the fawn had sought him out for protection! Taktuk tenderly lifted it and put it among some skins under the boat, where it would be safe.

But how would they break this "milling," Taktuk wondered. He knew that he would have got very dizzy going around like that; but the herd continued for a long while—the herders knew their work well. To crowd them at this time might have meant the loss of the herd. They must break the milling where the narrow neck joined the peninsula to the mainland.

Now the herders joined hands, and eighteen men crowded in on the herd, always moving toward them.

One fine-looking deer broke from the herd and looked beyond the camp toward the open peninsula—another followed—and at last, with a great dash, like liquid pouring from a bottle, the whole eighteen thousand flew at terrific speed down the narrow neck of land. Taktuk was watching a stampede.

The herders cried out in their joyous excitement and came running at full speed; the whole camp joined now in rushing behind the herd. Such yelling and running and waving of coats, removed in the heat of excitement! Taktuk and Fairy joined hands and ran with the rest—all for no special reason, but action was necessary after the strain of waiting so long. Soon the deer were over the "danger line" and safely corralled on the peninsula, although they imagined themselves on the open range, Taktuk was sure.

In a few minutes the herders had put up a burlap fence; the cloth hung limp and loose on improvised fence poles—a fawn could have pushed it over alone, but all eighteen thousand reindeer were safely shut behind that obstruction as though it had been a wall of rock.

Taktuk led Fairy over to the umiak where he had hidden the little fawn.

"See, my fawn has come to me," he proudly said, firmly believing that his father's promise had come true in this most miraculous way.

The fawn, which was mostly white, with a few brown spots,

looked up at him with large, soft brown eyes, and as he fondled and patted it, pushed out a soft, warm tongue and licked his cheek in a wet kiss. Taktuk was very proud as the other boys came up to admire his pet; the women, too, stood about asking how he had caught it.

"My father promised me I should have one—when the herd came this little one found me—my father must have worked magic."

The white man who had come on the engine boat, passing by, saw the little fawn. Taktuk was in great awe of the white man. Although he could speak a little English, learned in a few weeks at a government school, he was struck quite dumb when the white man was near, although he had heard his father and Ned talk on equal terms with him.

"Where did you get that, sonny?" kindly asked the white man.

Taktuk did not answer, but he grinned. He felt the kindness in the white man's voice.

The white man came over and patted the fawn's head.

"He will need to be fed," he said, still carrying on the one-sided conversation. "Wait here; I'll bring him something."

Taktuk did not understand a word of all this, but nothing could have dragged him away from the fawn just now, anyway.

Soon the white man was back, carrying a small tin can.

"Get me a pail of water, now." Taktuk at last began to comprehend. He brought the pail, but without the water.

"Water—in—the—pail—water," said the white man slowly.

Fairy could understand the white man's talk better than Taktuk; she whispered to him, acting as interpreter. Taktuk hurried to fill the pail from the makeshift well which had been dug for the camp. The white man opened the can with a wonderful knife he had in his pocket and poured a thick white liquid into the pail of water. He carefully rinsed the can and stirred the mixture.

The pail was held temptingly under the fawn's nose, but it only looked the other way. The white man dipped his fingers in the milk; the fawn licked them clean, then gradually began to lap up the milk from the pail.

Everyone sighed as the tension was over. The white man, as he left, called out: "We'll give him some more in the morning."

"This little one found me."

The silence broke among the children as soon as the white man was gone.

"Taktuk, let me pat him." —"See, he has drunk it all up!"—"Where are you going to keep him?" and many other questions were poured on Taktuk all at once.

Taktuk, disregarding their chatter, turned to them all with a grave air of importance.

"Do you know who that white man is?" and then, before they could answer, he slowly announced, "He is my partner."

"And I am your company!" proudly chimed in Fairy, never forgetting her title.

From that day on, Taktuk always referred to the white man as "Partner" although it was a long time before the white man could get Taktuk to overcome his shyness and talk with him as a partner should.

As Taktuk lay under the umiak that night he could hear the grunting of the mother reindeer anxiously searching for their lost fawns. At last they quieted down, as each found her own. Taktuk held his fawn a little closer, it was sleeping contentedly, and soon Taktuk was asleep, too, for he was tired after this, the biggest day of his life.

VII

THE "MARKING"

A pathetic little noise awoke Taktuk the next day. The fawn was begging for food and was now beginning to miss its mother. Nothing Taktuk could find would tempt it to eat.

"Will Partner come soon, do you think?" he anxiously asked Fairy.

"He said he would come in the morning," she assured him. "There he is now!"

Partner had another one of the mysterious cans with him. "Well, how is our fawn this morning, Taktuk?"

Taktuk grinned his appreciation. Partner had evidenly found out the boy's name from someone. Without being told, Taktuk ran to fill the pail with water. The admiring group of children from the neighboring umiak homes clustered about to watch the sticky mixture reluctantly leave the can.

This time Partner did not rinse it but left some of it still clinging to the sides. The fawn greedily lapped up the pailful. "Here, Taktuk," Partner called, giving him the can. "There is a lick left in it for you." Then he hurried off, for the marking would soon begin.

Taktuk ran his finger along the inner side of the can and licked it clean. What a sweet, delicious taste!

But he saw a group of eager little faces about him.

"Give us a lick, too," they begged.

Taktuk passed the can about, each one taking—a "lick."

Prunes, one of the older boys, boasted, "I've tasted it before!"

"What is its name?" Taktuk was keen for a new word.

"Kondenss—the white men had it here last year to put in the coffee."

"That is what I will name my fawn—'cause he is white nearly all over like the Kondenss," Taktuk declared, elated with the new name.

The men were shouting over at the corral—Pannigaluk called to Taktuk.

"Hurry up—it is time for the marking to begin!"

Taktuk tied Kondenss to a post near the umiaks and ran over to his father.

"What am I going to do to help?"

Pannigaluk was in a hurry. "I spoke to the white man; he said you could tend gate—the one from the pocket to the chute. He said he knew you."

"Yes—the white man is my partner. I know how to tend gate—Tom showed me," Taktuk eagerly assured him.

"Here, stand still," and Pannigaluk turned the hood of Taktuk's summer cloth parka up over his head and tied a red bandanna handkerchief over his nose and mouth. Taktuk had seen the other men dressed like this—he did not know why, nor did he ask. With only his eyes peering out over the bandanna, he looked like a regular reindeer man.

His shoulders squared, he climbed up on the high platform at the side of the heavy gate. The work of every man and boy was needed in the marking—the number of working people was small compared to the number of deer to be handled. Taktuk's gate was an important one; he realized his responsibility. He watched carefully. The moment would soon come for him to slide the gate.

The deer were peaceful and satisfied; all night they had grazed quietly and eaten of the choicest new willow shoots, tender grasses, mushrooms, and a great variety of reindeer lichens of different colors, green, pale gray, and dull gray like the sea gull's wing.

Now the rush of herding began again. The work, although hard, now became exciting play, for there was no longer any danger of losing the herd.

The older boys, led by George, shouted and waved their arms, cutting off from the main herd a few thousand deer, and driving them into the large "outer corral."

This led into the smaller one, the pen. Tom was tending the gate between the pen and the pocket. Then came Taktuk's gate, leading from the pocket to the chute. Here at the chute-end Pannigaluk and eighteen of the strongest young men in camp were ready to grab in turn the unmarked fawns and yearlings as they came through, throw them, and hold them down until their ears had been notched with their owner's mark.

Taktuk saw Partner there with his book to keep count of the number of deer marked for each owner.

The herders drove a few hundred deer from the first into the second corral. Taktuk watched from where he stood. They would soon be in the pocket, and then his work would commence. He trembled with joy and anticipation. There they came! Tom threw open the gate between the pen and the pocket—in they rushed, and before they could turn and seek safety again out of the little enclosure, Tom slammed shut the gate behind them.

From above, where he stood, Taktuk watched this assortment of reindeer—seventeen of them, of all ages and sizes. Four little fawns had come through, and three crowded to their mothers' sides, while the fourth ran about bewildered. Snorting in great excitement, one huge steer with his high crown of antlers rushed at the gate and struck at it, right at Taktuk's side. Taktuk was secretly glad that he was high and safe above them. Some day he knew he would join the "throwers," and gladly, but now he was satisfied to be where he was.

Taktuk was glad he was high above them.

Now the men at the end of the chute shouted and called for "Reindeer—reindeer!" That was the signal for Taktuk; he put his hand on the long wooden handle, carefully slid the gate to one side—and waited, breathlessly. The big steer, "king of the tundra," sniffed as he looked down the open chute, and, dashing forth with antlers tossed high, he fairly flew to his freedom. After him the deer, in a mass, flowed from the end of the chute.

Taktuk gazed in amazement, spellbound and thrilled by the sight.

"Shut the gate—shut the gate!" shouted Pannigaluk.

Taktuk slid it shut, but it was too late; all had gone through! He suddenly realized he was supposed to let only a few through at a time.

Pannigaluk came up to him.

"Don't forget again; remember only three or four at once!"

"Were there many lost?" asked Taktuk, terror-stricken.

"No; we got the fawns. All those that got away were deer that had been marked before."

Taktuk saw that four fawns were thrown and were being ear-marked. This did not seem to give them any apparent discomfort, for once they were up, off they ran at top speed, head and stub-tails high in the air, their new young horns like sticks of brown wood topping their cunning faces.

Tom had now let more deer into the pocket. Again came the call of "Reindeer!" from the men at the chute. This time Taktuk manipulated his gate in true deer-man fashion. Soon the work fell into routine, Taktuk doing his part carefully and well. He learned the reason for the bandanna. The milling deer raised clouds of dust from the dry, sandy ground. As they rubbed against each other their shedding hair fell like rain at their sides and was ground under foot until the pocket was deep with it. The day grew warmer. Mosquitoes came out in double force, attracted by the animal heat.

But Taktuk did not mind any of these discomforts. Protected from the hot sun and blowing dust and hair by his hood and bandanna, with his eyes peering brightly over it, he worked for hours, until his arms ached and the deer seemed to swim in the air before his eyes.

George came up then—"My turn now, Taktuk!"—and took over the gate.

Taktuk climbed stiffly down—he hadn't realized how tired he was—and joined the gathering of women and children who were watching near the end of the chute. They were very gay in their new bright-colored calico parkas. They shouted and called to the men, encouraging them, praising them when a particularly nice "throw" was made, or giggling when a steer, too strong and swift, would bound through the chute, upsetting his would-be thrower and dashing off over to the open range.

There was great rivalry among the men, urged on, no doubt, by the smiling audience of girls and women. Although warm and dusty, the men laughed often and made many throws to be proud of.

Now and then, Taktuk saw a deer come through with long strips of velvet hanging in red ribbons about his face, torn from his antlers in dashing madly against the sides of the corral.

"Why are the antlers so soft?" he asked Prunes, who was watching beside him.

"They are new, only grown out since May, but they will be strong hard bone by fall."

This was the "shopping season" for the Eskimo mothers and wives. They watched for unusually well-spotted fawns to come through the chute. These soft warm skins would supply the family wardrobe for the next winter for young and old, parkas, boots, mitts, and socks. The young meat supplied the food at the marking, and a feast it was going to be.

Taktuk watched Navaluk as she chose an unusually pretty fawn; he guessed that it was for a suit for him.

Then came a call of "Empty pocket!" and the last deer of the first "cut-off" which had been herded into the outer corral came through.

From the camp near appeared a welcome figure—the cook boy

with huge cans of hot coffee. He gave out tins cups and filled and refilled them many times.

Taktuk stood in line with the men. He drank two cups; he felt like a regular reindeer man, standing there, dusty and hot and tired, but so happy!

Then, with a shout, the men were off again. Taktuk started with them.

"It isn't your turn yet," Tom told him, so he went back to watch the others work.

Again three or four thousand deer were herded into the outer corral, and the work began again. This went on regardless of time, the men working day and night alike until they could work no longer and Taktuk bravely taking his turn each time. After the first three days of continuous work the men grew tired and exhausted in the white-hot sunlight of the daytime, so from then on they worked only at night, sleeping during the heat of the day.

All this time Partner had never forgotten to come daily with food for Kondenss and to talk to Taktuk for a few stolen moments. Taktuk had worked right through, snatching naps when he could.

Night after night the work continued in the strange bright light of the sun, which, taking only a few moments' rest, would rise up again in a red burst of glory.

Finally came the night when the last of the herd had been driven into the outer corral. One by one, they had dashed back to their freedom, until every deer had gone through the chute.

Then Partner called to Taktuk, "It is time to mark your fawn now; hurry and bring him here!"

Taktuk ran over the umiak. A strange feeling was in his throat. He had forgotten that Kondenss must leave him, leave him to follow over the open range with the herd. Picking the fawn up, he rubbed his cheek against the soft fur.

"Kondenss, you must go back to your mother now; but you will still be mine, they will put my mark on your ears, Taktuk's mark. I am your owner, you will still be mine!"

He could hardly manage the awkward weight of the fawn as he carried him over to the waiting men. The lump in his throat bothered him; his eyes felt blurry—he did so want to keep Kondenss with him! His pride in being an owner soon came to his rescue.

"See, this is your mark," Partner was explaining. "I will put your name in the book; here it is: Taktuk."

Taktuk felt like a proud owner now. The little-boy desire to keep Kondenss as a pet quite vanished. Pannigaluk held the frightened fawn while Ned deftly and quickly cut into the tiny ears—the mark which would always be Taktuk's. Then they all stood aside, waiting for Kondenss to make a dash toward the fast-disappearing herd. Instead, the fawn came over to Taktuk.

"Lead him over to where he can catch their scent," suggested Partner.

Gently Taktuk led the fawn past the camp, over the narrow land to where the last stragglers of the great herd were plainly in sight. Frisking up heels, head held high, the fawn ran toward the herd, crying out as it flew.

Tired and dusty, the whole camp stood watching the fawn skim over the earth. Then a mother deer, leaving the herd, ran calling softly to meet the fawn. Joyfully she smelled it over, happily; then, together, they raced back to join the herd!

Soon they became a part of the moving mass of brown bodies. Then, gradually slipping over the hill in the distance, the last of the huge herd was out of sight, to roam over the great open ranges for another year.

The round-up was over!

VIII

PLAYTIME

The tired camp rested during the heat of the next day. Taktuk missed the gentle little fawn. He had grown to love Kondenss, but he soon had little time to think about it, for everyone in camp was getting ready to play now, to play and feast just as hard as they had worked.

Taktuk and the boys gathered wood for the fires, and soon the big kettles of boiling meat filled the air with jolly smells. Taktuk ate until he thought he could eat no more, but Partner arrived with a box in his hands.

"Here is some candy for you and your friends, Taktuk."

Shyly Taktuk took the box. Immediately he was besieged by all the children of the camp, who had heard the magic word "candy." The box was soon empty and the children very quiet, each one busy with the round lump which filled his cheek. Taktuk had never had a "sucker" before; he had chosen a bright red one. Another new taste!

Now the men were putting up two long poles with a bar across them, like a football goal post. Taktuk knew what this meant.

"Kick ball," he cried. "They are going to play kick ball!"

The boys ran over, eager to watch this much-admired sport of the young men and girls. The women and old men crowded close.

A rag ball was suspended on a long string hanging from the bar, and dangled about four feet from the ground.

Pannigaluk was the first to try. Standing still, he jumped and with both feet at once kicked the ball. It was a double standing high kick. One by one the other men followed him, those missing the ball dropping out; then the ball was raised each time until only a few men were left who could reach it. Even Pannigaluk and George and Tom had finally dropped out, and at last only Ned was left. The ball was now lifted to about six feet from the ground, far above Ned's head. Fairy had pushed into the front row beside Taktuk. Breathlessly they watched Ned. He stood still, then jumped, almost turning a back somersault, but his feet touched the ball!

Everyone cheered, and Fairy beamed, so proud of her father!

Then came the tossing in a "skin." A circle of young men held a huge walrus skin tight all around. First Prunes stepped on the skin and the men raised it a few feet from the ground, and then, counting, raised and lowered it rhythmically; then with a powerful jerk tossed him in the air, but he landed in a tumble in the skin, much to everyone's delight.

Taktuk's turn came next. "One—two—three—four—" they counted; then came the jerk, and bump! Taktuk came down in a heap. He laughed with them and joined the crowd to watch Fairy try.

She stepped daintily on the skin, her little face serious and determined. Then, "one—two," up and down and up and down to the counting; then the powerful jerk—and the spring—up went Fairy far into the air, soaring almost birdlike high above their heads, and down again feet first without a tumble; then up again, balancing and flying with waving arms up and down like a real fairy.

Taktuk was proud of his company; he cheered her.

Everyone had a turn, some with success, breathlessly soaring in the air, while others only tumbled laughingly into the skin.

"Tum—tum—tum"—the sound of the dance drum beat monotonously on the clear air. Taktuk, with flying feet keeping time to its rhythm, ran to join the fast-growing circle of people. He hoped his mother Navaluk would sing the dance song he loved so much. Yes —there she was ready to begin.

He settled down on the ground and watched his mother as she danced and sang, fascinated by the beauty of her graceful motions. Her small, pretty hands waved above her head, behind her back, restless and fluttering like two little birds; while her body swayed to the constant rhythm of the drum; then slowly she knelt, and the fluttering restless hands were quiet beneath her chin.

"My arms they wave high in the air,
My hands they flutter behind my back;
They wave above my head like the wings of a bird,
Let me move my feet, let me dance, let me shrug
My shoulders; let me shake my body,
My arms, let me fold them, let me crouch down;
Let me hold my hands under my chin."

Noaluk, Fairy's mother, also had a song to sing—a new one—and she took her place in the center of the circle, swaying in time to the rhythm of the song—her song of rejoicing.

"A ya-a-a ye-e-ea-ye-a ee-a—
My song, this one, it begins to want to come out,
It begins to want to go out to my companions
Who ask for a song—who ask for a song—
Who ask for a dance;
My song, this one it comes,
For my companions ask to be made happy!
'Over here, at Choris, when we came from Buckland,
Even thus I found my man, even thus I found him;
I found him in good health; I found him in good health;
When he came, he wished you all plenty of good luck,
Hoorah! Hoorah!'
All of us, let us sing in unison."

Fairy eagerly followed every word, her lips moving. "I'll sing that song when I grow up," she whispered to Taktuk.

Then old Angnaurak, the greatest hunter of the Buckland country, sat down in the middle of the circle. A hush fell over the group as they waited for his story. Taktuk was quite in awe of Angnaurak, for he seemed to have stepped right out of a story himself, so wonderful were the things he could do.

In the winter he would wear a suit of white Arctic hare skin, so, at a distance, Taktuk could hardly see him against the snow. In the middle of the back of his coat he wore the symbol of luck—the tail of a cross-fox—and a lucky hunter he was, being about the only man of the village who dared go bear hunting.

The huge brown bears are greatly feared by the Buckland people, and many a time Taktuk had heard this warning given to the children: "Don't go far, or the bears will get you!" Angnaurak was the best story-teller of the village—no festivity was complete without him. Now they were all eager to hear this story which they loved best of all, for it was the old story of the founding of their own village.

The Story of the First Woman

Once there were but two men in all the world, and only one woman. One man lived at the Buckland River, and the other at the Kuskokwim Valley, to the south. The woman lived all alone in her house just halfway between these places.

One day, as these men were out hunting, they met at the woman's house. Never before had they seen a woman. The man from the south, when he saw her said, "This shall be my woman; I will take her with me." But the Buckland man cried, "She shall be mine!" and quickly did he catch hold of her by the shoulders and start to take her away. The man from the south got very angry, and just as the Buckland man was going out with her, he caught the woman by her feet and did try to pull her away from him, and they each pulled and pulled, and so strong were they, they pulled the woman so hard, she broke in two at the waist!

So the man from the south took home his part of the woman, which was only from her waist to her feet, but when he got home he carefully carved the upper part of her body from wood, giving her some arms and a very nice wooden head, so you see he had a whole woman after all!

And the man from Buckland, when he got home with the upper half of his woman, carved out of wood the rest of her, so that she could have some nice wooden legs to walk with.

In this way, both men were very happy ever after, and they had many children born to them, and so the village of Buckland grew, and also a village to the south.

Always, to this day, women of the village to the south dance very beautifully, but can do nothing so well in which they must use their hands or their heads.

But you will find that the women of Buckland Village are famous for the many clever things which they can do with their hands, and for their songs and bright ways.

Each one of the listening group knew every word of this story, and word by word they followed Angnaurak as he repeated it, but he had never been known to vary it. Taktuk was learning it, too. When at last the camp had gone to rest after hours and hours of revelry, Taktuk lay under the umiak and repeated the words he could remember over and over to himself.

"Once there were but two men in all the world—and only one woman. One man lived at Buckland River and the other at the Kuskokwim Valley. The woman lived all alone——" Thus on and on he repeated it in a whisper, sometimes beginning all over again, sometimes repeating one part again and again—until at last he was asleep.

When he waked, the white man's boat was getting ready to leave to go back to Nome.

"Why are we not going back home, too?" Taktuk asked Pannigaluk.

"We will all stay here for the rest of the summer; we have fish to catch, and the whale will be coming soon. You would not like to live in Buckland Village now, it would be too hot, and the mosquitoes are far too many."

Partner came over to say good-bye. He slipped a new shining belt knife into Taktuk's hand.

"Good-bye, Taktuk; study hard at school so you can talk more to me when we see each other next year!"

Taktuk silently grinned his appreciation—it was the first knife he had ever had!

Then, noisily puffing and snorting, the engine boat took Partner away.

IX

UNDER THE SUMMER SUN

Escholtz Bay is a whaler's paradise, and now old Angnaurak spent every day sitting watching the quiet blue water where it joined the deeper blue of Kotzebue Sound, watching for the coming of the beluga, or white whale. Taktuk and Fairy often sat with him, and he would tell them old folklore tales.

One day, as they were sitting with Angnaurak, Taktuk saw a bush near by move, move ever so little at the base, and then all was quiet again. He stole closer. "It's a mother ptarmigan," he whispered to Fairy. Taktuk loved these birds in the winter when they were pure white like the snow. He and Fairy had watched as they gradually took on dark feathers and became spotted brown and white like the earth itself, when the ground begins to appear between the lingering drifts in spring. Now the ptarmigan were entirely dark and could hardly be seen against the brown bushes and earth.

Taktuk crept up on Mother Ptarmigan for sport, to hear her cry of alarm and her voice giving orders to her nine babies who had wandered out to enjoy the sunshine—"Paq—paq!" ("Go back—go back!") She fluttered on, always away from the little family, who scurried under the brush in the opposite direction, obedient to the stern, "Paq—paq!" ("Go back—go back!")—"Paq! Paq!"

Then, when the two children returned, Angnaurak told them this story:

The Ptarmigan Thieves

Once there lived an old woman at Tin City with her two grandchildren, a boy and a girl. The boy was very skillful at catching ptarmigan in a net, and he kept the household well supplied with them; but after a time, when he visited his net each morning, he always found it empty—someone had stolen the ptarmigan in the night! He told his grandmother, "I can't catch any more ptarmigan because someone is always stealing them from the net." The old lady mumbled—she was so old she could hardly speak—"Well, never mind, my boy." "Oh, but I don't want you to go hungry," he said, "I'm going to find out who it is."

That night he lay in hiding near his net and watched. Soon two men came along. One said to the other, "I don't like this at all; I feel very frightened. Someone must be watching us, for I never felt like this before." His companion said, "You're dreaming—come on, let's take these ptarmigan out." So one held the net up on one side and the other on the other, and they took all the ptarmigan. The boy said to himself: "What right have they to steal my ptarmigan?" and suddenly called out, "Paq—paq—paq—paq—paq!" The men were so frightened, they dropped the ptarmigan and ran, but the boy ran after them, shouting all the time, "Paq—paq!" until he saw them enter a small round house. Quietly he stole onto the roof, lifted a corner of the window, and looked down. Inside was a medicine man sitting on the sleeping platform, and the two thieves were relating to him their adventure. Suddenly the boy called, "Paq—paq—paq—paq!" from his place on the roof.

The thieves sprang up, shrieking, "The Spirit—the Spirit!" and the medicine man, who was the real thief, as the men only stole at his bidding, called out: "Who will help me against the Spirit up there? Friend Black Bear, you come." Immediately a host of mice swarmed around the boy and threatened to eat him alive, but he sprang to his feet and stamped on them and killed them all. The medicine man called out again, "Who will help me against that Spirit up there? Friend White Bear, you come."

A host of lemmings then sprang up around the boy, but he tore them off him and stamped on them and killed them, just as he had killed the mice. Again the medicine man called out, "Who will help me against the Spirit up there? Friend Fire, you come." A great ball of fire suddenly rolled over toward the boy, who fled quickly. The fire rolled after him and had almost overtaken him when he drew his dogskin mitten from his left hand, saying, "My pup, help me." Immediately the fire and mitten began to fight, and the fire killed the mitten and consumed it. Then it ran after the boy again until it was almost on top of him. He drew off his other mitten and flung it back, saying, "My pup, help me." This time the mitten was victorious and the fire was destroyed. The boy reached home in safety, and always after that had no more trouble with his nets.

Taktuk, listening intently to the story, absent-mindedly watched the deep blue sea as it stretched flatly out before him. Now and then he noticed a sudden flash, but so quickly did it go he was not sure whether he had really seen it or not. As Angnaurak finished his story and began to puff on his pipe, Taktuk was sure he saw the flash again.

"Look—over there!" he exclaimed, pointing. "I saw a flash. Is it a whale?"

With eyes straining, they watched. It came again like a silver light flashing from the blue of the water, as the sun reflected from the wet round back of a white whale. Soon another flared up near it. "Whale! Whale come!" shouted Angnaurak, as he jumped up and rushed down to the shore to meet the hunters who had so anxiously been waiting for these words. Taktuk started to follow, but Tom and Prunes came running up the cliff.

"We can see them best from here!" panted Tom. "Look, there they go!"

Five kayaks had already started out from the beach.

"Angnaurak is leading!" exclaimed Taktuk in a hushed voice. The boys whispered in their excitement, although they knew the whale could not hear them. Angnaurak was leading the long-experienced hunters as he had led them for many years. He could be seen darting ahead of the others; not a ripple, not a sound broke the silence.

With sure easy dips of the paddles they skirted the rim of the bay, careful not to frighten the incoming herd of whale. The white glistening backs could be seen now at the entrance of the bay. Swiftly the silent kayaks worked their way in back of the herd, cutting off its only means of escape to the sound.

Then bedlam broke loose. Howls and shrieks shattered the silence; the men in the kayaks acted as if they had suddenly gone mad, bellowing at the top of their lungs, making hideous noises while they frantically beat the water with their paddles, sending great sprays of flashing water in the air. The whole world seemed to have gone mad as the hills answered them yell for yell, shriek for shriek, until the noise rebounded down the length and breadth of the bay.

Taktuk, trembling, carried away by this tremendous madness, shrieked and yelled with them hardly knowing what he was doing.

"They are driving them in—they are driving them in!" shouted Tom.

Beating the water continually, the hunters were chasing the frightened whales into shallow water.

The sharp report of a rifle shot broke the din—another and another—puffs of white smoke could be seen coming from the kayaks.

"They've got them!" shouted Tom, and started pell-mell down to the beach. Prunes and Taktuk, following, raced to get there in time to see them land.

The whole camp was at the beach by the time the boys reached it. Excitement was running high.

"Here they come—they've each got a big one," shouted Tom.

Behind each kayak a big beluga was being towed in.

The place was alive with activity in no time. The women immediately set to work to prepare the huge creatures for drying and eating.

Pannigaluk called to Taktuk, "Come with me; you can help with the building of the racks."

For years the Buckland people had caught their whale here.

The old drift timbers, used for drying racks, lay on the beach always in readiness for this great hunt, and now were swung into place for use. The men cut the tough hide from the sleek white body of the whale while the women prepared the tender white fat in long thin strips and hung them in great chains over the rack to dry. "Muktuk," they called it. The peninsula appeared decorated for some grand, gala occasion as these long festoons gleamed blue-white and red in the sun. The whale oil was stored in the ever-useful seal pokes for use in the coming winter. A feast, of course, was held in celebration, with dance songs and stories as the camp rejoiced.

The next few weeks slipped by quickly for Taktuk. There were so many pleasant things to do. Sometimes he went with Pannigaluk to take the salmon from the nets and to help spread the catch on the racks to dry in the sun.

Often he went berrying with the other boys. Quantities of berries grew on the peninsula; blueberries and moss berries, black and seedy; salmon berries, in shape like raspberries; and the Alaska cranberry. Some of these Navaluk packed in oil in seal pokes for use in the winter.

Navaluk was busy sewing the spotted fawn-skin she had selected during the reindeer marking into a serviceable winter suit for Taktuk. She measured him carefully with a measure taken from his own hand—the distance from the tip of his thumb to the end of his outstretched first finger; this was the correct length for the shoulder seam—and all other seams were measured the same way.

Fairy, who still remained a member of his household for the summer, would spend hours playing "measuring." She would measure baby Raisins for many imaginary suits. Raisins spent most of her time that summer crawling and rolling about on the reindeer skin spread on the ground, enjoying the warm sunshine. She wore hardly any clothes at all, in spite of the many suits of clothes that Fairy measured her for, and each day she grew fatter and browner and sweeter-tempered. No wonder Navaluk had named her for something very rare and precious!

X

HOME AGAIN!

The summer was ending. The sun had been in the sky day and night. Then it disappeared for five minutes, the next night for ten minutes, and at last for an hour. When Taktuk awoke in the morning it would be quite cold. The mosquitoes had disappeared, and the summer's work had been completed.

"We must be ready to start for home as soon as a fair wind comes," Pannigaluk announced to his family one day.

"Why do we have to wait for a fair wind?" asked Taktuk, as eager to get back home now as he had been to leave it.

"We have no engine boat to tow us home so we must put up the sail on the umiak and sail home ourselves. Will you be glad to get home and go to school again, Taktuk?"

"Oh, yes, because I am going to learn more white man's words so I can talk to my partner!"

Early the next morning the camp was astir, packing up its belongings. The fair wind had come!

Taktuk helped pack their umiak again this time with the dried fish, reindeer meat, whale oil, muktuk, and berries, besides all the things that they had brought with them, including Mission language books. Everything was in but the dogs.

"I'll bring them," offered Taktuk, and ran to untie them. They seemed glad to go into the boat, and started to yelp and howl, adding to the confusion. Taktuk's own dogs, Natsirk and Kopak, were arranged so he could sit beside them again.

The sail was hoisted.

"See how funny the circles look, Fairy!" Taktuk exclaimed as the last dog was loaded on the boat.

"What circles?"

"Why, the circles the dogs made from running around and around all summer—see over there."

He pointed to where each dog had worn a deep circular hole in the ground around the stake—these looked very strange now the dogs were removed from them.

The sail was hoisted, the wind filled it, and off they went, with Old Kuvnapuk steering; a kayak was being towed in back of the umiak. Taktuk looked at the deserted peninsula, fast being left behind.

"See, it begins to look like islands again," he observed. Their umiak was leading the other boats from the camp.

But they were only out a few hours or so when little waves restlessly began to lap-lap against the boat, splashing spray against Taktuk's face. Old Kuvnapuk, who was steering, sat up a little straighter and looked again and again at the southeastern sky. The water had turned from a beautiful blue to a cold, metallic gray, and each wave showed a splash of white at its throat.

Gray, purplish clouds began to scurry across the sky, meeting together to form one heavy mass overhead, shutting out the sun. The wind was beginning to blow in sharp gusts, causing the umiak to bob crazily. Kuvnapuk gave the word to the men to let down the sail and get out the paddles. Deftly they did this; and just in time, for now the wind was blowing at terrific speed from another direction. Rain splashed down in great drops, then pelted down in icy sheets. Taktuk pulled his hood over his face, while the women hurriedly covered everything over with the skins. Raisins and Fairy were tucked in under the skins, too. The men worked with all their strength paddling to keep the boat head on into the waves so as to prevent its swamping, as the waves were now growing larger and fiercer, constantly driving the boat from its course. Two sealskin pokes were blown up like balloons and hung over each side of the bow, to steady the boat.

Taktuk held tightly to Kopak and Natsirk; he buried his head in their fur. He tried to think of other things; he thought of his fawn and whispered softly to Natsirk: "Kondenss will be big when I see it next year. I wonder if it will remember me? It might leave the herd again and come to me."

He pictured a very large Kondenss with lofty antlers rushing from the herd to greet him.

Then—"I'll talk a lot to Partner—perhaps he will bring some more Kondenss for my fawn—no, I guess it will be too big for it then. My knife—I must not let anything happen to my knife, so I can show Partner how nicely I have kept it. The rain makes such a funny noise when it hits on my hood, Natsirk. The snow will come soon; you will like it. Remember what fun we had last winter! You are bigger now—I am bigger, too, Natsirk.

"I am an owner now. Maybe we will be big enough to go sealing next spring. I'll be glad to get back to school, 'cause I want to learn more words. Natsirk, do you suppose some spirit is angry with us to make this awful storm? Do you suppose we won't get home?"

Taktuk buried his face still farther in the warm comforting fur of the dog, who rubbed against him, also seeking comfort in this terrible rage of the elements.

The boat was rising and falling, pounding into the waves. Taktuk had the curious feeling that instead of the waves getting larger, the umiak was slowly shrinking in size, getting smaller and smaller, soon to disappear entirely.

"Kyana! Kyana!" ("Good! good!") shouted Kuvnapuk.

Quickly Taktuk jerked up his head. They were nearing shore, a rugged point of land with cliffs rising from it.

"Elephant Point!" cried Pannigaluk.

The umiak steadied as they drew into calmer water; with deft strokes of the paddles they touched the shore. It had grown quite dark by now—night was descending upon them earlier each day. Rapidly the umiak was turned over to form a shelter from the rain. A fire was made in the little sheet-iron stove. Navaluk made warm tea, and they ate some of the muktuk and dried reindeer meat.

"Why is this place called Elephant Point?" Taktuk asked Tom, who lay resting after the terrific strain of paddling.

"Once, long ago, longer ago than anyone can remember, a great big furry animal called Elephant roamed about here. The white men call them mammoths. They had great big tusks like the walrus, only much, much larger, because they were giant animals. They had long, funny noses that nearly reached to the ground; these were called trunks."

"Did they live at the same time as the big bad giant Elugoonik, who lived at Chamisso Island, who used to capture little boys and had webbed feet and hands?" Taktuk eagerly asked, referring to a myth which was told many times among the Buckland people.

"I don't know," Tom hesitated. "The white man said there wasn't any such giant, but"—here Tom was confident—"I know the big elephants were real, because their bones are found right here on this point."

"Maybe," Taktuk speculated, "maybe the big elephants belonged to the Elugoonik and helped him catch the little boys. Where are the bones?"

Tom parted the skins that hung down over the open side of the umiak. "Over there in those cliffs, frozen in the ice!"

Taktuk looked out. He could see faintly looming cliffs, black and forbidding against a sky almost as dark.

"Then how can I see the bones?" Taktuk was disappointed.

"Oh, you will see them all right in the morning; you can find lots of them scattered over the beach. The waves break away pieces of the cliff and then wash away the ice and dirt and leave tusks and teeth and bones all over the shore. You can get a nice piece of ivory to make a better handle for your new belt knife if you look careful, maybe."

Taktuk settled down under a warm reindeer skin. He called to Natsirk to come sleep close to him. His imagination, always ready to flare up, was aflame now, as he thought of the strange giant animals that lived here so long ago. "If they could be real, I don't see why the giant, Elugoonik, of Chamisso Island, could not have really lived, too. Anyway," he settled himself farther under the rug to sleep, "I don't think anyone knows."

He had a strange dream that night. It seemed to be morning, and he was running down along the beach to find the piece of ivory for his belt knife. As he neared the cliff he noticed the waves seemed to be talking as they rolled in from the sea.

They would shriek in taunting voices as they broke and rushed in, white foam rolling and creeping up toward the cliff, retreating only to come nearer the next time. "I'll find out your secret—your secret!" one would cry, and another echoed it as it rushed up. The high, rugged cliff seemed to grow even taller and colder as it answered in a distant voice: "No one shall know my secret—for hundreds of years I have kept it—more years than man can count—more years than the sea, more years than anyone knows, than—any—one—knows!"

A great wave rolled up. It flashed a violent green before it broke, and hissed: "We will know your secret—we will tell the world—we will tell the world—then it will not be a secret—the world—the world—the world!" With a mocking laugh, it ran in foaming white, stealthily creeping nearer and nearer the cliff, only to retreat with a shrill "The world!"

Taktuk in the dream was frightened by this strange behavior, and hid behind a rock, holding tight to Natsirk, who had followed him.

The cliff was turning a deep purple with rage.

"How could you tell my secret—silly babbling waves—if you knew it—silly waves—silly waves?"

Then the waves rushed forward pell-mell, one over the other, all in a tumult like a mad pack of dogs; rushed up the beach and clutched at the cliff—clutched and tore away great pieces of ice, leaving yawning gashes in its sides. They made a terrible noise, like the mad bellowing of the hunters as they chased the whale. The sound echoed and echoed from all sides of the universe. Then back to the sea the waves slid, carrying their stolen fragments with them.

Taktuk could hear the cliff, torn and jagged, wailing, lamenting in a high, plaintive voice like the sobbing of the wind:

"After all these years—years upon years—years upon year-r-r-rs!"

The waves were coming back again, laughing shrilly. The green one came bubbling up and rolled in on the beach, leaving a huge tusk behind it.

"For all the world to see," it shrilled as it slid back. "Nothing but bones—nothing but bones!"

The waves, now in order, danced and laughed and one by one rolled up and each left a tooth or a tusk or a bone behind, as they chorused: "Nothing but bones—bones—bones! For all the world to see—to see!"

And the cliff, somber and broken, wailed on:

"After all these years—years upon years—upon year-r-r-rs!"

Suddenly all the clamor hushed as a huge black shadow fell over them all.

Taktuk, dreaming on, felt terribly cold as the shadow enveloped him. Over the sea from the direction of Chamisso Island—a monstrous creature was coming—the Mammoth! He was coming directly toward Taktuk—the waves flattened glassily into the sea, and made a shining path for him. He lifted up his trunk and trumpeted like thunder: "I am looking for a boy to take to the Giant of Chamisso—a boy for the Giant of Chamisso!"

Taktuk was so overcome with fear he could not run. He buried his head in the fur of Natsirk and shut his eyes—nearer and nearer he could hear the voice—"A boy for the Giant of Chamisso!"

The dream was over.

Taktuk opened his eyes and lifted his head from Natsirk's neck. The sun was shining all about him; his mother was near, preparing whale meat for the morning meal. Natsirk was still sleeping curled up beside him. Taktuk awoke from his dream. What a joy to find everything normal again!

"Want to come with me to find the ivory for your knife?" Tom asked, coming up.

"Oh, yes." Taktuk jumped up.

"We must hurry, the boats will leave soon," Tom said, as they ran along the beach.

"The other boats landed here, too," observed Taktuk.

"Yes, they must have come in after we did; here we are."

The cliff seemed a bit sad and forbidding to Taktuk as he looked up at its muddy brown face. He could not help giving a frightened glance at the tiny waves which innocently lapped the shore.

"What is this?" he cried, as he picked up a huge piece of ivory almost too heavy for him to carry.

"That's a tooth," said Tom. "Here, I'll carry that; hurry up and find your piece for your knife."

"Here is one." Taktuk found a fragment of ivory just the right size. "What is this from?"

"A tusk," said Tom. "We must go back."

They hustled back; the boat was waiting for them, all ready to go. The water was calm and blue, and the little boat sailed gayly over it, sliding along. Taktuk drowsily watched the waves go by, Navaluk sang her lullaby, and Raisins nestled among the dogs.

"What do I see down there?
On the river—in the bend of the river,
A man jigging for a fish,
A man who is jigging!
A man who is jigging!"

That night they camped again at Igloo Point, feasting on some of the ducks they had stored there in the spring, on their way to Choris.

The next morning they started up the river. Paddling was not so easy this time, and they made slower progress.

"Why do we go so slow?" Taktuk asked Tom.

"We have to paddle against the current this way!"

Past the old village they went, on up the blue river that soon would be white with ice.

"Let's see who will see the schoolhouse first!" Taktuk said to Fairy. They kept their eyes straight ahead.

"I see it—I see it!" Fairy cried. "See, the flag is up; teacher must be there ahead of us!"

High in the air Taktuk could see the American flag flying from the schoolhouse pole. Sam Anaruk, the government teacher, was home before them. He was standing there, in the doorway, waving to them as he saw the boats of the village returning. The dogs set up a joyful barking as they caught the scent of familiar things.

"He is going in—listen, there goes the schoolhouse bell!" Taktuk exclaimed.

The familiar sound of the schoolhouse bell rang out, calling, calling to them—a Welcome Home!

WHAT HAPPENED TO INGER JOHANNE

By DIKKEN ZWILGMEYER
Translated from the Norwegian
By EMILIE POULSSON

Illustrations after
FLORENCE LILEY YOUNG

OURSELVES

THERE are four brothers and sisters of us at home, and as I am the eldest, it is natural that I should describe myself first. I am very tall and slim (Mother calls it "long and lanky"); and, sad to say, I have very large hands and very large feet. "My, what big feet!" our horrid old shoemaker always says when he measures me for a pair of new shoes. I feel like punching his tousled head for him as he kneels there taking my measure; for he has said that so often now that I am sick and tired of it.

My hair is in two long brown braids down my back. That is well enough, but my nose is too broad, I think; so sometimes when

I sit and study I put a doll's clothespin on it to make it smaller; but when I take the clothespin off, my nose springs right out again; so there is no help for it, probably.

Why people say such a thing is a puzzle; but they all, especially the boys, do say that I am so self-important. I say I am not—not in the least—and I must surely know best about myself, now that I am as old as I am. But I ask you girls whether it is pleasant to have boys pull your braids, or call you "Ginger," or to have them stand and whistle and give catcalls down by the garden wall, when they want you to come out. I have said that they must once for all understand that my braids must be let alone, that I will not be whistled for in that manner, and that I will come out when I am ready and not before. And then they call me self-important!

After me comes Karsten. He has a large, fair face, light hair, and big sticking-out ears. It is a shame to tease any one, but I do love to tease Karsten, for he gets so excited that he flushes scarlet out to the tips of his ears and looks awfully funny! Then he runs after me—which is, of course, just what I want—and if he catches me, gives me one or two good whacks; but usually we are the best of friends. Karsten likes to talk about wonderfully strong men and how much they can lift on their little finger with their arm stretched out; and he is great at exaggeration. People say I exaggerate and add a sauce to everything, but they ought to hear Karsten! Anyway, I don't exaggerate—I only have a lively imagination.

After Karsten there is a skip of five years; then comes Olaug, who is still so little that she goes to a "baby school" to learn her letters, and the Catechism. I often go to fetch Olaug home, for it is awfully funny there. When Miss Einarsen, the teacher, and her sister say anything they do not wish the children to understand, they use P-speech: Can-pan you-pou talk-palk it-pit? I went there often on purpose to learn it, for it is so ignorant to know only one language. But now I know both Norwegian and P-speech. Olaug always remembers exactly the days when the school money is to be paid, for on those days each child who brings the money gets a lump of brown sugar. Once a year the minister comes to Miss Einarsen's to catechize the children; but Miss Einarsen always stands behind the one who is being questioned and whispers the right answer. "Oh, Teacher is telling, Teacher is telling!" the children say to each other. "Yes, I am telling," says Miss Einarsen. "How do you think you would get along if I didn't?" On examination days Miss Einarsen always treats to thin chocolate in tiny cups, and the children drink about six cups apiece! Well, that's how it is at Olaug's school.

After Olaug comes Karl, but he is only a little midget. He thinks he can reach the moon if he stands on a chair by the window and stretches his arms away up high. He is perfectly wild to get hold of the moon because he thinks it would roll about so beautifully on the floor.

OUR TOWN

We live in a little town on the seacoast. It is much more fun to live in a little town than a big one, for then you know every one of the boys and girls, and there are many more good places to play in; and all the sea besides. Oh, yes! I know very well that there are lots of small towns that do not lie by the sea. They must be horrid!

Think how we have the great ocean thundering in against the shore, wave after wave. Oh, it is delightful! Anyone who has not seen that has missed a really beautiful sight. It is beautiful both in summer and winter; but I do believe it is most beautiful and wonderful in the time of the autumn storms. Go up on the hilltop some day in autumn, where the big beacon is, and look out over the sea! You have to hold on to your hat, hold on to your clothes, hold on to your body itself, almost. Whew-ew! the wind! How it blows! How it blows! And the whole ocean looks as if it were astir from the very bottom. Big black billows with broad white crests of foam come rolling, rolling, rolling in—one wave does not wait for the other. And how they break over the islands out where the lighthouse is! The lighthouse stands like a tall white ghost against the dark sea and the dark sky;—sinks behind an enormous wave, rises again, sinks and rises again. How swiftly the clouds fly! How the ocean seethes and roars! We hear it all over town, sobbing, roaring, thundering! Away in by the wharves of the market square the waters are all in a turmoil. The little boats rock and rock, and the big ships dip up and down. The wet rigging sparkles, the mooring chains strain and creak, and there is *such* a smell of salt in the air! You can almost taste the salt with your tongue.

In such weather the damaged ships come in. One autumn there came a Spanish steamship, with a green funnel and a white hull. It lay with almost its whole stern under water when the pilot from Krabbesund brought it in. That was jolly; not for the people on board—it was anything but jolly for them—but for us children.

When we choose, we go out into the harbor in boats and row round and round among the strange ships. At last, very likely, the sailors call out to us and ask us to come on board, and then it doesn't take us long to scramble up the ladder, you may be sure! On board, it is awfully jolly. Once a French skipper gave us some pineapple preserves; but generally we only get crackers. When the Spanish ship was in, the streets swarmed with foreign sailors, with long brown necks and burning black eyes. Then the old policeman

Mr. Weiby, strutted about, and sent Father long written reports about street rows and disturbances. The Spaniards didn't bother themselves a mite about old Weiby, puffing around with his chin high in the air!

Sometimes on summer afternoons when the water lies calm and shining, we slip off and borrow a boat (Mr. Terkelsen's, quite often) and go rowing around the island. Then, afterwards, we float about—dabbling and splashing in the darkened water until evening comes on. Ah! that is pleasure!

AN ADVENTURE

One summer evening Massa Peckell, Mina Trap and I saved two people from drowning; and we were praised for it in the newspapers. Really it is most delightful to see your name in print! I should like ever so much to do something else that the papers would praise me for, but I don't know what it could be!

This is how it happened that time. We had borrowed old Terkelsen's boat and rowed quite a way out. From a wharf on one of the islands another boat laden with wood came toward us. The wood was in slabs and chips and was piled high fore and aft. Down between the piles sat two children rowing. As they came nearer we saw that it was Lisa and George, the lighthouse-keeper's children. Mina and I were rowing, but I was so much stronger that I kept rowing her round and round, so that we were laughing and having a jolly time. Probably George and Lisa were watching us and forgetting all about their top-heavy boat; for, the next thing we knew, both piles of wood, George and Lisa, and the boat were all upset in the water. It was a dreadful thing to see!

"We—we'll go ashore and get help!" shrieked Massa. Humph!

A pretty time they would have if we did that! Mina and I had more sense, so we turned our boat quickly and were over to the spot in two or three strokes of the oars. The boat was completely capsized and the chips floated over the water as thick as a floor. But George and Lisa were nowhere to be seen!

Then you may believe that Mina and I yelled with all our might! You know how it sounds over the water. My! how we did shriek! It must have been heard all over town. I saw people away back on the wharves running to the water to see what was the matter.

Then, there bobbed Lisa's head up among the chips, and Mina and I hauled her up by the arms into the boat. Massa had to hang away over on the starboard so that *our* boat shouldn't upset, too. Old Terkelsen is always so mad when we take his boat without leave. I can't imagine, for the life of me, why he should get so provoked over it. We always bring it back just as good as ever! Massa and Mina and I have no desire, forsooth, to set out to sea through the Skagerrak and sail away with it! But on that day it was fortunate that we had taken his boat, and not some miserable little thing belonging to anybody else.

As soon as Lisa got her breath, she cried out: "Oh! the chips! the chips!" But just then George's head appeared, and Mina and I made a grab for him; but he was so stupidly heavy that we could n't pull him in; so we only held him fast and screamed and screamed. Out from the wharves and from the islands came ever so many boats and lots of people. Those minutes that we hung over the edge of that boat and held on with all our might to the half-drowned George, who was as heavy as lead—shall I ever forget? George was drawn up into another boat and they took us in tow. Lisa sat like a drowned rat and cried till she choked. Then Massa began to cry, too;—and so we came to the wharf.

For several days after the rescue I couldn't go into the street without people's stopping me and wanting a full account of how it all happened. Really, it is quite troublesome to be famous; but I like it pretty well, nevertheless.

When Mina and I met that stout, lighthouse-Lisa on the street next time, we couldn't imagine how we had ever been able to drag her into the boat! But you mustn't expect *gratitude* in this world. Many a time since then has Lisa come tiptoeing along after us on the street, tossing her head this way and that, mimicking us, to show how self-important we are! And *that* after we saved the stupid creature from drowning!

OUR HOME

We live up on a hill in a lovely old house. People call it an old rattletrap of a house, but that is nothing but envy because they don't live there themselves. There are big old elm trees around the house which shade it and make the back part of the deep rooms quite dark. The rafters show overhead, and the floors rock up and down when you walk hard on them, just because they are so old. There is one place in the parlor floor where it rocks especially. When no one is in there except Karsten and myself, we often tramp with all our might where the floor rocks most, for we want dreadfully to see whether we can't break through into the cellar.

There are several gardens belonging to our house. One big garden has only plum trees with slender trunks and a little cluster of branches and leaves high, high up. When I walk down there under the plum trees, I often imagine that I am down in the tropics, wandering under palm trees. I have a garden of my own, too. I wouldn't have mentioned it particularly if there weren't one remarkable fact about it. Really and truly, nothing will grow in it but that dark blue toadflax—you know what that is. Every single spring I buy seeds with my pocket money, and plant and water and

Mina and I hauled her up by the arms into the boat.

take care of them, but when summer comes there is nothing in the garden but great big toadflax stalks all gone to seed. It is awfully tiresome, especially when they have such a horrid name.

PLAYMATES

Now I think it is time to describe all of us boys and girls who play together, and whom I am going to tell about in my book.

There is Peter, the dean's son, with his sleepy brown eyes and freckles as big as barleycorns. Peter is a cowardly chap. He never has any opinion of his own. And if he had one he would never dare to stand by it if you contradicted him. He's terribly afraid of the cold, too, and goes about with a scarf wound around his neck, and mittens if a single snowflake falls. Still, Peter is very nice indeed; he does everything that I want him to.

Then there is my brother Karsten, but I've told you about him. He is a little younger than the rest of us.

Another boy is Ezekiel Weiby. He is fourteen years old and has an awfully narrow face—not much broader than a ruler. He is very clever and reads every sort of book. But when he is out with the rest of us, he wants us all to sit still and hear him tell about everything he has been reading. For a while that is very pleasant, but I get tired of it pretty soon, for I hate to sit still long at a time. That is a very funny thing. Other people get tired of walking or running about, but I can't stand it to sit still.

Nils Trap is the bravest of all the boys. He never wears an overcoat, but goes around with his hands in his pockets whistling a funny tune:

"Ho, hei for Laaringa!"

which you probably don't know. Nils Trap clambers like a cat up in the rigging of the vessels. Some people say that they have seen him lie out straight on the ball at the top of the big mast of the

Palmerston and spin himself round. But others say that is a whopper, for the *Palmerston* is the biggest ship in town with the very highest masts. Perhaps he could lie and balance himself on top of it, but spin himself round! That he could n't do if he tried till he was blue in the face.

Then there are Massa, and Mina, and I. Mina is Nils's sister and my best friend. She has a gold filling in one of her front teeth. Oh, if I could only have such a shining little spot as that in my teeth! Mine are only plain straight white ones and they look really dull beside hers.

Massa Peckell is plump and easy-going. She thinks the most beautiful thing is to be pale and thin. She heard that it would give you a delicate pale skin if you drank vinegar and ate rice soup, so she tried it as hard as she could. But her beauty-cure only gave her the stomach-ache. Her fat, red cheeks are just like Baldwin apples still.

Every day, summer and winter, we are together, all of us that I have written about here. In summer there is a lot of fun to be had everywhere, but especially on the delightful hill back of our house—I will tell you all about that hill some other time—but in winter, humph! What can girls and boys do in such horrid mild winters as we are now having, I should really like to know! Last year we had no snow to speak of, and here it is now after New Year's and I haven't yet, to my recollection, seen a single snowflake which didn't melt in five minutes, or any ice that didn't break through as soon as you stamped your heel on it. If I could only make a journey to the North Pole and do what I wanted to there, I should send down some lovely soft snowdrifts and some smooth blue glistening ice in a jiffy, to all the boys and girls who are wishing for them day after day.

In the meantime I am glad that I have begun to write this book in winter, otherwise I should be bored to death.

Of course we go out-of-doors now too, even though the mild weather is disgusting; but when it storms as hard as it did in the autumn, making the old elm trees crash and swish so that we can scarcely hear ourselves talk, then it is not comfortable to play out-of-doors, I assure you. At such times we often shut ourselves up in the little room over the wood-shed. There is nothing up there but a keg of red ochre which we paint ourselves with, but really we have lots of fun there, nevertheless.

Ezekiel aways seizes the chance to give a lecture in the wood-shed, and his words gush out like water from a fountain. When I get tired of it, I sneak around behind him and give him a little English punch in the back, for I am very clever at boxing, you must know. "Come on! Can you use your fists like an Englishman?" And then I roll my hands round very fast, just as I have seen the English sailors do, and give him a quick punch in the stomach with my fist.

Ezekiel squirms about like a worm, and defends himself with his small weak fingers. The others laugh, and Ezekiel and I laugh with them, and so we all laugh together.

Well, now you know us all, and you know what it is like around here.

WHAT HAPPENED ONE ST. JOHN'S DAY

Well; what I am going to tell about now has n't the least thing to do with St. John's Day itself—you must n't think it has; not the least connection with fresh young birch leaves and strong sunshine and Whitsuntide lilies and all that. Far from it. It is only that a certain St. John's Day stands out in my memory because of what happened to me then.

Yes, now you shall hear about it. First I must tell you of the weather. It was just exactly what it should be on St. John's Day. The sky looked high and deep, with tiniest white clouds sprinkled over the whole circle of the heavens, and the sunshine was glorious on the hills and mountains and on the blue, blue sea.

Since it was Sunday as well as St. John's Day, I was all dressed up. To be sure my dress was an old one of Mother's made over, but the insertion was spandy new and there was a lot of it. I'd love to draw a picture of that dress for you, if you wanted to have one made like it.

Perhaps I had best begin at the very beginning, which was really Karsten's stamp collection. He does nothing but collect stamps, and talk and jabber about stamps the whole day long. He swaps and bargains, and has a whole heap of "dubelkits," as he calls them. These duplicates he keeps in a tiny little box. He means to be very orderly, you see.

To tell the truth, Karsten is perfectly stupid about swapping. The other boys can fool him like everything. He does n't understand a bit how to do business, and so I always feel like taking charge of these stamp bargainings myself. If I see a boy I don't know very well, peeping around the corner or sneaking up the hill, I am right on hand, for boys that want to trade never come running; they act as if they were spying round and lying in wait for some one.

The instant Karsten sees them he comes out with his stamp album. He stands there and expounds and explains about his stamps, with such a trustful look on his round pink face, while the other boys watch their chance to fool him; and before he knows it, some of his best specimens are gone. That's why I have taken hold.

As soon as I see a suspicious-looking boy on the horizon—that is to say on the hill—I go out and stand at the corner in all my dignity and won't budge, and I always put in my word you may be sure. Karsten doesn't like it, but anyway, he had me to thank for a rare Chili stamp.

But it was that very same rare stamp that brought about all my trouble on St. John's Day, because Nils Peter cheated that stupid donkey of a Karsten out of it the next time he saw him. And that was on St. John's Day, the very day after I had got it for him.

"I believe you would give them your nose, if they asked for it," I said to Karsten. "You'd stand perfectly still and let them cut your nose nicely off, if they wished."

"You think you are smart, don't you?" said Karsten fiercely.

As Olaug came out just then (she is my little sister, you remember), I shouted to her:

"Run as fast as you can to Nils Peter and tell him Inger Johanne says for him to give up that Chili stamp instantly. I'll hold Karsten while you run."

He would have run after Olaug to catch her before she should have time to ask Nils Peter for the stamp, for he thought that would be too embarrassing.

Just as I got a good grip on Karsten, Olaug started. Oh, how she ran!—just like a race horse, with her head high. Her hat fell off and hung by its elastic round her neck. She ran down the hill and up over Kranheia at top speed.

But you may believe I had a job of it standing there and holding fast to Karsten. He pushed and he struck and he scolded. My! how he did behave!

But I held on and watched Olaug to see how far she had got. I was high on the hill, you know, and could see a long way.

"O dear! Olaug will burst a blood vessel running like that," I thought. My! now she is there—now away off there. Karsten squirmed and struggled; now Olaug is on the path up Kranheia—she's slowing down a little.

Impossible for me to hold Karsten any longer. I had to let go. He was off like an arrow, his hair standing up straight and his feet pounding the ground like a young elephant's.

O pshaw! Running like that he would soon catch Olaug. It was frightfully exciting, like a horse race or a hunt after wild animals.

Well, that isn't a very good comparison, for nothing could be less like a wild animal than Olaug; but it was awfully exciting to see if she would keep ahead and get the Chili stamp from Nils Peter.

So that I might see better how the race ended I sprang up to our chicken-yard, or rather beyond it, on our own hill. You could see the whole path up over Kranheia better from there than from any other place. But just where I must be to see best was that awfully high board fence, too high for me to see over, that went from the chicken-yard quite a long way beyond on the hill.

Pooh! What of it? I just wiggled a board that was already loose, pulled it away and stuck my head in the opening. It was a little narrow but I got my head through. Oh—oh! Karsten had caught up to Olaug and run past her like an ostrich at full speed—I've always heard that an ostrich runs faster than anything else in the world—yes, there he was swinging in towards Nils Peter's house.

O pshaw! Now that Chili stamp was lost for ever and ever.

Olaug had pumped herself right down; she had to sit still and get her breath, poor thing!

Now that there was nothing more for me to watch, I started to draw my head back out of the narrow opening between the thick boards. But, O horrors! It stuck fast! I couldn't possibly get it back. I turned and twisted my head this way and that, and up and down; I tried to pull and squeeze it back, but no, that was utterly impossible. How in the world I had ever got my head through the opening in the first place I can't understand to this day, but that I had got it through was only too sure.

New struggles to get loose—I thought I should tear my ears off—Goodness gracious, what should I do!

At first I wasn't a speck afraid. I just wriggled and pulled as hard as I could. But when I realized that I simply could not free myself, a sort of terror came over me.

Just think—if I never got my head out? Or suppose there came a cross dog and bit me while my head was as if nailed fast in the fence! And suppose nobody found me—(for of course nobody would know that I had run up here beyond the chicken-yard)—and perhaps I should have to stay caught in the fence the whole night, when it was dark.

I cried and sobbed, then I called; at last I screamed and roared. I heard the hens in the yard flap their wings and run about wildly, evidently frightened by the noise I made.

Down on the road, people stood still and gazed upward; then of course I shrieked the louder. But no one looked up to the chicken-yard; and even if they had, they couldn't very well see, from so far down, a round brown head sticking through a brown fence. I roared incessantly, and at last I saw a woman start to run up the hill—and then a man started—but they did not see me and soon disappeared among the trees, although I kept on bawling, "Help! I am right here! I am caught in the fence!"

Just then I saw Karsten and Nils Peter come out of Nils Peter's house. They stood a moment as if listening, and naturally they recognized my voice.

Then they started running. If Karsten had raced over there, he certainly raced back again, too.

I kept bawling the whole time: "Here! here! in the fence! I am stuck fast in the fence!" It wasn't many minutes before both Karsten and Nils Peter stood behind me.

"Have you gone altogether crazy?" said Karsten in the greatest astonishment.

I felt a little offended, but there's no use in being offended when you haven't command over your own head, so I said very meekly:

"Ugh! such a nuisance! My head is stuck fast in here. Can't you help me?"

Would you believe it? They didn't laugh a bit—awfully kind, I call that—they just hauled and pulled me as hard as they could; it fairly scraped the skin off behind my ears and I thought I should be scalped if they kept on.

"No, it's no use," I said, crying again. "Run after Father, run after Mother, get everybody to come—uh, hu, hu!"

Well, they came. I couldn't see them, but I could hear the whole lot of them behind me.

Now there *was* a scene! The same story began again; they pulled and twisted my head, Father gave directions, I cried and Olaug cried and everybody talked at once.

"No," said Father at last, "it can't be done. Hurry down to Carpenter Wenzel and ask him to come and to bring his saw with him."

"Uh, huh! He'll saw my head off!" I wailed.

But Mother patted me on the back and comforted me, and all the others standing behind kept saying it would be all right soon, while I stood there like a mouse in a trap and cried and cried.

But it was Sunday and the carpenter was not at home.

"Run after my little kitchen saw then," said Mother. "Bring the meat-ax, too," called Father.

They just hauled and pulled me as hard as they could.

Oh, how would they manage? It seemed to me my head would surely be sawed or chopped to pieces.

Well, now began a sawing and hammering around me. When Mother sawed I was not afraid, but when Father began I was in terror, for Father, who is so awfully clever with his head, is so unpractical with his hands that he can't even drive a nail straight. So you can imagine how clumsy he would be about getting a head out of a board fence.

The others all had to laugh finally, but I truly had no desire to laugh until my head was well out. In fact, I didn't feel much like laughing then either, for really it had been horrid.

Ever since that time Karsten and Nils Peter have teased me about that Chili stamp. They say that getting my head stuck fast was a punishment for putting my oar in everywhere. Think of it—as if I *did* try to manage other people's affairs so very much!

But it certainly is horrid when you can't control your own head. You just try it and see.

CHRISTMAS MUMMING

It was Christmas Eve when we went mumming, and oh! how glorious the moonlight was! Down in our streets and up over our hills the moon shines clearer than it does anywhere else on the face of the globe, I'll wager.

Massa, Mina and I had dressed ourselves up in fancy costumes. "If any one asks where you are from," said Mother, when we were ready to start, "you can safely say, 'From the Land of Fantasy.' You certainly look as if you came from there."

Massa had on a light blue dress trimmed with gold-colored cord. It was one of Mother's heirlooms from Great-grandmother Krag, and had a tiny short waist and big puffed sleeves. Massa wore also a green velvet hat, and her thick long flaxen hair hung loose down her back.

Mina was dressed in silk from top to toe; an old-time dress of flowered brown silk with a train, a green silk shawl and a big white silk bonnet that came away out beyond her face.

When the others were ready, there was nothing fine left for me, so I had to take a white petticoat, and a dressing sacque, and a big old-fashioned Leghorn hat that Mother had worn when she was young. To decorate myself a little, I carried a beautifully carved *tine* in one hand and a red parasol in the other. We all wore masks, of course—big pasteboard masks, which came away down over our chins, with enormous noses and highly colored red cheeks.

Well, off we went and soon stood at the foot of our hill in a most daring mood, ready for all sorts of pranks.

I don't know who proposed that we should go first to Mrs. Berg's, but we all chimed in at once. We crept softly up to her door-step.

Unluckily for us, as it happened, Mrs. Berg has a great iron weight on her street door—so that it will shut of itself, you know. What the matter was, I can't imagine, but as soon as we had given one knock at the door, down fell that iron weight to the floor with a thundering crash. We were so frightened that we were on the point of running away when Mrs. Berg and her husband came bustling out to the door with a lighted lamp.

"No, thanks," said Mrs. Berg, as soon as she caught sight of us. "I don't want anything to do with such jugglery as this! Out with you, and that quickly!"

"Oh, no, little Marie," said her husband. "You ought to ask the little young ladies in. They are not street children, don't you see?" Mina's magnificent clothes evidently made an impression on him.

Mrs. Berg mumbled something about its being all the same to

her what sort of people we were, but Mr. Berg had already opened the door and respectfully asked us to walk in.

It was as hot as a bake-oven in the sitting room, and so stuffy and thick with tobacco smoke that I thought I should smother behind my mask. Mr. Berg bowed and bowed and set out three chairs for us in the middle of the room. Now we had planned at home that we would use only P-speech while mumming, for then no one would know us.

"May I ask where these three elegant ladies come from?" asked Mr. Berg.

Massa undertook to answer, but she was never very clever at P-speech and she got all mixed up:

"From-prom. Fan-tan-*pan*—pi-ta—sa-si p-p-p——" she stammered, in a hopeless tangle, while Mina and I were ready to burst with laughter.

"Bless us! These must be foreigners from some very distant land—they speak such a curious language. You must treat them with something, Marie."

Marie didn't appear very willing to treat us to anything, but she went over to a corner cupboard and brought out a few cookies—pale, baked-to-death "poor man's cookies." They looked poor, indeed! I shuddered before I stuck a piece into my mouth.

To eat with a mask on, when the mouth is no wider than the slit in a savings-bank, has its difficulties, I can tell you. The little I did get in tasted of camphor. Mrs. Berg must have kept her medicines in the same closet with the cakes.

"Perhaps the little ladies would like something more," said Mr. Berg.

"No, thanks—No-po, thanks-panks." And we all three rose to go. We curtsied and curtsied. Mr. Berg bowed and bowed. Mrs.

Berg turned the key in the street door after us with a snap, and I heard her say something about "that long-legged young one of the judge's!"

Oh! how we laughed! "Now we will go to Mrs. Pirk's," said I.

"Inger Johanne! Are you crazy? She is worse than Mrs. Berg!"

"That makes it all the more wildly exciting! Come on!"

We crept stealthily into Mrs. Pirk's kitchen. It was pitch dark in there except for a little light through the keyhole of the sitting room. "Hush! Keep still!"

Mrs. Pirk coughed suddenly and we all quaked.

"Now she will surely come!" Silence again. We were half-choked with laughter.

"I am going to clear my throat," said I. "Ahem!"

"Ahem!" I gave a very loud, strong one the second time.

A chair was hastily shoved aside in the sitting room, the door opened, a sharp light fell on our three fantastic figures, and Mrs. Pirk stood in the doorway with her spectacles on her nose. I stepped forward. "Good-pood day-pay!"

Mrs. Pirk went like a flash to the fireplace and grabbed a broomstick. "Get out!" she cried. "Out with you!"

So out of the door we ran, stumbling and tumbling over each other, Mrs. Pirk after us with her uplifted broom, out into the moonlit street. Oh! it was unspeakable fun to be chased out-of-doors that way by Mrs. Pirk!

Well—then we went on to the Macks'.

They were sitting alone in their big light sitting room, as we went in. Mrs. Mack was playing "patience" and Mr. Mack sat by her side smoking his long pipe and pointing out with the end of it which card he thought she ought to take next.

We pressed close together around the door and curtsied.

"Why, see! Welcome to youth and joy!" said Mrs. Mack, rising. "What nice young people these are to come to visit a pair of old folks like us!"

Mr. Mack came forward and pointed with the end of his pipe over our heads, saying:

"Up on the sofa with you! Up on the sofa with you, all three!"

So there we sat, as if we were distinguished guests, with the lamp shining full upon us.

"I see you have a *tine* with you," said Mr. Mack, looking at the *tine* I carried. "Have you something to sell, perhaps? And where may these pretty little ladies be from?"

"I-pi sell-pell butter-putter," said I.

"We are from the Land of Fantasy," said Massa, without attempting P-speech again.

"Why! They don't make butter in the Land of Fantasy, do they?" asked Mrs. Mack.

Just then the servant came in with an immense tray, and on it was something very different from Mrs. Berg's camphorated cookies, I assure you! I thought with grief of my mask mouth no bigger than a savings-bank slit.

"And now what about unmasking?" said Mr. Mack. "That is, if these ladies from the Land of Fantasy are willing to liven up an evening for a couple of old people."

Were *willing!* We took our masks off in a jiffy. But, would you believe it? Mr. Mack said he knew me the very minute we came in!

Mrs. Mack took a glass of Christmas mead and recited:

"Oh! I remember the happy ways
Of my gay and innocent childhood days.
And I love to feel that my old heart swells,
With the same pure joy that in childhood dwells."

"Mamma composed that herself," said Mr. Mack, gazing admiringly at his wife.

Later in the evening, Mrs. Mack danced the minuet for us, holding up her skirt and singing in a delicate old-lady voice. Then she said:

"Do you remember, Mack? Do you remember that they were playing that air the evening you asked me to marry you?"

"Do I *remember?*" And Mr. Mack and his wife beamed tenderly at each other.

"Think! That such a homely woman as I should get married!" said Mrs. Mack to us on the sofa.

"You homely!" and Mr. Mack gave the dear old lady a kiss right on the mouth.

"Now we shall see, children, whether, when you get old, you have done like Mack and me. We have danced a minuet our whole life through, and the memories of youth have been our music."

When we went home at the end of the evening, we had our pockets crammed full of apples and nuts and cakes.

It is jolly fun to go out mumming at Christmas! Just try it!

MOTHER BRITA'S GRANDCHILD

It was an afternoon in the spring. There had been a heavy fall of snow the day before and then suddenly a thaw set in. So very warm was the air and the sun so burning hot that the water from the roof gutters came rushing and tumbling out in regular waterfalls; and big snowslides from the housetops thumped down everywhere, making a rumbling noise all along the streets.

The walking I won't try to describe. There were no paths made, just the frightfully soft melting snow, so deep that it came exactly half-way to your knees. So there was n't much pleasure in walking, I assure you; and we had n't a thing to do.

The steamships from both east and west were delayed by the snow-storm, so there was no fun in going to the wharf and hanging around there. Usually it is amusing enough—always something new to see and something happening; and now and then we have fun seeing the queer seasick people on board the ships. Just outside of our town there is a horribly rough place in the sea where cross currents meet, and the passengers look forlorn enough when the ship gets to the wharf.

But all this isn't really what I meant to tell about now: I started to tell about the afternoon when we played a lot of pranks simply because there was n't a thing else to do. Truly, that was the reason. Now you shall hear.

Karen, Mina, Munda, and I were together that afternoon. Not a person was to be seen on the street and it was disgustingly quiet and dull everywhere. The only pleasant thing was that there came a tremendously big, heavy snowslide right down on the little shoemaker. Jorgen.

Well, I don't mean that that was a pleasure exactly, you understand, but it made a little variety.

Just as he came around the corner, by Madam Lindeland's, b-r-r-r! there was a rumbling above, and down upon him slid a whole mass of snow from Madam Lindeland's steep sloping roof. He was knocked completely over, and all we could see of him was a bit of his old brown blouse sticking up through the snow.

In a flash, Mina, Munda, Karen, and I were on the spot, digging him out with our hands. Before you could count ten, he was up, but you had better believe he was angry! Not at us exactly, but at the snow, and the thaw, and the town itself that was so badly arranged that people walking in the streets might be killed before they knew it.

"Preposterous, the whole business," grumbled the shoemaker. "Who would dream that there would be such a thaw right on

There came a tremendously big, heavy snowslide right down on the little shoemaker.

top of such an unreasonable snowstorm—and in March, too!"

Then he noticed that he had lost his cap, so we dug in the snow again, searching for it, and had lots of fun before we finally found it.

All this excitement over the snowslide made us crazy for more fun, and we decided that we would go to Madam Graaberg and ask her if she had white velvet to sell. Madam Graaberg has a little shop in a basement and sells almost nothing but *lu-de-fisk* (fish soaked in lye, with a rank odor).

First we peeped in the window between the glasses of groats. Yes, there were many people in the shop and Madam Graaberg stood behind the counter as usual. She is as big as three ordinary women and her eyes are as black as two bits of coal; and my! how they can flash!

We plumped ourselves down into the shop, all four of us. It smelled frightfully of *lu-de-fisk* and the whole floor was like a puddle from all the wet feet. A fine place to go to ask for white velvet! And Madam Graaberg has an awful temper, let me tell you!

There were many customers to be waited on before us, so we stood together in a bunch at the farthest end of the counter. The time dragged on and on before they had all got their *lu-de-fisk,* for that was what they wanted, the whole swarm of them.

On the counter beside me, there was a big new ball of string in an iron frame, the kind that whirls around when you pull the string. The end of the string dangled so invitingly close to me, and waiting for Madam Graaberg to be ready to attend to us was so tedious, that I busied myself with taking the end of the string and slyly tying it fast to one of the buttons on the back of Munda's coat. Of course I meant to untie the string before we went out, but Madam Graaberg turned suddenly to us.

"What do you want, children?" asked she, portly and dignified, towering over the counter.

We were all a little bewildered because she had come to us so abruptly, but we pushed Munda forward. My, how uncomfortable she looked!

"Have you any white velvet for sale?" asked Munda feebly.

I gave a spring toward the door, for it seemed best to get away at once. Two maids stood there, who roared with laughter. "Ha ha! Ha ha! Madam Graaberg, that's pretty good. Ha ha!"

"White velvet," hissed Madam Graaberg. "White velvet! Make a fool of me in my own lawful business, will you? Out of my shop this instant!"

She didn't need to tell us twice. We dashed helter-skelter out of the door, all four of us, splashing the mud and slush recklessly.

Suddenly Munda cried out, "Oh, I'm fast to something! I'm fast to something behind!"

Just think! I had forgotten to untie the string from the button! I thought I heard a buzzing noise when we flew out of the door, but it never occurred to me that it could be the string-ball whirling around in its frame.

There was no time now to untie the knot, for Madam Graaberg was right out in the street and calling after us. They were not exactly gentle words she was using, either, you may well believe!

"Oh, but I'm fast—I'm fast!" shrieked Munda again.

"Tear off the button!" I shouted. Munda made some desperate efforts to get hold of her own back. No use; so I took hold of the string and gave a great jerk and off came the button. Munda was free and we dashed round the street corner.

"Uh, uh huh!" sobbed Munda. "Mother'll be so angry about that button!"

"Pooh!" said I. "Just sew the hole up, and you can always find a button to put over it. But oh, girls! How jolly angry Madam Graaberg was!"

"Yes, and was n't she funny when she said, 'Out of my shop this instant'?"

We were tremendously pleased with our joke. We talked and laughed—enjoying ourselves immensely; but we had n't had enough tomfoolery yet.

"Girls," I said, "now let's go to Nibb's shop and ask whether he has white velvet."

All were willing. To think of asking that queer Mr. Nibb for white velvet, when he kept only shoe-strings and paraffin for sale! My! but that would be fun! Mr. Nibb always has the window shades tight down over his shop windows, so that not the least thing can be seen from the street. He isn't exactly right in his mind—and do you know what he did once?

It was in church and I sat just in front of him and had on my flat fur cap. He is a great one to sing in church and he stands bolt upright and sings at the top of his voice. And just think! He laid his hymn-book on top of my cap just as if it were a reading desk, and I didn't dare to move my head because he might get in a rage if I did. So he sang and sang and sang, and I sat and sat there with the hymn-book on the top of my head.

Well—that was that time—but now we stood there in the street considering as to whether we should go in and ask him if he had white velvet.

"No, we surely don't dare to," said Karen.

"Oh, yes, we do," said I. "He can't kill us."

"Who knows?" said Karen. "He isn't just like other people."

"Pooh! When there are four of us together—" No, they did n't want to—so I suddenly threw the shop door wide open and then we had to go in. Mr. Nibb came toward us bowing and bowing. We pushed Munda forward again.

"Have you any white—" began Munda in a shaking voice. And then our courage suddenly gave way and Karen, Mina, and I sprang to the door as quick as lightning, slamming the door after us, and not stopping until we were at the farther corner of the street. And then we saw that Munda was n't with us! Why in the world had n't she come out? What was happening to her? We rushed back and listened outside the shop door. Not a sound was to be heard. Karen and Mina were both as white as chalk.

"It's all your fault," they whispered to me. "Who knows what danger Munda is in?"

At that I was so frightened that I did n't know what I was doing, and I threw the door open at once.

There sat Munda on a chair in the middle of the shop, holding a big apple, and Mr. Nibb stood with his legs crossed, leaning against the counter in a jaunty attitude and talking to her.

"Are there many dances in the town nowadays—young ladies?" asked Mr. Nibb, turning to us, as we, pale as death, entered the shop.

No answer.

"Or engagements among the young people perhaps," he continued —polite to the last degree.

"People live so quietly in this town—one might call himself buried alive here, so that a visit from four promising young beauties is—ahem—an adventure!"

Dear me! how comical he was! None of us said a word. Suddenly Munda got up.

"A thousand thanks," she said and curtsied—the apple in her hand.

"Thank you," we echoed, all curtseying; though really I have n't the least idea what we were thanking him for!

"Ah—bah!" said Mr. Nibb waving his hand. "It is I who must thank you. I am much indebted to the young ladies for this delightful call."

With this he opened the door, and came away out on the steps and bowed.

Oh, how we laughed when he had gone in and the door was shut again. We laughed so we could scarcely stand.

"What did he do when you were alone, Munda?"

"He sprang after a chair," said Munda. "And then he sprang after an apple—and then he stood himself there by the counter just as you saw him and began to talk—oh! how frightened I was!"

"What did he say?"

"Ha ha! he—ha ha!—he asked me if I were engaged!"

"Ha ha ha! that was splendid."

"And just then you all came in."

"Ha ha! Ha ha ha!"

By this time it was so late that we must start for home and we took the quickest way, over High Street. It was almost dark and there was scarcely a person in sight, as we ran up the street through the March slush and mud.

"Oh, let's knock on Mother Brita's windows!" said I, and we knocked gayly on the little panes as we ran past the house.

At that moment Mother Brita called from her doorway.

"Halloa!" she called. "Come here a minute. God be praised that any one should come! Let me speak to you."

We went slowly back. Perhaps she was angry with us for knocking on her windows.

"Here I am as if I were in prison," said Mother Brita. "My little grandchild is sick with bronchitis and I can't leave him a single minute; and my son John, you know him, is out there at Stony Point with his ship, and is going to sail away this very evening, and he sails to China to be gone two years—and I want so much to say good-bye to him—two whole years—to China—but I can't leave that poor sick baby in there, for he chokes if some one does n't lift him up when the coughing spells come on—oh, there he's coughing again!"

Mother Brita hurried in, and all four of us after her. A tiny baby lay there in a cradle, and Mother Brita lifted him and held him up while the coughing spell lasted. He coughed so hard that he got quite blue in the face.

"O dear! You see how it is! Now he'll go away—my son John—this very evening, and I may never see him again in this world, uh-huh-huh!"

Poor Mother Brita! It seemed a sin and a shame that she should not at least see her son to bid him good-bye.

"I'll sit here with the baby until you come back, Mother Brita," said I.

"Yes, I will, too."

"So will I, and I." All four of us wanted to stay.

"Oh, oh! What kind little girls!" said Mother Brita. "I will fly like the wind. Just raise him up when the spells come on. I won't be long on the way either going or coming. Well, good-bye, and I'm much obliged to you." With that Mother Brita was out of the house, having barely taken time to throw a handkerchief over her head.

There we sat. It was a strange ending to an afternoon of fun and mischief. The room was very stuffy; a small candle stood on the table and burned with a long, smoky flame, and back in a corner an old clock ticked very slowly, tick—tock!—tick—tock!

We talked only in whispers. Very soon the baby had another coughing fit. We raised him up and he choked and strangled as before, and after the coughing, cried as if in pain, without opening his eyes. Poor little thing! Poor baby!

Again we sat still for a while without speaking; then—"I'm so frightened—everything is so dismal," whispered Karen.

Deep silence broken only by the clock's ticking and the baby's breathing.

"I think I must go," she added after a minute.

"That is mean of you," whispered I.

"I must go, too," whispered Munda. "They are always so anxious at home when I don't come."

"I must go, too," whispered Mina.

Then I got a little angry. "Oh, well, all right, go, every one of you! All right, go on, if you want to be so mean."

And only think, they did go! They ran out of the door, all three, without a word more. Just then the baby had another attack and I had to hold him up quite a long time before he could get his breath again.

And now I was all alone in Mother Brita's little house. Never in my life had I been in there before, and it was anything but pleasant, you may well believe. It was very dark in all the corners, and the poor baby coughed and coughed; the candle burned lower and lower and the clock ticked on slowly and solemnly. No sign of Mother Brita.

Well, I would sit here. I would n't stir from here even if Mother Brita did n't come back before it was pitch-dark night—no, indeed, I would not. I would not. Not for anything would I leave this pitiful little suffering baby alone.

He was certainly very sick, very, very sick; perhaps God would come to take him tonight. Just think, if He should come while I sat there!—

At first this made me feel afraid, but then I thought that I need not be afraid of God—of Him who is kinder than anyone in the world! The baby coughed painfully and I lifted him up again.

Everything was so queer, so wonderfully queer! First had we four been racing about, playing pranks and thinking only of fun all the afternoon—perhaps it was wrong to play such mischievous pranks—and now here was I alone taking care of a little baby I had never known anything about—a little baby that God or His angels might soon come for and take away. I had not the least bit of fear now. I only felt as if I were in church—it was so solemn and so still. In a little while, this poor baby might be in Heaven—in that beautiful place flooded with glorious light—with God. And I, just a little girl down here on earth, was I to be allowed to sit beside the baby until the angels came for him?

I looked around the bare, gloomy room. It might be that the angels who were to take away Mother Brita's grandchild were already here. Oh, how good it would be for the poor little baby who coughed so dreadfully!

The clock had struck for half-past seven, for eight o'clock, and half-past eight, and there was just a small bit left of the candle. The sick baby had quieted down at last, and now lay very still.

There came a rattling at the door; some one fumbled at the latch and I stared through the gloom with straining eyes, making up my mind not to be afraid. The door opened slowly a little way, and Ingeborg, our cook, put her round face into the opening.

"Well, have I found you at last? And is it here you are? I was to tell you to betake yourself home. Your mother and father have been worrying themselves to pieces about you, and—"

"Hush, Ingeborg! Be still. He is so sick, so very sick."

Ingeborg came over to the cradle and bent down. Then she hurriedly brought the bit of candle to the cradle.

"Oh, he is dead," she said slowly. "Poor little thing! He is dead—poor little chap!"

"Oh, no, Ingeborg, no!" I sobbed. "Is he dead? For I lifted him up every single time he coughed. Oh, it is beautiful that he is dead, he suffered so, and yet—oh, it seems sad, too!"

"I will stay here with him now until Mother Brita comes home," said Ingeborg. "For you—"

"How did you know I was here?"

"Why, Karen and Munda came into the kitchen just a few minutes ago, and told me."

She said again that she would stay in my place, but I could n't bear to go before Mother Brita came back.

Shortly after, Mother Brita hurried in, warm and out of breath. "Oh, oh! how long you have had to wait," she said in distress. "I could n't find John at Stony Point, I had to go away into town. I suppose you are angry that I stayed so long."

"The baby had to give up the fight, Mother Brita," said Ingeborg.

"Give up? What? What do you say?"

"I lifted him up, Mother Brita, every time he coughed, I did truly," said I, and then I burst out crying again. I could n't help it.

"Yes, I am sure you did, my jewel," said Mother Brita, "and God be praised that He has taken the baby out of this poor little body. Never can pain or sin touch him now."

Mother and Father said that I had done just right to stay, and when Mother kissed me good night she said she was sure that the dear God himself had been with me and the poor little baby. And that seemed so wonderful and beautiful and solemn that I could never tell anyone, even Mother, how beautiful it was.

Up in the churchyard there is a tiny grave, the grave of Mother Brita's grandchild. I know very well just were it is and I often put flowers upon it in the summer. What I like best to put there are rosebuds, fresh, lovely, pink rosebuds.

TRAVELING WITH A BILLY-GOAT

The next summer we spent in the country; and when we were coming home, would you believe it? Karsten got a live billy-goat as a present from Mother Goodfields, and I got a live wild forest-cat from Jens Kverum's mother. Of course I wanted something alive since Karsten had the goat, so I begged and teased Agnete Kverum until she finally said I might have the yellow-brown cat I wanted. Not that I would not rather have had the goat, you may be sure, though naturally I would n't let Karsten know that. He was puffed up enough already.

Well, anyway, we took both the goat and the cat with us when we went home; but anything so difficult to travel with you can't possibly imagine. Now you shall hear the whole story from first to last; for if anybody else has a desire to take a real live goat or cat with them on the train or into the ladies' cabin of the steamboat, they had better know all the bother and row-de-dow it will make. I advise everyone against doing it. All the people who are traveling with you get angry, although it is scarcely to be expected that a billy-goat or a wild cat will behave nicely in a ladies' cabin. At any rate, ours did n't. Listen now.

Mother Goodfields had any number of goats. They were all up at the saeter except two, and these roamed in the forest with the cows, because each of them had an injured leg. But one day one goat was missing and nobody in the world could find it.

Old Kari mourned for it constantly and talked of nothing else. Every day she pictured to herself a new horrible way it had met its death. Either it had got caught in a mountain crevice and starved to death, or a wolf had taken it, or Beata Oppistuen had butchered it without any right to. "That Beata. You could expect any kind of doings from her." Old Kari went to and fro in the forest seeking the goat till far into the night.

But one fine day there on the forest side of the farm fence stood the lost goat with a tiny little baby-goat at her side. And that kid was the prettiest and cunningest you ever set eyes on. It had a soft silky little beard, and it stood on its hind legs and hopped and skipped as if it would jump over into the field.

The cows came and sniffed at it; the other goat, that had stayed at home with them, examined it very particularly; and the little kid danced, zigzag and every which way; and so it was introduced to society, you might say.

How we children ran after that little billy-goat! But Karsten was the worst, for he went to the forest every single day to tend it and brought it home every single night.

"I rather think I shall have to give you that kid," said Mother Goodfields to Karsten one night as he came along carrying it.

From that time Karsten was a changed boy altogether, for he didn't give a thought to the big lake that he had cared so much about all summer. In his brain there was absolutely nothing but that billy-goat. It ate bread and butter and drank out of a teacup; and one night when Mother went up to bed she caught a glimpse of Billy-goat's beard above the blanket beside Karsten's head. Just imagine! Karsten was going to let the kid sleep with him. But Mother put a stop to that and Karsten had to hurry downstairs and out to the barn with the goat.

Karsten never allowed me to touch Billy-goat and so I wanted to have a pet animal of my own. I considered seriously for a day or two as to whether I should not ask Mother Goodfields for a brown calf that was kept out in the pasture; but one fine morning it was slaughtered, so there was an end to that plan. Then I brought my desire down to Agnete Kverum's cat. It was golden-brown and had long hair and was exactly like a big cosy muff; and in the muff were two great yellow eyes. Whenever I went up to the Kverum place it sat curled together on the door-sill and purred and was perfectly charming. I did n't give Agnete a minute's rest or peace, and so, as you know, I got the cat.

Strangely enough, Mother was not in the least overjoyed when I came back carrying the forest-cat.

"I don't like these presents," said Mother. "There will only be tears and heartbreak when you have to leave them."

"Leave them!" exclaimed Karsten and I in one breath. "Oh, but you know they must go back home with us!"

"The goat is so smart about going up and down stairs," said Karsten. "And it likes to drink out of a teacup and it can perfectly well stay in the hotel garden over night in the city."

"Are you crazy, you two?" said Mother. "It would never do in the world."

But we teased and begged so, that Mother finally said yes—we might take them. For the potato-cellar was full of rats, she said, that the cat might take care of; and you could always get rid of a goat in our town. And I promised that I would hold on to the cat through the whole journey, and Karsten would hold on to the kid, and Mother need n't think they would be any worry or nuisance to her at all. No indeed—far from it.

Well, off we went. When Mother talks of our journey home from the country that time, she both laughs and cries. First we had to drive nearly twenty-five miles. Mother and Karl and Olaug, and the kid and Karsten, and the forest-cat and I, and the hold-all and lunch-basket and bundle of shawls—all were in one carriage. Nobody kept quiet an instant, for Karlie boy wanted to know who lived in every single house along the road, and Olaug whimpered and wanted to eat all the time, and the forest-cat could not by hook or crook be made to stay in any basket, but would sit on the driver's seat and look around; so you see, I had to stand and hold it so it should not fall out of the carriage. And the goat kicked into the air with all its four legs and would not lie in Karsten's lap a minute. You had better believe there was a rumpus!

Mother said afterwards that she just sat and wished that both the cat and the goat would fall out of the carriage; she would then whip up the horse and drive away from them, she was so sick of the whole business.

At last we came to the first place where we were to stay over night. Karsten and I took our pets with us to our rooms. They should not be put into a strange barn and be frightened, poor things! But oh, how those rooms looked in the morning! I can't possibly describe it.

Mother was desperate.

"Do let us get away from this place," she said. "There's no knowing how much I shall have to pay; it will be a costly reckoning, I'll warrant you."

It was.

Well, we all hurried, and flew down to the little steamer. It was cram-jam full of passengers—ladies who sat with their opera-glasses and were very elegant and looked sideways at you; and sunburnt gentlemen with tiny little traveling caps. They all looked hard at Karsten and me with our animals in our arms.

The billy-goat bleated and was determined to get down on to the deck, and the cat miaowed and the ladies drew their skirts close and looked indignant.

"Go into the cabin!" said Mother.

Karsten and I scrambled down below with the goat and the cat.

There wasn't a living soul there, nothing but bad air and red velvet sofas. We let go of both the goat and the cat. It would be good for them to stir their legs a little, poor creatures!

Pit-pat! pit-pat! Away went the goat to a sofa, and snatched a big bite out of a bouquet of stock that lay there. One long lavender spray hung dangling from Billy-goat's mouth.

"Oh, are you crazy? Catch your goat! Catch your goat!"

But the flowers were gone and the goat was dancing sideways over the cabin floor.

From the sideboard sounded a thud and a horrible rattle-te-bang of glass and silver. The cat had sprung right up into a big bowl of cream and all the cream was running down on the sofa.

It is a horrible sight to see two quarts of cream flowing over a red velvet sofa! Oh, how frightened I was!

"Hold the door shut, Karsten!" I said. "I'll try to dry it up."

With shaking hands I tried to mop up the cream with my pocket-handkerchief, while the cat and the kid lapped and drank the cream that trickled down to the floor; and Karsten held the door shut with all his might.

But it was like an ocean of cream. It was impossible—impossible for me to dry it up.

"Oh, Karsten! what shall we do?"

"It was your cat that did it."

"Yes, but your goat ate the stock."

"Let's run away," said Karsten; and carrying the goat and the cat we rushed up the narrow cabin stairs. But, O horrors! There wasn't any sort of a place where we could hide. And how it did look down in the cabin! And Mother didn't know the least thing about it. Oh, dear! Oh, dear! "If they only don't throw Billy-goat and the cat overboard!" said Karsten thoughtfully.

"Are you up here again?" called Mother.

"Ye-es."

We ran away out forward, away to the bow of the boat. Usually I think there is nothing so jolly as to sit far, far out in the bow, seeing nothing of the boat back of me, just as if I were gliding forward high up in the air. But today it wasn't the least bit jolly, for all that cream down on the sofa was frightful to think of. Karsten and I couldn't talk of anything else. He was angry, however, because I hadn't mopped it up.

"Well, but I couldn't wipe it up with nothing."

"Oh, you could have taken your waterproof or something out of our trunk."

I was really struck by that thought. Perhaps—perhaps I could get hold of something to wipe up all that disgusting cream with. We both got up from the box where we had been sitting. O horrors! There stood the dining room stewardess facing us. No sight could have been more terrible to me.

"Oh, here you are, are you? Of course it was you who have got things in such a condition in the dining saloon."

I looked at Karsten and Karsten looked at me.

"Yes, the cat upset the bowl," I said faintly.

"Well, it's a pretty business," said the stewardess. "And we are in a fine fix and no mistake. Dinner spoiled, no more cream for the multerberries, and they're nothing without it, the whole cabin running over with cream, the sofa absolutely ruined, glasses broken—oh, you'll have a handsome sum to pay! Well, you've got to go to the Captain," and she swaggered across the deck.

But now Mother had heard about it, and she came toward us with a face I can't describe—and the Captain came; and there Karsten and I stood holding the goat and the cat in our arms.

Oh, it was an awful interview! The Captain wasn't gentle, not he, and Mother had to pay heaps of money.

"There is no sense in traveling with such a menagerie," said the Captain.

The passengers who had nothing but dry multerberries for dessert were certainly angry with us, and Mother was most unhappy. But the cat lay in my lap and blinked with its yellow eyes and purred like far-away thunder—it was so happy; and Billy-goat rubbed its head with that silky beard against Karsten's jacket and looked up at him with its trustful black eyes; so neither Karsten nor I had the heart to scold. And it wouldn't have done any good, anyway.

At the train, trouble began again, for just imagine! No one knew what the freight charges should be for a kid. The ticket-agent stuck his head out of his window to stare at the innocent little creature, and the station-master pulled at his mustache and stared too; and they turned over page after page in their books and whispered together. At last they made out that the cost would be the same as for a cow. Mother shook her head but paid. (I was glad I had my cat in a basket where no one noticed it, and it slept like a log.)

Since the kid was so very tiny, Karsten was allowed to take it into the compartment with us, for it was absolutely impossible to let that baby go alone into the cattle-car.

"Thank goodness!" said Mother when she finally got us all settled. "Now there are only five hours more of this part of the journey."

Two ladies were in the compartment—one very severe-looking who had a lorgnette, the other fat and jolly, with awfully pretty red cherries on her hat. Little Billy-goat stood on the seat and ate crackers, making a great crunching. The fat lady laughed at it till she shook all over, but the severe lady drew the corners of her mouth down, looking crosser than ever.

Karsten was so glad to have some one admire the kid that he made it do all the tricks it could. However, that was soon over, for it could not do anything except stand on two legs.

Just as it stood there on two legs, with the most innocent face you can imagine, it gave a little leap—oh, oh! up toward the hat of the fat lady; and that very instant the beautiful red cherries crackled in Billy-goat's mouth.

"Oh, my new hat!" screamed the fat lady.

"It is outrageous that one should be liable to such treatment," said the cross lady.

"That's the time you got fooled, Billygoat," said Karl, "for you got glass cherries instead of real cherries."

Mother had lost all patience now and no mistake; and the kid had to go under the seat and lie there the whole time. And Mother offered the fat lady some chocolates and some of Mother Goodfields' home-made cakes that we had brought for luncheon, and begged her pardon again and again for Billy-goat's behavior; so that finally the fat lady was a little appeased. The goat had eaten four of the glass cherries, and there were eight still left on the hat, so it was n't wholly spoiled.

"Well, all I know is I would never have stood it," said the lady with the lorgnette.

The forest-cat behaved beautifully, sleeping the whole time on the train; and we all grew tired, oh! so tired. I could n't look out of the window at last, I was so utterly tired out. And I did not bother myself about either the cat or the billy-goat.

Finally we rumbled into the city and to the station platform.

But Mother was altogether right in saying that it would never do in the world to have a billy-goat in the city. When we got to the hotel where we were to spend that night, there stood the host at the door.

He is a very cross man. When he saw Billy-goat in Karsten's arms he was furious at once. He had not fitted up his rooms for animals, he said, and the goat would please be so good as to keep itself entirely

The beautiful red cherries crackled in Billy-goat's mouth.

outside of them. So Billy-goat was put into the pitch-dark coal-cellar —and had to stay there the whole night.

When we went down the next morning it stood on two legs and danced sideways from pure joy. But when Karsten took it out into the court, pop! away went the goat over the low fence into the hotel-keeper's garden, then out by an unlatched gate into the wide, wide world.

"No," said Mother firmly, "you may not go to look for it, nor will I ask the police to find it. If I have n't suffered and paid enough for that creature—"

Poor little Billy-goat! It was a sin and a shame that we ever took you away from the forest at Goodfields!

IN SCHOOL

Oh, such fun as we had in school that time when Mr. Gorrisen was our teacher! It was a regular comedy. He was a tiny little man. Antoinette and I were taller than he, so you can judge for yourself. And I never in my life saw anyone with such round eyes as he had.

You should just have seen those eyes when we were having a little fun at our desks. With a hard, fixed stare, not letting his gaze wander for an instant, his eyes bored themselves right into the culprit.

Down from the platform he came, with slow, measured step across the floor—his eyes not moving for a second—came nearer and nearer and nearer; ugh! then his finger tips grabbed the very tip-end of your ear and there they held tight like a vise. No one can have the faintest idea how painful it was. And all without one word; not a syllable came over Mr. Gorrisen's lips. I wonder, I really do, that there is anything left of the tips of my ears since then, considering the many times Mr. Gorrisen took hold of them!

And he was mighty quick about giving us poor marks! If I did n't know every single thing in the lesson by heart, so that I could rattle it off, I got a "4" immediately.

It was at that time, however, that I hit upon the plan of cutting out the bad marks from my report book, for a "4" or "5" looks perfectly disgusting in a report. But an innocent little square hole—that's no harm, as it were.

"But, Inger Johanne," said Father, "what is that?"

"Oh, well, Father, there was a bad mark there," I answered. "And I didn't dare come home with such a mark, so I just cut it out."

The first time I did it, Father wasn't so very angry; but when I did it again and again, he was furious. So I had to give it up. Then when I really came to think about it, I saw it was wrong, so I would not do it any more, anyway.

Once we had Mr. Gorrisen on Examination Day. Mrs. White, with her light kid gloves on, sat in a chair on the platform and listened, holding Karen's dirty German reading book by the tip edge. She looked continually at the book but she didn't understand a word—I'll wager anything you like she didn't—for she never turned over the page when she should have. I saw that plainly. On a seat near the door sat Madam Tellefsen, who had come to listen to Mina; she did not put on any airs, though. She never once pretended to understand German, but laid the book down beside her on the seat and sat there sweltering in her French shawl and looking rather helpless.

Enough of that. I was just carving my name on my desk-lid—very deep and nice it was to be—when all at once I noticed that Mr. Gorrisen was looking at me. He stared as if he were staring right through me, stared steadily as he came across the room.

Oh, my unlucky ear-tip! His fingers held it as tight as a vise. Up I must get from my seat and across the floor was I led by the ear to the corner of the room. There he let go of me.

Well! Imagine that! A pretty sight I made standing in the corner on Examination Day! If only Mrs. White and Madam Tellefsen had not been sitting there! They would surely go and tattle about it all over town.

Truly I would not stand there any longer. Mr. Gorrisen was reading a piece aloud just then, so all at once I lay flat down on the floor and crept over to the desks. Once I had got under the desks, it was easy enough. Kima Pirk gave me a horrid kick in the back, and Karen whacked my head when I was directly under her desk, but that was only because I pinched them as I passed. I could hear them all whispering and whispering above me—it was great fun—and I crept farther and farther. I thought I would go to the last desk, you see. There, now I had reached it. I got up and settled myself in the seat, wearing a most innocent expression.

I looked at Mrs. White. Her face seemed to get sharper and narrower just from severity; but Madam Tellefsen laughed so that she had to hold the end of her French shawl over her face. I had got very warm and my hair was very dusty from that expedition under the desks, but I didn't mind that.

Fully five minutes passed before Mr. Gorrisen saw me. But all at once when I had begun to feel pretty safe, came:

"Why, Inger Johanne! Have you walked out of the corner without permission?"

"No, I have not walked, Mr. Gorrisen," said I.

"She crept," the others murmured faintly.

"She crept," said Kima aloud from her desk in the front row.

"What is this, Inger Johanne?" asked Mr. Gorrisen severely.

"It was so tedious to stand there, Mr. Gorrisen," I said.

"Yes, that was exactly why you were put there."

"And so I crept over here when you didn't see me."

Without another word, down across the floor he came. I turned my right ear toward him, for the left ear burned horribly even yet from the other time. But he evidently thought that an ear-pinch was too gentle a punishment for creeping through the whole classroom. I was taken by the arm and led along out of the door. Outside in the hall he shook me by the arm. Oh, well! it was just a little shake anyway—but then I had to hang around in that hall until the lesson was all over.

I can't understand now how I ever dared to creep that way in Mr. Gorrisen's class. O dear! I have been awfully foolish many times—unbelievably foolish!

Then there was that day Mr. Gorrisen fell off his chair. I was put out in the hall that day, too. But all the others ought to have been sent out as well, for we all laughed together. It was just because I couldn't stop laughing that I had to go. I surely have spasms in my cheeks, for long after all the others have stopped I keep on—I can't help it.

We were having our geography lesson. Mr. Gorrisen sat in an armchair by the table and stared at us, for he was not the kind of teacher that sharpens pencils or polishes his finger nails or does anything like that. He just sits and sways back and forth in his chair and stares incessantly. Well, never mind that. The lesson was on the peninsula of Korea. I remember distinctly.

"Now, Minka, Korea lies—" He swayed and swayed in his chair. "Korea lies—ahem! Ko-re-a lies—"

Minka glanced anxiously around to see whether any one would whisper to her—"Korea lies between—"

There came a frightful explosive bang; the chair had gone over backward, making a horrible noise, and Mr. Gorrisen's small legs were up in the air above the corner of the table.

Oh, what shrieks of laughter pealed out through the classroom! But quick as a flash Mr. Gorrisen was up again. He sat himself in the armchair as if nothing had happened, only his face was flaming red up to his hair. It was exactly as if there had been no interruption whatever, to say nothing of such a noisy comical topsy-turvy.

"Korea lies where, Minka?"

But that was more than I could bear. I burst out laughing again—he, he! ha, ha!—and all the others joined in. If he had only laughed himself, I don't believe it would have seemed so funny—but he was as solemn as an owl.

"Stop laughing instantly." He struck the table with his ruler so that the room rang. We quieted down at once except for a hiccough here and there, but the worst of it was that Mr. Gorrisen stared only at me. I fixed my eyes on an old map on the wall and thought of all the saddest things I could, but it was of no use. My laughter burst out again; I was so full of it that it just bubbled over.

Mr. Gorrisen swayed back and forth in his chair as usual as if to show how perfectly unembarrassed he was. But suddenly—true as Gospel—if he did n't almost tip over again! He clutched frantically at the table, gave a guilty glance at me. "Ha, ha! Ha, ha!" I could hear my own laughter above all the rest.

Mr. Gorrisen was up in a trice, and I was hurried out of the door so quickly that, almost before I knew it, I stood out in the cold hall. I nearly froze, it was so bitterly cold there; for it was nearly Christmas time, you see.

I opened the door a tiny bit just far enough to put my nose through the crack.

"Mr. Gorrisen."

"Well?"

"It's so cold out here. I won't laugh any more."

"Very well. Come in."

And so I went in again. At recess they all said they wondered how

I ever dared ask Mr. Gorrisen to let me come in from the hall.

"Pooh!" said I. "I dare do anything with Mr. Gorrisen."

"Oh-h! you don't either! Far from it!"

"Well, I'd really dare pretty nearly anything. I'm not afraid of him."

"Would you dare sing right out loud in his class?" asked Karen.

Pooh! that wouldn't be anything much to do," said Minka. Then they all began to tease me.

"Fie, for shame! She is so brave and yet she does not dare to do such a little thing as that!"

"You shall see whether I dare or not," I said. And, would you believe it? I did sing aloud one time in Mr. Gorrisen's geography class.

It was several days after he had tipped over. I had been watching my chance in all his classes, but somehow it didn't seem to come. One day, however, I was just in the humor, and in the midst of the silence, while Mr. Gorrisen sat and wrote down marks in the record book, I sang out at the top of my voice:

" 'Sons of Norway, that ancient kingdom' "—

I did not once glance at Mr. Gorrisen but looked around at all the others who lay over their desks and laughed till they choked. And I sang on:

" 'Manly and solemn, let the sound rise!' "

Not a sound had come from the platform till that instant. Then I heard behind me the click, click, click of Mr. Gorrisen's heels across the floor and out of the door.

"You'll catch it! oh, you'll catch it, Inger Johanne."

"Oh, I wouldn't be in your shoes for a good deal!"

"Well, it was you who teased me to do it," I said.

"Yes, but to think that you should be so stupid as to do such a thing."

I did really get a little scared, especially because it was so long before Mr. Gorrisen came back.

"Run away!" said one.

"Hide under your desk," said another.

But there he was in the doorway and the Principal with him.

"What is all this, Inger Johanne?" said the Principal. "You are too big to be so wild now. You are not such a bad girl, but you are altogether too thoughtless and use no judgment."

"Yes," I said. I was so glad the Principal didn't scold any harder.

"Of course you will be marked for this in your report book; and remember this," the Principal shook his finger at me threateningly, "it won't do for you to behave like this many times, Inger Johanne. You won't get off so easily again." But as he went out of the door I saw that he smiled. Yes, he did, really.

But Mother didn't smile when she saw the marks.

"Are you going to bring sorrow to your father and mother?" she said. And those beautiful brown eyes of hers looked sad and troubled.

Just think! It had never occurred to me that it would be a sorrow to Father and Mother for me to sing out loud in class. Oh, I was awfully, awfully disgusted with myself. I hung around Mother all the afternoon.

First and foremost I must beg Mr. Gorrisen's pardon, Mother said. It seemed to me I could ask the whole world's pardon if only Mother's eyes wouldn't look so sorrowful. I wanted very much to go right down to Mr. Gorrisen's lodgings; but Mother said she thought it was only right that I should beg his pardon at school, so that all the class should hear. It was embarrassing, frightfully embarrassing, to ask Mr.

Gorrisen's pardon—but I did it notwithstanding. I said, "Please excuse me for singing out in class."

"H'm, h'm," said Mr. Gorrisen. "Well, go back now and take your seat."

Since then I have sat like a lamp-post in his classes—yes, I really have. Many a time I should have liked to have some fun—but then I would think of Mother's sorrowful eyes and so I have held myself in and kept from any more skylarking.

WHEN THE CIRCUS CAME

I was going to school one day, but was pretty late in getting started. The trouble was that our yellow hen, Valpurga, had been sick, and since, of course, I could n't trust any one else to attend to her, I had made myself late.

When hens begin to mope, keeping still under a bush, drawing their heads way down into their feathers, and just rolling their eyes about, that's enough—it is anything but pleasant when it is a hen you are fond of. That's the way Valpurga was behaving. I gave her butter and pepper, for that is good for hens.

But it was n't about Valpurga I wanted to tell. It was about the circus-riders being here.

The clock in the dining room said five minutes of nine, and I had n't eaten my breakfast, had n't studied any of my German grammar lesson, and had to get to school besides. Things went with a rush, I can tell you; with a piece of bread and butter in one hand, the German grammar open in the other, I dashed down the hill.

"Prepositions which govern the dative: *aus, ausser, bei, binnen—aus, ausser, bei*"—pshaw, the ragged old book! There went a leaf over the fence, down into Madam Land's yard. It was best to be careful in going after it, for Madam Land's windows looked out to this side, and she was furious when any one trod down her grass. I expected every moment to hear her knock sharply on the window pane with her thimble. She did n't see me though, and I climbed back over the fence with the missing leaf.

—"aus, ausser—"

Round the corner swung Policeman Weiby with a stranger, a queer-looking man. The stranger was absolutely deep yellow in the face, with black-as-midnight hair, and black piercing eyes. On his head he wore a little green cap, very foreign-looking, and on his feet patent leather riding boots that reached above his knees.

Weiby puffed, threw his chest out even more than usual and looked very much worried. It must be something really important, for day in and day out Weiby has seldom anything else to do than to poke his stick among the children playing hopscotch in the street.

Though I was so terribly late, of course I had to stand still and look after Weiby and the strange man until they disappeared around the corner up by the office. Something interesting had come to town, that was plain. Either a panorama, or a man who swallowed swords, or one who had no arms and sewed with his toes. Hurrah, there was surely to be some entertainment!

I got to school eleven minutes late. A normal-school pupil, Mr. Holmesland, had the arithmetic class that morning. He sat on the platform with his hand under his cheek supporting his big heavy head, and looked at me reproachfully as I came in. I slipped in behind the rack where all the outside things hung, to take off my things, and to finish the last mouthful of my bread and butter.

Pooh, I never bother myself a bit about Mr. Holmesland. I walked boldly out and took my seat. Another long reproachful look from the platform. "Do you know what time it is, Inger Johanne?"

"Yes, but I could n't possibly come before, Mr. Holmesland, because I had to attend to someone who was sick."

"Indeed—is your mother sick?"

"Oh, no." He did n't ask anything more, and I was glad of it.

"What example are you doing?" I asked Netta, who sat beside me.

"This," she showed me her slate, but above the example was written in big letters: *"The circus has come!"*

The arithmetic hour was frightfully long. At recess we talked of nothing but the circus. Netta had seen an awfully fat, black-haired lady, in a fiery red dress, and a fat pug dog on her arm; they certainly belonged to the circus troupe, for there was no such dark lady and no such dog in the whole town. Mina had seen a little slender boy, with rough black hair and gold earrings—and had n't I myself seen the director of the whole concern? It was queer that I was the one who had most to tell, though, as you know, all I had seen of the circus troupe was the strange man with Policeman Weiby as I passed them on the hill.

We had sat down to dinner at home; Karsten had n't come; we did n't know whether it was the circus or our having *"lu-de-fisk"* for dinner that kept him away. Suddenly the dining-room door was thrown open, and there he stood in the doorway, very red in the face and so excited he could hardly speak.

"Can the circus-riders keep their horses in our barn?" he asked, all out of breath. You know we had a big, old barn that was never used. Karsten had to repeat what he had said; we always have to speak awfully clearly to Father; he won't stand any slovenly talk.

Father and Mother looked at each other across the table.

"Well, I don't see any objection," said Father.

"But is it worth while to have all that hubbub in our barn?"

said Mother. I was burning with eagerness as I listened to her.

"It is probably not very easy for them to find a place for all their horses here in town," said Father, "and I shall make the condition that they behave themselves there."

"Well, as you like," said Mother.

Outside in the hall stood the same man I had seen in the morning, and another fellow of just the same sort, but smaller and rougher-looking. Father went out and talked with them; the one in the green cap mixed in a lot of German. *"Danke schön—danke schön,"* they said as they went away.

Hurrah!—the circus-riders were to keep their horses in our barn, right here on our place—hurrah!—hurrah! what fun!

The horses were to come by land from the nearest town, nobody knew just when. I took my geography up on the barn steps that afternoon to study my lesson. I didn't want to miss seeing them come.

Little by little, a whole lot of children collected up there. Away out on the Point they had heard that the circus-riders were to have our barn. Some of the boys began to try to run things, and to push us girls away, but they learned better soon enough.

"No, sir," I gave one a thump—"be off with you; get away, and be quick about it, or you'll catch it."

Most of the boys in the town are afraid of me, I can tell you, because I have strong hands and a quick tongue, and behind me, like an invisible support, is always Father, and all the police, who are under him—so it's not often any one makes a fuss. Besides, I should like to know when you should have the say about things if not on your own barn steps.

More and more children gathered; they swarmed up the hill. I stood on the barn steps with a whip. If anyone came near—swish!

At last—here came the horses! First a big white horse that a groom was leading by the bridle, then two small shaggy ponies, then a big red horse that carried his head high, and then the whole troop following. Some were loose and jumped in among us children; the

I stood on the barn steps with a whip.

grooms scolded and shouted both in German and in Polish; a few small, rough-coated dogs rushed around catching hold of the skirts of some of the girls, who ran and screamed.

Suddenly a little swarthy groom got furious at all of us children who were standing around and drove us down the hill. It made me angry to have him chase me away too, especially because all the others saw it. At first I thought of making a speech to him in German and telling him who I was and that the barn was mine; but I did n't know at all what barn was in German, so I had to give it up.

In the moonlight that evening the fat lady in the red dress, and two little girls came to see to the horses. Afterwards they sat for a long time out on the barn steps watching the moon. The two little girls had long light hair down their backs and short dresses above their knees.

I leaned against the dining-room window with my nose pressed flat, and stared at them. Oh, what a delightful time those little girls had! Think! to travel that way—just travel—travel—travel, to ride on those lovely horses, and wear such short fancy skirts, and have your hair flowing loose over your back.

I never was allowed to go with my hair loose—and I suppose I shall have to stay in this poky town all my days; and never in the world shall I get a chance to ride on a horse, I thought.

At night I lay awake and heard the horses stamping and thumping up in the barn. After all, even this was good fun, almost like being in the midst of a fairy tale.

The next day I was again late to school. There was not a single one of the swarthy fellows to be seen around the barn, so I climbed up on the wall and stuck grass through a broken window-pane to the big white horse. I patted him on his smooth pinky nose: "Oh, you sweet, lovely horse!"—I must go down for more grass, the very best grass to be found he should have.

"Inger Johanne, will you be so good as to go to school? It's very late"—it was Father calling from the office window; so there was an end to that pleasure.

Down by the steamboat-landing, in the big open square, the circus tent had been set up. Karsten and I were down there two hours before the performance was to begin. I was the first of all the spectators to go inside. It was a tremendously big, high tent, three rows of seats around it, and a staging of rough boards for the orchestra. Anything so magnificent you never saw. At last the performance began.

But to describe what goes on at a circus, that I won't do. About ordinary things, such as are happening every day at home, I can write very well, as you know, but anything so magnificent as that circus I can't describe.

I was nearly out of my wits, people said afterwards. I stood up on the seat—those behind me were angry, but that didn't bother me at all—clapped my hands and shouted "Bravo!" and "Hurrah!" Toward the last the riders, when they came in, gave me a special salute in that elegant way, you know, holding up their whips before one eye. I liked that awfully well. I was fairly beside myself with joy.

Well, now I knew what I wanted to be: I wanted to be a circus-rider! For that was the grandest and jolliest thing in the whole world. Did you ever feel about yourself that you were going to be something great, something more than everyone else, as if you stood on a high mountain with all the other people far below you? Well, I had felt like that, and now I knew what it was that I should be.

I lay awake far into the night and thought and thought. Yes, it was plain, I should have to run away with the circus-riders. I could not have a better opportunity. Certainly Father and Mother would never let me go. It would be horrid to run away, but that was nothing; a circus-rider I must be, I saw that plainly. The worst was, all the oil I had heard that circus-riders must drink to keep themselves limber and light. Ugh! no, I would not drink oil; I would be light all the same, and awfully quick about hopping and dancing on the horses. And after many years I would come back to the town. No one would know me at first, and everyone would be so terribly surprised to learn that the graceful rider in blue velvet was the judge's Inger Johanne.

I forgot to say that we were to have two free tickets every evening because Father was town judge. The first evening Karsten and I went, but the second evening Mother said that the maids should go.

"You were there last night," said Mother. "We can't spend money on such foolishness; tomorrow evening you may go again."

Oh, how broken-hearted I was because I couldn't go to the circus that evening! and Mother called it foolishness! If she only knew I was going to be a circus-rider! I wouldn't tell her for the world.

In the evening, when it was time for the performance to begin, I went down to the steamboat-landing just the same. The fat lady with the shining black eyes sat there selling tickets; the people crowded about the entrance, some had already begun to stream in; the big flag which served as a door was constantly being drawn aside to let people in, and at every chance I peeked behind the flag. To think that I wasn't going to get in tonight! Suppose I ran home and asked Father very nicely for a ticket; perhaps there was still time.

"Won't you have a ticket?" asked the black-eyed lady. She said she remembered me from the evening before when I had been so delighted.

"No, I have no money," said I, and my whole face grew red. It really was embarrassing, but since she asked me I had to tell the truth.

"If you will stand there by the door and take the tickets, you may come in and look on," she said.

Wouldn't I! Just the thing for me! Not even a cat should slip in without a ticket. I was very strict at the door and pushed away the sailors who wanted to crowd in. I was terribly clever, the lady said.

And so I went in again, and enjoyed it just as much as I had the evening before. I was tremendously proud of having earned my ticket, for in that way it was as if I were taken at once right into the circus troupe. Every single night they performed I would take the tickets—yet no one in the whole town would know that Inger Johanne meant to go away with the circus. I would wait till the very last day it was in town before I asked the fat dark lady, who was the director's wife, if I might go. Of course I knew her now.

And I must say good-bye to Father and Mother and my brothers and sister, or I couldn't bear it. I wouldn't stay away forever, no, far from it, only a little while, until I was a perfectly splendid performer.

All at once it occurred to me that I ought to practice a little on horseback before I offered myself to the circus troupe. I ought at least to know what it was like to sit on a horse.

There certainly couldn't be any better opportunity than there was now, when our whole barn was full of horses. But I must take Karsten into my confidence; he would have to help me to climb through a hole in the back of the barn, for the grooms always fastened the barn door when they went away. At noon there was never any one up there, so I planned to crawl in then and practice getting on and off of a horse. Yes, I would stand up on him, too—on one leg—stretch out my arms, and throw kisses as they do at the circus.

"Karsten," said I the next day, "what should you say if I became a circus-rider?"

"You—when you're knock-kneed!—you would look nice, Inger Johanne, you would."

"You look after your own knees, Karsten, I'm going to be a circus-rider, all the same, I really am."

"Oh, what bosh!"

"Well, you'll see; when the circus-riders go I'm going with them. You must n't tell a soul, Karsten, but a circus-rider is what I'm going to be."

Karsten looked at me rather doubtfully.

"But you must help me to get into the barn through that hole at the back, for I shall have to practice, you understand."

"Well, will you give me that red-and-blue pencil of yours then?"

"Oh, yes, only come along."

We stole behind the barn. Karsten kept hold of me while I climbed up—there, now I was in the barn. How it looked! When twelve horses must stand in five stalls, there isn't much room left, you know, and they had been put every which way—one pony stood in the calf-pen.

All the horses except two were lying down resting. The white horse over by the window was standing up; he turned around and looked at me with big sorrowful eyes. It had really been my plan to get on him, for he was the handsomest of them all, but I did n't dare to venture among the big shining bodies of the horses lying all over the floor. No, I should have to be satisfied with the little black one that stood in the calf-pen. Karsten had thrust the upper part of his body in through the hole. I went up to the black horse.

"He is angry; he is putting his ears back; look out, Inger Johanne!" called Karsten.

"Pooh—do you think I mind that?" I climbed up on the calf-pen. For a moment I wondered whether I should try to stand on the horse at once. I put out my foot and touched him—no, he was so smooth and slippery, it would certainly be best to sit the first time I got on a horse. I gave a little jump, and there I sat.

Oh, dear! What in the world was happening? I did n't know, but I thought the horse had gone crazy. First he stood on his fore legs with his hind legs in the air, and then on his hind legs, and threw me off as if I were nothing at all. I fell across the edge of the calf-pen—oh, what a whack my arm got! I literally couldn't move it for a whole minute; and there was a grand rumpus in the barn; some of the horses got up and whinnied, and the black one that I had sat on kicked and kicked with his hind legs every instant.

I could just see the top of Karsten's head at the hole now.

"Oh, Karsten—Karsten."

"Are you dead, Inger Johanne?"

I don't really know how I got out through the hole with my injured arm. But outside of the barn I sat down right among all the nettles and cried.

When I went into the house there was a great commotion. Everybody was scared and the doctor was sent for. My sleeve was cut up to the shoulder, and the doctor said I had broken a small bone in my wrist, and besides had sprained and bruised my arm about as much as I could.

"You do everything so thoroughly, Inger Johanne," said the doctor.

When I was in bed with my arm in splints and bandages, I began to cry violently. Not so much because of my arm—though I cried a little about that, too—but most that I should have thought I could run away from Father and Mother, who were so good. I told Mother the whole thing.

"But now I'll never—never—never think of running away again, Mother."

The day the circus-riders left with the horses, I stood at the window with my arm in a sling and watched them.

But only think! Karsten wouldn't give up, and I had to hand over my red-and-blue pencil to him even though I didn't run away with the circus-riders!

MOVING

Twice, that I can remember, Father had tried to get a position off in the country, and each time I had been so sure we were going to move that I had imagined exactly how everything would be in our new home. A big old farmhouse, yes, for I like old, old houses; an immense garden, with empress pears and every possible kind of berry; big red barns and outhouses; big pastures all around; cows and calves, and horses to go driving with wherever I wished. I should like best a red horse with a white mane, a horse that looked wild; and a little light basket-phaeton. And I would drive, and crack my whip—oh, how I would snap it! And there would be a lot of hens that I would take care of myself, for I am so interested in hens.

Once, I told all around town that we were to move to Telemarken. I really believed it myself. Everybody in town heard of it and at last it got into the paper, and, O dear! it wasn't true at all, and it was I who had told it. That time Father was furious with me.

After that I never heard a word about Father's looking for a position; I suppose they were afraid I should tell of it again. And so it was like lightning from a clear sky and I was completely astounded when Mother told me one morning at breakfast that Father had got a position in Christiania, and that we were to move away.

"Well, may I tell about it now?" I asked.

"Yes, now you may say all you like," said Mother.

I couldn't get another mouthful down after hearing the news, but hurried off to school. Not a soul had come when I got there, so I had to wait, alone with my great news, for five long minutes. The first to come was Antoinette Wium; she had hardly opened the door when I called out: "I am going to move away from town."

Then I planted myself firmly at the door, and told every single one that came in. Before the first recess was over, the whole school and all the teachers knew that we were to move to Christiania.

I was so glad, I did n't know what to do. The first few days I just went around telling it down on the wharves and everywhere.

All at once everything seemed so tedious in town. I did n't care any longer about what my friends were talking of; all I wanted was to talk about Christiania. When I was alone I sang to myself: "We shall travel, travel, travel," mostly to the tune of

"Ja, vi elsker dette landet,"

for that has such a swing to it.

I must say that now, for the first time, I understood how Lawyer Cold felt. He is a fat young man from Christiania who has settled in our town, but is in despair because he has to live here. He comes up to Father's office and sits and talks by the hour, complaining, until he puts Father in a bad humor, too. It is Karl Johan Street that he misses so frightfully, he says. And to think that now I was going to Karl Johan Street and should see all the cadets and all the fun! I could understand Lawyer Cold's feelings perfectly now. Oh, oh, how delightful it will be!

I began at once to go around to say good-bye, although we were not to leave for three or four months. I went to all the cottages and huts round about. One day I went by Ellef Kulaas' house up on the hill. He was standing by his door. He is tall, and his whole body seems to be warped, and he never looks at people, but off anywhere else.

"Good-bye, Ellef, I am going away," said I.

Ellef did n't answer; he only turned his quid in his mouth.

"We are going to Christiania," I went on.

"Yes, I was there once," said Ellef. "It's a dangerous Sodom."

"But aren't there plenty of splendid things to see, Ellef?"

"Oh, yes—I wanted most to see that big mountain Gausta. They told me I'd have to take a horse and wagon to get there; but I went to see the old dean that used to be here—he lived high up—and when I looked out of his skylight I saw everything, Gausta and the churches and the whole kit and boodle. I saved a lot of money that way. I went up there twice and looked through the skylight, and so I saw the whole show—for nothing, too. I suppose hardly anybody sees it any better."

Humph! As if I'd be satisfied like Ellef Kulaas with seeing things through the dean's skylight!

There were many places where I said good-bye several times. At last they laughed at me, and I had to laugh too. One day I went by Madam Guldahl's house. Madam Guldahl always stands at her garden gate and talks with people who are passing.

"Good-bye, Madam Guldahl, we are going to Christiania," said I.

"You may if you want to. I am thankful to live here rather than there."

"Why is that?"

"Oh, I was there six weeks on account of my bad leg—such hurrying and running in the streets you never saw. I didn't know a soul in the streets; what pleasure could there be in that, I'd like to know! One day I saw Ellef Kulaas on the street there, and I was so glad I wanted to throw my arms around his neck. People went by each other without once looking at each other—not at all as though it was immortal souls they were passing."

I wondered a little whether I should want to throw my arms round Ellef Kulaas' neck if I met him on Karl Johan Street; but I hardly thought I should.

There were three farewell parties for me in the town, with tables loaded with good things at all the places, and at table they always "toasted" me, singing:

"Og dette skal vaere Inger Johanne's skaal! Hurrah!"

I sang with them myself, and it was quite ceremonious. It's awfully good fun to be made so much of. The girls all wanted to walk arm in arm with me and be awfully good friends, and I promised to write to them all.

At home all the floors were covered with straw and big packing-cases; chairs and sofas were wrapped in matting; a policeman went around sorting and packing for several days, and Mother wore her morning dress all day long. It was all horribly uncomfortable and awfully pleasant at the same time.

I packed a box of crockery, and it was really very well done, but the policeman packed it all over again. After that I wasn't allowed to do anything except run errands.

At school I gave away my scholar's-companion and my eraser and my pencils and penholders, and an old torn map, as keepsakes.

On Saturday, after prayers, the Principal said:

"There is a little girl here who is soon to leave us. It is Inger Johanne, as we all know. We shall miss you, Inger Johanne. You are a good girl in spite of all your pranks. May everything go well with you. God bless you."

This was terribly unexpected. Oh, what a beautiful speech—I began to cry—oh, how I cried! The very moment the Principal said: "There is a little girl here who is soon to leave us," everything seemed perfectly horrid all at once.

Just think, to leave the school and my friends, and the town, and everything, and never, never come back!

I laid my head down on the desk and cried, and cried, and

couldn't stop. I had thought only of all the new things I was going to, and not that I should never in the world live here again—here where I had been so happy.

Oh, dear! if we were only not going, if we were just to stay here all our lives. At last the Principal came down and patted me on the head, and then I cried all the more.

When I got home they could hardly see my eyes, I had cried so.

"Now you see, Inger Johanne, it's not all pleasure, either," said Mother.

The last day, I ran up on the hill, and said good-bye to all the places where we used to play, to Rome and Japan, to Kongsberg and the North Cape—for we had given names to some of them.

"Good-bye!" I shouted across the rocks and the heather and the juniper. "Good-bye!" I ran and ran, for I wanted to see all the places where we had played, before I went away forever. At home, on the outside wall of our old house, I wrote in pencil, "Good-bye, my beloved home!"

But I didn't cry, except that time at school.

At the steamboat-wharf, when we were leaving, it was only fun. The wharf was packed full of people, and they all wanted to talk to us and shake hands, and they gave Mother bouquets and gave me bouquets; and there was such a crowd and bustle and talk and noise before all our things were finally on board! Only one thing was horrid, and that was that Ingeborg the maid cried so sorrowfully. She was not going with us; she stood on the wharf by herself and cried and cried.

"Don't cry, Ingeborg; you must come and visit us—yes, you must, you must; don't cry!"

"I can't do anything else," said Ingeborg, sobbing aloud.

Now I had to go on board and the steamboat started.

"Good-bye, good-bye"—I ran to the very stern right by the flag, and waved and waved. I could see Massa and Mina on the wharf all the way to where we swung around the islands.

I stood staring back at the town.

Now Peckell's big yellow house vanished, and now the custom-house; now I could see nothing but the little red house high up on the hill; and at last that vanished too.

But I still stood there, looking back and looking back at the gray hills. Among them I had lived my whole life long!

Other hills and islands came into view, and the sea splashed up over them, but not one of them did I know.

How strange that was!

Nevertheless, I suddenly felt awfully glad, and I began to sing at the top of my voice to the old tune (no one heard me, the sea roared so mightily):

"Oh! I love to travel, travel!"

EMBELLISHMENT

ONE day Beechnut, who had been ill, was taken by Phonny and Madeline for a drive. When Phonny and Madeline found themselves riding quietly along in the wagon in Beechnut's company, the first thought which occurred to them, after the interest and excitement awakened by the setting out had passed in some measure away, was that they would ask him to tell them a story. This was a request which they almost always made in similar circumstances. In all their rides and rambles Beechnut's stories were an unfailing resource, furnishing them with an inexhaustible fund of amusement sometimes, and sometimes of instruction.

"Well," said Beechnut, in answer to their request, "I will tell you now about my voyage across the Atlantic Ocean."

"Yes," exclaimed Madeline, "I should like to hear about that very much indeed."

"Shall I tell the story to you just as it was," asked Beechnut, "as a sober matter of fact, or shall I embellish it a little?"

"I don't know what you mean by embellishing it," said Madeline.

"Why, not telling exactly what is true," said Beechnut, "but inventing something to add to it, to make it interesting."

"I want to have it true," said Madeline, "and interesting, too."

By

JACOB ABBOTT

Illustrations by
FRANCIS D. BEDFORD
and
WARREN CHAPPELL

"But sometimes," replied Beechnut, "interesting things don't happen, and in such cases, if we should only relate what actually does happen, the story would be likely to be dull."

"I think you had better embellish the story a little," said Phonny—"just a *little,* you know."

"I don't think I can do that very well," replied Beechnut. "If I attempt to relate the actual facts, I depend simply on my memory, and I can confine myself to what my memory teaches; but if I undertake to follow my invention, I must go wherever it leads me."

"Well," said Phonny, "I think you had better embellish the story, at any rate, for I want it to be interesting."

"So do I," said Madeline.

"Then," said Beechnut, "I will give you an embellished account of my voyage across the Atlantic. But, in the first place, I must tell you how it happened that my father decided to leave Paris and come to America. It was mainly on my account. My father was well enough contented with his situation so far as he himself was concerned, and he was able to save a large part of his salary, so as to lay up a considerable sum of money every year; but he was anxious about me.

"There seemed to be nothing," continued Beechnut, "for me to do, and nothing desirable for me to look forward to, when I should become a man. My father thought, therefore, that, though it would perhaps be better for *him* to remain in France, it would probably be better for *me* if he should come to America, where he said people might rise in the world, according to their talents, thrift, and industry. He was sure, he said, that I should rise, for you must understand, he considered me an extraordinary boy."

"Well," said Phonny, "*I* think you were an extraordinary boy."

"Yes, but my father thought," rejoined Beechnut, "that I was something very extraordinary indeed. He thought I was a genius."

"So do I," said Phonny.

"He said," continued Beechnut, "he thought it would in the end be a great deal better for him to come to America, where I might become a man of some consequence in the world, and he said that he should enjoy his own old age a great deal better, even in a strange land, if he could see me going on prosperously in life, than to remain all his days in that porter's lodge.

"All the money that my father had saved," Beechnut continued, "he got changed into gold at an office in the Boulevards; but then he was very much perplexed to decide how it was best to carry it."

"Why did he not pack it up in his chest?" asked Phonny.

"He was afraid," replied Beechnut, "that his chest might be broken open, or unlocked by false keys, on the voyage, and that the money might be thus stolen away; so he thought that he would try to hide it somewhere in some small thing that he could keep with him all the voyage."

"Could not he keep his chest with him all the voyage?" asked Phonny.

"No," said Beechnut; "the chests, and all large parcels of baggage belonging to the passengers, must be sent down into the hold of the ship out of the way. It is only a very little baggage that the people are allowed to keep with them between the decks. My father wished very much to keep his gold with him, and yet he was afraid to keep it in a bag, or in any other similar package, in his little trunk, for then whoever saw it would know that it was gold, and so perhaps form some plan to rob him of it.

"While we were considering what plan it would be best to adopt for the gold, Arielle, who was the daughter of a friend of ours, proposed to hide it in my *top*. I had a very large top which my father had made for me. It was painted yellow outside, with four stripes of bright blue passing down over it from the stem to the point. When the top was in motion, both the yellow ground and the blue stripes entirely disappeared, and the top appeared to be of a uniform green color. Then, when it came to its rest again, the original colors would reappear."

"How curious!" said Madeline. "Why would it do so?"

"Why, when it was revolving," said Beechnut, "the yellow and the blue were blended together in the eye, and that made green. Yellow and blue always make green. Arielle colored my top, after my father had made it, and then my father varnished it over the colors, and that fixed them.

"This top of mine was a monstrous large one, and being hollow, Arielle thought that the gold could all be put inside. She said she thought that that would be a very safe hiding-place, too, since nobody would think of looking into a top for gold. But my father said that he thought that the space would not be quite large enough, and then if anybody should happen to see the top, and should touch it, the weight of it would immediately reveal the secret.

"At last my father thought of a plan which he believed would answer the purpose very perfectly. We had a very curious old clock. It was made by my grandfather, who was a clockmaker in Geneva. There was a little door in the face of the clock, and whenever the time came for striking the hours, this door would open, and a little platform would come out with a tree upon it. There was a beautiful little bird on the tree, and when the clock had done striking, the bird would flap its wings and sing. Then the platform would slide back into its place, the door would shut, and the clock go on ticking quietly for another hour.

"This clock was made to go," continued Beechnut, "as many other clocks are, by two heavy weights, which were hung to the wheelwork by strong cords. The cords were wound round some of the wheels, and as they slowly descended by their weight they made the wheels go round. There was a contrivance inside the clock to make the wheels go slowly and regularly, and not spin round too fast, as they would have done if the weights had been left to themselves. This is the way that clocks are often made.

"Now, my father," continued Beechnut, "had intended to take this old family clock with him to America, and he now conceived the idea of hiding his treasure in the weights. The weights were formed of two round tin canisters filled with something very heavy. My father said he did not know whether it was shot or sand. He unsoldered the bottom from these canisters and found that the filling was shot. He poured out the shot, put his gold pieces in in place of it, and then filled up all the interstices between and around the gold pieces with sand, to prevent the money from jingling. Then he soldered the bottom of the canisters on again, and no one would have known that the weights were anything more than ordinary clockweights. He then packed the clock in a box, and put the box in his trunk. It did not take up a great deal of room, for he did not take the case of the clock, but only the face and the works and the two weights, which last he packed carefully and securely in the box, one on each side of the clock itself.

"When we got to Havre, all our baggage was examined at the custom-house, and the officers allowed it all to pass. When they came to the clock, my father showed them the little door and the bird inside, and they said it was very curious. They did not pay any attention to the weights at all.

"When we went on board the vessel our chests were put by the side of an immense heap of baggage upon the deck, where some seamen were at work lowering it down into the hold through a square opening in the deck of the ship. As for the trunk, my father took that with him to the place where he was going to be himself during the voyage. This place was called the steerage. It was crowded full of men, women, and children, all going to America. Some talked French, some German, some Dutch, and there were ever so many babies that were too little to talk at all. Pretty soon the vessel sailed.

"We did not meet with anything remarkable on the voyage, except that once we saw an iceberg."

"What is that?" asked Madeline.

"It is a great mountain of ice," replied Beechnut, "floating about

The clock ready for packing.

in the sea on the top of the water. I don't know how it comes to be there."

"I should not think it would float upon the top of the water," said Phonny. "All the ice that I ever saw in the water sinks into it."

"It does not sink to the bottom," said Madeline.

"No," replied Phonny, "but it sinks down until the top of the ice is just level with the water. But Beechnut says that his iceberg rose up like a mountain."

"Yes," said Beechnut, "it was several hundred feet high above the water, all glittering in the sun. And I think that if you look at any small piece of ice floating in the water, you will see that a small part of it rises above the surface."

"Yes," said Phonny, "a very little."

"It is a certain proportion of the whole mass," rejoined Beechnut. "They told us on board our vessel that about one-tenth part of the iceberg was above the water; the rest—that is, nine-tenths—was under it; so you see what an enormous big piece of ice it must have been to have only one-tenth part of it tower up so high.

"There was one thing very curious and beautiful about our iceberg," said Beechnut. "We came in sight of it one day about sunset, just after a shower. The cloud, which was very large and black, had passed off into the west, and there was a splendid rainbow upon it. It happened, too, that when we were nearest to the iceberg it lay toward the west, and, of course, toward the cloud, and it appeared directly under the rainbow, and the iceberg and the rainbow made a most magnificent spectacle. The iceberg, which was very bright and dazzling in the evening sun, looked like an enormous diamond, with the rainbow for the setting."

"How curious!" said Phonny.

"Yes," said Beechnut, "and to make it more remarkable still, a whale just then came along directly before the iceberg, and spouted there two or three times; and as the sun shone very brilliantly upon the jet of water which the whale threw into the air, it made a sort of silver rainbow below in the center of the picture."

"How beautiful it must have been!" said Phonny.

"Yes," rejoined Beechnut, "very beautiful indeed. We saw a great many beautiful spectacles on the sea; but then, on the other hand, we saw some that were dreadful."

"Did you?" asked Phonny. "What?"

"Why, we had a terrible storm and shipwreck at the end," said

Beechnut. "For three days and three nights the wind blew almost a hurricane. They took in all the sails, and let the ship drive before the gale under bare poles. She went on over the seas for five hundred miles, howling all the way like a frightened dog."

"Were you frightened?" asked Phonny.

"Yes," said Beechnut. "When the storm first came on, several of the passengers came up the hatchways and got up on the deck to see it; and then we could not get down again, for the ship gave a sudden pitch just after we came up, and knocked away the step-ladder. We were terribly frightened. The seas were breaking over the forecastle and sweeping along the decks, and the shouts and outcries of the captain and the sailors made a dreadful din. At last they put the step-ladder in its place again, and we got down. Then they put the hatches on, and we could not come out any more."

"The hatches?" said Phonny. "What are they?"

"The hatches," replied Beechnut, "are a sort of scuttle-doors that cover over the square openings in the deck of a ship. They always have to put them on and fasten them down in a great storm."

Just at this time the party happened to arrive at a place where two roads met, and as there was a broad and level space of ground at the junction, where it would be easy to turn the wagon, Beechnut said that he thought it would be better to make that the end of their ride, and so turn round and go home. Phonny and Madeline were quite desirous of going a little farther, but Beechnut thought that he should be tired by the time he reached the house again.

"But you will not have time to finish the story," said Phonny.

"Yes," replied Beechnut; "there is very little more to tell. It is only to give an account of our shipwreck."

"Why, did you have a shipwreck?" exclaimed Phonny.

"Yes," said Beechnut. "When you have turned the wagon, I will tell you about it."

So Phonny, taking a great sweep, turned the wagon round, and the party set their faces toward home. The Marshal was immediately going to set out upon a trot, but Phonny held him back by pulling upon the reins and saying:

"Steady, Marshal! steady! You have got to walk all the way home."

"The storm drove us upon the Nova Scotia coast," said Beechnut, resuming his story. "We did not know anything about the great danger that we were in until just before the ship went ashore. When we got near the shore the sailors put down all the anchors; but they would not hold, and at length the ship struck. Then there followed a dreadful scene of consternation and confusion. Some jumped into the sea in their terror, and were drowned. Some cried and screamed, and acted as if they were insane. Some were calm, and behaved rationally. The sailors opened the hatches and let the passengers come up, and we got into the most sheltered places that we could find about the decks and rigging and tied ourselves to whatever was nearest at hand. My father opened his trunk and took out his two clock-weights, and gave me one of them; the other he kept himself. He told me that we might as well try to save them, though he did not suppose that we should be able to do so.

"Pretty soon after we struck the storm seemed to abate a little. The people of the country came down to the shore and stood upon the rocks to see if they could do anything to save us. We were very near the shore, but the breakers and the boiling surf were so violent between us and the land that whoever took to the water was sure to be dashed to pieces. So everybody clung to the ship, waiting for the captain to contrive some way to get us to the shore."

"And what did he do?" asked Phonny.

"He first got a long line and a cask, and he fastened the end of the long line to the cask, and then threw the cask overboard. The other end of the line was kept on board the ship. The cask was tossed about upon the waves, every successive surge driving it in nearer and nearer to the shore, until at last it was thrown up high upon the rocks. The men upon the shore ran to seize it, but before they could get hold of it the receding wave carried it back again among the breakers, where it was tossed about as if it had been a feather, and overwhelmed with the spray. Presently away it went again up upon the shore, and the men again attempted to seize it. This was repeated two or three times. At last they succeeded in grasping hold of it, and they ran up with it upon the rocks, out of the reach of the seas.

"The captain then made signs to the men to pull the line in toward the shore. He was obliged to use signs, because the roaring and thundering of the seas made such a noise that nothing could be heard. The sailors had before this, under the captain's direction, fastened a much stronger line—a small cable, in fact—to the end of the line which had been attached to the barrel. Thus, by pulling upon the smaller line, the men drew one end of the cable to the shore. The other end remained on board the ship, while the middle of it lay tossing among the breakers between the ship and the shore.

"The seamen then carried that part of the cable which was on shipboard up to the masthead, while the men on shore made their end fast to a very strong post which they set in the ground. The seamen drew the cable as tight as they could, and fastened their end very strongly to the masthead. Thus the line of the cable passed in a gentle slope from the top of the mast to the land, high above all the surges and spray. The captain then rigged what he called a sling, which was a sort of loop of ropes that a person could be put into and made to slide down in it on the cable to the shore. A great many of the passengers were afraid to go in this way, but they were still more afraid to remain on board the ship."

"What were they afraid of?" asked Phonny.

Sliding down the cable to safety.

"They were afraid," replied Beechnut, "that the shocks of the seas would soon break the ship to pieces, and then they would all be thrown into the sea together. In this case they would certainly be destroyed, for if they were not drowned, they would be dashed to pieces on the rocks which lined the shore.

"Sliding down the line seemed thus a very dangerous attempt, but they consented one after another to make the trial, and thus we all escaped safe to land."

"And did you get the clock-weights safe to the shore?" asked Phonny.

"Yes," replied Beechnut, "and as soon as we landed we hid them in the sand. My father took me to a little cove close by, where there was not much surf, as the place was protected by a rocky point of land which bounded it on one side. Behind this point of land the waves rolled up quietly upon a sandy beach. My father went down upon the slope of this beach, to a place a little below where the highest waves came, and began to dig a hole in the sand. He called me to come and help him. The waves impeded our work a little, but we persevered until we had dug a hole about a foot deep. We put our clock-weights into this hole and covered them over. We then ran back up upon the beach. The waves that came up every moment over the place soon smoothed the surface of the sand again, and made it look as if nothing had been done there. My father measured the distance from the place where he had deposited his treasure up to a certain great white rock upon the shore exactly opposite to it, so as to be able to find the place again, and then we went back to our company. They were collected on the rocks in little groups, wet and tired, and in great confusion, but rejoiced at having escaped with their lives. Some of the last of the sailors were then coming over in the sling. The captain himself came last of all.

"There were some huts near the place on the shore, where the men made good fires, and we warmed and dried ourselves. The storm abated a great deal in a few hours, and the tide went down, so that we could go off to the ship before night to get some provisions. The next morning the men could work at the ship very easily, and they brought all the passengers' baggage on shore. My father got his trunk with the clock in it. A day or two afterwards some sloops came to the place, and took us all away to carry us to Quebec. Just before we embarked on board the sloops, my father and I, watching a good opportunity, dug up our weights out of the sand, and put them back safely in their places in the clock-box."

"Is that the end?" asked Phonny, when Beechnut paused.

"Yes," replied Beechnut, "I believe I had better make that the end."

"I think it is a very interesting and well-told story," said Madeline. "And do you feel very tired?"

"No," said Beechnut. "On the contrary, I feel all the better for my ride. I believe I will sit up a little while."

So saying, he raised himself in the wagon and sat up, and began to look about him.

"What a wonderful voyage you had, Beechnut!" said Phonny. "But I never knew before that you were shipwrecked."

"Well, in point of fact," replied Beechnut, "I never was shipwrecked."

"Never was!" exclaimed Phonny. "Why, what is all this story that you have been telling us, then?"

"Embellishment," said Beechnut quietly.

"Embellishment!" repeated Phonny, more and more amazed.

"Yes," said Beechnut.

"Then you were not wrecked at all?" said Phonny.

"No," replied Beechnut.

"And how did you get to the land?" asked Phonny.

"Why, we sailed quietly up the St. Lawrence," replied Beechnut, "and landed safely at Quebec, as other vessels do."

"And the clock-weights?" asked Phonny.

"All embellishment," said Beechnut. "My father had no such clock, in point of fact. He put his money in a bag, his bag in his chest, and his chest in the hold, and it came as safe as the captain's sextant."

"And the iceberg and the rainbow?" said Madeline.

"Embellishment, all embellishment," said Beechnut.

"Dear me!" said Phonny, "I thought it was all true."

"Did you?" said Beechnut. "I am sorry that you were so deceived, and I am sure it was not my fault, for I gave you your choice of a true story or an invention, and you chose the invention."

"Yes," said Phonny, "so we did."

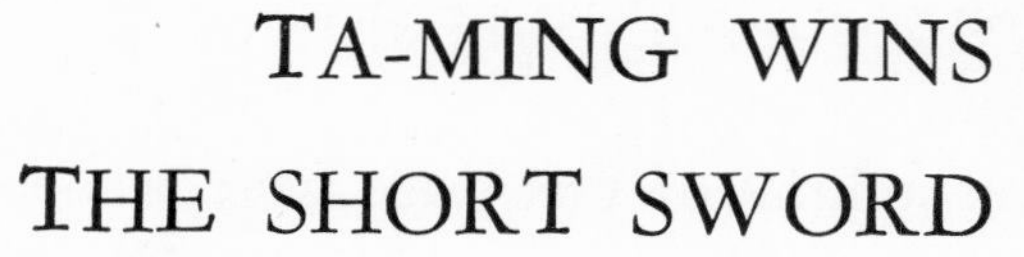

TA-MING WINS THE SHORT SWORD

By VIOLET M. IRWIN

Illustrations by
WARREN CHAPPELL

TWO GOOD FIGHTERS

"HOU AH!"

The monk who was carrying the water buckets from the open well to the monastery kitchen stopped with this exclamation of approval to watch a Chinese boy jumping in iron shoes. In spite of the great weight of the shoes which retarded his movement, his leaps were noticeably wide and high.

Sympathetic murmurs ran among the other monks gathered as impromptu spectators. All wore gray cotton gowns folded over and tied at one side, exposing their chests in an irregular V-shaped opening, black cloth shoes and homemade white cotton stockings, with the seams carefully run up the fronts so that they would not hurt their feet.

"Assuredly he will not remain on the farm, this boy," said one.

"You have lifted the remark out of my mouth. It was a mighty leap. His honorable legs must have the strength of steel. There will surely be wider activities found for them than treading the irrigation pump."

The performer was Chang Ta-ming, the son of Chang the farmer, who worked on shares the fertile fields belonging to Fan Ju-Lung. This farm, lying in a wide valley, extended up to a harsh rib of rocky soil. At the summit of this ridge were wooded heights, among the trees of which the monastery hid.

At fifteen Ta-ming had mastered such education as the village school afforded. But it was not in book learning his soul delighted. The ardor of his youth poured itself out in physical expression. For years every stretch of spare time had seen him toiling up the steep slope to the monastery gate, running swiftly along the ornamental paths, over the arched bridge that spanned the foot of the waterfall and around to a side door giving on the athletic court. Here, at first under the tuition of a friendly monk and later instructed by the lama himself, he had learned the strengthening exercises, the lightning twists of sword and spear, and the intricacies of the boxing method which made him an adversary to be feared. The monks themselves were surprised at the boy's dexterity and endurance.

He removed the iron shoes which had weighted his feet in practice, developing his leg muscles to unbelievable toughness and, freed from this hindrance, made a leap at once and so high and so broad that the holy men exclaimed aloud in admiration.

Without waiting to rest or perceptibly savor their praise, Ta-ming set the shoes aside and brought out the heavy iron bar which was to be his opponent in a thigh and ankle exercise. The stout rod of iron, measuring about five inches across and four feet in length, he set upright, burying it a foot deep in the earth, tramping the soil solidly around the buried end. Then he took his place opposite and, standing hands on hips, raised one leg with stiff knee and swung it easily but mightily, knocking the iron pole flat on the ground.

Let anyone who doubts the extreme difficulty of this feat try it. Again exclamations of amazement sprang from the spectators.

"Prosperity lies beneath his heavy heel."

"There will come a moment of well-achieved triumph for the spirits of his illustrious ancestors."

"The boy takes honorable precedence for his age!"

But the monk who had drawn the water gave Ta-ming a more satisfactory compliment by offering him a drink.

The athlete accepted gladly. Green leaves had been placed on top of the water to steady it and to keep it from spilling, for the pails, which were hung from a bamboo stick laid across the monk's shoulders, swayed at each step and washed the contents to and fro. Raising these leaves, the boy drank.

Swinging on his heel, the young enthusiast next challenged the monk Wu to a unique exhibition. The monk, armed with a heavy spear sharply pointed with steel and made gay for its ghastly work by a thin fringe of red horsehair fastened below the barbs of the tip, sought to pierce the defender's neck, while Ta-ming protected himself by twirling a sword in either hand and by constantly swinging his head from side to side in a neck play designed to elude his enemy's onslaughts. He did it magnificently. Around and around, faster and faster, to right, to left, spun the swords. Though the spear pressed him, it never once touched his flesh. But that was not enough. Presently, at a signal, the boy threw himself on the ground and rolled about, still putting up his defense with the whirling swords, their blades flashing in the sunlight, while Wu's long weapon menaced his heart.

From an open shutter in the gray brick wall the lama watched them. No sooner was the bout ended than his face vanished, and shortly a young monk came out with a summons for Ta-ming to go to the armor room.

No sting of surprise lurked in this message. The lama was fond of the farmer's boy. He had personally instructed him in boxing,

Though the spear pressed him, it never touched his flesh.

and the supreme skill which the monks admired so much Ta-ming owed entirely to his patron's tuition. It was a signal pleasure to be called before him. The delighted youth hastily donned his blue cotton coat and, with a wave of farewell to his companions, disappeared into the building. He knew every turn of room and corridor under that gray-tiled roof. To the right he went through the refectory and across an inner court. His black cloth shoes made no sound on the wide gray paving stones. A moment he hesitated outside the door leading to the armor room, then quickly pushed aside a curtain of split bamboo and entered.

It was a silent, stern chamber, all gray brick and gray stone. Cold northern light fell through its paper windows and glinted from the spears and shields and helmets decorating its walls. Arrows of many shapes and sizes hung there in rows, flanked by long knives and swords of curious design. On a stone bench at one side sat the lama—a man well past middle age, clad in a long gray cotton gown, light in color and fashioned after the Ming period. His arms were now folded in its flowing sleeves. His head with its graying hair had sunk on his chest. So cataleptic seemed his stillness he might well have been a statue carved all of a piece out of the grayness of that gray interior.

But the lama's mind remained alert. The rattling bamboo curtain roused him. He came forward and greeted Ta-ming.

"Welcome, my son, I have watched you today from the window and am pleased with the excellent performance you have given, not only in the muscle tests, but later when in boxing you pitted your skill against that of the monk Wu."

Ta-ming bowed over his clasped hands. "I am grateful for the heartening words of your praise," he said modestly. And added in a rounder voice, "That Wu has a lightning hand, Eminence!"

Owing to his constant association with the monks, Ta-ming spoke excellent Mandarin, though he seldom indulged in the flowery form of speech used by his more intellectual companions.

The lama smiled. "Your adversary would not have pressed you so hard had you recollected that rotary thrust from the lower position a little earlier. No. Do not look mortified," for the boy's glance had fallen. "You did remember it in time and put your knowledge to good use. The next engagement will bring it to you sooner and so on until the motion becomes an instinct. However, I have not called you here today to lecture, but to compliment you. To inform you that I see I have taught you all I know."

"Master!" protested Ta-ming, breathless.

"It is surely true. I have imparted to you the principles of the boxing art, seen you well grounded in the right method, watched you add the touches of a master hand. Today you are the fleetest runner in the province, the strongest youth of your age in the whole of Manchuria, as well as the most skillful with the sword. All you need is a weapon fine enough to justify your use of it."

"Ah, if I had a sword of my own!" sighed Ta-ming. Immediately his face brightened. "I shall have one some day. I am saving up for one. A few cash are already in my sleeve, Reverend Father."

The lama's wise eyes smiled. He could estimate very well how few were likely to be the cash in the sleeve of a farmer's boy, and he knew something of the price of good steel. Rising, he went to the wall and detached a short sword that hung there by an embroidered scarlet belt.

Ta-ming stepped closer. His eyes, like twin carnelians set in a face of old ivory, glowed brightly. He was not often permitted to handle the weapons belonging to the monastery, many of which were ancient treasures. When the lama held out the sword, the boy's muscular, well-formed, large hand reached for it eagerly. At the moment, attention being concentrated in his eyes, he scarcely heard the chief priest's voice.

"I find much gratification in giving into the keeping of such an admirable pupil this hereditary sword. It was made by Ta Yeh, the famous sword maker, many hundred years ago. I feel sure your worthy hands will never disgrace the beauty and dignity which should belong to a superior weapon."

Ta-ming's mouth fell a little open. "To keep?" The words came with a gasp. "Mine! Do you mean—to keep?"

"You have earned it by diligence."

The boy took his tutor's gift reverently. "Always it will companion me through life, Supreme One. We will be two good fighters made by two great masters."

The lama was pleased by the well-turned tribute, but he answered gravely, "Fighters. Yes, it may be so. The future is an unwritten sheet. You will perhaps journey into far places and find strange adventures, but wherever you go, or however you fare, recollect, my son, that the art of boxing is learned for self-defense, not for aggression. Let the decoration of lotus flowers on the sword blade remind you of the beauty of mercy."

Ta-ming's eyes were already devouring the splendid gift. It was a bloodthirsty-looking weapon, not at all suggesting mercy. The thin bright knife curved back from the short handle, presenting on its outer side a death-edge of sharpness. The flat sides were chased in a design employing the flowers the lama mentioned. But the ivory handle had been carved to simulate two bats. This indicated a double blessing. The bat forms, moreover, had been stained bright Chinese red, which is the color of happiness.

"Mercy sheds a double blessing that leads to happiness," counseled the lama.

"I shall not forget, honorable master," Ta-ming answered.

Now that he had examined the appearance of his sword, he could control himself no longer, but must try the heft of it. Stepping back to the hall's wide center, he swung the glittering steel, cutting a silver arc through the gray air. He swept his arm upward, whirled with demoniacal swiftness, and lunged at an imaginary enemy.

Critically alert, the lama watched every movement and signified approval with a nod.

"It would be well to strike lower," he suggested again, waving an indicative hand the long nails of which extended the fingers to uncanny length.

Ta-ming swung and lunged a second time.

"It is well, my boy," said the venerable man. "Come often to practice with us. What you have so ably learned from me you can hereafter impress upon the monks. Until the next meeting gladdens our expectant gaze, farewell."

Ta-ming fastened the scarlet sword belt about his waist, then, bowing low, passed from the room. His mien was humble enough till the bamboo curtain fell behind him. Then he threw out his chest, his firm chin jerked up. Pride stiffened his back. He turned to go out the way he had come. But remembering it must be near the hour of evening prayer and that he would encounter none of the monks at this time, he decided on a shorter route and strode through an open arch into the monastery garden.

The world lay before him poetically serene. A zigzag path descended between shrubs not yet in flower to the bridge and the waterfall and the stream. Farther down, beyond a rock wall, nature ran riot in moss and trees. Below stretched the loamy soil of the farm, and his father's house in the center of a grove of pine and willow trees. Mother Chang and Father Chang—what faces would be theirs when he displayed his prize! And little Fa Fai—how round her black eyes would grow as she watched him executing swirls and passes in the yard. And Lung, and Po-ling, and baby

Yan—they must learn to keep their distance. Swordplay is dangerous play to the unwary.

The boy's pulse quickened in anticipation of showing off his treasure, and he hurried on. It was a fine day for walking. A brisk wind streamed off the mountain side. The sun, just about to set, laid its red shaft of light across the roof of a pagoda standing farther down the path. The sound of somebody beating a wooden drum fell on his ears, and the voices of monks singing an evening hymn. Ta-ming drew forth his sword to admire it. He carried the blade naked in his hand for the thrill of its glory. But at the wall bounding the monastery property he stopped to thrust the slim steel back into its scabbard. Once away from the path, the ground was far too rough for safe going with an unsheathed knife—besides, he wanted to run.

He leaped the wall at a handspring and scrambled and slithered down the steep hillside. As soon as his feet touched flat ground he started away at a deer's pace, springing over the ditches, spurred on by joyous expectation of Mother Chang's sure sympathy. The sword swung and bobbed against his body, and its unaccustomed touch made him feel every inch a man.

"I ought to have a uniform," the boy thought. "A uniform naturally goes with a sword."

That was the first time Ta-ming ever thought about wearing a uniform, but it was not to be the last.

THE LITTLE GREEN GOD

The landscape seemed to have been painted with a wash of blue and a wash of green. The vivid color of fresh crops challenged a cloudless sky. One white heron drifted across, flapping its wide wings lazily. Centering the picture, a grove of pine and willow trees indicated Chang's house. In the middle distance Ta-ming, a blot of bright cobalt several shades deeper than the azure heavens, bent over an irrigation pump, pedaling for dear life. The youth was so intent on his work, so deafened by its clatter, he did not hear the raucous noise of an approaching airplane till it was almost over him. Then he leaped from the pump and stood gazing upward, eyes and mouth open.

Rumor of these strange sky-carts in which men traveled had come to the farm, but this was the first one Ta-ming had ever seen. It was flying very high and looked extremely small, scarcely bigger than a swallow skimming the ground. He wished it would come down.

Always in Ta-ming's generous heart sprang an impulse to share good luck. He tore his fascinated eyes from the strange machine and cast a hasty glance toward the farmhouse. Around at the back he had left his brothers and sister busily weaving hempen rope, while little Yan ran in the yard, safe behind the bamboo fence, flying his kite. Yan's pigtail was tied with knots of red silk and his blue cotton trousers flapped wide in the breeze, where the tailor, for convenience' sake, had omitted to sew up the back seam. Now the kite tugged at its string, forgotten, while its navigator watched this strange new bird in the bright sky. He had raised an alarm with the shrill pipe of his four-year-old lungs:

"Foon Jiang! Da Foon Jiang! Flying kite!"

Mother Chang had run to him and, head thrown back, followed the direction of his glance. The children dropped their rope-weaving to gaze upward. Even Father Chang, hearing his wife's voice raised in excited "Quei Lai! Come quickly!" appeared at the door followed by old Fan Ju-lung, who had come that day to collect the rent and to inspect certain recent improvements in the farm sheds.

As if drawn by a single spell, the older people and the children began to move forward from the shelter of the trees. Ta-ming took it all in at a glance, then riveted his attention on the airplane. He felt glad to be out in the fields with a clear view. If only the thing would come down instead of passing out of sight beyond the wooded mountain!

The airplane banked and turned, began to circle slowly—ah! it was coming down. It grew in size as it descended in a gentle spiral. It was large now—threateningly large. The noise rushed at the watchers like a furious dragon beating fear into their brains—a harsh, unsteady, jerking noise. The machine seemed to be falling on them. Men crouched. Yan ran to his mother, crying. The children bolted for the shelter of the trees. Ta-ming stood rooted to the spot in a petrification of frantic joy as the plane raced clamorously above his head. He felt his hair rise at the roots, but he did not budge. His heart almost burst with excitement.

Suddenly the noise ceased. The great, ungainly, stiff-winged thing glided down and bumped hard on the ground. It rebounded and jarred down again, ran the whole length of the field and stopped, its wheels a foot from the lip of an irrigation ditch, its still propeller hanging perilously beyond the sluggish water.

Instantly the whole landscape seemed to come alive. The farmer's family and Fan Ju-lung dashed from the house. Neighbors ran from their fields. The women washing clothes by the stream which flowed from the monastery hill down the side of Chang's property, left their work and hurried over. But Ta-ming had the start of them all. The airplane was only a couple of plots from him. He bounded forward at top speed—*his* top speed, fast as a racing colt—and arrived as the aviator stepped from the fuselage.

"Great daddy! Here's a narrow escape from eternity!" the man sang out in a big, hearty voice when he saw how near the wheels stood to the brink of the ditch. "It takes some doing to land safely on these cursed checkerboards of wheat and rice."

This large person, in flying coat and helmet, was an American all the way from Illinois. Though he had been stationed a couple of months in China, flying his Curtis plane over and around Peking, he knew not a word of the language—not even a little pidgin English—so he delivered himself in outright, middle-west American. Ta-ming blinked as the stranger talked. He stared like a life-sized idol. But the second man, who was still sitting in a seat near the tail of the airplane, seemed to understand. Removing a cumbersome pair of goggles, he craned his neck over the side:

"What brought us down here, Bill?"

"Marksmanship—marksmanship—the hand of genius on the controls. You betcha! Nothing less would have landed us safely. These bed quilts of patchwork fields ain't so good, but that ridge of rock and evergreens might have been worse. And the engine was kicking like a doggone mule."

By this time the various storming parties had converged on the spot. They babbled at the aviator till his answering pantomime would have convinced any moron he was a deaf-mute. Then, as the passenger stepped from the plane, they suddenly realized he was Chinese and mobbed him, knocking from his hand a small box he was carrying.

"Greetings, wayfarer!" "Are you hurt?" "Have you eaten your rice?" "Is there anything we can do?" "Would you have some tea, honorable sir?"

"No, no, thank you. We are all right. Buddha is merciful!"

The stranger seemed more concerned about the safety of his

parcel than about his own comfort. He raised the box, which was bound in red fiber paper, and shook it gently, listening. Ta-ming suddenly felt a great curiosity to know what the parcel contained. He thought the owner, who was a young man, twenty-one or two, with a remarkably smooth and tranquil face, looked good-natured enough to tell him. He might have so far forgotten his manners as to ask, but at that moment Fan Ju-lung created a diversion. Older and stiffer-jointed than the farmers, the landowner could not run at the same speed, and being outdistanced had not improved his temper. Now he came hobbling up with a full-throated outcry against the damage done to his crops.

"Chia La Wu! Chia La Wu! What a mess you have made! Good grain ruined! These foreign devils bring destruction on our country. Who is going to pay me for my wheat?"

He glared at the long, double track the airplane had cut through his young crop, at the crowd trampling it underfoot, and at the aviator, while he shook his fists and raised his voice louder and louder. Nobody paid much attention, least of all the American. Grinning, Bill Carson jerked his head toward his passenger, and throwing off his heavy coat, turned to examine the engine. The growing throng of Chinese pressed around him, yelling to one another at the tops of their voices.

A moment later he spoke. "I've got one or two hours' work here, Mr. Yi. If you want to settle out of court with old Goat's Beard, you'd better move on up to the house and take the whole hive of them off my back or I'll go loco."

The Chinese gentleman bowed to Fan Ju-lung. "Do not distress yourself, worthy sir. The damage which has been done by our despicable machine will be adequately repaid. Let us proceed to the house of——"

He hesitated, looking about. Chang was pushed forward, several neighbors crying his name.

"—To the house of Chang, whose dutiful wife will perhaps make us a cup of tea while we discuss the fair amount of the damage."

Fan Ju-lung, mollified by these words, assumed a less belligerent attitude and, falling in beside the stranger, began to retrace his steps to the grove. Father Chang followed them, Mother Chang having run ahead, the children scuttling with her like a flock of chickens. The neighbors, who found a prospect of greater interest in the settlement of a damage case in good understandable Chinese than in watching a foreigner monkey with the inside of his machine, followed in a long line tailing out across the landscape.

According to the dictates of Chinese politeness, Fan began by asking the stranger a raft of highly personal questions, and those walking within hearing had their curiosity satisfied. They learned the gentleman who had so unexpectedly descended from heaven was Yi Putung of Shanghai. Despite his foreign clothes and fine manners, his serene face and hands as delicate as a lady's, he seemed to be in a forlorn position. His grandfather had been Tao Tai of a rich province—that is, a high official, next door to and in line for the governorship—but owing to political intrigues his promotion had failed. Both the father and the mother of the young man were dead, after many calamities, social and financial. He was now on his way to Mukden to interview the war lord, Marshal Wai, hoping to persuade that wealthy man to purchase the rare jade figure of the fire god, Fu Sen, which he carried in the red parcel under his arm.

Ta-ming was dogging his father's footsteps, ears alert. At the last news his face fell. Only a god in that thrilling-looking package! Every family in the countryside possessed at least one god. They were commonplace. The boy knew no art standard by which to distinguish the good from the inferior, the ordinary from the rare and beautiful, so he dismissed the parcel with a snort. Though he was disappointed in that matter, the person of Yi Putung thrilled him. This man with whom they talked was really going to meet the war lord! Amazing thought! His young heart burned with envy. "Oh, to be great," ambition cried in him. "A great man of the great world, able to ride in airplanes and meet marshals—and everything." What earthly use was there in working on a farm all one's life, when the world spread so wide and its possibilities seemed so breath-catching?

The youth still struggled with the overwhelming emotion of these thoughts when Yi Putung and his host entered the house. At one stride they stepped from the sweet spring odor of young crops and damp earth into heavy air tainted with incense. Ta-ming pushed his way in, hard on their heels, determined not to lose a word of the stranger's conversation.

The room ran into the pitch of the roof, for the house boasted only one story. It was meagerly furnished in unvarnished pine, and an image of Kwan Yin, Goddess of Mercy, occupied a niche in the central wall, with joss sticks burning before it. Mother Chang awaited her guests, beaming. She dusted off the best chair with her cotton sleeves and offered it to Yi Putung, then busied herself preparing tea.

The stranger was at first too preoccupied with anxiety over the safety of his treasured god to bother about eating or drinking. Placing the parcel on the table, he unknotted its fiber string and removed the paper. Underneath a second wrapping of silk lay a smooth wooden box, silk-lined and with a sliding top, such as is customarily used to protect the treasures of the Far East. Yi Putung's hands trembled as he opened the lid. The safety of this precious curio was very important to him. He lifted out a piece of dark green jade, and after examining it carefully set it on the table, sighing:

"Oi-ye! Unbroken. Buddha is indeed merciful."

None of the farmers crowding the room knew enough to appreciate the beauty of this rare carving, but Fan Ju-lung looked at it with interest. The figure, which stood about ten inches high, represented an elderly man clad in a graceful robe. His arms were folded. The thin lines of his long nails lay over his voluminous sleeves. His beard flowed across his breast as if driven by a strong wind, and his benevolent face regarded the world with the tranquil look of a philosopher.

"Old," said Fan Ju-lung, touching the cold jade reverently. "This doubtless belongs to the days of your illustrious grandfather's remote youth?"

"The carving was made originally for Yang Kwei-fei, the favorite of the Emperor Tang," Yi answered with the air of one conscious of making an impression, for those emperors had reigned from about 600 A.D. to 900.

That sent the landowner's brows up. "Indeed! A veritable antique. You are to be congratulated, worthy sir, on the possession of such an heirloom."

Yi Putung grimaced. "I am not so sure of it; the god is supposed to carry a malignant spell. Yang Kwei-fei was so fond of this carving that at the hour of her tragic death she ordered it to be buried with her. Whether her commands were disregarded, and Fu Sen retained by trickery or theft, or whether the god was recovered later from the tomb is not known. But certainly ill chance has haunted our house since the incomparable work of art fell into my ancestor's hands."

This speech roused indignation. Fan spoke sharply:

"You cannot expect success nor advancement from the powers which rule the Upper World so long as you dicker with Fi Gi—those cursed flying machines—and encourage the destruction by modern inventions which now menaces our land." He eyed with great disfavor the European clothes worn by Yi.

That gentleman, busy packing away his god, looked up surprised.

"Everything that is best in China is old," the landowner added combatively.

Yi smiled. "I cannot agree with you there, wise elder. China has too long been bound by such stick-in-the-mud philosophy. Under its spell she has withered and almost died. But gradually we improve. Take for instance the old system of education now happily replaced by modern schools."

"Hold your tongue, ill-begotten son of a ruined father!" Fan screamed, suddenly enraged.

The listening farmers grinned and winked at one another, for they knew old Fan Ju-lung was a crank on the subject of the great government examinations which for centuries had been held every third year. Students had come from all over the country to try their luck and skill, since success in these searching tests had meant place, power, and wealth. The examination ground, now destroyed, had been a vast area built over with small detached huts, each student having one to himself. There the would-be scholar entered in high hope and trembling expectation at the beginning of the examination period, and did not emerge again until the writing was completed, receiving his food in the hut, sleeping in it, and attending only to his papers.

Yi, knowing nothing of the landowner's peculiarities, regarded him blankly as he delivered his tirade.

"Mark my words. There will never be anything arranged to take adequately the place of the old system thrown out by this rash generation of nitwits like you. Your modern schools, your modern sciences are wasted time—all of them! The ancient knowledge which has raised our scholars to the pinnacle of wisdom for four thousand years is good enough for me—"

"But—" stammered the amazed and peacefully minded Yi Putung.

"My ears refrain from argument. I understand all you can say. My unworthy brain is not entirely devoid of learning. Did I not pass my provisional examination at Mukden and twice fail in the national competition——"

"Small blame to you for that," answered Yi with spirit. "To be shut up in a little hut, badly ventilated and worse lighted, lacking air and exercise for ten days, is a poor means of fitting a man to do his best brain work or display the extreme limit of what he knows——"

"Ah, you admit we knew something then. I tell you one needed to know everything for that test——"

"Everything—yes. And nothing—nothing of practical value. No science—no——"

"Science—pish! What benefit does science confer? When I failed the second time in the national examination I returned to live on the property my father left me, and since then every six months I have made the round of the farms, collecting rents and inspecting the stock and buildings. Would I have been better racing from end to end of the empire in a flying machine? All science does is to bring on us scourges of foreign devils with their calamities. You here—ruining my crops."

So it went on, Yi Putung praising the new, Fan defending the old. Ta-ming was bored. All at once he remembered the aviator and rushed out into the field again to learn how things were progressing. A few men had stayed by the American, watching with dull eyes and uncomprehending faces while he fiddled with his motor. The Chinese are essentially lacking in any turn for mechanism; moreover, these men and their ancestors had been occupied in agriculture through many generations. They were as dead to the language of wheels and cogs as to the words Bill Carson used.

At last the job was done. The engine ran like silk unrolling from a spool, and Carson, with vivid pantomime, tried to show the men that he wanted help in turning the machine around so that the ditch would lie behind her and her nose point up the field ready to take off.

He was getting the ideas over to them, slowly but surely, when a too willing helper suddenly thrust his shoulder against the fuselage and gave a mighty heave. Maybe he had just grasped the thought that Carson wanted the plane moved, maybe he was trying his strength to show off; anyway, the lurch started the unchocked wheels standing on the slight down grade. In a second they slid over the lip of the ditch and settled comfortably into the mud.

For the next five minutes the distracted aviator made the air red-hot with profanity. The ugly import of his words was lost upon his hearers, but his manner left no doubt about his wrath. The Chinese stood around stoically calm and let him rave away. He was still raving when Ta-ming arrived.

A live-wire mind did not need language to grasp what had happened. One glance told all. With intelligent gestures the boy suggested hoisting the plane out of the creek on the far side, so that it would stand facing up the second field. The ditch had been a natural stream before it was deepened and turned into part of the irrigation system, and it lay between two gentle slopes. Carson saw Ta-ming's plan would save the trouble of turning the plane around and nodded approval. The boy began jabbering Mandarin for a while, then walked away toward the farm shed, followed by several men. Carson waited, wondering. Presently they returned with a timber as heavy as lead. Using this for a lever, they pried the plane up, hauling, pushing, pulling it, till the wheels rolled over the far bank. From start to finish Ta-ming worked like an ox. He took command, too, barking directions at his helpers with the self-assurance of a general.

When it was done Carson fell back, mopping his face. He slapped Ta-ming on the shoulder, crying, "Bully for you, kid. You're a he-man!" He beamed on the boy, tested his biceps and felt his legs, hard as iron. "Gosh! What a youngster! He's the build of a heavy-weight, if not the size. Never saw anything to equal it."

The Chinese youth understood admiration in spite of the taboo on language. He flung off his cotton coat and exhibited the muscles flowing under his skin, smooth as a piece of polished jade. At that moment he longed, as never before, to show his skill with the sword and to give a boxing exhibition. But his sword hung at the bed head in his little room. There were no iron bars to bend beneath his heel and there was not a fighting man among the onlookers. All he could do was grin and stiffen his arm muscles till the aviator's grip fell from them.

"Any time you want a buddy, come to Illinois," said Carson, taking up his pilot coat.

Ta-ming understood that, also. With a swift access of impudent bravado he pointed from himself to the machine. The gesture was assertive, but his eyes pleaded like an expectant pup's. Bill read in them fierce desire, concentrated longing.

"Want to take a flip? Well—it's a risk coming down, and we'll have to turn her around. But I guess joy-riding always is risky. You've been a good, useful kid—hop in."

Tone, smile, gesture conveyed the sense lacking in his foreign words. He showed the watchers how to swing the propeller and how to pull the chocks. He threw Yi's jacket to the trembling boy, helped him climb into the cockpit, and saw the strap was buckled close. Then

Ta-ming climbed into the cockpit.

he took his own place. The engine started its throaty roar, the propeller cut its dangerous swath, the machine ran over the second field, zoomed and soared.

They were actually in the air only a few minutes. For Ta-ming it seemed two hours, a year, an incarnation. He stuck out his hand to feel the blast of the wind, and jerked it back quickly. He peered over the side. That world below him was another world—vaster, different, more magnificent. What a tiny pocket handkerchief the fields—the whole farm—looked! Ah! He would never be content on it again.

A sort of madness seized the boy. Like the lust of a carnivorous animal that first tastes blood, the flavor of romance burst upon Ta-ming's knowledge, upsetting all judgment, customs, calculation. Forms and traditions were grave clothes. Life teemed with adventure for those who went to it. Well—he would go. The great choice presented itself and found settlement all in a moment, swift as an arrow's flight. He would go.

Down again. There was no banging and bumping this time. Carson knew his bearings. They alighted as softly as a petal on the grass, and Ta-ming, stepping to the ground, was at once surrounded, for everybody had rushed out of the house as soon as they heard the motor roar.

The grain indemnity was settled, and the man from Shanghai had paid, leaving his purse perilously empty. He had offered to pay Mother Chang for her tea, which was politely repudiated. Then, picking up his red parcel, he had set out for the plane. The entire company followed him, trailing across the damaged crop and on into the second field. Fan Ju-lung had not counted on that. But, owing to the heat of their argument about schools, he had charged a staggering price for the original damage, so it was fair enough.

Placidly Yi Putung donned his coat and goggles and seated himself. The course was cleared of onlookers. With a rush and a roar the plane took off. The prophet of modernity had left them. Up—up—up she rose, then turned and headed for the land beyond the monastery hills. As soon as the plane vanished, a storm of chatter, question, and cackle broke loose on Ta-ming, deluging his ears. They asked him every conceivable thing about his sensations, and he answered politely, with never a word of his new hope or the set plan in his heart.

By twos and threes the neighbors returned to their farms. The women went back to their washing and Ta-ming to his pump. But his mind was no longer with the work.

Ambition boiled in him. He wanted to get away out of this valley, where crops were the beginning and end and middle of life, out into the real world where real things happened—big things! To Mukden, perhaps, but better still—Peking. Why should he not go to Peking and write his life in distinguished characters? The boy knew himself superior to all the people of those parts, except Fan Ju-lung. He had a brighter brain than any, and a far better body. Had not the lama called him the strongest boy in Manchuria?

When Ta-ming had finished his work, he started toward his home. Then, for the first time, he saw it as it was—a meager little place standing in the square of bamboo fence behind which pigs and chickens roamed. The house was built of mud and straw with a ridge-pole turned up saucily at both ends. Its yellow walls made a gay background for the weathered red posters on either side of the front door, crying aloud in gigantic characters for fair weather and heavy harvests. Shelter, security, peace, and a certain amount of comfort were all there. But the boy's heart turned from it. "Not large enough," was the verdict. "I've got to get out of this," he thought, as he trudged along the edge of the field. "Tomorrow, or maybe tonight after the hour of evening rice, I will speak to my father."

TA-MING DISOBEYS

Supper was served. The farmer's family, all but little Yan, sat around the table. Each held his bowl of rice close to his mouth and fed himself with chop-sticks at incredible speed. They all drank tea —quantities of strong, clear "green" tea. When the sharp edge of appetite had been lessened the boys began to pelt Ta-ming with questions.

"How did it feel up in the sky?"

"Could you see any birds?"

"Was it cold?"

"You had my mind torn to pieces in fright," said his mother as she set a dish of salted turnips and cabbage in the middle of the table. Yan, who had a tooth for cabbage, shoved into the circle and clamored to be served.

Ta-ming ladled a generous portion into the child's bowl. For a time the business of eating progressed undisturbed. Dusk was falling beneath the beams. Little light filtered through the paper panes of the small windows, both of which were carefully closed, as was the door. Under the table a fat chow dog gnawed an old bone, chickens pecked for crumbs. A piglet, which for some reason had refused to eat till its frame showed through its skin, lay in one corner wrapped in an old cotton quilt. When he had finished his own supper, Father Chang tried to make the creature eat out of an earthen pan, for a pig is a pig to a poor farmer. The animal only snorted, however, and rested on its side, stretching its legs out in hopeless fashion.

"The Fi Gi has caused us all to lose the best part of a day from our work," grumbled Chang.

That reminded the boys how rare such excitement was, and they rattled away with their string of questions faster than ever:

"Did you see us staring up at you, Ta-ming?"

"Did you see me put out my tongue and make a cat's face?"

"What's on the other side of the hills?"

"How big did the house look from up there?"

Ta-ming answered the last query without hesitation. "Big! The whole farm looked but a patch on a pair of kutes. It's a poor little place."

"It's plenty large enough when one has to sow the wheat," observed Chang.

Ta-ming took no notice of that remark. He went to his room to

Fed himself with chopsticks at an incredible speed.

get his sword. His room was a tiny place built on, like the outhouses, at right angles to the main wall. In crossing the court formed by the three wings of the house, and called the "well of heaven," he stopped to twitter to his blackbird. These birds, which have the appearance of crows and can be taught to talk like parrots, are rare Chinese pets. Ta-ming had caught Huk Fei (Black Queen) while she was very young, and prized her highly. His heart's allegiance was divided between his bird and his sword, now favoring one, now the other. They seemed equally alive to him and both needed his care. Returning with the sword, he sat down on the k'ang, a sort of brick bed built into the room, and began to polish the blade and rub up the carving on the handle.

"Come and play cat's cradle with me," teased Fa Fai.

"Oh, I can't tonight. I haven't the time tonight. Get Lung to do it," her elder brother answered.

"Lung occupies himself with his studies. Besides, his worthless fingers are stiff as a goat's horns," she said fretfully.

It was almost dark by now. Lung, a couple of years younger than Ta-ming and much smaller, lighted one of those little tin lamps which the Standard Oil Company has spread from one end of China to the other, and placed it on the table. He settled himself with an abacus, the small wooden frame and lines of counters used by the Chinese in doing arithmetic, and concentrated his mind on his work. The farmer smoked his water pipe in silence. Mother Chang moved into the small circle of the lamplight with her endless sewing in her hand. Yan had fallen asleep in his cotton day clothes on the pig's bed and would not wake till morning. Fa Fei and Po-ling quarreled quietly.

It was the hour of rest and relaxation, but Ta-ming's busy mind worked faster than before. He was turning over and over his big idea of a new life. His heart pounded. The pulses in his temples showed how the blood swept through his veins. This might be a good time to speak to his father. He wished the youngsters would go to bed, but knew there was no chance of that. Po-ling's voice came softly now, telling Fa Fei, for the thousandth time, the story of Wu Chung, the tiger killer:

In the remote ages this terrible person, Wu, known as the greatest hunter of his day, traveled through the grassy plains toward the home of his reverend grandmother, for time approached the New Year and all who could returned to the tombs of their ancestors to worship their imperishable memory. As Wu journeyed, he came to a branch of the forest and threw himself down under its tall trees to rest from the glare of the noonday sun. Being weary beyond enduring, he fell asleep and slept heavily until the evening.

The spot where Wu had carelessly flung himself lay near the mouth of a grass tunnel which was a tiger runway leading into the flat country. In his exalted dreams the honorable hunter heard a rustling as of a stealthy body moving through grass. He awoke and listened, staring up at the stars blinking through the open spaces of the branches. That rustle—rustle—in the grass drew nearer.

"Every road leads in two directions," thought Wu, and turned his sight from the contemplation of the upper heaven toward the path opposite that by which he had approached. There stretched the dim grayness of the starlit plain. Between him and its expanse hung two amber eyes burning like fire coals.

Wu rose on his elbow to take a better look. As he did so, he realized the tiger saw him and was about to spring. He leaped to his feet, slapping one hand on his honorable thigh for his knife. But before he could draw the blade a tawny streak launched itself into the air. Having no time to draw his weapon, defenseless save for his iron muscles, the great hunter received the savage enemy. He closed upon the animal with his naked hands and, exercising his almost superhuman strength, tore the great jaws apart. At the end of the memorable encounter the beast's carcass lay bleeding on the ground.

Thus runs the story of Wu, the tiger killer. A Chinese classic, as well known throughout the empire as is the story of Samson and the lion, or of Little Red Riding Hood, in English-speaking countries.

Ta-ming had seen it on the stage. He wondered if the tale were true. He had been told it was familiar all over China. Was that so? Who could say? What did he know about the rest of his vast country?

Realization of his ignorance shot through him like a twinge of pain and suddenly he spoke:

"When you have climbed Tai Shan the whole world looks small below——" Lung jerked his head around at this quotation from the Four Books of Confucius, but his brother went right on without taking any notice:

"It is the greatest sensation in life to be up high and look down, and see the smallness of the old place. To look out and discover the land extending on every side. To feel that you could get away there and—and do something there—something big!"

The outburst fell among them like a bomb. Mother Chang started and looked up alarmed. Po-ling's voice abruptly ceased.

"What do you mean by 'big'?" asked Chang in a quiet tone.

"Anything's better than working on a farm."

"Our family have always been farmers. Would you presume to improve on the pursuits of your noble ancestors?"

"I want to go away," said the boy stubbornly. "I want to get out and do something and see the world—and—oh, what's the use of sticking here forever like a frog in a hole!"

"But it is here you earn your food." His mother's voice held a note of pleading.

"I could earn it elsewhere." The full pride of his physical strength welled in Ta-ming's tone.

Chang asked impassively, "What would you do?"

His son was scarcely prepared for the straight thrust of that question. His mind had not settled details yet. The entire possible future hung like a lovely mirage half revealed and half obscured by distance. So he stammered the first thing that came into his mind:

"I—I could be a soldier."

The farmer frowned, quoting:

"Good iron will not be a nail.
A good man will not be a soldier."

"That's the old army!" cried Ta-ming. "Soldiers learn a lot of things now. I might learn to drive a Fi Gi."

Lung laughed outright. "Ha, ha, ha! Listen to his unqualified impertinence. Ta-ming thinks because he can swing a sword he may compete with students. None but a leper would contend that brawn has ever equaled brain. I am the one who must penetrate the Outer Spaces——"

"Do not disturb our consultation with your ill-considered speech," Chang remarked mildly. Then he said to his eldest son, "Have you thought, my boy, of what it would mean to me to lose you?"

Ta-ming hung his head, for he had been thinking of nothing else all the afternoon. His amazing strength enabled him to do, even at his age, a full man's work on the farm. For years he had been his father's right hand. Lung, being small and thinking only of books, was as good as useless in such matters. The modern system of education adopted in the village school had not altered the Chinese reverence for the student, nor did Lung intend to give up his privilege of idleness and alternate learning with physical work. In this he heartily seconded Fan Ju-lung's protest that the old ways are the best ways. There was but one answer to give to the farmer's question and Ta-ming did not give it.

A long silence fell in the close little room—a potent hush wrapping them around like a fog. It seemed to muffle and shut in the small sounds of family life which had filled the place ten minutes earlier. Mother Chang's hands lay idle. The children's story was untold.

All at once the pig gave a snort. Chang rose to look at it, but before he crossed the room he spoke: "It is better to put from your mind for all time this idea of leaving the tablets of your fathers."

Ta-ming's face paled. His heart dropped into his cloth shoes. In China the word of the head of the house is law. It would be as useful to open a paper umbrella in a thunderstorm as to try to reason against Chang's decision. Since his father said he could not go, he could not. Independence swept into the boy's spirit like a flash of lightning. Why should it mean he could not go?

He put the evil thought from him instantly. The teachings of Confucius enjoin the strict observance of the parent's word. Supreme obedience is the ideal laid down in the Writings. Ta-ming had always been a good boy. He was alarmed at his own audacity in even thinking of taking his own way. But once thought has started, it acts too often like a wild colt holding the bit in its teeth, plunging on unrestrained.

That idea of liberty went with Ta-ming when he strode away to his room. It dogged him while he took off his outer clothes. It sat on a reach of his mind like a bird on a limb as he lay in his wooden bunk under the old cotton pad.

"Filial piety is good, doubtless—but to remain a farmer grubbing in the ground one's whole life is a hard thing for a dragon who longs to soar in the heavens. If I go out and make a place for myself, that will amply repay my disobedience. The credit of having a talented son would surely straighten the past with my parents." Long hours Ta-ming tossed about. He had confused and noble visions of himself—at times a great aviator, at times a general in a glittering uniform. Whatever his father might say against soldiers, he would never object to his son's being a general!

Ta-ming rose and lighted a wax candle. He took from a carved redwood box, the only furniture in his room except his bunk, a small toy arrow. This was his third treasure. His arrow, his sword, and his bird made up the sum of his possessions. But the arrow, now preserved for sentimental reasons, had once been his only joy. It was of wood, rather blunted at the point and having a scrap of a feather still jauntily stuck to the other end. His aunt, Ah Mu, had brought it to him once when she returned for her periodical visit before his grandmother's death. It had been bought in a stall at a great festival and had always shone for its young owner with the glamour of those imagined gayeties. Now he held it in his hand, regarding it silently. The flight of the arrow—the flight of the Fi Gi—his own flight. They seemed to lead on naturally, each but an enlargement of the last. Fate seemed at that moment to be forcing him out into the world—out and up.

For an instant the boy's spirit recoiled. Assurance of the farm's homely comfort and security overflowed him. To have no bed in which to lie, no rice waiting in the morning. How would he like that?

His eyes turned from side to side of the little enclosure, his room. Not often did a Chinese farm boy have a room to himself. To be sure, he had cleaned it out, patched the roof, repaired the walls—what one works for intelligently one can enjoy. Suddenly the walls seemed to stifle him. He must go—he must go! His father would miss him, of course, and he would miss his mother. Between Ta-ming and the placid-faced woman, Chang's wife, who was so abundantly contented, a daughter of the soil, soaked with the illusive forces of nature, there existed one of those great loves of parent for children and children for parent which are the strong romance of China. He would miss his mother. And his mother—would her heart break? Ta-ming felt she had too much confidence in him to worry about him. While his feet were carrying him abroad into immense adventure, her mind would already be welcoming him back. She would forgive him, for she would understand. Swiftly it was born in on Ta-ming that his mother not only understood but longed for him to go. He recalled the look in her soft brown eyes last night as she had sat hands folded, listening.

Tenderness filled his spirit. He would have liked to hug her once for good-bye. Years had passed since their last embrace. It is not the custom in China for boys to caress their mothers after they have passed out of young childhood. Besides, she would be asleep and Ta-ming dare not risk waking her. But he would leave her a message—a message she could read, if no other.

He slid back the frame of his paper window and peered out. A lopsided moon had risen and bathed the sleeping world in light. The strong draft extinguished his candle, but Ta-ming's eyes were avid as a cat's. He could see quite well by the sky lantern. He fastened on his sword and stuck the arrow into his belt. Then he took from the redwood chest a clay box into which he had slipped one by one the few cash he had bragged of to the lama. This was his own money—his life savings. A sharp tap with the back of his sword broke the box. Ta-ming did not wait to count. However little it was, it must do. He hurried to fasten it securely into his cotton coat.

Then he opened the door and moved across the court to his pet. The bird slept on her perch, a ball of feathers, her head hidden under one wing. Ta-ming inserted his hand and lifted Huk Fei gently from the cage. Still holding the startled creature, he set her quivering feet on his finger and laid his cheek against her frightened heart. This was the supreme sacrifice necessary to his going. His mother he would see again, but, once at large, Huk Fei would not return. Sentiment bade Ta-ming let the captive free to celebrate her master's freedom. Moreover, he was afraid to leave her in the cage lest she be neglected and maybe die. In his absence who would take care of the bird? His mother was busy from morning till night. Lung heeded nothing but his everlasting books. Po-ling would laugh and shirk the duty. Fa Fai would forget. No, he must let the prisoner free. The blackbird was strutting on his wrist now. Slowly Ta-ming raised the hand above his head and swung it from him. Huk Fei took flight. An instant her dark form blotted the moon, then vanished among the willow trees.

With a lump in his throat, Ta-ming turned toward the house. Silent as a ghost he entered. His parents slept on the k'ang, joined in the winter by most of their children, for the brick bed had a fire underneath it and was the most comfortable spot in cold weather. Tonight only Fa Fai snuggled at their feet.

The room looked eerie in the stifled moonlight struggling through the closed paper panes and the partly open door. The clumsy cotton loom on one side and the agricultural implements stacked opposite rose like grim dragons. Baskets and jars of grain littered the floor against the walls, and a queer variety of things dangled from the sooty roof. These, swayed by the draft of the open door, seemed to beckon Ta-ming to enter.

On tiptoe the boy approached the sleepers. His father's form was turned to the wall, his face hidden by one upflung arm. His mother reposed on her back, the cotton cover drawn to her chin. Her breath came evenly. Fascinated, Ta-ming stood a long time watching the blur of her round face, the closed beloved almond eyes, the slightly open mouth. At last he took his little arrow, the treasure of his childhood, and laid it lightly on the bed between his parents. This was his message to her. When his mother saw his open window she would know he was a captive freed. The empty bird cage would tell her how he intended to soar for the family honor. And the arrow promised that he meant to make use of his talents in a direct course.

Softly Ta-ming closed the house door behind him and struck across under the trees by the path to the road. The moon had slid down the heavens. Its oblique shining laid tree shadows in long, dark tiger stripes over the brown earth. Frogs croaked in the ditches, mysteriously obscured by a thin mist lying over the fields. Nowhere was any trace of yesterday's strange visitors but in the boy's strange going.

A sturdy figure he looked, clad in a blue cotton coat and trousers. A close-fitting black cloth hat with a black button on top covered his head, and white cotton stockings and his best black cloth shoes covered his feet, while his short sword swung on his hip. Ta-ming paid no heed to the scarred fields or the noisy frogs as he marched away to seek his destiny.

ABOUT ELIZABETH ELIZA'S PIANO

By LUCRETIA P. HALE

Illustrations by HAROLD BRETT

ELIZABETH ELIZA had a present of a piano, and she was to take lessons of the postmaster's daughter. They decided to have the piano set across the window in the parlor, and the carters brought it in, and went away.

After they had gone the family all came in to look at the piano; but they found the carters had placed it with its back turned toward the middle of the room, standing close against the window.

How could Elizabeth Eliza open it? How could she reach the keys to play upon it?

Solomon John proposed that they should open the window, which Agamemnon could do with his long arms. Then Elizabeth Eliza should go round upon the piazza, and open the piano. Then she could have her music-stool on the piazza, and play upon the piano there.

So they tried this; and they all thought it was a very pretty sight to see Elizabeth Eliza playing on the piano, while she sat on the piazza, with the honeysuckle vines behind her.

It was very pleasant, too, moonlight evenings. Mr. Peterkin liked to take a doze on his sofa in the room; but the rest of the family liked to sit on the piazza. So did Elizabeth Eliza, only she had to have her back to the moon.

All this did very well through the summer; but, when the fall came, Mr. Peterkin thought the air was too cold from the open window, and the family did not want to sit out on the piazza.

Elizabeth Eliza practised in the mornings with her cloak on; but she was obliged to give up her music in the evenings, the family shivered so.

One day, when she was talking with the lady from Philadelphia, she spoke of this trouble.

The lady from Philadelphia looked surprised, and then said, "But why don't you turn the piano round?"

One of the little boys pertly said, "It is a square piano."

But Elizabeth Eliza went home directly, and, with the help of Agamemnon and Solomon John, turned the piano round.

"Why did we not think of that before?" said Mrs. Peterkin. "What shall we do when the lady from Philadelphia goes home again?"

SOLOMON JOHN GOES FOR APPLES

By LUCRETIA P. HALE

Illustrations by WARREN CHAPPELL

SOLOMON JOHN agreed to ride to Farmer Jones's for a basket of apples, and he decided to go on horseback. The horse was brought round to the door. Now he had not ridden for a great while; and, though the little boys were there to help him, he had great trouble in getting on the horse.

He tried a great many times, but always found himself facing the wrong way, looking at the horse's tail. They turned the horse's head, first up the street, then down the street; it made no difference; he always made some mistake, and found himself sitting the wrong way.

"Well," said he, at last, "I don't know as I care. If the horse has his head in the right direction, that is the main thing. Sometimes I ride this way in the cars, because I like it better. I can turn my head easily enough, to see where we are going." So off he went, and the little boys said he looked like a circus-rider, and they were much pleased.

He rode along out of the village, under the elms, very quietly. Pretty soon he came to a bridge, where the road went across a little stream. There was a road at the side, leading down to the stream, because sometimes wagoners watered their horses there. Solomon John's horse turned off, too, to drink of the water.

"Very well," said Solomon John, "I don't blame him for wanting to wet his feet, and to take a drink, this hot day."

When they reached the middle of the stream, the horse bent over his head.

"How far his neck comes into his back!" exclaimed Solomon John; and at that very moment he found he had slid down over the horse's head, and was sitting on a stone, looking into the horse's face. There were two frogs, one on each side of him, sitting just as he was, which pleased Solomon John, so he began to laugh instead of to cry. But the two frogs jumped into the water.

"It is time for me to go on," said Solomon John. So he gave a jump, as he had seen the frogs do; and this time he came all right on the horse's back, facing the way he was going.

"It is a little pleasanter," said he.

The horse wanted to nibble a little of the grass by the side of the way; but Solomon John remembered what a long neck he had, and would not let him stop.

At last he reached Farmer Jones, who gave him his basket of apples.

Next he was to go on to a cider-mill, up a little lane by Farmer Jones's house, to get a jug of cider. But as soon as the horse was turned into the lane, he began to walk very slowly—so slowly that Solomon John thought he would not get there before night. He whistled, and shouted, and thrust his knees into the horse, but still he would not go.

"Perhaps the apples are too heavy for him," said he. So he began by throwing one of the apples out of the basket. It hit the fence by the side of the road, and that started up the horse and he went on merrily.

"That was the trouble," said Solomon John; "that apple was too heavy for him."

But very soon the horse began to go slower and slower.

So Solomon John thought he would try another apple. This hit a large rock, and bounded back under the horse's feet and sent him off at a great pace. But very soon he fell again into a slow walk.

Solomon John had to try another apple. This time it fell into a pool of water and made a great splash, and set the horse off again for a little while; he soon returned to a slow walk—so slow that Solomon John thought it would be tomorrow morning before he got to the cider-mill.

"It is rather a waste of apples," thought he; "but I can pick them up as I come back, because the horse will be going home at a quick pace."

So he flung out another apple; that fell among a party of ducks, and they began to make such a quacking and a waddling that it frightened the horse into a quick trot.

So the only way Solomon John could make his horse go was by flinging his apples, now on one side, now on the other. One time he frightened a cow, that ran along by the side of the road while the horse raced with her. Another time he started up a brood of turkeys that gobbled and strutted enough to startle twenty horses. In another place he came near hitting a boy, who gave such a scream that it sent the horse off at a furious rate.

And Solomon John got quite excited himself, and he did not stop till he had thrown away all his apples and had reached the corner of the cider-mill.

"Very well," said he, "if the horse is so lazy, he won't mind my stopping to pick up the apples on the way home. And I am not sure but I shall prefer walking a little to riding the beast."

The man came out to meet him from the cider-mill, and reached him the jug. He was just going to take it, when he turned his horse's head round, and, delighted at the idea of going home, the horse set off at a full run without waiting for the jug. Solomon John clung to the reins, and his knees held fast to the horse. He called out "Whoa! whoa!" but the horse would not stop.

He went galloping on past the boy, who stopped and flung an apple at him; past the turkeys, that came and gobbled at him; by the cow, that turned and ran back in a race with them until her breath gave out; by the ducks, that came and quacked at him; by an old donkey, that brayed over the wall at him; by some hens, that ran into the road under the horse's feet and clucked at him; by a great rooster, that stood up on a fence and crowed at him; by Farmer Jones, who looked out to see what had become of him; down the village street, and he never stopped till he had reached the door of the house.

Out came Mr. and Mrs. Peterkin, Agamemnon, Elizabeth Eliza, and the little boys.

Solomon John got off his horse all out of breath.

"Where is the jug of cider?" asked Mrs. Peterkin.

"It is at the cider-mill," said Solomon John.

"At the mill!" exclaimed Mrs. Peterkin.

"Yes," said Solomon John; "the little boys had better walk out for it; they will enjoy it; and they had better take a basket; for on the way they will find plenty of apples scattered all along on either side of the lane, and hens, and ducks, and turkeys, and a donkey."

The little boys looked at each other, and went; but they stopped first, and put on their India-rubber boots.

A TRAGEDY IN MILLINERY

By
KATE DOUGLAS WIGGIN

I

EMMA JANE PERKINS'S new winter dress was a blue and green Scotch plaid poplin, trimmed with narrow green velvet ribbon and steel nail-heads. She had a gray jacket of thick furry cloth with large steel buttons up the front, a pair of green kid gloves, and a gray felt hat with an encircling band of bright green feathers. The band began in front with a bird's head and ended behind with a bird's tail, and angels could have desired no more beautiful toilette. That was her opinion, and it was shared to the full by Rebecca.

But Emma Jane, as Rebecca had once described her to Mr. Adam Ladd, was a rich blacksmith's daughter, and she, Rebecca, was a little half-orphan from a mortgaged farm "up Temperance way," dependent upon her spinster aunts for board, clothes, and schooling. Scotch plaid poplins were manifestly not for her, but dark-colored woolen stuffs were, and mittens, and last winter's coats and furs.

And how about hats? Was there hope in store for her there? she wondered, as she walked home from the Perkins house, full of admiration for Emma Jane's winter outfit, and loyally trying to keep that admiration free from wicked envy. Her red-winged black hat was her second best, and although it was shabby she still liked it, but it would never do for church, even in Aunt Miranda's strange and never-to-be-comprehended views of suitable raiment.

There was a brown felt turban in existence, if one could call it existence when it had been rained on, snowed on, and hailed on for two seasons; but the trimmings had at any rate perished quite off the face of the earth, that was one comfort!

Emma Jane had said, rather indiscreetly, that at the village milliner's at Milliken's Mills there was a perfectly elegant pink breast to be had, a breast that began in a perfectly elegant solferino and terminated in a perfectly elegant magenta: two colors much in vogue at that time. If the old brown hat was to be her portion yet another winter, would Aunt Miranda conceal its deficiencies from a carping world beneath the shaded solferino breast? *Would* she, that was the question?

Filled with these perplexing thoughts, Rebecca entered the brick house, hung up her hood in the entry, and went into the dining room.

Miss Jane was not there, but Aunt Miranda sat by the window with her lap full of sewing things, and a chair piled with pasteboard boxes by her side. In one hand was the ancient, battered, brown felt turban, and in the other were the orange and black porcupine quills from Rebecca's last summer's hat; from the hat of the summer before that, and the summer before that, and so on back to prehistoric ages of which her childish memory kept no specific record, though she was sure that Temperance and Riverboro society did. Truly a sight to chill the blood of any eager young dreamer who had been looking at gayer plumage!

Miss Sawyer glanced up for a second with a satisfied expression, and then bent her eyes again upon her work.

"If I was going to buy a hat trimming," she said, "I could n't select anything better or more economical than these quills! Your mother had them when she was married, and you wore them the day you come to the brick house from the farm; and I said to myself then that they looked kind of outlandish, but I've grown to like 'em now I've got used to 'em. You've been here for goin' on two years and they've hardly be'n out o' wear, summer or winter, more'n a month to a time! I declare they do beat all for service! It don't seem as if your mother could 'a' chose 'em—Aurelia was always such a poor buyer! The black spills are 'bout as good as new, but the orange ones are gittin' a little mite faded and shabby. I wonder if I could n't dip all of 'em in shoe blackin'? It seems real queer to put a porcupine into hat trimmin', though I declare I don't know jest what the animiles are like, it's be'n so long sence I looked at the pictures of 'em in a geography. I always thought their quills stood out straight and angry, but these kind o' curls round some at the ends, and that makes 'em stand the wind better. How do you like 'em on the brown felt?" she asked, inclining her head in a discriminating attitude and poising them awkwardly on the hat with her work-stained hand.

How did she like them on the brown felt indeed?

Miss Sawyer had not been looking at Rebecca, but the child's eyes were flashing, her bosom heaving, and her cheeks glowing with sudden rage and despair. All at once something happened. She forgot that she was speaking to an older person; forgot that she was dependent; forgot everything but her disappointment at losing the solferino breast, remembering nothing but the enchanting, dazzling beauty of Emma Jane Perkins's winter outfit; and, suddenly, quite without warning, she burst into a torrent of protest.

"I will *not* wear those hateful porcupine quills again this winter! I will not! It's wicked, *wicked* to expect me to! Oh! how I wish there never had been any porcupines in the world, or that all of them had died before silly, hateful people ever thought of trimming hats with them! They curl round and tickle my ear! They blow against my cheek and sting it like needles! They do look outlandish, you said so yourself a minute ago. Nobody ever had any but only just me! The only porcupine was made into the only quills for me and nobody else! I wish instead of sticking *out* of the nasty beasts, that they stuck *into* them, same as they do into my cheek! I suffer, suffer, suffer, wearing them and hating them, and they will last forever and forever, and when I'm dead and can't help myself, somebody'll rip them out of my last year's hat and stick them on my head, and I'll be buried in them! Well, when *I* am buried *they* will be, that's one good thing! Oh, if I ever have a child I'll let her choose her own feathers and not make her wear ugly things like pigs' bristles and porcupine quills!"

With this lengthy tirade Rebecca vanished like a meteor, through the door and down the street, while Miranda Sawyer gasped for breath, and prayed to Heaven to help her understand such human whirlwinds as this Randall niece of hers.

This was at three o'clock, and at half-past three Rebecca was kneeling on the rag carpet with her head in her aunt's apron, sobbing her contrition.

"Oh! Aunt Miranda, do forgive me if you can. It's the only time I've been bad for months! You know it is! You know you said last week I had n't been any trouble lately. Something broke inside of me and came tumbling out of my mouth in ugly words! The porcupine quills make me feel just as a bull does when he sees a red cloth; nobody understands how I suffer with them!"

Miranda Sawyer had learned a few lessons in the last two years, lessons which were making her (at least on her "good days") a trifle kinder, and at any rate a juster woman than she used to be. When she alighted on the wrong side of her four-poster in the morning, or felt an extra touch of rheumatism, she was still grim and unyielding; but sometimes a curious sort of melting process seemed to go on within her, when her whole bony structure softened, and her eyes grew less vitreous. At such moments Rebecca used to feel as if a superincumbent iron pot had been lifted off her head, allowing her to breathe freely and enjoy the sunshine.

"Well," she said finally, after staring first at Rebecca and then at the porcupine quills, as if to gain some insight into the situation—"well, I never, sence I was born int' the world, heerd such a speech as you've spoke, an' I guess there probably never was one. You'd better tell the minister what you said and see what he thinks of his prize Sunday-school scholar. But I'm too old and tired to scold and fuss, and try to train you same as I did at first. You can punish yourself this time, like you used to. Go fire something down the well, same as you did your pink parasol! You've apologized and we won't say no more about it today, but I expect you to show by extry good conduct how sorry you be! You care altogether too much about your looks and your clothes for a child, and you've got a temper that'll certainly land you in state's prison some o' these days!"

Rebecca wiped her eyes and laughed aloud. "No, no, Aunt Miranda, it won't really! That was n't temper; I don't get angry with *people;* but only, once in a long while, with things; like those—cover them up quick before I begin again! I'm all right! Shower's over, sun's out!"

Miss Miranda looked at her searchingly and uncomprehendingly. Rebecca's state of mind came perilously near to disease, she thought.

"Have you seen me buyin' any new bunnits, or your Aunt Jane?" she asked cuttingly. "Is there any particular reason why you should dress better than your elders? You might as well know that we're short of cash just now, your Aunt Jane and me, and have no intention of riggin' you out like a Milltown fact'ry girl."

"Oh-h!" cried Rebecca, the quick tears starting again to her eyes and the color fading out of her cheeks, as she scrambled up from her knees to a seat on the sofa beside her aunt. "Oh-h! how ashamed I am! Quick, sew those quills on to the brown turban while I'm good! If I can't stand them I'll make a neat little gingham bag and slip it over them!"

And so the matter ended, not as it customarily did, with cold words on Miss Miranda's part and bitter feelings on Rebecca's, but with a gleam of mutual understanding.

Mrs. Cobb, who was a master hand at coloring, dipped the offending quills in brown dye and left them to soak in it all night, not only making them a nice warm color, but somewhat weakening their rocky spines, so that they were not quite as rampantly hideous as before, in Rebecca's opinion.

Then Mrs. Perkins went to her bandbox in the attic and gave Miss Dearborn some pale blue velvet, with which she bound the brim of the brown turban and made a wonderful rosette, out of which the porcupine's defensive armor sprang, buoyantly and gallantly, like the plume of Henry of Navarre.

Rebecca was resigned, if not greatly comforted, but she had grace enough to conceal her feelings, now that she knew economy was at the root of some of her aunt's decrees in matters of dress; and she managed to forget the solferino breast, save in sleep, where a vision of it had a way of appearing to her, dangling from the ceiling, and dazzling her so with its rich color that she used to hope the milliner would sell it that she might never be tempted with it when she passed the shop window.

One day, not long afterwards, Miss Miranda borrowed Mr. Perkins's horse and wagon and took Rebecca with her on a drive to Union, to see about some sausage meat and head cheese. She intended to call on Mrs. Cobb, order a load of pine wood from Mr. Strout on the way, and leave some rags for a rug with old Mrs. Pease, so that the journey could be made as profitable as possible, consistent with the loss of time and the wear and tear on her second-best black dress.

The red-winged black hat was forcibly removed from Rebecca's head just before starting, and the nightmare turban substituted.

"You might as well begin to wear it first as last," remarked Miranda, while Jane stood in the side door and sympathized secretly with Rebecca.

"I will!" said Rebecca, ramming the stiff turban down on her head with a vindictive grimace, and snapping the elastic under her long braids; "but it makes me think of what Mr. Robinson said when the minister told him his mother-in-law would ride in the same buggy with him at his wife's funeral."

"I can't see how any speech of Mr. Robinson's, made years an' years ago, can have anything to do with wearin' your turban down to Union," said Miranda, settling the lap robe over her knees.

"Well, it can; because he said: 'Have it that way, then, but it'll spile the hull blamed trip for me!' "

Jane closed the door suddenly, partly because she experienced a desire to smile (a desire she had not felt for years before Rebecca came to the brick house to live), and partly because she had no wish to overhear what her sister would say when she took in the full significance of Rebecca's anecdote, which was a favorite one with Mr. Perkins.

It was a cold blustering day, with a high wind that promised to bring an early fall of snow. The trees were stripped bare of leaves, the ground was hard, and the wagon wheels rattled noisily over the thank-you-ma'ams.

"I'm glad I wore my Paisley shawl over my cloak," said Miranda. "Be you warm enough, Rebecca? Tie that white rigolette tighter round your neck. The wind fairly blows through my bones. I most wish 't we'd waited till a pleasanter day, for this Union road is all up hill or down, and we shan't get over the ground fast, it's so rough. Don't forget, when you go into Scott's, to say I want all the trimmin's when they send me the pork, for mebbe I can try out a little mite o' lard. The last load o' pine's gone turrible quick; I must see if 'Bijah Flagg can't get us some cut-rounds at the Mills, when he hauls for Squire Bean next time. Keep your mind on your drivin', Rebecca, and don't look at the trees and the sky so much. It's the same sky and same trees that have been here right along. Go awful slow down this hill and walk the hoss over Cook's Brook bridge, for I always suspicion it's goin' to break down under me, an' I should n't want to be dropped into that fast runnin' water this cold day. It'll be froze stiff by this time next week. Had n't you better get out and lead"—

The rest of the sentence was very possibly not vital, but at any rate it was never completed, for in the middle of the bridge a fierce gale of wind took Miss Miranda's Paisley shawl and blew it over her head. The long heavy ends whirled in opposite directions and wrapped themselves tightly about her wavering bonnet. Rebecca had the whip and the reins, and in trying to rescue her struggling aunt could not steady her own hat, which was suddenly torn from her head and tossed against the bridge rail, where it trembled and flapped for an instant.

"My hat! oh! Aunt Miranda, my hateful hat!" cried Rebecca, never remembering at the instant how often she had prayed that the "fretful porcupine" might some time vanish in this violent manner, since it refused to die a natural death.

She had already stopped the horse, so, giving her aunt's shawl one last desperate twitch, she slipped out between the wagon wheels, and darted in the direction of the hated object, the loss of which had dignified it with a temporary value and importance.

The stiff brown turban rose in the air, then dropped and flew along the bridge; Rebecca pursued; it danced along and stuck between two of the railings; Rebecca flew after it, her long braids floating in the wind.

"Come back! Come back! Don't leave me alone with the team. I won't have it! Come back, and leave your hat!"

Miranda had at length extricated herself from the submerging shawl, but she was so blinded by the wind, and so confused that she did not measure the financial loss involved in her commands.

Rebecca heard, but her spirit being in arms, she made one more mad scramble for the vagrant hat, which now seemed possessed with an evil spirit, for it flew back and forth, and bounded here and there, like a living thing, finally distinguishing itself by blowing between the horse's front and hind legs, Rebecca trying to circumvent it by going around the wagon, and meeting it on the other side.

It was no use; as she darted from behind the wheels the wind gave the hat an extra whirl, and scurrying in the opposite direction it soared above the bridge rail and disappeared into the rapid water below.

"Get in again!" cried Miranda, holding on her bonnet, "You

done your best and it can't be helped, I only wish't I'd let you wear your black hat as you wanted to; and I wish't we'd never come such a day! The shawl has broke the stems of the velvet geraniums in my bonnet, and the wind has blowed away my shawl pin and my back comb. I'd like to give up and turn right back this minute, but I don't like to borrer Perkins's hoss again this month. When we get up in the woods you can smooth your hair down and tie the rigolette over your head and settle what's left of my bonnet; it'll be an expensive errant, this will!"

II

It was not till next morning that Rebecca's heart really began its song of thanksgiving. Her Aunt Miranda announced at breakfast, that as Mrs. Perkins was going to Milliken's Mills, Rebecca might go too, and buy a serviceable hat.

"You must n't pay over two dollars and a half, and you must n't get the pink bird without Mrs. Perkins says, and the milliner says, that it won't fade nor moult. Don't buy a light-colored felt because you'll get sick of it in two or three years, same as you did the brown one. I always liked the shape of the brown one, and you'll never get another trimmin' that'll wear you like them quills."

"I hope not!" thought Rebecca.

"If you had put your elastic under your chin, same as you used to, and not worn it behind because you think it's more grown-up an' fash'onable, the wind never'd 'a' took the hat off your head, and you would n't 'a' lost it; but the mischief's done and you can go right over to Mis' Perkins now, so you won't miss her nor keep her waitin'. The two dollars and a half is in an envelope side o' the clock."

Rebecca swallowed the last spoonful of picked-up codfish on her plate, wiped her lips, and rose from her chair happier than the seraphs in Paradise.

The porcupine quills had disappeared from her life, and without any fault or violence on her part. She was wholly innocent and virtuous, but nevertheless she was going to have a new hat with the solferino breast, should the adored object prove, under rigorous examination, to be practically indestructible.

> "Whene'er I take my walks abroad,
> How many hats I'll see;
> But if they 're trimmed with hedgehog quills
> They'll not belong to me!"

So she improvised, secretly and ecstatically, as she went toward the side entry.

"There's 'Bijah Flagg drivin' in," said Miss Miranda, going to the window. "Step out and see what he's got, Jane; some passel from the Squire, I guess. It's a paper bag and it may be a punkin, though he would n't wrop up a punkin, come to think of it! Shet the dinin' room door, Jane; it's turrible drafty. Make haste, for the Squire's hoss never stan's still a minute 'cept when he's goin'!"

Abijah Flagg alighted and approached the side door with a grin.

"Guess what I've got for ye, Rebecky?"

No throb of prophetic soul warned Rebecca of her approaching doom.

"Nodhead apples?" she sparkled, looking as bright and rosy and satin-skinned as an apple herself.

"No; guess again."

"A flowering geranium?"

"Guess again!"

"Nuts? Oh! I can't, 'Bijah; I'm just going to Milliken's Mills on an errand, and I'm afraid of missing Mrs. Perkins. Show me quick! Is it really for me, or for Aunt Miranda?"

"Reely for you, I guess!" and he opened the large brown paper bag and drew from it the remains of a water-soaked hat!

They *were* remains, but there was no doubt of their nature and substance. They had clearly been a hat in the past, and one could even suppose that, when resuscitated, they might again assume their original form in some near and happy future.

Miss Miranda, full of curiosity, joined the group in the side entry at this dramatic moment.

"Well, I never!" she exclaimed. "Where, and how under the canopy, did you ever?"—

"I was working on the dam at Union Falls yesterday," chuckled Abijah, with a pleased glance at each of the trio in turn, "an' I seen this little bunnit skippin' over the water jest as Becky does over the road. It's shaped kind o' like a boat, an' gorry, ef it wa'n't sailin' jest like a boat! 'Where hev I seen that kind of bristlin' plume?' thinks I."

("Where indeed!" thought Rebecca stormily.)

"Then it come to me that I'd drove that plume to school and drove it to meetin' an' drove it to the Fair an' drove it most everywheres on Becky. So I reached out a pole an' ketched it 'fore it got in amongst the logs an' come to any damage, an' here it is! The hat's passed in its checks, I guess; looks kind as if a wet elephant had stepped on it; but the plume's 'bout's good as new! I reely fetched the hat back for the sake o' the plume."

"It was real good of you, 'Bijah, an' we're all of us obliged to you," said Miranda, as she poised the hat on one hand and turned it slowly with the other.

"Well, I do say," she exclaimed, "and I guess I've said it before, that of all the wearin' plumes that ever I see, that one's the wearin'est! Seems though it just would n't give up. Look at the way it's held Mis' Cobb's dye; it's about as brown's when it went int' the water."

"Dyed, but not a mite dead," grinned Abijah, who was somewhat celebrated for his puns.

"And I declare," Miranda continued, "when you think o' the fuss they make about ostriches, killin' 'em off by hundreds for the sake o' their feathers that'll string out and spoil in one hard rain-storm—an' all the time lettin' useful porcupines run round with their quills on, why I can't hardly understand it, without milliners have found out jest how good they do last, an' so they won't use 'em for trimmin'. 'Bijah's right; the hat ain't no more use, Rebecca, but you can buy you another this mornin'—any color or shape you fancy—an' have Miss Morton sew these brown quills on to it with some kind of a buckle or a bow, jest to hide the roots. Then you'll be fixed for another season, thanks to 'Bijah."

Uncle Jerry and Aunt Sarah Cobb were made acquainted before very long with the part that destiny, or Abijah Flagg, had played in Rebecca's affairs, for, accompanied by the teacher, she walked to the old stage-driver's that same afternoon. Taking off her new hat with the venerable trimming, she laid it somewhat ostentatiously upside down on the kitchen table and left the room, dimpling a little more than usual.

Uncle Jerry rose from his seat, and, crossing the room, looked curiously into the hat and found that a circular paper lining was neatly pinned in the crown, and that it bore these lines, which were read aloud with great effect by Miss Dearborn, and with her approval were copied in the Thought Book for the benefit of posterity:—

"It was the bristling porcupine,
As he stood on his native heath,
He said, 'I'll pluck me some immortelles
And make me up a wreath.
For tho' I may not live myself
To more than a hundred and ten,
My quills will last till crack of doom
And maybe after then.
They can be colored blue or green
Or orange, brown, or red,
But often as they may be dyed
They never will be dead.'
And so the bristling porcupine
As he stood on his native heath,
Said, 'I think I'll pluck me some immortelles
And make me up a wreath.'

"R. R. R."

TOM SAWYER WHITEWASHES THE FENCE

By MARK TWAIN

Illustrations by
WARREN CHAPPELL

I

"TOM!"

No answer.

"Tom!"

No answer.

"What's gone with that boy, I wonder! You TOM!"

No answer.

The old lady pulled her spectacles down and looked over them about the room; then she put them up and looked out under them. She seldom or never looked *through* them for so small a thing as a boy; they were her state pair, the pride of her heart, and were built for "style," not service—she could have seen through a pair of stove-lids just as well. She looked perplexed for a moment, and then said, not fiercely, but still loud enough for the furniture to hear:

"Well, I lay if I get hold of you I'll—"

She did not finish, for by this time she was bending down and punching under the bed with the broom, and so she needed breath to punctuate the punches with. She resurrected nothing but the cat.

"I never did see the beat of that boy!"

She went to the open door and stood in it and looked out among the tomato vines and "jimpson" weeds that constituted the garden. No Tom. So she lifted up her voice at an angle calculated for distance, and shouted:

"Y-o-u-u *Tom!*"

There was a slight noise behind her and she turned just in time to seize a small boy by the slack of his roundabout and arrest his flight.

"There! I might 'a' thought of that closet. What you been doing in there?"

"Nothing."

"Nothing! Look at your hands. And look at your mouth. What *is* that truck?"

"*I* don't know, aunt."

"Well, *I* know. It's jam—that's what it is. Forty times I've said if you did n't let that jam alone I'd skin you. Hand me that switch."

The switch hovered in the air—the peril was desperate—

"My! Look behind you, aunt!"

The old lady whirled round, and snatched her skirts out of danger. The lad fled, on the instant, scrambled up the high board fence, and disappeared over it.

His Aunt Polly stood surprised a moment, and then broke into a gentle laugh.

"Hang the boy, can't I never learn anything? Ain't he played me tricks enough like that for me to be looking out for him by this time? But old fools is the biggest fools there is. Can't learn an old dog new tricks, as the saying is. But my goodness, he never plays them alike, two days, and how is a body to know what's coming? He 'pears to know just how long he can torment me before I get my dander up, and he knows if he can make out to put me off for a minute or make me laugh, it's all down again and I can't hit him a lick. I ain't doing my duty by that boy, and that's the Lord's truth, goodness knows. Spare the rod and spile the child, as the Good Book says. I'm a-laying up sin and suffering for us both, *I* know. He's full of the Old Scratch, but laws-a-me! he's my own dead sister's boy, poor thing, and I ain't got the heart to lash him, somehow. Every time I let him off, my conscience does hurt me so, and every time I hit him my old heart most breaks. Well-a-well, man that is born of woman is of few days and full of trouble, as the Scripture says, and I reckon it's so. He'll play hookey this evening,[1] and I'll be obleeged to make him work, tomorrow, to punish him. It's mighty hard to make him work Saturdays, when all the boys is having holiday, but he hates work more than he hates anything else, and I've *got* to do some of my duty by him, or I'll be the ruination of the child."

Tom did play hookey, and he had a very good time. He got back home barely in season to help Jim, the small colored boy, saw next-day's wood and split the kindlings before supper—at least he was there in time to tell his adventures to Jim while Jim did three-fourths of the work. Tom's younger brother (or rather, half-brother), Sid, was already through with his part of the work (picking up chips), for he was a quiet boy, and had no adventurous, troublesome ways.

While Tom was eating his supper, and stealing sugar as opportunity offered, Aunt Polly asked him questions that were full of guile, and very deep—for she wanted to trap him into damaging revealments. Like many other simple-hearted souls, it was her pet

[1] Southwestern for "afternoon."

vanity to believe she was endowed with a talent for dark and mysterious diplomacy, and she loved to contemplate her most transparent devices as marvels of low cunning. Said she:

"Tom, it was middling warm in school, war n't it?"

"Yes'm."

"Powerful warm, war n't it?"

"Yes'm."

"Did n't you want to go in a-swimming, Tom?"

A bit of a scare shot through Tom—a touch of uncomfortable suspicion. He searched Aunt Polly's face, but it told him nothing. So he said:

"No'm—well, not very much."

The old lady reached out her hand and felt Tom's shirt, and said:

"But you ain't too warm now, though." And it flattered her to reflect that she had discovered that the shirt was dry without anybody knowing that that was what she had in her mind. But in spite of her, Tom knew where the wind lay, now. So he forestalled what might be the next move:

"Some of us pumped on our heads—mine's damp yet. See?"

Aunt Polly was vexed to think she had overlooked that bit of circumstantial evidence, and missed a trick. Then she had a new inspiration:

"Tom, you did n't have to undo your shirt-collar where I sewed it, to pump on your head, did you? Unbutton your jacket!"

The trouble vanished out of Tom's face. He opened his jacket. His shirt-collar was securely sewed.

"Bother! Well, go 'long with you. I'd made sure you'd played hookey and been a-swimming. But I forgive ye, Tom. I reckon you're a kind of a singed cat, as the saying is—better'n you look. *This* time."

She was half sorry her sagacity had miscarried, and half glad that Tom had stumbled into obedient conduct for once.

But Sidney said: "Well, now, if I didn't think you sewed his collar with white thread, but it's black."

"Why, I did sew it with white! Tom!"

But Tom did not wait for the rest. As he went out at the door he said: "Siddy, I'll lick you for that."

In a safe place Tom examined two large needles which were thrust into the lapels of his jacket, and had thread bound about them—one needle carried white thread and the other black. He said:

"She'd never noticed if it hadn't been for Sid. Confound it! sometimes she sews it with white, and sometimes she sews it with black. I wish to gee-miny she'd stick to one or t'other—*I* can't keep the run of 'em. But I bet you I'll lam Sid for that. I'll learn him!"

He was not the Model Boy of the village. He knew the model boy very well though—and loathed him.

Within two minutes, or even less, he had forgotten all his troubles. Not because his troubles were one whit less heavy and bitter to him than a man's are to a man, but because a new and powerful interest bore them down and drove them out of his mind for the time—just as men's misfortunes are forgotten in the excitement of new enterprises. This new interest was a valued novelty in whistling, which he had just acquired from a negro, and he was suffering to practise it undisturbed. It consisted in a peculiar birdlike turn, a sort of liquid warble, produced by touching the tongue to the roof of the mouth at short intervals in the midst of the music—the reader probably remembers how to do it, if he has ever been a boy. Diligence and attention soon gave him the knack of it, and he strode down the street with his mouth full of harmony and his soul full of gratitude.

He felt much as an astronomer feels who has discovered a new planet—no doubt, as far as strong, deep, unalloyed pleasure is concerned, the advantage was with the boy, not the astronomer.

Tom Sawyer.

The summer evenings were long. It was not dark, yet. Presently Tom checked his whistle. A stranger was before him—a boy a shade larger than himself. A newcomer of any age or either sex was an impressive curiosity in the poor little shabby village of St. Petersburg. This boy was well dressed, too—well dressed on a week-day. This was simply astounding. His cap was a dainty thing, his close-buttoned blue cloth roundabout was new and natty, and so were his pantaloons. He had shoes on—and it was only Friday. He even wore a necktie, a bright bit of ribbon. He had a citified air about him that ate into Tom's vitals. The more Tom stared at the splendid marvel, the higher he turned up his nose at his finery and the shabbier and shabbier his own outfit seemed to him to grow. Neither boy spoke. If one moved, the other moved—but only sidewise, in a circle; they kept face to face and eye to eye all the time. Finally Tom said:

"I can lick you!"

"I'd like to see you try it."

"Well, I can do it."

"No you can't, either."

"Yes I can."

"No you can't."

"I can."

"You can't."

"Can!"

"Can't!"

An uncomfortable pause. Then Tom said:

"What's your name?"

" 'Tisn't any of your business, maybe."

"Well, I 'low I'll *make* it my business."

"Well, why don't you?"

"If you say much, I will."

"Much—much—*much*. There now."

"Oh, you think you're mighty smart, *don't* you? I could lick you with one hand tied behind me, if I wanted to."

"Well, why don't you *do* it? You *say* you can do it."

"Well, I *will,* if you fool with me."

"Oh, yes—I've seen whole families in the same fix."

"Smarty! You think you're *some,* now, *don't* you? Oh, what a hat!"

"You can lump that hat if you don't like it. I dare you to knock it off—and anybody that 'll take a dare will suck eggs."

"You're a liar!"

"You're another."

"You're a fighting liar and dasn't take it up."

"Aw—take a walk!"

"Say—if you give me much more of your sass I'll take and bounce a rock off'n your head."

"Oh, of *course* you will."

"Well, I *will.*"

"Well, why don't you *do* it then? What do you keep *saying* you will for? Why don't you *do* it? It's because you're afraid."

"I *ain't* afraid."

"You are."

"I ain't."

"You are."

Another pause, and more eyeing and sidling around each other. Presently they were shoulder to shoulder. Tom said:

"Get away from here!"

"Go away yourself!"

"I won't."

"*I* won't either."

So they stood, each with a foot placed at an angle as a brace, and both shoving with might and main, and glowering at each other with hate. But neither could get an advantage. After struggling till both were hot and flushed, each relaxed his strain with watchful caution, and Tom said:

"You're a coward and a pup. I'll tell my big brother on you, and he can thrash you with his little finger, and I'll make him do it, too."

"What do I care for your big brother? I've got a brother that's bigger than he is—and what's more, he can throw him over that fence, too." [Both brothers were imaginary.]

"That's a lie."

"*Your* saying so don't make it so."

Tom drew a line in the dust with his big toe, and said:

"I dare you to step over that, and I'll lick you till you can't stand up. Anybody that'll take a dare will steal sheep."

The new boy stepped over promptly, and said:

"Now you said you'd do it, now let's see you do it."

"Don't you crowd me now; you better look out."

"Well, you *said* you'd do it—why don't you do it?"

"By jingo! for two cents I *will* do it."

The new boy took two broad coppers out of his pocket and held them out with derision. Tom struck them to the ground. In an instant both boys were rolling and tumbling in the dirt, gripped together like cats; and for the space of a minute they tugged and tore at each other's hair and clothes, punched and scratched each other's noses, and covered themselves with dust and glory. Presently the confusion took form and through the fog of battle Tom appeared, seated astride the new boy, and pounding him with his fists.

"Holler 'nuff!" said he.

The boy only struggled to free himself. He was crying—mainly from rage.

"Holler 'nuff!"—and the pounding went on.

At last the stranger got out a smothered "'Nuff!" and Tom let him up and said:

"Now that'll learn you. Better look out who you're fooling with next time."

The new boy went off brushing the dust from his clothes, sobbing, snuffling, and occasionally looking back and shaking his head and threatening what he would do to Tom the "next time he caught him out." To which Tom responded with jeers, and started off in high feather, and as soon as his back was turned the new boy snatched up a stone, threw it and hit him between the shoulders and then turned tail and ran like an antelope. Tom chased the traitor home, and thus found out where he lived. He then held a position at the gate for some time, daring the enemy to come outside, but the enemy only made faces at him through the window and declined. At last the enemy's mother appeared, and called Tom a bad, vicious, vulgar child, and ordered him away. So he went away, but he said he "'lowed to lay" for that boy.

He got home pretty late, that night, and when he climbed cautiously in at the window, he uncovered an ambuscade, in the person of his aunt; and when she saw the state his clothes were in her resolution to turn his Saturday holiday into capitivity at hard labor became adamantine in its firmness.

II

Saturday morning was come, and all the summer world was bright and fresh, and brimming with life. There was a song in every heart; and if the heart was young the music issued at the lips. There was cheer in every face and a spring in every step. The locust trees were in bloom and the fragrance of the blossoms filled the air. Cardiff Hill, beyond the village and above it, was green with vegetation, and it lay just far enough away to seem a Delectable Land, dreamy, reposeful, and inviting.

Tom appeared on the sidewalk with a bucket of whitewash and a long-handled brush. He surveyed the fence, and all gladness left him and a deep melancholy settled down upon his spirit. Thirty yards of board fence nine feet high. Life to him seemed hollow, and existence but a burden. Sighing he dipped his brush and passed it along the topmost plank; repeated the operation; did it again; compared the insignificant whitewashed streak with the far-reaching continent of unwhitewashed fence, and sat down on a tree-box discouraged. Jim came skipping out at the gate with a tin pail, and singing "Buffalo Gals." Bringing water from the town pump had always been hateful work in Tom's eyes, before, but now it did not strike him so. He remembered that there was company at the pump. White, mulatto, and negro boys and girls were always there waiting their turns, resting, trading playthings, quarreling, fighting, skylarking. And he remembered that although the pump was only a hundred and fifty yards off, Jim never got back with a bucket of water under an hour—and even then somebody generally had to go after him. Tom said:

"Say, Jim, I'll fetch the water if you'll whitewash some."

Jim shook his head and said:

"Can't, Mars Tom. Ole missis, she tole me I got to go an' git dis water an' not stop foolin' roun' wid anybody. She says she spec' Mars Tom gwine to ax me to whitewash, an' so she tole me go 'long an' 'tend to my own busines—she 'lowed *she'd* 'tend to de whitewashin'."

"Oh, never you mind what she said, Jim. That's the way she always talks. Gimme the bucket—I won't be gone only a minute. *She* won't ever know."

"Oh, I dasn't, Mars Tom. Ole missis she'd take an' tar de head off'n me. 'Deed she would."

"*She!* She never licks anybody—whacks 'em over the head with her thimble—and who cares for that, I'd like to know. She talks awful, but talk don't hurt—anyways it don't if she don't cry. Jim, I'll give you a marvel. I'll give you a white alley!"

Jim began to waver.

"White alley, Jim! And it's a bully taw."

"My! Dat's a might gay marvel, *I* tell you! But Mars Tom I's powerful 'fraid ole missis—"

"And besides, if you will I'll show you my sore toe."

Jim was only human—this attraction was too much for him. He put down his pail, took the white alley, and bent over the toe with absorbing interest while the bandage was being unwound. In another moment he was flying down the street with his pail and a tingling rear, Tom was whitewashing with vigor, and Aunt Polly was retiring from the field with a slipper in her hand and triumph in her eye.

But Tom's energy did not last. He began to think of the fun he had planned for this day, and his sorrows multiplied. Soon the free boys would come tripping along on all sorts of delicious expeditions, and they would make a world of fun of him for having to work—the very thought of it burnt him like fire. He got out his worldly wealth and examined it—bits of toys, marbles, and trash; enough to buy an exchange of *work*, maybe, but not half enough to buy so much as half an hour of pure freedom. So he returned his straitened means to his pocket, and gave up the idea of trying to buy the boys. At this dark and hopeless moment an inspiration burst upon him! Nothing less than a great, magnificent inspiration.

He took up his brush and went tranquilly to work. Ben Rogers hove in sight presently—the very boy, of all boys, whose ridicule he had been dreading. Ben's gait was the hop-skip-and-jump—proof enough that his heart was light and his anticipations high. He was eating an apple, and giving a long, melodious whoop, at intervals, followed by a deep-toned ding-dong-dong, ding-dong-dong, for he was personating a steamboat. As he drew near, he slackened speed, took the middle of the street, leaned far over to starboard and rounded to ponderously and with laborious pomp and circumstance—for he was personating the *Big Missouri,* and considered himself to be drawing nine feet of water. He was boat and captain and engine-bells combined, so he had to imagine himself standing on his own hurricane-deck giving the orders and executing them:

"Stop her, sir! Ting-a-ling-ling!" The headway ran almost out and he drew up slowly toward the sidewalk.

"Ship up to back! Ting-a-ling-ling!" His arms straightened and stiffened down his sides.

"Set her back on the stabbard! Ting-a-ling-ling! Chow! Ch-chow-wow! Chow!" His right hand meantime, describing stately circles—for it was representing a forty-foot wheel.

"Let her go back on the labboard! Ting-a-ling-ling! Chow-ch-chow-chow!" The left hand began to describe circles.

"Stop the stabboard! Ting-a-ling-ling! Stop the labboard! Come ahead on the stabbard! Stop her! Let your outside turn over slow! Ting-a-ling-ling! Chow-ow-ow! Get out that headline! *Lively* now! Come—out with your springline—what're you about there! Take a turn round that stump with the bight of it! Stand by that stage, now—let her go! Done with the engines, sir! Ting-a-ling-ling! *Sh't! s'h't! sh't!"* (trying the gauge-cocks).

Tom went on whitewashing—paid no attention to the steamboat. Ben stared a moment and then said:

"Hi-*yi! You're* up a stump, ain't you!"

No answer. Tom surveyed his last touch with the eye of an artist, then he gave his brush another gentle sweep and surveyed the result, as before. Ben ranged up alongside of him. Tom's mouth watered for the apple, but he stuck to his work. Ben said:

"Hello, old chap, you got to work, hey?"

Tom wheeled suddenly and said:

"Why, it's you, Ben! I warn't noticing."

"Say—*I'm* going in a-swimming, *I* am. Don't you wish you could? But of course you'd druther *work*—wouldn't you? Course you would!"

Tom contemplated the boy a bit, and said:

"What do you call work?"

"Why, ain't *that* work?"

Tom resumed his whitewashing and answered carelessly:

"Well, maybe it is, and maybe it ain't. All I know, is, it suits Tom Sawyer."

Sat on a barrel, munched his apple, and planned more slaughter.

"Oh come, now, you don't mean to let on that you *like* it?"

The brush continued to move.

"Like it? Well, I don't see why I ought n't to like it. Does a boy get a chance to whitewash a fence every day?"

That put the thing in a new light. Ben stopped nibbling his apple. Tom swept his brush daintily back and forth—stepped back to note the effect—added a touch here and there—criticized the effect again—Ben watching every move and getting more and more interested, more and more absorbed. Presently he said:

"Say, Tom, let *me* whitewash a little."

Tom considered, was about to consent; but he altered his mind:

"No—no—I reckon it would n't hardly do, Ben. You see, Aunt Polly's awful particular about this fence—right here on the street, you know—but if it was the back fence I would n't mind and *she* would n't. Yes, she's awful particular about this fence; it's got to be done very careful; I reckon there ain't one boy in a thousand, maybe two thousand, that can do it the way it's got to be done."

"No—is that so? Oh come, now—lemme just try. Only just a little—I'd let *you*, if you was me, Tom."

"Ben, I'd like to, honest injun; but Aunt Polly—well, Jim wanted to do it, but she would n't let him; Sid wanted to do it, and she would n't let Sid. Now don't you see how I'm fixed? If you was to tackle this fence and anything was to happen to it—"

"Oh, shucks, I'll be just as careful. Now lemme try. Say—I'll give you the core of my apple."

"Well, here— No, Ben, now don't. I'm afeard—"

"I'll give you *all* of it!"

Tom gave up the brush with reluctance in his face, but alacrity in his heart. And while the late steamer *Big Missouri* worked and sweated in the sun the retired artist sat on a barrel in the shade close by, dangled his legs, munched his apple, and planned the slaughter of more innocents. There was no lack of material; boys happened along every little while; they came to jeer, but remained to whitewash. By the time Ben was fagged out, Tom had traded the next chance to Billy Fisher for a kite, in good repair; and when *he* played out, Johnny Miller bought in for a dead rat and a string to swing it with—and so on, and so on, hour after hour. And when the middle of the afternoon came, from being a poor poverty-stricken boy in the morning, Tom was literally rolling in wealth. He had beside the things before mentioned, twelve marbles, part of a jew's-harp, a piece of blue bottle-glass to look through, a spool cannon, a key that would n't unlock anything, a fragment of chalk, a glass stopper of a decanter, a tin soldier, a couple of tadpoles, six firecrackers, a kitten with only one eye, a brass door-knob, a dog-collar—but no dog —the handle of a knife, four pieces of orange-peel, and a dilapidated old window-sash.

He had had a nice, good, idle time all the while—plenty of company—and the fence had three coats of whitewash on it! If he had n't run out of whitewash, he would have bankrupted every boy in the village.

Tom said to himself that it was not such a hollow world, after all. He had discovered a great law of human action, without knowing it—namely, that in order to make a man or a boy covet a thing, it is only necessary to make the thing difficult to attain. If he had been a great wise philosopher, like the writer of this book, he would now have comprehended that Work consists of whatever a body is *obliged* to do, and that Play consists of whatever a body is not obliged to do. And this would help him to understand why constructing artificial flowers or performing on a treadmill is work, while rolling tenpins or climbing Mont Blanc is only amusement. There are wealthy gentlemen in England who drive four-horse passenger-coaches twenty or thirty miles on a daily line, in the summer, because the privilege costs them considerable money; but if they were offered wages for the service, that would turn it into work and then they would resign.

The boy mused awhile over the substantial change which had taken place in his worldly circumstances, and then wended toward headquarters to report.

ONE MEMORABLE FOURTH

From THE STORY OF A BAD BOY

By THOMAS
BAILEY ALDRICH

Illustrations by A. B. FROST

I

TWO months had elapsed since my arrival at Rivermouth, when the approach of an important celebration produced the greatest excitement among the juvenile population of the town.

There was very little hard study done in the Temple Grammar School the week preceding the Fourth of July. For my part, my heart and brain were so full of fire-crackers, Roman candles, rockets, pin-wheels, squibs, and gunpowder in various seductive forms, that I wonder I did n't explode under Mr. Grimshaw's very nose. I could n't do a sum to save me; I could n't tell, for love or money, whether Tallahassee was the capital of Tennessee or of Florida; the present and the pluperfect tenses were inextricably mixed in my memory, and I did n't know a verb from an adjective when I met one. This was not alone my condition, but that of every boy in the school.

Mr. Grimshaw considerately made allowances for our temporary distraction, and sought to fix our interest on the lessons by connecting them directly or indirectly with the coming Event. The class in arithmetic, for instance, was requested to state how many boxes of fire-crackers, each box measuring sixteen inches square, could be stored in a room of such and such dimensions. He gave us the Declaration of Independence for a parsing exercise, and in geography confined his questions almost exclusively to localities rendered famous in the Revolutionary War.

"What did the people of Boston do with the tea on board the English vessels?" asked our wily instructor.

"Threw it into the river!" shrieked the smaller boys, with an impetuosity that made Mr. Grimshaw smile in spite of himself. One luckless urchin said, "Chucked it," for which happy expression he was kept in at recess.

Notwithstanding these clever stratagems, there was not much solid work done by anybody. The trail of the serpent (an inexpensive but dangerous fire-toy) was over us all. We went round deformed by quantities of Chinese crackers artlessly concealed in our trousers pockets; and if a boy whipped out his handkerchief without proper precaution, he was sure to let off two or three torpedoes.

Even Mr. Grimshaw was made a sort of accessory to the universal demoralization. In calling the school to order, he always rapped on the table with a heavy ruler. Under the green baize tablecloth, on the exact spot where he usually struck, a certain boy, whose name I withhold, placed a fat torpedo. The result was a loud explosion, which caused Mr. Grimshaw to look queer. Charley Marden was at the water-pail, at the time, and directed general attention to himself by strangling for several seconds and then squirting a slender thread of water over the blackboard.

Mr. Grimshaw fixed his eyes reproachfully on Charley, but said nothing. The real culprit (it wasn't Charley Marden, but the boy whose name I withhold) instantly regretted his badness, and after school confessed the whole thing to Mr. Grimshaw, who heaped coals of fire upon the nameless boy's head by giving him five cents for the Fourth of July. If Mr. Grimhsaw had caned this unknown youth, the punishment would not have been half so severe.

On the last day of June the Captain received a letter from my father, enclosing five dollars "for my son Tom," which enabled that young gentleman to make regal preparations for the celebration of our national independence. A portion of this money, two dollars, I hastened to invest in fireworks; the balance I put by for contingencies. In placing the fund in my possession, the Captain imposed one condition that dampened my ardor considerably—I was to buy no gunpowder. I might have all the snapping-crackers and torpedoes I wanted; but gunpowder was out of the question.

I thought this rather hard, for all my young friends were provided with pistols of various sizes. Pepper Whitcomb had a horse-pistol nearly as large as himself, and Jack Harris—though he, to be sure, was a big boy—was going to have a real old-fashioned flintlock musket. However, I did n't mean to let this drawback destroy my happiness. I had one charge of powder stowed away in the little brass pistol which I brought from New Orleans, and was bound to make a noise in the world once, if I never did again.

It was a custom observed from time immemorial for the town's boys to have a bonfire on the Square on the midnight before the Fourth. I did n't ask the Captain's leave to attend this ceremony, for I had a general idea that he would n't give it. If the Captain, I reasoned, does n't forbid me, I break no orders by going. Now this was a specious line of argument, and the mishaps that befell me in consequence of adopting it were richly deserved.

On the evening of the 3rd I retired to bed very early, in order to disarm suspicion. I did n't sleep a wink, waiting for eleven o'clock to come round; and I thought it never would come round, as I lay counting from time to time the slow strokes of the ponderous bell in the steeple of the Old North Church. At length the laggard hour arrived. While the clock was striking I jumped out of bed and began dressing.

My grandfather and Miss Abigail were heavy sleepers, and I might have stolen downstairs and out at the front door undetected; but such a commonplace proceeding did not suit my adventurous disposition. I fastened one end of a rope (it was a few yards cut from Kitty Collins' clothesline) to the bedpost nearest the window, and cautiously climbed out on the wide pediment over the hall door. I had neglected to knot the rope; the result was, that, the moment I swung clear of the pediment, I descended like a flash of lightning, and warmed both my hands smartly. The rope, moreover, was four or five feet too short; so I got a fall that would have proved serious had I not tumbled into the middle of one of the big rose-bushes growing on either side of the steps.

I scrambled out of that without delay, and was congratulating myself on my good luck, when I saw by the light of the setting moon the form of a man leaning over the garden gate. It was one of the town watch, who had probably been observing my operations with curiosity. Seeing no chance of escape, I put a bold face on the matter and walked directly up to him.

"What on airth air you a-doin'?" asked the man, grasping the collar of my jacket.

"I live here, sir, if you please," I replied, "and am going to the bonfire. I did n't want to wake up the old folks, that's all."

The man cocked his eye at me in the most amiable manner, and released his hold.

"Boys is boys," he muttered. He did n't attempt to stop me as I slipped through the gate.

Once beyond his clutches, I took to my heels and soon reached the Square, where I found forty or fifty fellows assembled, engaged in building a pyramid of tar-barrels. The palms of my hands still tingled so that I couldn't join in the sport. I stood in the doorway of the Nautilus Bank, watching the workers, among whom I recognized lots of my schoolmates. They looked like a legion of imps, coming and going in the twilight, busy in raising some infernal edifice. What a Babel of voices it was, everybody directing everybody else, and everybody doing everything wrong!

When all was prepared, someone applied a match to the somber pile. A fiery tongue thrust itself out here and there, then suddenly the whole fabric burst into flames, blazing and crackling beautifully. This was a signal for the boys to join hands and dance around the burning barrels, which they did, shouting like mad creatures. When the fire had burnt down a little, fresh staves were brought and heaped on the pyre. In the excitement of the moment I forgot my tingling palms, and found myself in the thick of the carousal.

Before we were half ready, our combustible material was expended, and a disheartening kind of darkness settled down upon us. The boys collected together here and there in knots, consulting as to what should be done. It yet lacked four or five hours of daybreak, and none of us were in the humor to return to bed. I approached one of the groups standing near the town-pump, and discovered in the uncertain light of the dying brands the figures of Jack Harris, Phil Adams, Harry Blake, and Pepper Whitcomb, their faces streaked with perspiration and tar, and their whole appearance suggestive of New Zealand chiefs.

"Hullo! here's Tom Bailey!" shouted Pepper Whitcomb; "he'll join in!"

Of course he would. The sting had gone out of my hands, and I was ripe for anything—none the less ripe for not knowing what was on the *tapis*. After whispering together for a moment, the boys motioned me to follow them.

We glided out from the crowd and silently wended our way through a neighboring alley, at the head of which stood a tumble-down old barn, owned by one Ezra Wingate. In former days this was the stable of the mail-coach that ran between Rivermouth and Boston. When the railroad superseded that primitive mode of travel, the lumbering vehicle was rolled into the barn, and there it stayed. The stage-driver, after prophesying the immediate downfall of the nation, died of grief and apoplexy, and the old coach followed in his wake as fast as it could by quietly dropping to pieces. The barn had the reputation of being haunted, and I think we all kept very close together when we found ourselves standing in the black shadow cast by the tall gable. Here, in a low voice, Jack Harris laid bare his plan, which was to burn the ancient stage-coach.

"The old trundle-cart isn't worth twenty-five cents," said Jack Harris, "and Ezra Wingate ought to thank us for getting the rubbish out of the way. But if any fellow here does n't want to have a hand in it, let him cut and run, and keep a quiet tongue in his head ever after."

With this he pulled out the staples that held the rusty padlock, and the big barn door swung slowly open. The interior of the stable was pitch-dark, of course. As we made a movement to enter, a sudden scrambling, and the sound of heavy bodies leaping in all directions, caused us to start back in terror.

"Rats!" cried Phil Adams.

"Bats!" exclaimed Harry Blake.

"Cats!" suggested Jack Harris. "Who's afraid?"

Well, the truth is, we were all afraid; and if the pole of the stage had not been lying close to the threshold, I don't believe anything on earth would have induced us to cross it. We seized hold of the pole-straps and succeeded with great trouble in dragging the coach out. The two fore wheels had rusted to the axle tree, and refused to revolve. It was the merest skeleton of a coach. The cushions had long since been removed, and the leather hangings, where they had not crumbled away, dangled in shreds from the worm-eaten frame. A load of ghosts and a span of phantom horses to drag them would have made the ghastly thing complete.

Luckily for our undertaking, the stable stood at the top of a very steep hill. With three boys to push behind, and two in front to steer, we started the old coach on its last trip with little or no difficulty. Our speed increased every moment, and, the fore wheels becoming unlocked as we arrived at the foot of the declivity, we charged upon the crowd like a regiment of cavalry, scattering the people right and left. Before reaching the bonfire, to which someone had added several bushels of shavings, Jack Harris and Phil Adams, who were steering, dropped on the ground, and allowed the vehicle to pass over them, which it did without injuring them; but the boys who were clinging for dear life to the trunk-rack behind fell over the prostrate steersmen, and there we all lay in a heap, two or three of us quite picturesque with the nose-bleed.

The coach, with an intuitive perception of what was expected of it, plunged into the center of the kindling shavings, and stopped. The flames sprung up and clung to the rotten woodwork, which burned like tinder. At this moment a figure was seen leaping wildly from the inside of the blazing coach. The figure made three bounds toward us, and tripped over Harry Blake. It was Pepper Whitcomb, with his hair somewhat singed, and his eyebrows completely scorched off!

Pepper had slyly ensconced himself on the back seat before we started, intending to have a neat little ride down hill, and a laugh at us afterwards. But the laugh, as it happened, was on our side, or would have been, if half a dozen watchmen had not suddenly pounced down upon us, as we lay scrambling on the ground, weak with mirth over Pepper's misfortune. We were collared and marched off before we well knew what had happened.

The abrupt transition from the noise and light of the Square to the silent, gloomy brick room in the rear of the Meat Market seemed like the work of enchantment. We stared at each other aghast.

"Well," remarked Jack Harris, with a sickly smile, "this *is* a go!"

"No go, I should say," whimpered Harry Blake, glancing at the bare brick walls and the heavy iron-plated door.

"Never say die," muttered Phil Adams, dolefully.

The Bridewell was a small low-studded chamber built up against the rear end of the Meat Market, and approached from the Square by a narrow passageway. A portion of the room was partitioned off into eight cells, numbered, each capable of holding two persons. The cells were full at the time, as we presently discovered by seeing several hideous faces leering out at us through the gratings of the doors.

A smoky oil lamp in a lantern suspended from the ceiling threw a flickering light over the apartment, which contained no furniture excepting a couple of stout wooden benches. It was a dismal place by night, and only little less dismal by day, for the tall houses surrounding "the lock-up" prevented the faintest ray of sunshine from penetrating the ventilator over the door—a long narrow window opening inward and propped up by a piece of lath.

As we seated ourselves in a row on one of the benches, I imagine that our aspect was anything but cheerful. Adams and Harris looked very anxious, and Harry Blake, whose nose had just stopped bleeding, was mournfully carving his name, by sheer force of habit, on

"Ef I was a youngster like you, this spot would n't hold me long."

the prison bench. I don't think I ever saw a more "wrecked" expression on any human countenance than Pepper Whitcomb's presented. His look of natural astonishment at finding himself incarcerated in a jail was considerably heightened by his lack of eyebrows.

As for me, it was only by thinking how the late Baron Trenck would have conducted himself under similar circumstances that I was able to restrain my tears.

None of us were inclined to conversation. A deep silence, broken now and then by a startling snore from the cells, reigned throughout the chamber. By and by Pepper Whitcomb glanced nervously toward Phil Adams and said, "Phil, do you think they will—*hang us?"*

"Hang your grandmother!" returned Adams, impatiently; "what I'm afraid of is that they'll keep us locked up until the Fourth is over."

"You ain't smart ef they do!" cried a voice from one of the cells. It was a deep bass voice that sent a chill through me.

"Who are you?" said Jack Harris, addressing the cells in general; for the echoing qualities of the room made it difficult to locate the voice.

"That don't matter," replied the speaker, putting his face close up to the gratings of No. 3, "but ef I was a youngster like you, free an' easy outside there, this spot would n't hold *me* long."

"That's so!" chimed several of the prison-birds, wagging their heads behind the iron lattices.

"Hush!" whispered Jack Harris, rising from his seat and walking on tiptoe to the door of cell No. 3. "What would you do?"

"Do? Why, I'd pile them 'ere benches up agin that 'ere door, an' crawl out of that 'ere winder in no time. That's my advice."

"And werry good adwice it is, Jim," said the occupant of No. 5, approvingly.

Jack Harris seemed to be of the same opinion, for he hastily placed the benches one on the top of another under the ventilator, and, climbing up on the highest bench, peeped out into the passageway.

"If any gent happens to have a ninepence about him," said the man in cell No. 3, "there's a sufferin' family here as could make use of it. Smallest favors gratefully received, an' no questions axed."

This appeal touched a new silver quarter of a dollar in my trousers-pocket; I fished out the coin from a mass of fireworks, and gave it to the prisoner. He appeared to be so good-natured a fellow that I ventured to ask what he had done to get into jail.

"Entirely innocent. I was clapped in here by a rascally nevew as wishes to enjoy my wealth afore I'm dead."

"Your name, sir?" I inquired, with a view of reporting the outrage to my grandfather and having the injured person reinstated in society.

"Git out, you insolent young reptyle!" shouted the man, in a passion.

I retreated precipitately, amid a roar of laughter from the other cells.

"Can't you keep still?" exclaimed Harris, withdrawing his head from the window.

A portly watchman usually sat on a stool outside the door day and night; but on this particular occasion, his services being required elsewhere, the Bridewell had been left to guard itself.

"All clear," whispered Jack Harris, as he vanished through the aperture and dropped softly on the ground outside. We all followed him expeditiously—Pepper Whitcomb and myself getting stuck in the window for a moment in our frantic efforts not to be last.

"Now, boys, everybody for himself!"

II

The sun cast a broad column of quivering gold across the river at the foot of our street, just as I reached the doorstep of the Nutter House. Kitty Collins, with her dress tucked about her so that she looked as if she had on a pair of calico trousers, was washing off the sidewalk.

"Arrah, you bad boy!" cried Kitty, leaning on the mop-handle, "the Capen has jist been askin' for you. He's gone uptown, now. It's a nate thing you done with my clothesline, and it's me you may thank for gettin' it out of the way before the Capen came down."

The kind creature had hauled in the rope, and my escapade had not been discovered by the family; but I knew very well that the burning of the stagecoach, and the arrest of the boys concerned in the mischief, were sure to reach my grandfather's ears sooner or later.

"Well, Thomas," said the old gentleman, an hour or so afterwards, beaming upon me benevolently across the breakfast table, "you didn't wait to be called this morning."

"No, sir," I replied, growing very warm, "I took a little run uptown to see what was going on."

I didn't say anything about the little run I took home again!

"They had quite a time on the Square last night," remarked Captain Nutter, looking up from the *Rivermouth Barnacle,* which was always placed beside his coffee cup at breakfast.

I felt that my hair was preparing to stand on end.

"Quite a time," continued my grandfather. "Some boys broke into Ezra Wingate's barn and carried off the old stagecoach. The young rascals! I do believe they'd burn up the whole town if they had their way."

With this he resumed the paper. After a long silence he exclaimed, "Hullo!"—upon which I nearly fell off the chair.

" 'Miscreants unknown,' " read my grandfather, following the paragraph with his forefinger; " 'escaped from the Bridewell, leaving no clue to their identity, except the letter H, cut on one of the benches. Five dollars reward offered for the apprehension of the perpetrators.' Sho! I hope Wingate will catch them."

"Miscreants unknown . . . Escaped from the Bridewell."

I don't see how I continued to live, for on hearing this the breath went entirely out of my body. I beat a retreat from the room as soon as I could, and flew to the stable with a misty intention of mounting Gypsy and escaping from the place. I was pondering what steps to take, when Jack Harris and Charley Marden entered the yard.

"I say," said Harris, as blithe as a lark, "has old Wingate been here?"

"Been here?" I cried. "I should hope not!"

"The whole thing's out, you know," said Harris, pulling Gypsy's forelock over her eyes and blowing playfully into her nostrils.

"You don't mean it!" I gasped.

"Yes, I do, and we are to pay Wingate three dollars apiece. He'll make rather a good spec out of it."

"But how did he discover that we were the—the miscreants?"

I asked, quoting mechanically from the *Rivermouth Barnacle.*

"Why, he saw us take the old ark, confound him! He's been trying to sell it any time these ten years. Now he has sold it to us. When he found that we had slipped out of the Meat Market he went right off and wrote the advertisement offering five dollars reward, though he knew well enough who had taken the coach, for he came round to my father's house before the paper was printed to talk the matter over. Wasn't the governor mad, though! But it's all settled, I tell you. We're to pay Wingate fifteen dollars for the old go-car, which he wanted to sell the other day for seventy-five cents, and couldn't. It's a downright swindle. But the funny part of it is to come."

"Oh, there's a funny part to it, is there?" I remarked bitterly.

"Yes. The moment Bill Conway saw the advertisement, he knew it was Harry Blake who cut that letter H on the bench; so off he rushes up to Wingate—kind of him, wasn't it?—and claims the reward. 'Too late, young man,' says old Wingate, 'the culprits have been discovered.' You see, Sly-Boots hadn't any intention of paying that five dollars."

Jack Harris' statement lifted a weight from my bosom. The article in the *Rivermouth Barnacle* had placed the affair before me in a new light. I had thoughtlessly committed a grave offense. Though the property in question was valueless, we were clearly wrong in destroying it. At the same time Mr. Wingate *had* tacitly sanctioned the act by not preventing it when he might easily have done so. He had allowed his property to be destroyed in order that he might realize a large profit.

Without waiting to hear more, I went straight to Captain Nutter, and, laying my remaining three dollars on his knee, confessed my share in the previous night's transaction.

The Captain heard me through in profound silence, pocketed the bank-notes, and walked off without speaking a word. He had punished me in his own whimsical fashion at the breakfast table, for, at the very moment he was harrowing up my soul by reading the extracts from the *Rivermouth Barnacle,* he not only knew all about the bonfire, but had paid Ezra Wingate his three dollars. Such was the duplicity of that aged impostor!

I think Captain Nutter was justified in retaining my pocket-money, as additional punishment, though the possession of it later in the day would have got me out of a difficult position, as the reader will see further on.

I returned with a light heart and a large piece of punk to my friends in the stable-yard, where we celebrated the termination of our trouble by setting off two packs of fire-crackers in an empty wine-cask. They made a prodigious racket, but failed somehow to fully express my feelings. The little brass pistol in my bedroom suddenly occurred to me. It had been loaded I don't know how many months, long before I left New Orleans, and now was the time, if ever, to fire it off. Muskets, blunderbusses, and pistols were banging away lively all over town, and the smell of gunpowder, floating on the air, set me wild to add something respectable to the universal din.

When the pistol was produced, Jack Harris examined the rusty cap and prophesied that it would not explode.

"Never mind," said I, "let's try it."

I had fired the pistol once, secretly, in New Orleans, and, remembering the noise it gave birth to on that occasion, I shut both eyes tight as I pulled the trigger. The hammer clicked on the cap with a dull, dead sound. Then Harris tried it; then Charley Marden; then I took it again, and after three or four trials was on the point of giving it up as a bad job, when the obstinate thing went off with a tremendous explosion, nearly jerking my arm from the socket. The smoke cleared away, and there I stood with the stock of the pistol clutched convulsively in my hand—the barrel, lock, trigger, and ramrod having vanished into thin air.

The obstinate thing went off with a tremendous explosion.

"Are you hurt?" cried the boys, in one breath.

"N—no," I replied, dubiously, for the concussion had bewildered me a little.

When I realized the nature of the calamity, my grief was excessive. I can't imagine what led me to do so ridiculous a thing, but I gravely buried the remains of my beloved pistol in our back garden, and erected over the mound a slate tablet to the effect that "Mr.

Barker, formerly of new orleans, was Killed accidently on the Fourth of July, 18—in the 2nd year of his age."[1] Binny Wallace, arriving on the spot just after the disaster, and Charley Marden (who enjoyed the obsequies immensely), acted with me as chief mourners. I, for my part, was a very sincere one.

As I turned away in a disconsolate mood from the garden, Charley Marden remarked that he should n't be surprised if the pistol-butt took root and grew into a mahogany tree or something. He said he once planted an old musket-stock, and shortly afterwards a lot of *shoots* sprung up! Jack Harris laughed; but neither I nor Binny Wallace saw Charley's wicked joke.

We were now joined by Pepper Whitcomb, Fred Langdon, and several other desperate characters, on their way to the Square, which was always a busy place when public festivities were going on. Feeling that I was still in disgrace with the Captain, I thought it politic to ask his consent before accompanying the boys.

A booth on the outskirts of the crowd.

He gave it with some hesitation, advising me to be careful not to get in front of the firearms. Once he put his fingers mechanically into his vest-pocket and half drew forth some dollar bills, then slowly thrust them back again as his sense of justice overcame his genial dis-

[1] This inscription is copied from a triangular-shaped piece of slate, still preserved in the garret of the Nutter House, together with the pistol-butt itself, which was subsequently dug up for a *post-mortem* examination.

position. I guess it cut the old gentleman to the heart to be obliged to keep me out of my pocket-money. I know it did me. However, as I was passing through the hall, Miss Abigail, with a very severe cast of countenance, slipped a brand-new quarter into my hand. We had silver currency in those days, thank Heaven!

Great were the bustle and confusion on the Square. By the way, I don't know why they called this large open space a square, unless because it was an oval—an oval formed by the confluence of half a dozen streets, now thronged by crowds of smartly dressed town's-people and country folk; for Rivermouth on the Fourth was the center of attraction to the inhabitants of the neighboring villages.

On one side of the Square were twenty or thirty booths arranged in a semicircle, gay with little flags and seductive with lemonade, ginger-beer, and seed-cakes. Here and there were tables at which could be purchased the smaller sort of fireworks, such as pin-wheels, serpents, double-headers, and punk warranted not to go out. Many of the adjacent houses made a pretty display of bunting, and across each of the streets opening on the Square was an arch of spruce and evergreen, blossoming all over with patriotic mottoes and paper roses.

It was a noisy, merry, bewildering scene as we came upon the ground. The incessant rattle of small arms, the booming of the twelve-pounder firing on the Mill Dam, and the silvery clangor of the church-bells ringing simultaneously — not to mention an ambitious brass band that was blowing itself to pieces on a balcony—were enough to drive one distracted. We amused ourselves for an hour or two, darting in and out among the crowd and setting off our crackers. At one o'clock the Honorable Hezekiah Elkins mounted a platform in the middle of the Square and delivered an oration, to which his "feller-citizens" did n't pay much attention having all they could do to dodge the squibs that were set loose upon them by mischievous boys stationed on the surrounding housetops.

Our little party which had picked up recruits here and there, not being swayed by eloquence, withdrew to a booth on the outskirts of the crowd, where we regaled ourselves with root beer at two cents a glass. I recollect being much struck by the placard surmounting this tent:

ROOT BEER
SOLD HERE.

It seemed to me the perfection of pith and poetry. What could be more terse? Not a word to spare, and yet everything fully expressed. Rhyme and rhythm faultless. It was a delightful poet who made those verses. As for the beer itself—that, I think, must have been made from the root of all evil! A single glass of it insured an uninterrupted pain for twenty-four hours.

The influence of my liberality working on Charley Marden—for it was I who paid for the beer—he presently invited us all to take an ice cream with him at Pettingil's saloon. Pettingil was the Delmonico of Rivermouth. He furnished ices and confectionery for aristocratic balls and parties, and didn't disdain to officiate as leader of the orchestra at the same; for Pettingil played on the violin, as Pepper Whitcomb described it, "like Old Scratch."

Pettingil's confectionery store was on the corner of Willow and High Streets. The saloon, separated from the shop by a flight of three steps leading to a door hung with faded red drapery, had about it an air of mystery and seclusion quite delightful. Four windows, also draped, faced the side-street, affording an unobstructed view of Marm Hatch's back yard, where a number of inexplicable garments on a clothesline were always to be seen careering in the wind.

There was a lull just then in the ice cream business, it being dinner time, and we found the saloon unoccupied. When we had seated ourselves around the largest marble-topped table. Charley Marden in a manly voice ordered twelve sixpenny ice creams, "strawberry and verneller mixed."

It was a magnificent sight, those twelve chilly glasses entering the room on a waiter, the red and white custard rising from each glass like a church steeple, and the spoon handle shooting up from the apex like a spire. I doubt if a person of the nicest palate could have distinguished, with his eyes shut, which was the vanilla and which the strawberry; but if I could at this moment obtain a cream tasting as that did, I would give five dollars for a very small quantity.

We fell to with a will, and so evenly balanced were our capabilities that we finished our creams together, the spoons clinking in the glasses like one spoon.

"Let's have some more!" cried Charley Marden, with the air of Aladdin ordering up a fresh hogshead of pearls and rubies. "Tom Bailey, tell Pettingil to send in another round."

Could I credit my ears? I looked at him to see if he were in earnest. He meant it. In a moment more I was leaning over the counter giving directions for a second supply. Thinking it would make no difference to such a gorgeous young sybarite as Marden, I took the liberty of ordering ninepenny creams this time.

On returning to the saloon, what was my horror at finding it empty!

There were the twelve cloudy glasses, standing in a circle on the sticky marble slab, and not a boy to be seen. A pair of hands letting go their hold on the window sill outside explained matters. I had been made a victim.

I couldn't stay and face Pettingil, whose peppery temper was well known among the boys. I hadn't a cent in the world to appease him. What should I do? I heard the clink of approaching glasses —the ninepenny creams. I rushed to the nearest window. It was only five feet to the ground. I threw myself out as if I had been an old hat.

Landing on my feet, I fled breathlessly down High Street, through Willow, and was turning into Brierwood Place when the sound of several voices, calling to me in distress, stopped my progress.

"Look out, you fool! the mine! the mine!" yelled the warning voices.

Several men and boys were standing at the head of the street, making insane gestures to me to avoid something. But I saw no mine, only in the middle of the road in front of me was a common flour barrel, which, as I gazed at it, suddenly rose into the air with a terrific explosion. I felt myself thrown violently off my feet. I

remember nothing else, excepting that, as I went up, I caught a momentary glimpse of Ezra Wingate leering through his shop-window like an avenging spirit.

The mine that had wrought me woe was not properly a mine at all, but merely a few ounces of powder placed under an empty keg or barrel and fired with a slow-match. Boys who did n't happen to have pistols or cannon generally burnt their powder in this fashion.

For an account of what followed I am indebted to hearsay, for I was insensible when the people picked me up and carried me home on a shutter borrowed from the proprietor of Pettingil's saloon. I was supposed to be killed, but happily (happily for me at least) I was merely stunned. I lay in a semi-unconscious state until eight o'clock that night, when I attempted to speak. Miss Abigail, who watched by the bedside, put her ear down to my lips and was saluted with these remarkable words:

"Strawberry and verneller mixed!"

"Mercy on us! What is the boy saying?" cried Miss Abigail.

"ROOTBEERSOLDHERE!"

THE NEW PUP: A PENROD STORY

By *BOOTH TARKINGTON*

Illustrations by GORDON GRANT

I

ON A Friday in April, Penrod Schofield, having returned from school at noon promptly, on account of an earnest appetite, found lunch considerably delayed and himself (after a bit of simple technique) alone in the pantry with a large, open, metal receptacle containing about two-thirds of a peck of perfect doughnuts just come into the world.

The history of catastrophe is merely the history of irresistible juxtapositions. When Penrod left the pantry he walked slowly. In the large metal receptacle were left a small number of untouched doughnuts; while upon the shelf beside it were two further doughnuts, each with a small bite experimentally removed—and one of these bites, itself, lay, little mangled, beside the parent doughnut.

Nothing having been discovered, he seated himself gently at the lunch-table, and, making no attempt to take part in the family conversation, avoided rather than sought attention. This decorum on his part was so unusual as to be the means of defeating its object, for his mother and father and Margaret naturally began to stare at him. Nevertheless, his presence continued to be unobtrusive and his manner preoccupied. Rallied by Margaret, he offered for reply only a smile, faint, courteous and strange, followed, upon further badinage, by an almost imperceptible shake of the head, which he seemed to fear might come off if more decisively agitated.

"But, Penrod dear," his mother insisted, "you *must* eat a little something or other."

For the sake of appearances, Penrod made a terrible effort to eat a little something or other.

When they had got him to his bed, he said, with what resentful strength remained to him, that it was all the fault of his mother, and she was indeed convinced that her insistence had been a mistake. For several hours the consequences continued to be more or less demonstrative; then they verged from physical to mental, as the thoughts of Penrod and the thoughts of his insides merged into one. Their decision was unanimous—a conclusive horror of doughnuts. Throughout ghastly durations of time there was no thought possible to him but the intolerable thought of doughnuts. There was no past but doughnuts; there was no future but doughnuts. He descended into the bottomest pit of an abyss of doughnuts; he lay suffocating in a universe of doughnuts. He looked back over his dreadful life to that time, before lunch, when he had been alone with the doughnuts in the pantry, and it seemed to him that he must have been out of his mind. How could he have endured even the noxious smell of the things? It was incredible to him that any human being could ever become hardy enough to bear the mere sight of a doughnut.

Not until the next morning did Penrod Schofield quit his bed and come out into the fair ways of mankind again, and then his step was cautious; there was upon his brow the trace of an experience.

For a little while after his emergence to the air he had the look of one who has discovered something alarming in the pleasant places of life, the look of one who has found a scorpion hiding under a violet. He went out into the yard through the front door, and, even with his eyes, avoided the kitchen.

"Yay, Penrod!" a shout greeted him. "Look! Looky here! Look what *I* got!"

Upon the sidewalk was Sam Williams in a state of unmistakable elation. His right hand grasped one end of a taut piece of clothes-line; the other end had been tied round the neck of a pup; but, owing to the pup's reluctance, the makeshift collar was now just behind his ears, so that his brow was furrowed, his throat elongated and his head horizontal. As a matter of fact, he was sitting down; nevertheless, Sam evidently held that the pup was being led.

"This good ole dog o' mine not so easy to *lead,* I can tell you!"

These were Sam's words, in spite of the pup's seated attitude. On the other hand, to support the use of "lead," the pup was certainly moving along at a fair rate of speed. In regard to his state of mind, any beholder must have hesitated between two guesses: his expression denoted either resignation or profound obstinacy, and, by maintaining silence throughout what could not possibly have been other than a spiritual and bodily trial, he produced an impression of reserve altogether deceptive. There do exist reserved pups, of course; but this was not one of them.

Sam brought him into the yard. "How's *that* for high, Penrod?" he cried.

Penrod forgot doughnuts temporarily. "Where'd you get him?" he asked. "Where'd you get that fellow, Sam?"

"Yay!" shouted Master Williams. "He belongs to me."

"Where'd you *get* him? Didn't you hear me?"

"You just look him over," Sam said importantly. "Take a good ole look at him and see what you got to say. He's a full-blooded dog, all right! You just look this good ole dog over."

With warm interest, Penrod complied. He looked the good ole dog over. The pup, released from the stress of the rope, lay placidly upon the grass. He was tan-colored over most of him, though interspersed with black; and the fact that he had nearly attained his adolescence was demonstrated by the cumbersomeness of his feet and the half-knowing look of his eye. He was large; already he was much taller and heavier than Duke.

"How do you know he's full-blooded?" asked Penrod cautiously, before expressing any opinion.

"My goodness!" Sam exclaimed. "Can't you look at him? Don't you know a full-blooded dog when you see one?"

Penrod frowned. "Well, who told you he was?"

"John Carmichael."

"Who's John Carmichael?"

"He's the man works on my uncle's farm. John Carmichael owns the mother o' this dog here; and he said he took a fancy to me and he was goin' to give me this dog's mother and all the other pups besides this one, too, only my fam'ly would n't let me. John says they were all pretty full-blooded, except the runt; but this one was the best. This one is the most full-blooded of the whole kitamaboodle."

For the moment Penrod's attention was distracted from the pup. "Of the whole what?" he inquired.

"Of the whole kitamaboodle," Sam repeated carelessly.

"Oh," said Penrod, and he again considered the pup. "I bet he isn't as full-blooded as Duke. I bet he isn't anywhere *near* as full-blooded as Duke."

Sam hooted. "Duke!" he cried. "Why, I bet Duke isn't a *quarter* full-blooded! I bet Duke hasn't got any full blood in him at all! All you'd haf to do'd be look at Duke and this dog together; then you'd see in a minute. I bet you, when this dog grows up, he could whip Duke four times out o' five. I bet he could whip Duke now, only pups won't fight. All I ast is, you go get Duke and just *look* which is the most full-blooded."

"All right," said Penrod. "I'll get him, and I guess maybe you'll have sense enough to see yourself which is. Duke's got more full blood in his hind feet than that dog's got all over him."

He departed hotly, calling and whistling for his own, and Duke, roused from a nap on the back porch, loyally obeyed the summons. A moment or two later, he made his appearance, following his master to the front yard, where Sam and the new pup were waiting. However, upon his first sight of this conjuncture, Duke paused at the corner of the house, then quietly turned to withdraw. Penrod was obliged to take him by the collar.

"Well, *now* you're satisfied, I guess!" said Sam Williams, when Penrod had dragged Duke to a spot about five feet from the pup. "I expect you can tell which is the full-bloodedest now, can't you?"

"Yes; I guess I can!" Penrod retorted. "Look at that ole cur beside good ole Dukie, and anybody can see he isn't full-blooded a-*tall!*"

"He isn't?" Sam cried indignantly, and, as a conclusive test, he gathered in both hands a large, apparently unoccupied area of the pup's back, lifting it and displaying it proudly, much as a clerk shows goods upon a counter. "Look at that!" he shouted. "Look how loose his hide is! You never saw a looser-hided dog in your life, and you can't any more do that with Duke'n you could with a potato-bug! Just try it once; that's all I ast."

"That's nothing. Any pup can do that. When Duke was a pup——"

"Just try it once, I said. That's all I ast."

"I got a right to talk, haven't I?" Penrod demanded bitterly. "I guess this is my own father's yard, and I got a ri——"

"Just try it, once," Sam repeated, perhaps a little irritatingly. "That's all I ast."

"My goodness HEAVENS!" Penrod bellowed. "I never heard such a crazy racket as you're makin'! Haven't you got enough sense to——"

"Just try it once. That's all I——"

"Dry UP!" Penrod was furious.

Sam relapsed into indignant silence. Penrod similarly relapsed. Each felt that the other knew nothing whatever about full-blooded dogs.

"Well," Sam said finally, "what you want to keep aholt o' Duke for? *My* dog ain't goin' to hurt him."

"I guess not! You said yourself he couldn't fight."

"I did not! I said *no* pup will——"

"All right then," said Penrod. "I was only holdin' him to keep him from chewin' up that poor cur. Better let him loose so's he can get away if good ole Dukie takes after him."

"Let's let 'em both loose," Sam said, forgetting animosity. "Let's see what they'll do."

"All right," Penrod, likewise suddenly amiable, agreed. "I expeck they kind of like each other, anyways."

Released, both animals shook themselves. Then Duke approached the pup and sniffed carelessly and without much interest at the back of his neck. Duke was so bored by the information thus obtained that he yawned and once more made evident his intention to retire to the backyard. The new pup, however, after having presented up to this moment an appearance uninterruptedly lethargic, suddenly took it into his head to play the jolly rogue. At a pup's gallop, he proceeded to a point directly in Duke's line of march, and halted. Then he placed his muzzle flat upon the ground between his wide-spread paws and showed the whites of his eyes in a waggish manner. Duke also halted, confronting the joker and emitting low sounds of warning and detestation.

Then, for the sake of peace, he decided to go round the house the other way; in fact, he was in the act of turning to do so when the pup rushed upon him and frolicsomely upset him. Thereupon, Duke swore, cursing all the pups in the world and claiming blasphemously to be a dangerous person whom it were safer not again to jostle. For a moment, the pup was startled by the elderly dog's intensive oratory; then he decided that Duke was joking, too, and returned to his clowning. Again and again he charged ponderously upon, into and over Duke, whose words and actions now grew wild indeed. But he was helpless. The pup's humor expressed itself in a fever of physical badinage, and Duke no sooner rose than he was upset again. When he lay upon his back, raving and snapping, the disregardful pup's large feet would flop weightily upon the pit of his stomach or upon his very face with equal unconcern. Duke had about as much chance with him as an elderly gentleman would have with a jocular horse. Never before was a creature of settled life so badgered.

Both boys were captivated by the pup's display of gaiety, and Penrod, naturally prejudiced against the blithe animal, unwillingly felt his heart warming. It was impossible to preserve any coldness of feeling toward so engaging a creature, and, besides, no boy can long resist a pup. Penrod began to yearn toward this one. He wished that John Carmichael had worked on a farm belonging to *his* uncle.

"That *is* a pretty good dog, Sam," he said, his eyes following the pup's merry violence. "I guess you're right— he's proba'ly *part* full-blooded, maybe not as much as Duke, but a good deal, anyhow. What you goin' to name him?"

"John Carmichael."

"I wouldn't," said Penrod. "I'd name him sumpthing nice. I'd name him Frank, or Walter or sumpthing."

"No, sir," Sam said firmly. "I'm goin' to name him John Carmichael. I told John Carmichael I would."

"Well, all right," Penrod returned, a little peevishly. "Always got to have your own way!"

"Well, haven't I got a right to?" Sam inquired, with justifiable heat. "I'd like to know why I oughtn't to have my own way about my own dog!"

"I don't care," said Penrod. "You can call him John Carmichael when you speak to him; but, when *I* speak to him, I'm goin' to call him Walter."

"You can if you want to," Sam returned. "It won't be his name."

"Well, Walter'll be his name long as I'm talkin' to him."

"It won't, either!"

"Why won't it? Just answer me, why."

"Because," said Sam, "his name'll be John Carmichael all the time, no matter who's talkin' to him."

"That's what you think," said Penrod, and he added, in a tone of determination, "His name'll be Walter whenever I say a word to him."

Sam began to wear a baffled expression, for the controversy was unusual and confusing. "It won't," he said. "Do you s'pose Duke's name'd be Walter, if you called him Walter while you were talkin' to him, and then change back to Duke the rest o' the time when you aren't talkin' to him?"

"What?"

"I said—well, suppose Duke's name was Walter"—Sam paused, finding himself unable to recall the details of the argumentative illustration he had offered.

"What's all that stuff you were talkin' about?" Penrod insisted.

"His name's John Carmichael," Sam said curtly. "Hyuh, John!"

"Hyuh, Walter!" cried Penrod.

"Hyuh, John! Hyuh, John Carmichael!"

"Hyuh, Walter, Walter! *Come* here, good ole Walter, Walter, Walter!"

"Hyuh, John! *Good* ole Johnny!"

The pup paid no attention to either of the rival godfathers, but continued to clown it over Duke, whose mood was beginning to change. His bad temper had exhausted itself, and, little by little, the pup's antics began to stir the elderly dog's memory of his own puphood. He remembered the glad unconventionality, the long days of irresponsible romping, and he wished that he might live those days again. By imperceptible degrees, his indignation diminished; he grew milder and milder until, finally, he found himself actually collaborating in the pup's hoydenish assaults. Duke's tone of voice became whimsical; he lay upon his back and pretended to swear and snap; but the swearing and snapping were now burlesque and meant to be understood as such. Duke ended by taking a decided fancy to Walter-John Carmichael.

The moral influence of dogs upon one another is profound—a matter seldom estimated at its value. People are often mystified by a change of character in a known and tried dog; they should seek to discover with whom he has been associating himself. Sometimes the change in a dog's character is permanent; sometimes it is merely temporary. In the latter case, when the animal returns to his former habit of mind, it is usually a sign that the source of influence has vanished—the other dog has moved away. Or it may be merely that the influenced dog has concluded that his new manner does not pay. One thing, however, is certain: when a dog goes wrong late in life, it is almost invariably due to the influence and example of some other dog—usually a younger one, odd as that may seem.

Walter-John Carmichael proved his light-headedness by forgetting Duke abruptly and galloping off after a sparrow that had flown near the ground. The sparrow betook himself to the limb of a tree, while the pup continued to careen and zigzag over the grass in the lunatic belief that he was still chasing the sparrow. Duke thereupon scampered upon an imaginary track, shaped like a large figure eight, and then made a jovial rush at Walter-John, bowling him over and over. Finding that the thing could be done, Duke knocked Walter-John over as often as the latter rose to his feet. Duke had caught the infection of youth; he had been lifted out of himself by Walter-John's simple happiness, and the little old dog was in great spirits. Of course, he did not weigh the question of his conduct carefully; later events proved that he acted on the spur of emotion and paused neither to reason nor to estimate consequences. His promptings were, indeed, physical rather than mental—simply, he felt like a pup once more and in all things behaved like one.

Meanwhile, the two boys sat upon the grass and watched the friendly battle. "I'm goin' to train John to be a trick dog," Sam said.

"What you goin' to train him?"

"Oh, like dogs in the dog show," Sam replied, with careless ease. "I'm goin' to make him do all those tricks."

"Yes, you are!"

"I am, too!"

"Well, *how* are you?" asked the skeptical Penrod. "How you goin' to train him?"

"Lots o' ways."

"Well, what are they?"

"Why, it's the easist thing in the world to train a pup," said Sam. "Take an ole dog like Duke, and 'course you can't train him. First thing I'm goin' to train John is to catch a ball when I throw it to him."

"You mean catch it in his mouth the same as a baseball player does with his hands?"

"Yes, sir!"

Penrod laughed scornfully.

"You wait and see!" Sam cried.

"Well, how are you goin' to? Just answer me that!"

"You'll *see* how."

"Well, why can't you answer how you're goin' to do so much? Just answer me that; that's all I——"

"Well, I'll tell you how," Sam began, speaking thoughtfully.

"Well, why'n't you *tell* me, then, instead o' talkin' so mu——"

"How can I, when you won't let me? You talk yourself all the ti——"

"You don't *know* how! That's the reason you talk so much," Penrod asserted. "You could n't any more teach a dog to catch a ball than——"

"I could, too! I'd put sumpthing on it."

Penrod's loud laugh was again scornful. "'Put sumpthing on it!'" he mocked. "*That'd* teach a dog to catch a ball, would n't it? What you goin' to put on it? Tar? So it'd stick in his mouth?" And overcome by the humor of this satire, Penrod rolled in the grass, shouting derisively.

Not at all disconcerted, his friend explained: "No; I would n't put any ole tar on it. I'd take a ball and rub sumpthing that tastes good to him on the ball."

"What for?"

"Then I'd throw it to him, and he'd catch it just like he would a piece o' beefsteak. Have n't you ever seen a dog catch meat?"

Penrod's laughter ceased; the idea fascinated him at once. "Look here, Sam," he said. "Let's teach both our dogs to do that. Let's go round to the barn and start gettin' 'em all trained up so's we can have a dog show."

"*That's* the ticket!" cried Sam.

Within five minutes, the unfortunate Duke and Walter-John, interrupted in their gambols, were beginning to undergo a course of instruction. The two trainers agreed to avoid all harshness; the new method of teaching by attractive deceptions was to be followed throughout the course, and, for a while, they were consistently persuasive and diplomatic. Penrod brought a bit of raw meat and a solid-rubber ball from the house. The meat was rubbed on the ball, which was then presented to the two dogs for inspection and sniffing. Both took some interest in it, and Duke licked it casually.

The ball was tossed first to Duke, who moved aside and would have taken his unobstrusive departure had he not been detained. Next, Sam tossed the ball to Walter-John, who, without budging, placidly watched its approach through the air, and yet seemed surprised and troubled when it concluded its flight upon his right eye. Meat was freshly rubbed upon the ball and the experiment repeated again and again, so that after a little experience Walter-John learned to watch the ball and to move as soon as he saw it coming toward him. After half an hour, he was almost as able to dodge as Duke.

It may not be denied that by this the trainers were irritated. Their theory was so plausible—it had sounded so simple, so inevitable—that the illogical conduct of the two dogs could not fail to get more and more upon the theorist's nerves. Naturally, then, in spite of all agreements never to resort to harshness, there were times when, instead of tossing, Penrod threw the ball to Duke, and Sam to Walter-John. In fact, to an observer who had no knowledge of dog-training, the instruction finally might have seemed to be a contest in accuracy between the two trainers, especially as they had found it necessary to tie both Walter-John and Duke rather closely to the stable wall. Indeed, that was the view of the matter ignorantly taken by Della.

"I niver see th' beat!" she exclaimed, coming out upon the back porch from the kitchen. "Chainin' thim two poor dogs ag'inst the wall and throwin' big rocks at 'em to see which can hit 'em the most times and——"

"Rocks!" Penrod interrupted angrily. "Who's throwin' rocks? You tell me who's throwin' any rocks!"

"I'll tell you to come to lunch," Della retorted. "And Mrs. Williams has been telephonin' a quawter'v an hour. They're waitin' lunch at the Williamses; so you let thim two poor dogs go—if they still got the strenk to walk. Are you comin' to yer lunch, Musther Penrod, or not? Come in and try to eat like a human person and not like a rhinoceros the way you did yesterday, and you know what you got fer it, too—I'm glad, praise hiven!" She returned into the house, slamming the door.

"What's she mean, Penrod?" Sam inquired, as he released Walter-John from the wall. "What did you get for what, that she says she was so glad about?"

"Nothin'," said Penrod, though his expression had become momentarily unpleasant. "Those Irish always got to be sayin' sumpthing or other."

"Yey," Sam agreed. "Let's go ahead and train our dogs some more this afternoon. You bring Duke over to our yard, Penrod, and let's get started early."

II

Penrod assented, and, at a little after one o'clock, the training began again in the Williams's yard. Duke and Walter-John passed two hours comparable to hours human beings pass at the dentist's, and both the trainers gradually became hoarse, though they still maintained that their method continued to be humane and persuasive. Experiments with the ball were finally postponed to another day, as both dogs persisted in their dodging and each refused to grasp the idea of a ball's purpose—even when it was forcibly placed in his mouth and held there for minutes at a time.

Duke had long ago mastered the art of "sitting-up," and today, upon command, he "sat up" till he was ready to drop, while Walter-John was held up in a similar position and bidden to learn from the example of Duke, but would not even look at him. No progress being perceptible in this, a barrel-hoop was procured, and one trainer held the hoop, while the other accustomed the dogs to passing through it. Patiently, until his back ached, Penrod again and again threw Duke and the cumbersome Walter-John in turn through the hoop; then held it while Sam manipulated the dogs.

"*Now* I expeck they unnerstand what we want 'em to do," said Sam, at last, straightening up with a gasp. "Anyways, they cert'nly ought to!"

"Jump, Dukie!" Penrod urged. "Jump through the hoop just like you been doin'! *Come* on, old Dukie— *jump!*"

Again the patience of the instructors was strained. Both Duke and Walter-John could be coaxed to pass under the hoop or upon either side of it; but each refused to pass through it of his free will. Manifestly, they had, for inexplicable reasons, conceived a prejudice against hoop-jumping, and nothing served to remove their aversion.

"I'll tell you what we can train 'em," Penrod suggested, after a long pause of discouragement. "We can train 'em to walk the tight-rope. We could do that, anyway!"

After the setbacks received in processes apparently so much simpler (especially for dogs) than tight-rope walking, Penrod's proposal naturally produced a feeling of surprise in Sam. "What on earth you talkin' about now?"

"Why, look!" said Penrod. "Listen, Sam—you listen here a minute! We can teach 'em to walk the tight-rope *easy!* It won't be anything at all, the way *I* got fixed up to do it. *Then* just look where we'll be, when our good ole dogs get so's all we got to do'll just be to say, 'Hyuh, Dukie, jump up on that clo'esline and walk it!' And then you can say, 'Hyuh, Walter, jump up——' "

"I would n't, neither!" Sam interrupted. "His name's John!"

"Well, anyway," Penrod continued evasively, "you could tell him to jump up on a clo'esline and walk it just like Duke, and he'd do it. *Oh,* oh!" Penrod's eyes sparkled; he gesticulated joyously—to his mind, the gorgeous performance was already taking place. "*Oh,* oh! That would n't be any good ole show—I guess not! Why, we could charge a *dollar* for anybody to come in! *Oh,* oh! Laydeez and gentlemun, the big show is about to commence! *Get* up on that tight-rope now, you good ole Duke! Laydeez and gentlemun, you now see before your very eyes the only two tight-rope-walking dogs ever trained to——"

"Well, can't you wait a minute?" Sam cried. "I'd like to know how we're goin' to train 'em to walk any tight-rope when they don't show any more sense'n they did about that hoop and catchin' a ball and——"

"Listen, I told you, did n't I?" said Penrod. "Look, Sam! First, we'll train 'em to walk the fence-rail here in your yard. We'll take one of 'em at a time and put him on the rail. Then one of us'll hold him from jumpin' off while the other pushes him along from behind so's he's got to keep goin'. Well, if he *can't* get off, and if he's *got* to keep goin'—so, well, if we do that enough, say so often a day for so many weeks—well, he can't *help* himself from learning how to walk a fence-rail, can he?"

"No. But how——"

"Listen—did n't I tell you? Well, when he's got that much good and learned, all we do is get a board half the size of the fence-rail and do the same thing with him on *it*—and then get another one half the size of that one, and so on till we get him trained to walk on a board that's just the same size as a rope. I'd like to know *then* if he could n't walk just as well on a rope as on a board he could n't tell the *difference* from a rope from."

"Well, I don't care," Sam said. "I bet it'll take pretty near forever."

"It would if we just sit around here and never do anything."

"Oh, I'm willing to give it a *try*," Sam said.

Sam's mother, coming out into the yard, half an hour later, preserved her composure, though given cause for abandoning it. Walter-John was seated upon the fence-rail but moving steadily. Sam distrained him from leaving the rail, while Penrod's two extended hands, applying serious and constant pressure at the base of Walter-

John's spine, compelled Walter-John to progress along the fence-rail. Walter-John's expression was concerned and inquiring, and Duke, tied to a tree, near by, stood in an attitude of depression.

"Let the dogs go now, boys," Mrs. Williams called. "I've got something for you, and then Sam has to come in and get dressed to go and spend an hour or so at his grandmother's. It's after three o'clock."

"What you got for us?" Sam asked.

She displayed a plate covered with a napkin.

"*Oh,* oh!" Both boys trotted to Mrs. Williams.

"What's under that napkin?" cried the eager Sam.

"Look!" and she withdrew the napkin, while Sam shouted.

"Doughnuts!"

He dashed at them; but his mother fended him off. "Wait, Sam!" she said. "Shame on you! See how polite Penrod is! *He* does n't grab and——"

"That's only because he's company," Sam interrupted. "Gimme those doughnuts!"

"No," she said. "There are five apiece, and you'll divide evenly. Here, Penrod; you take your five first."

"Ma'am?" said Penrod, his face flushing painfully.

"Don't be bashful." Mrs. Williams laughed, and she extended the plate toward him. "You're Sam's guest and you must choose your five first."

Penrod was anxious to prevent his recent misfortune from becoming known, and he felt that to decline these doughnuts would arouse suspicion. Yet he was uncertain whether or not he could, with physical security, hold five doughnuts even in his hands.

"Hurry, Penrod! I know you want them."

At arm's length he took five doughnuts, two in one hand and three in the other. Then his arms fell at his sides, and he stood very straight, holding his head high and his nose to the clouds.

"There!" said Mrs. Williams, departing. "All right, Sammy! As soon as you've finished them, you must come to dress. Not more than ten minutes."

Sam carolled and capered with his doughnuts, stuffing his mouth full, so that he carolled no more, but capered still, in greater ecstasy. No pleasures of contemplation for Sam, or dwelling long and delicately upon morsels! What was sweet to his flesh he took, and consumed as he took. The five doughnuts sped to the interior almost *en masse*. Within four minutes there remained of them but impalpable tokens upon Sam's cheeks.

"Hah!" he shouted. "Those were *good!*" Then, his eye falling upon Penrod's drooping hands, "Well, for gray-*shus* sakes!" he exclaimed. "Are n't you goin' to *eat* 'em?"

Penrod's voice was lifeless. He responded: "Well, some days I kind o' like to save mine up and eat 'em when I feel like it." He swallowed twice, coughed twice.

"I wish I'd saved mine," Sam said. "Come on, John, ole doggie!" he added, beginning to drag the pup toward the house.

"What you goin' to do with him?" Penrod asked.

"I'm goin' to lock him up in the cellar while I'm gone. That's where they said I could keep him."

"What for? Let me have him till you get back. I'll bring him over here before dinner time."

Sam thought this request outrageous. "*No,* sir!" he cried. "Haven't you got a dog o' your own? You want to go and get mine so's he knows you better'n he would me? I guess not! John Carmichael's goin' to stay right in our cellar every minute I'm not here to be trainin' him!"

"Oh, come on, Sam!" Penrod urged, for he had become more and more fascinated by Walter-John throughout the day. "It isn't goin' to *hurt* him any, is it?"

"I won't do it."

"Oh, come on, Sam! What's the use actin' that way to a poor dog—lockin' him up in a dark ole cellar when he ought to be out in the fresh air so's he could keep strong? He likes Duke, and he ought to be allowed to stay with him. I call it mighty mean, lockin' him up in that ole ugly cellar just because *you* want to go and have a good time at your grandmother's."

"I don't care what you call it; he's goin' to be locked up," Sam said. "And I don't either want to go and have a good time at my grandmother's. I *got* to go."

Whereupon, having thus uttered his final decision in the matter, and defended his character against the charge of selfishness, Sam towed Walter-John as far as the cellar door.

"Wait a minute, Sam," Penrod urged. "If you'll let me have him till you get back, I'll give you some o' these doughnuts."

"How many?"

"I'll give you," said Penrod, "the whole kitamaboodle!"

"*Yay!*"

Blithely the doughnuts passed from Penrod's hands to Sam's, and the end of the bit of clothesline from Sam's to Penrod's.

"Come on, Walter!" Penrod cried.

Though his utterance was already thick, Sam protested instantly. "Stop that!" he commanded. "His name's John Carmichael, and you got to call him John. You can't have him if you're going to call him Walter."

Penrod began to argue rather bitterly. "My goodness, gracious heavens! He's just the same as *my* dog till you get back, isn't he?"

"He is not!"

"Didn't I just pay you for him? It's just the same as buyin' him till you get back from your grandmother's, and whatever time he's my dog, he's got to be named Walter. If you don't like it, you can give me back my doughnuts!"

"Oh, goodness!" Sam groaned. "Well, you got to quit callin' him Walter after today, anyways. The poor dog's got to learn his name *some* time."

Penrod, wearing an unassuming air of triumph, released Duke from the tree to which he had been tied, and, leading both dogs, proceeded toward the back gate; but before he went out into the alley Sam was amazed to see him pause at the hydrant and wash his hands exhaustively. Then Penrod opened the alley gate and passed from sight with his two charges, leaving Sam staring, open-mouthed.

Duke trotted obediently after his master; but Walter-John still misconceived the purposes of a leash and progressed for the most part in his seated or semi-seated attitude. However, Penrod reached his own yard—the front yard, away from the kitchen—without much difficulty, and paused there, regarding Walter-John with pleasure and affection.

He sat down on the grass, a dog under each arm. His imagination stepped quietly out of the present into the gold-clouded future. He saw himself in the filtered light of a great tent, addressing in a magnificent bass voice the fanning multitude.

"Laydeez and gentlemun—"

"Laydeez and gentlemun, allow me to interdoos to your attainshon, the great tight-rope-walking dog, Walter!" And straightway, from the "dressing-room tent," Walter-John came hopping on hind legs, white ruff about his neck. Then Penrod proclaimed: "And now, laydeez and gentlemun, let me interdoos to your attainshon, Walter's little boy, Duke, the greatest tight-rope dog on EARTH!" Whereupon, Duke, similarly hopping and similarly be-ruffed, came forward to the side of the ringmaster in the ring, and the three bowed low, to twenty-thousand plaudits. Anxious attendants in uniform ran to their posts to support the tight-rope, and Penrod, smiling negligently——

His bubble broke. The clatter of a brazen gong and a staccato of iron-shod hoofs—sounds increasing, coming nearer—startled him from the proud daydream. A hose-cart, then a fire-engine, then a hook-and-ladder wagon careened in turn round the corner, passed furiously and roared up the street, followed by panting boys with faces alight.

Penrod leaped to his feet. The stable was too far. He dragged Duke and Walter-John up the front steps and across the verandah; he tried the front door, found it unlocked, opened it, thrust Walter-John and Duke into the hall, slammed the door and made off to the fire.

In the cool hall, Duke and Walter-John looked at each other vaguely; then discovered that they were free. A frolicsome look bloomed upon the fertile face of Walter-John. With no motive, he dashed into a large room that opened from the hall, and knocked over a tall silver vase of lilies that somebody had set upon the floor directly in his way. Then he charged upon Duke, upset him, left him kicking at the air, and scampered to and fro for the love of motion. Duke was instantly infected; his puphood of the morning returned in full flood, and he, in his turn, charged upon Walter-John.

Both dogs had been through a great deal that day; in fact, their trainers had shown them a poor time, and nothing could have been more natural than that Duke and Walter-John should wish to liven things up after their protracted experience as apprentices in baseball, sitting-up, hoop-jumping and tight-rope-walking. They made it an orgy. The house was empty of human life, upstairs and down, as far as the kitchen door, which was closed. Walter-John and Duke engaged in mimic battle all over this empty house, and wherever there was anything that could be upset, they upset it, for Walter-John was undoubtedly cumbersome.

Exhausting for a time this pleasure, Walter-John found matter of interest on a low table in the library. This consisted of a new encyclopedia, limp-leather covers, gilt tops, thin paper, seven volumes, purchased by Mr. Schofield the week before. Walter-John dragged down two volumes, one labelled "Ala-Con," the other, "Mon-Pyx." Walter-

John began to eat "Ala-Con," and Duke—all culture fallen from him now in his rejuvenation—Duke began to eat "Mon-Pyx." That is, they did not eat except accidentally, for neither of them actually swallowed much of the paper; but the effect upon "Ala-Con" and "Mon-Pyx" was none the less radical.

Growing tired of this learned work, they found some semi-edible slippers in Margaret's room upstairs, also a table-cover—which frightened Walter-John on account of the noise the things made when he dragged the cover from the table. Next, he discovered, hanging in an open closet in the same room, a beady substance that proved enjoyable. In this, as in everything, the senile Duke joined him with gusto. The orgy continued.

Penrod found the fire an unusually satisfactory one. In fact, a large warehouse, almost full of hides and leather, burned all up, and dusk was falling when Penrod, smelling intensely, again reached his place of residence. As he opened the gate, he saw Duke coming round a corner of the house with a peculiar air. There was something regretful and haunted about the little old dog; he advanced hesitatingly, seeming to be without confidence, and when Penrod spoke to him, he disappeared instantly. In the darkness, his young master could not see where or even in which direction he went. Suddenly a chill struck upon Penrod's spine. He remembered. Where, oh, where, was Walter-John?

Penrod entered the front hall impetuously; but paused there at once—and more cold chills touched his young spine. A sound of lamentation—his mother's voice—came from the library, and evidently she was addressing Mr. Schofield.

"You never *saw* such a house! *Oh,* if I'd only followed my instinct and not let Margaret persuade me to go to that reception with her! We had Della give Duke a whipping, because he had a shred of

Margaret's best party dress sticking to his nose, and he *must* have helped that horrible pup! Della threw lumps of coal at *him* when she chased him out, and I do hope she hit him. It seems utterly impossible that there were only *two* dogs in the house. Look at that encyclopedia—why anybody would think it must have taken two of them all afternoon to do just *that* much damage, let alone all the other awful things! Della says she's sure Penrod let them into the house, and this time I certainly don't intend to say one word against it if you think you ought to——"

"Yes, of course I ought to," Mr. Schofield said; and, to the dismayed ears listening in the hallway, his voice was the executioner's.

With infinite precaution, Penrod returned to the front door, let himself out, and no one could have heard a footfall as he crossed the verandah.

He found Sam closing the door of the Williams's cellar upon Walter-John. "Where'd you come across him?" Penrod asked, in a preoccupied tone. He was not much interested.

"*Nice* way to bring him home like you promised, wasn't it?" Sam returned indignantly. "I found him out in the alley, 'way up by the corner, and he acted like he was scared to death. He didn't even act like he knew me."

"See here a minute, Sam," Penrod said, in a friendly though still preoccupied tone. "On account of all those doughnuts I gave you, and everything, I don't s'pose your mother would mind if I stayed over here for dinner much, would she?"

GALLEGHER

By RICHARD HARDING DAVIS

Illustrations by CHARLES DANA GIBSON

WE had had so many office-boys before Gallegher came among us that they had begun to lose the characteristics of individuals, and became merged in a composite photograph of small boys, to whom we applied the generic title of "Here, you"; or "You, boy." We had had sleepy boys, and lazy boys, and bright, "smart" boys, who became so familiar on so short an acquaintance that we were forced to part with them to save our own self-respect.

They generally graduated into district-messenger boys, and occasionally returned to us in blue coats with nickel-plated buttons, and patronized us.

But Gallegher was something different from anything we had experienced before. Gallegher was short and broad in build, with a solid, muscular broadness, and not a fat and dumpy shortness. He wore perpetually on his face a happy and knowing smile, as if you and the world in general were not impressing him as seriously as you thought you were, and his eyes, which were very black and very bright, snapped intelligently at you like those of a little black-and-tan terrier.

All Gallegher knew had been learnt on the streets; not a very good school in itself, but one that turns out very knowing scholars. And Gallegher had attended both morning and evening sessions. He could not tell you who the Pilgrim Fathers were, nor could he name the thirteen original States, but he knew all the officers of the twenty-second police district by name, and he could distinguish the clang of a fire engine's gong from that of a patrol wagon or an ambulance fully two blocks distant. It was Gallegher who rang the alarm when the Woolwich Mills caught fire, while the officer on the beat was asleep, and it was Gallegher who led the "Black Diamonds" against the "Wharf Rats," when they used to stone each other to their heart's content on the coal-wharves of Richmond.

I am afraid, now that I see these facts written down, that Gallegher was not a reputable character; but he was so very young and so very old for his years that we all liked him very much nevertheless. He lived in the extreme northern part of Philadelphia, where the cotton and woolen mills run down to the river, and how he ever got home after leaving the *Press* building at two in the morning, was one of the mysteries of the office. Sometimes he caught a night car, and sometimes he walked all the way, arriving at the little house, where his mother and himself lived alone, at four in the morning. Occasionally he was given a ride on an early milk cart, or on one of the newspaper delivery wagons, with its high piles of papers still damp and sticky from the press. He knew several drivers of "night hawks"—those cabs that prowl the streets at night looking for belated passengers—and when it was a very cold morning he would not go home at all, but would crawl into one of these cabs and sleep, curled up on the cushions, until daylight.

Besides being quick and cheerful, Gallegher possessed a power of amusing the *Press's* young men to a degree seldom attained by the ordinary mortal. His clog-dancing on the city editor's desk, when that gentleman was upstairs fighting for two more columns of space, was always a source of innocent joy to us, and his imitations of the comedians of the variety halls delighted even the dramatic critic, from whom the comedians themselves failed to force a smile.

But Gallegher's chief characteristic was his love for that element of news generically classed as "crime."

Not that he ever did anything criminal himself. On the contrary, his was rather the work of the criminal specialist, and his morbid interest in the doings of all queer characters, his knowledge of their methods, their present whereabouts, and their past deeds of transgression often rendered him a valuable ally to our police reporter, whose daily feuilletons were the only portion of the paper Gallegher deigned to read.

In Gallegher the detective element was abnormally developed. He had shown this on several occasions, and to excellent purpose.

Once the paper had sent him into a Home for Destitute Orphans which was believed to be grievously mismanaged, and Gallegher, while playing the part of a destitute orphan, kept his eyes open to what was going on around him so faithfully that the story he told of the treatment meted out to the real orphans was sufficient to rescue the unhappy little wretches from the individual who had them in charge, and to have the individual himself sent to jail.

Gallegher's knowledge of the aliases, terms of imprisonment, and various misdoings of the leading criminals in Philadelphia was almost as thorough as that of the chief of police himself, and he could tell to an hour when "Dutchy Mack" was to be let out of prison, and could identify at a glance "Dick Oxford, confidence man," as "Gentleman Dan, petty thief."

There were, at this time, only two pieces of news in any of the papers. The least important of the two was the big fight between the Champion of the United States and the Would-be Champion, arranged to take place near Philadelphia; the second was the Burrbank murder, which was filling space in newspapers all over the world, from New York to Bombay.

Richard F. Burrbank was one of the most prominent of New York's railroad lawyers; he was also, as a matter of course, an owner of much railroad stock, and a very wealthy man. He had been spoken of as a political possibility for many high offices, and, as the counsel for a great railroad, was known even further than the great railroad itself had stretched its system.

At six o'clock one morning he was found by his butler lying at the foot of the hall stairs with two pistol wounds above his heart. He was quite dead. His safe, to which only he and his secretary had the keys, was found open, and $200,000 in bonds, stocks, and money, which had been placed there only the night before, was found missing. The secretary was missing also. His name was Stephen S. Hade, and his name and his description had been telegraphed and cabled to all parts of the world. There was enough circumstantial evidence to show, beyond any question of possibility of mistake, that he was the murderer.

It made an enormous amount of talk, and unhappy individuals were being arrested all over the country, and sent on to New York for identification. Three had been arrested at Liverpool, and one man just as he landed at Sydney, Australia. But so far the murderer had escaped.

We were all talking about it one night, as everybody else was all over the country, in the local room, and the city editor said it was worth a fortune to any one who chanced to run across Hade and succeeded in handing him over to the police. Some of us thought Hade had taken passage from some one of the smaller seaports, and others were of the opinion that he had buried himself in some cheap lodging house in New York, or in one of the smaller towns in New Jersey.

"I should n't be surprised to meet him out walking, right here in Philadelphia," said one of the staff. "He'll be disguised, of course, but you could always tell him by the absence of the trigger finger on his right hand. It's missing, you know; shot off when he was a boy."

"You want to look for a man dressed like a tough," said the city editor; "for as this fellow is to all appearances a gentleman, he will try to look as little like a gentleman as possible."

"No, he won't," said Gallegher with that calm impertinence that made him dear to us. "He'll dress just like a gentleman. Toughs don't wear gloves, and you see he's got to wear 'em. The first thing he thought of after doing for Burrbank was of that gone finger, and how he was to hide it. He stuffed the finger of that glove with cotton so's to make it look like a whole finger, and the first time he takes off that glove they've got him—see, and he knows it. So what youse want to do is to look for a man with gloves on. I've been a-doing it for two weeks now, and I can tell you it's hard work, for everybody wears gloves this kind of weather. But if you look long enough you'll find him. And when you think it's him, go up to him and hold out your hand in a friendly way, like a bunco-steerer, and shake his hand; if you feel that his forefinger ain't real flesh, but just wadded cotton, then grip to it with your right and grab his throat with your left, and holler for help."

There was an appreciative pause.

"I see, gentlemen," said the city editor, dryly, "that Gallegher's reasoning has impressed you; and I also see that before the week is out all of my young men will be under bonds for assaulting innocent pedestrians whose only offense is that they wear gloves in mid-winter."

• • •

It was about a week after this that Detective Hefflefinger, of Inspector Byrnes's staff, came over to Philadelphia after a burglar, of whose whereabouts he had been misinformed by telegraph. He brought the warrant, requisition, and other necessary papers with him, but the burglar had flown. One of our reporters had worked on a New York paper, and knew Hefflefinger, and the detective came to the office to see if he could help him in his so far unsuccessful search.

He gave Gallegher his card, and after Gallegher read it, and had discovered who the visitor was, he became so demoralized that he was absolutely useless.

"One of Byrnes's men" was a much more awe-inspiring individual to Gallegher than a member of the Cabinet. He accordingly seized his hat and overcoat, and leaving his duties to be looked after by others, hastened out after the object of his admiration, who found his suggestions and knowledge of the city so valuable, and his company so entertaining, that they became very intimate, and spent the rest of the day together.

In the meanwhile the managing editor had instructed his subordinates to inform Gallegher, when he condescended to return, that his services were no longer needed. Gallegher had played truant once too often. Unconscious of this, he remained with his new friend until late the same evening, and started the next afternoon toward the *Press* office.

As I have said, Gallegher lived in the most distant part of the city not many minutes' walk from the Kensington railroad station, where trains ran into the suburbs and on to New York.

It was in front of this station that a smoothly shaven, well-dressed man brushed past Gallegher and hurried up the steps to the ticket office.

He held a walking-stick in his right hand, and Gallegher, who now patiently scrutinized the hands of every one who wore gloves, saw that while three fingers of the man's hand were closed around the cane, the fourth stood out in almost a straight line with his palm.

Gallegher stopped with a gasp and with a trembling all over his little body, and his brain asked with a throb if it could be possible. But possibilities and probabilities were to be discovered later. Now was the time for action.

He was after the man in a moment, hanging at his heels and his eyes moist with excitement.

He heard the man ask for a ticket to Torresdale, a little station just outside of Philadelphia, and when he was out of hearing, but not out of sight, purchased one for the same place.

The stranger went into the smoking car, and seated himself at one end toward the door. Gallegher took his place at the opposite end.

He was trembling all over, and suffered from a slight feeling of nausea. He guessed it came from fright, not of any bodily harm that might come to him, but of the probability of failure in his adventure and of its most momentous possibilities.

The stranger pulled his coat collar up around his ears, hiding the lower portion of his face, but not concealing the resemblance in his troubled eyes and close-shut lips to the likenesses of the murderer Hade.

They reached Torresdale in half an hour, and the stranger, alighting quickly, struck off at a rapid pace down the country road leading to the station.

Gallegher gave him a hundred yards' start, and then followed slowly after. The road ran between fields and past a few frame houses set far from the road in kitchen gardens.

Once or twice the man looked back over his shoulder, but he saw only a dreary length of road with a small boy splashing through the slush in the midst of it and stopping every now and again to throw snowballs at belated sparrows.

After a ten minutes' walk the stranger turned into a side road which led to only one place, the Eagle Inn, an old roadside hostelry known now as the headquarters for pothunters from the Philadelphia game market and the battleground of many a cock-fight.

Gallegher knew the place well. He and his young companions had often stopped there when out chestnutting on holidays in the autumn.

The son of the man who kept it had often accompanied them on their excursions, and though the boys of the city streets considered him a dumb lout, they respected him somewhat owing to his inside knowledge of dog- and cock-fights.

The stranger entered the inn at a side door, and Gallegher, reaching it a few minutes later, let him go for the time being, and set about finding his occasional playmate, young Keppler.

Keppler's offspring was found in the woodshed.

" 'Taint hard to guess what brings you out here," said the tavern-keeper's son, with a grin; "it's the fight."

"What fight?" asked Gallegher, unguardedly.

"What fight? Why, *the* fight," returned his companion, with the slow contempt of superior knowledge. "It's to come off here tonight. You know that as well as me; anyway your sportin' editor knows it. He got the tip last night, but that won't help you any. You need n't think there's any chance of your getting a peep at it. Why, tickets is two hundred and fifty apiece!"

"Whew!" whistled Gallegher, "where's it to be?"

"In the barn," whispered Keppler. "I helped 'em fix the ropes this morning, I did."

"Gosh, but you're in luck," exclaimed Gallegher, with flattering envy. "Could n't I jest get a peep at it?"

"Maybe," said the gratified Keppler. "There's a winder with a wooden shutter at the back of the barn. You can get in by it, if you have some one to boost you up to the sill."

"Sa-ay," drawled Gallegher, as if something had but just that moment reminded him. "Who's that gent who come down the road just a bit ahead of me—him with the cape-coat! Has he got anything to do with the fight?"

"Him?" repeated Keppler in tones of sincere disgust. "No-oh, he ain't no sport. He's queer, Dad thinks. He come here one day last week about ten in the morning, said his doctor told him to go out 'en the country for his health. He's stuck up and citified, and wears gloves, and takes his meals private in his room, and all that sort of ruck. They was saying in the saloon last night that they thought he was hiding from something, and Dad, just to try him, asks him last night if he was coming to see the fight. He looked sort of scared, and said he did n't want to see no fight. And then Dad says, 'I guess you mean you don't want no fighters to see you.' Dad did n't mean no harm by it, just passed it as a joke; but Mr. Carleton, as he calls himself, got white as a ghost an' says, 'I'll go to the fight willing enough,' and begins to laugh and joke. And this morning he went right into the bar-room, where all the sports were setting, and said he was going into town to see some friends; and as he starts off he laughs an' says, 'This don't look as if I was afraid of seeing people, does it?' but Dad says it was just bluff that made him do it, and Dad thinks that if he had n't said what he did, this Mr. Carleton would n't have left his room at all."

Gallegher had got all he wanted, and much more than he had hoped for—so much more that his walk back to the station was in the nature of a triumphal march.

He had twenty minutes to wait for the next train, and it seemed an hour. While waiting he sent a telegram to Hefflefinger at his hotel. It read:

> Your man is near the Torresdale station, on Pennsylvania railroad; take cab, and meet me at station. Wait until I come.
>
> GALLEGHER.

With the exception of one at midnight, no other train stopped at Torresdale that evening, hence the direction to take a cab.

The train to the city seemed to Gallegher to drag itself by inches.

It stopped and backed at purposeless intervals, waited for an express to precede it, and dallied at stations, and when, at last, it reached the terminus, Gallegher was out before it had stopped and was in the cab and off on his way to the home of the sporting editor.

The sporting editor was at dinner and came out in the hall to see him, with his napkin in his hand. Gallegher explained breathlessly that he had located the murderer for whom the police of two continents were looking, and that he believed, in order to quiet the suspicions of the people with whom he was hiding, that he would be present at the fight that night.

The sporting editor led Gallegher into his library and shut the door. "Now," he said, "go over all that again."

Gallegher went over it again in detail, and added how he had sent for Hefflefinger to make the arrest in order that it might be kept from the knowledge of the local police and from the Philadelphia reporters.

"What I want Hefflefinger to do is to arrest Hade with the warrant he has for the burglar," explained Gallegher; "and to take him on to New York on the owl train that passes Torresdale at one. It don't get to Jersey City until four o'clock, one hour after the morning papers go to press. Of course, we must fix Hefflefinger so's he'll keep quiet and not tell who his prisoner really is."

The sporting editor reached his hand out to pat Gallegher on the head, but changed his mind and shook hands with him instead.

"My boy," he said, "you are an infant phenomenon. If I can pull the rest of this thing off tonight it will mean the $5,000 reward and fame galore for you and the paper. Now, I'm going to write a note to the managing editor, and you can take it around to him and tell him what you've done and what I am going to do, and he'll take you back on the paper and raise your salary. Perhaps you did n't know you've been discharged?"

"Do you think you ain't a-going to take me with you?" demanded Gallegher.

"Why, certainly not. Why should I? It all lies with the detective and myself now. You've done your share, and done it well. If the man's caught, the reward's yours. But you'd only be in the way now. You'd better go to the office and make your peace with the chief."

"If the paper can get along without me, I can get along without the old paper," said Gallegher, hotly. "And if I ain't a-going with you, you ain't neither, for I know where Hefflefinger is to be, and you don't, and I won't tell you."

"Oh, very well, very well," replied the sporting editor, weakly capitulating. "I'll send the note by a messenger; only mind, if you lose your place, don't blame me."

Gallegher wondered how this man could value a week's salary against the excitement of seeing a noted criminal run down, and of getting the news to the paper, and to that one paper alone.

From that moment the sporting editor sank in Gallegher's estimation.

Mr. Dwyer sat down at his desk and scribbled off the following note:

> I have received reliable information that Hade, the Burrbank murderer, will be present at the fight tonight. We have arranged it so that he will be arrested quietly and in such a manner that the fact may be kept from all other papers. I need not point out to you that this will be the most important piece of news in the country tomorrow. Yours, etc.,
>
> MICHAEL E. DWYER.

The sporting editor stepped into the waiting cab, while Gallegher whispered the directions to the driver. He was told to go first to a district-messenger office, and from there up to the Ridge Avenue Road, out Broad Street, and on to the old Eagle Inn, near Torresdale.

It was a miserable night. The rain and snow were falling together, and freezing as they fell. The sporting editor got out to send his message to the *Press* office, and then lighting a cigar, and turning up the collar of his great-coat, curled up in the corner of the cab.

"Wake me when we get there, Gallegher," he said. He knew he had a long ride, and much rapid work before him, and he was preparing for the strain.

To Gallegher the idea of going to sleep seemed almost criminal. From the dark corner of the cab his eyes shone with excitement, and with the awful joy of anticipation. He glanced every now and then to where the sporting editor's cigar shone in the darkness, and watched it as it gradually burnt more dimly and went out. The light in the shop windows threw a broad glare across the ice on the pavements, and the lights from the lamp-posts tossed the distorted shadow of the cab, and the horse, and the motionless driver, sometimes before and sometimes behind them.

After half an hour Gallegher slipped down to the bottom of the cab and dragged out a lap-robe, in which he wrapped himself. It was growing colder, and the damp, keen wind swept in through the cracks until the window-frames and woodwork were cold to the touch.

An hour passed, and the cab was still moving more slowly over the rough surface of partly paved streets, and by single rows of new houses standing at different angles to each other in fields covered with ash-heaps and brick-kilns. Here and there the gaudy lights of a drug-store, and the forerunner of suburban civilization, shone from the end of a new block of houses, and the rubber cape of an occasional policeman showed in the light of the lamp-post that he hugged for comfort.

Then even the houses disappeared, and the cab dragged its way between truck farms, with desolate-looking glass-covered beds, and pools of water, half-caked with ice, and bare trees, and interminable fences.

Once or twice the cab stopped altogether, and Gallegher could hear the driver swearing to himself, or at the horse, or the roads. At last they drew up before the station at Torresdale. It was quite deserted, and only a single light cut a swath in the darkness and showed a portion of the platform, the ties, and the rails glistening in the rain. They walked twice past the light before a figure stepped out of the shadow and greeted them cautiously.

"I am Mr. Dwyer, of the *Press*," said the sporting editor, briskly. "You 've heard of me, perhaps. Well, there should n't be any difficulty in our making a deal, should there? This boy here has found Hade, and we have reason to believe he will be among the spectators at the fight tonight. We want you to arrest him quietly, and as secretly as possible. You can do it with your papers and your badge easily enough. We want you to pretend that you believe he is this burglar you came over after. If you will do this, and take him away without any one so much as suspecting who he really is, and on the train that passes here at 1.20 for New York, we will give you $500 out of the $5,000 reward. If, however, one other paper, either in New York or Philadelphia, or anywhere else, knows of the arrest, you won't get a cent. Now, what do you say?"

The detective had a great deal to say. He was n't at all sure the man Gallegher suspected was Hade; he feared he might get himself into trouble by making a false arrest, and if it should be the man, he was afraid the local police would interfere.

"We've no time to argue or debate this matter," said Dwyer, warmly. "We agree to point Hade out to you in the crowd. After the fight is over you arrest him as we have directed, and you get the money and the credit of the arrest. If you don't like this, I will arrest the man myself, and have him driven to town, with a pistol for a warrant."

Hefflefinger considered in silence and then agreed unconditionally. "As you say, Mr. Dwyer," he returned. "I've heard of you for a thoroughbred sport. I know you'll do what you say you'll do; and as for me I'll do what you say and just as you say, and it's a very pretty piece of work as it stands."

They all stepped back into the cab, and then it was that they were met by a fresh difficulty, how to get the detective into the barn where the fight was to take place, for neither of the two men had $250 to pay for his admittance.

But this was overcome when Gallegher remembered the window of which young Keppler had told him.

In the event of Hade's losing courage and not daring to show himself in the crowd around the ring, it was agreed that Dwyer should come to the barn and warn Hefflefinger; but if he should come, Dwyer was merely to keep near him and to signify by a prearranged gesture which one of the crowd he was.

They drew up before a great black shadow of a house, dark, forbidding, and apparently deserted. But at the sound of the wheels on the gravel the door opened, letting out a stream of warm, cheerful light, and a man's voice said, "Put out those lights. Don't youse know no better than that?"

This was Keppler, and he welcomed Mr. Dwyer with effusive courtesy.

The two men showed in the stream of light, and the door closed on them, leaving the house as it was at first, black and silent, save for the dripping of the rain and snow from the eaves.

The detective and Gallegher put out the cab's lamps and led the horse toward a long, low shed in the rear of the yard, which they now noticed was almost filled with teams of many different makes, from the Hobson's choice of a livery stable to the brougham of the man about town.

"No," said Gallegher, as the cabman stopped to hitch the horse beside the other, "we want it nearest that lower gate. When we newspaper men leave this place we'll leave it in a hurry, and the man who is nearest town is likely to get there first. You won't be a-following of no hearse when you make your return trip."

Gallegher tied the horse to the very gatepost itself, leaving the gate open and allowing a clear road and a flying start for the prospective race to Newspaper Row.

The driver disappeared under the shelter of the porch, and Gallegher and the detective moved off cautiously to the rear of the barn. "This must be the window," said Hefflefinger, pointing to a broad wooden shutter some feet from the ground.

"Just you give me a boost once, and I'll get that open in a jiffy," said Gallegher.

The detective placed his hands on his knees, and Gallegher stood upon his shoulders, and with the blade of his knife lifted the wooden button that fastened the window on the inside, and pulled the shutter open.

Then he put one leg inside over the sill, and leaning down helped to draw his fellow conspirator up to a level with the window. "I feel

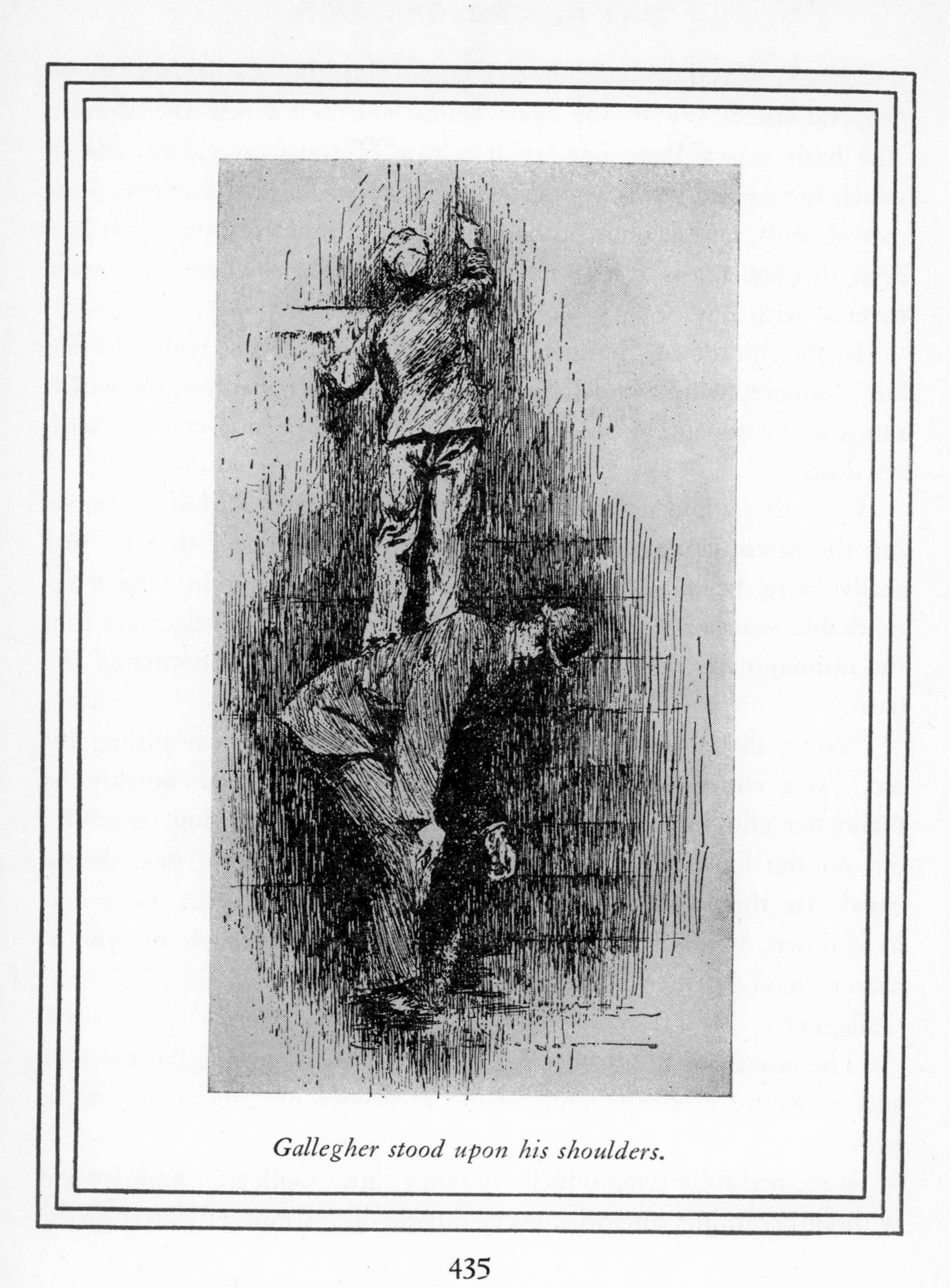

Gallegher stood upon his shoulders.

just like I was burglarizing a house," chuckled Gallegher, as he dropped noiselessly to the floor below and refastened the shutter. The barn was a large one, with a row of stalls on either side in which horses and cows were dozing. There was a haymow over each row of stalls, and at one end of the barn a number of fence rails had been thrown across from one mow to the other. These rails were covered with hay.

In the middle of the floor was the ring. It was not really a ring, but a square, with wooden posts at its four corners through which ran a heavy rope. The space enclosed by the rope was covered with sawdust.

Gallegher could not resist stepping into the ring, and after stamping the sawdust once or twice, as if to assure himself that he was really there, began dancing around it, and indulging in such a remarkable series of fistic manœuvres with an imaginary adversary that the unimaginative detective precipitately backed into a corner of the barn.

"Now, then," said Gallegher, having apparently vanquished his foe, "you come with me." His companion followed quickly as Gallegher climbed to one of the haymows, and, crawling carefully out on the fence rail, stretched himself at full length, face downward. In this position, by moving the straw a little, he could look down, without being himself seen, upon the heads of whomsoever stood below. "This is better'n a private box, ain't it?" said Gallegher.

The boy from the newspaper office and the detective lay there in silence, biting at straws and tossing anxiously on their comfortable bed.

It seemed fully two hours before they came. Gallegher had listened without breathing, and with every muscle on a strain, at least a dozen times, when some movement in the yard had led him to believe that they were at the door.

And he had numerous doubts and fears. Sometimes it was that the police had learnt of the fight, and had raided Keppler's in his absence, and again it was that the fight had been postponed, or, worst of all, that it would be put off until so late that Mr. Dwyer could not get back in time for the last edition of the paper. Their coming, when at last they came, was heralded by an advance guard of two sporting men, who stationed themselves at either side of the big door.

"Hurry up, now, gents," one of the men said with a shiver, "don't keep this door open no longer 'n is needful."

It was not a very large crowd, but it was wonderfully well selected. It ran, in the majority of its component parts, to heavy white coats with pearl buttons. The white coats were shouldered by long blue coats with astrakhan fur trimmings, the wearers of which preserved a cliqueness not remarkable when one considers that they believed every one else present to be either a crook or a prize-fighter.

There were well-fed, well-groomed club-men and brokers in the crowd, a politician or two, a popular comedian with his manager, amateur boxers from the athletic clubs, and quiet, close-mouthed sporting men from every city in the country. Their names if printed in the papers would have been as familiar as the types of the papers themselves.

And among these men, whose only thought was of the brutal sport to come, was Hade, with Dwyer standing at ease at his shoulder—Hade, white, and visibly in deep anxiety, hiding his pale face beneath a cloth traveling-cap, and with his chin muffled in a woolen scarf. He had dared to come because he feared his danger from the already suspicious Keppler was less than if he stayed away. And so he was there, hovering restlessly on the border of the crowd, feeling his danger and sick with fear.

When Hefflefinger first saw him he started up on his hands and elbows and made a movement forward as if he would leap down then and there and carry off his prisoner single-handed.

"Lie down," growled Gallegher; "an officer of any sort would n't live three minutes in that crowd."

The detective drew back slowly and buried himself again in the straw, but never once through the long fight which followed did his eyes leave the person of the murderer. The newspaper men took their places in the foremost row close around the ring, and kept looking at their watches and begging the master of ceremonies to "shake it up, do."

There was a great deal of betting, and all of the men handled the great rolls of bills they wagered with a flippant recklessness which could only be accounted for in Gallegher's mind by temporary mental derangement. Some one pulled a box out into the ring and the master of ceremonies mounted it, and pointed out in forcible language that as they were almost all already under bonds to keep the peace, it behooved all to curb their excitement and to maintain a severe silence, unless they wanted to bring the police upon them and have themselves "sent down" for a year or two.

Then two very disreputable-looking persons tossed their respective principals' high hats into the ring, and the crowd, recognizing in this relic of the days when brave knights threw down their gauntlets in the lists as only a sign that the fight was about to begin, cheered tumultuously.

This was followed by a sudden surging forward, and a mutter of admiration much more flattering than the cheers had been, when the principals followed their hats and, slipping out of their greatcoats, stood forth in all the physical beauty of the perfect brute.

Their pink skin was as soft and healthy-looking as a baby's, and glowed in the lights of the lanterns like tinted ivory, and underneath this silken covering the great biceps and muscles moved in and out and looked like the coils of a snake around the branch of a tree.

Gentleman and blackguard shouldered each other for a nearer view; the coachmen, whose metal buttons were unpleasantly suggestive of police, put their hands, in the excitement of the moment, on the shoulders of their masters; the perspiration stood out in great drops on the foreheads of the backers, and the newspaper men bit somewhat nervously at the ends of their pencils.

And in the stalls the cows munched contentedly at their cuds and gazed with gentle curiosity at their two fellow brutes, who stood waiting the signal to fall upon and kill each other, if need be, for the delectation of their brothers.

"Take your places," commanded the master of ceremonies.

In the moment in which the two men faced each other the crowd became so still that, save for the beating of the rain upon the shingled roof and the stamping of a horse in one of the stalls, the place was as silent as a church.

"Time," shouted the master of ceremonies.

The two men sprang into a posture of defense, which was lost as quickly as it was taken, one great arm shot out like a piston rod; there was the sound of bare fists beating on naked flesh; there was an exultant indrawn gasp of savage pleasure and relief from the crowd, and the great fight had begun.

How the fortunes of war rose and fell, and changed and rechanged that night, is an old story to those who listen to such stories; and those who do not will be glad to be spared the telling of it. It was, they say, one of the bitterest fights between two men that this country has ever known.

But all that is of interest here is that after an hour of this desperate, brutal business the champion ceased to be the favorite; the man whom he had taunted and bullied, and for whom the public had but little sympathy, was proving himself a likely winner, and under his cruel blows, as sharp and clean as those from a cutlass, his opponent was rapidly giving way.

The men about the ropes were past all control now; they drowned Keppler's petitions for silence with oaths and in inarticulate shouts of anger, as if the blows had fallen upon them, and in mad rejoicings. They swept from one end of the ring to the other, with every muscle leaping in unison with those of the man they favored, and when a New York correspondent muttered over his shoulder that this would be the biggest sporting surprise since the Heenan-Sayers fight, Mr. Dwyer nodded his head sympathetically in assent.

In the excitement and tumult it is doubtful if any heard the three quickly repeated blows that fell heavily from the outside upon the big doors of the barn. If they did, it was already too late to mend matters, for the door fell, torn from its hinges, and as it fell a captain of police sprang into the light from out of the storm, with his lieutenants and their men crowding close at his shoulder.

In the panic and stampede that followed, several of the men stood as helplessly immovable as though they had seen a ghost; others made a mad rush into the arms of the officers and were beaten back against the ropes of the ring; others dived headlong into the stalls, among the horses and cattle, and still others shoved the rolls of money they held into the hands of the police and begged like children to be allowed to escape.

The instant the door fell and the raid was declared Hefflefinger slipped over the cross rails on which he had been lying, hung for an instant by his hands, and then dropped into the center of the fighting mob on the floor. He was out of it in an instant with the agility of a pickpocket, was across the room and at Hade's throat like a dog. The murderer, for the moment, was the calmer man of the two.

"Here," he panted, "hands off, now. There's no need for all this violence. There's no great harm in looking at a fight, is there? There's a hundred-dollar bill in my right hand; take it and let me slip out of this. No one is looking. Here."

But the detective only held him the closer.

"I want you for burglary," he whispered under his breath. "You've got to come with me now, and quick. The less fuss you make, the better for both of us. If you don't know who I am, you can feel my badge under my coat there. I've got the authority. It's all regular, and when we're out of this d—d row I'll show you the papers." He took one hand from Hade's throat and pulled a pair of handcuffs from his pocket.

"It's a mistake. This is an outrage," gasped the murderer, white and trembling, but dreadfully alive and desperate for his liberty. "Let me go, I tell you! Take your hands off me! Do I look like a burglar, you fool?"

"I know who you look like," whispered the detective, with his face close to the face of his prisoner. "Now, will you go easy as a burglar, or shall I tell these men who you are and what I *do* want you for? Shall I call out your real name or not? Shall I tell them? Quick, speak up; shall I?"

There was something so exultant—something so unnecessarily savage in the officer's face that the man he held saw that the detective knew him for what he really was, and the hands that had held his

The detective only held him closer.

throat slipped down around his shoulders, or he would have fallen. The man's eyes opened and closed again, and he swayed weakly backward and forward, and choked as if his throat were dry and burning. Even to such a hardened connoisseur in crime as Gallegher, who stood closely by, drinking it in, there was something so abject in the man's terror that he regarded him with what was almost a touch of pity.

"For God's sake," Hade begged, "let me go. Come with me to my room and I'll give you half the money. I'll divide with you fairly. We can both get away. There's a fortune for both of us there. We both can get away. You'll be rich for life. Do you understand—for life!"

But the detective, to his credit, only shut his lips the tighter.

"That's enough," he whispered, in return. "That's more than I expected. You've sentenced yourself already. Come!"

Two officers in uniform barred their exit at the door, but Hefflefinger smiled easily and showed his badge.

"One of Byrnes's men," he said, in explanation; "came over expressly to take this chap. He's a burglar; 'Arlie' Lane, *alias* Carleton. I've shown the papers to the captain. It's all regular. I'm just going to get his traps at the hotel and walk him over to the station. I guess we'll push right on to New York tonight."

The officers nodded and smiled their admiration for the representative of what is, perhaps, the best detective force in the world, and let him pass.

Then Hefflefinger turned and spoke to Gallegher, who still stood as watchful as a dog at his side. "I'm going to his room to get the bonds and stuff," he whispered; "then I'll march him to the station and take that train. I've done my share; don't forget yours!"

"Oh, you'll get your money right enough," said Gallegher. "And, sa-ay," he added, with the appreciative nod of an expert, "do you know, you did it rather well."

Mr. Dwyer had been writing while the raid was settling down, as he had been writing while waiting for the fight to begin. Now he walked over to where the other correspondents stood in angry conclave.

The newspaper men had informed the officers who hemmed them in that they represented the principal papers of the country, and were expostulating vigorously with the captain, who had planned the raid, and who declared they were under arrest.

"Don't be an ass, Scott," said Mr. Dwyer, who was too excited to be polite or politic. "You know our being here isn't a matter of choice. We came here on business, as you did, and you've no right to hold us."

"If we don't get our stuff on the wire at once," protested a New York man, "we'll be too late for tomorrow's paper, and——"

Captain Scott said he did not care a profanely small amount for tomorrow's paper, and that all he knew was that to the station house the newspaper men would go. There they would have a hearing, and if the magistrate chose to let them off, that was the magistrate's business, but that his duty was to take them into custody.

"But then it will be too late, don't you understand?" shouted Mr. Dwyer. "You've got to let us go *now,* at once."

"I can't do it, Mr. Dwyer," said the captain, "and that's all there is to it. Why, haven't I just sent the president of the Junior Republican Club to the patrol wagon, the man that put this coat on me, and do you think I can let you fellows go after that? You were all put under bonds to keep the peace not three days ago, and here you're at it—fighting like badgers. It's worth my place to let one of you off."

What Mr. Dwyer said next was so uncomplimentary to the gallant Captain Scott that that overwrought individual seized the sporting editor by the shoulder, and shoved him into the hands of two of his men.

This was more than the distinguished Mr. Dwyer could brook, and he excitedly raised his hand in resistance. But before he had time to do anything foolish his wrist was gripped by one strong little hand, and he was conscious that another was picking the pocket of his great-coat.

He slapped his hands to his sides, and, looking down, saw Gallegher standing close behind him and holding him by the wrist. Mr. Dwyer had forgotten the boy's existence, and would have spoken sharply if something in Gallegher's innocent eyes had not stopped him.

Gallegher's hand was still in that pocket in which Mr. Dwyer had shoved his notebook filled with what he had written of Gallegher's work and Hade's final capture, and with a running descriptive account of the fight. With his eyes fixed on Mr. Dwyer, Gallegher drew it out, and with a quick movement shoved it inside his waistcoat. Mr. Dwyer gave a nod of comprehension. Then glancing at his two guardsmen, and finding that they were still interested in the wordy battle of the correspondents with their chief, and had seen nothing, he stooped and whispered to Gallegher: "The forms are locked at twenty minutes to three. If you don't get there by that time it will be of no use, but if you're on time you'll beat the town—and the country, too."

Gallegher's eyes flashed significantly, and, nodding his head to show he understood, he started boldly on a run toward the door. But the officers who guarded it brought him to an abrupt halt, and, much to Mr. Dwyer's astonishment, drew from him what was apparently a torrent of tears.

"Let me go to me father. I want me father," the boy shrieked hysterically. "They've 'rested father. Oh, daddy, daddy. They're a-goin' to take you to prison."

"Who is your father, sonny?" asked one of the guardians of the gate.

"Keppler's me father," sobbed Gallegher. "They're a-goin' to lock him up, and I'll never see him no more."

"Oh, yes, you will," said the officer, good-naturedly; "he's there in that first patrol wagon. You can run over and say good night to him, and then you'd better get to bed. This ain't no place for kids of your age."

"Thank you, sir," sniffed Gallegher, tearfully, as the two officers raised their clubs, and let him pass out into the darkness.

The yard outside was in a tumult, horses were stamping, and plunging, and backing the carriages into one another; lights were flashing from every window of what had been apparently an uninhabited house, and the voices of the prisoners were still raised in angry expostulation.

Three police patrol wagons were moving about the yard, filled with unwilling passengers, who sat or stood, packed together like sheep and with no protection from the sleet and rain.

Gallegher stole off into a dark corner, and watched the scene until his eyesight became familiar with the position of the land.

Then with his eyes fixed fearfully on the swinging light of a lantern with which an officer was searching among the carriages, he groped his way between horses' hoofs and behind the wheels of carriages to the cab which he had himself placed at the furthermost gate. It was still there, and the horse, as he had left it, with its head turned toward the city. Gallegher opened the big gate noiselessly, and worked nervously at the hitching strap. The knot was covered with a thin coating of ice, and it was several minutes before he could loosen it. But his teeth finally pulled it apart, and with the reins in his hands he sprang upon the wheel. And as he stood so, a shock of fear ran down his back like an electric current, his breath left him, and he stood immovable, gazing wide-eyed into the dark.

The officer with the lantern had suddenly loomed up from behind a carriage not fifty feet distant, and was standing perfectly still, with his lantern held over his head, peering so directly toward Gallegher that the boy felt that he must see him. Gallegher stood with one foot on the hub of the wheel and with the other on the box waiting to spring. It seemed a minute before either of them moved, and then the officer took a step forward, and demanded sternly, "Who is that? What are you doing there?"

There was no time for parley then. Gallegher felt that he had been taken in the act, and that his only chance lay in open flight. He leaped up on the box, pulling out the whip as he did so, and with a quick sweep lashed the horse across the head and back. The animal sprang forward with a snort, narrowly clearing the gatepost, and plunged off into the darkness.

"Stop!" cried the officer.

So many of Gallegher's acquaintances among the 'longshoremen and mill hands had been challenged in so much the same manner that Gallegher knew what would probably follow if the challenge was disregarded. So he slipped from his seat to the footboard below, and ducked his head.

The three reports of a pistol, which rang out briskly from behind him, proved that his early training had given him a valuable fund of useful miscellaneous knowledge.

"Don't you be scared," he said, reassuringly, to the horse; "he's firing in the air."

The pistol-shots were answered by the impatient clangor of a patrol wagon's gong, and glancing over his shoulder Gallegher saw its red and green lanterns tossing from side to side and looking in the darkness like the side lights of a yacht plunging forward in a storm.

"I had n't bargained to race you against no patrol wagons," said Gallegher to his animal; "but if they want a race, we'll give them a tough tussle for it, won't we?"

Philadelphia, lying four miles to the south, sent up a faint yellow glow to the sky. It seemed very far away, and Gallegher's braggadocio grew cold within him at the loneliness of his adventure and the thought of the long ride before him.

It was still bitterly cold.

The rain and sleet beat through his clothes, and struck his skin with a sharp, chilling touch that set him trembling.

Even the thought of the over-weighted patrol-wagon probably sticking in the mud some safe distance in the rear, failed to cheer him, and the excitement that had so far made him callous to the cold died out and left him weaker and nervous.

But his horse was chilled with the long standing, and now leaped eagerly forward, only too willing to warm the half-frozen blood in its veins.

"You're a good beast," said Gallegher, plaintively. "You've got more nerve than me. Don't you go back on me now. Mr. Dwyer says we've got to beat the town." Gallegher had no idea what time it was as he rode through the night, but he knew he would be able to find out from a big clock over a manufactory at a point nearly three-quarters of the distance from Keppler's to the goal.

He was still in the open country and driving recklessly, for he knew the best part of his ride must be made outside the city limits.

He raced between desolate-looking cornfields with bare stalks and patches of muddy earth rising above the thin covering of snow; truck farms and brickyards fell behind him on either side. It was very lonely work, and once or twice the dogs ran yelping to the gates and barked after him.

Part of his way lay parallel with the railroad tracks, and he drove for some time besides long lines of freight and coal cars as they stood resting for the night. The fantastic Queen Anne suburban stations were dark and deserted, but in one or two of the block-towers he could see the operators writing at their desks, and the sight in some way comforted him.

Once he thought of stopping to get out the blanket in which he had wrapped himself on the first trip, but he feared to spare the time, and drove on with his teeth chattering and his shoulders shaking with the cold.

He welcomed the first solitary row of darkened houses with a faint cheer of recognition. The scattered lamp-posts lightened his spirits, and even the badly paved streets rang under the beats of his horse's feet like music. Great mills and manufactories, with only a night-watchman's light in the lowest of their many stories, began to take the place of the gloomy farmhouses and gaunt trees that had startled him with their grotesque shapes. He had been driving nearly an hour, he calculated, and in that time the rain had changed to a wet snow, that fell heavily and clung to whatever it touched. He passed block after block of trim workmen's houses, and still and silent as the sleepers within them, and at last he turned the horse's head into Broad Street, the city's great thoroughfare, that stretches from its one end to the other and cuts it evenly in two.

He was driving noiselessly over the snow and slush in the street, with his thoughts bent only on the clockface he wished so much to see, when a hoarse voice challenged him from the sidewalk. "Hey, you, stop there, hold up!" said the voice.

Gallegher turned his head, and though he saw that the voice came from under a policeman's helmet, his only answer was to hit his horse sharply over the head with his whip and to urge it into a gallop.

This, on his part, was followed by a sharp, shrill whistle from the policeman. Another whistle answered it from a street corner one block ahead of him. "Whoa," said Gallegher, pulling on the reins. "There's one too many of them," he added, in apologetic explanation. The horse stopped, and stood, breathing heavily, with great clouds of steam rising from its flanks.

"Why in hell did n't you stop when I told you to?" demanded the voice, now close at the cab's side.

"I did n't hear you," returned Gallegher, sweetly. "But I heard you whistle, and I heard your partner whistle, and I thought maybe it was me you wanted to speak to, so I just stopped."

"You heard me well enough. Why are n't your lights lit?" demanded the voice.

"Should I have 'em lit?" asked Gallegher, bending over and regarding them with sudden interest.

"You know you should, and if you don't, you've no right to be driving that cab. I don't believe you're the regular driver, anyway. Where'd you get it?"

"It ain't my cab, of course," said Gallegher, with an easy laugh. "It's Luke McGovern's. He left it outside Cronin's while he went in to get a drink, and he took too much, and me father told me to drive it round to the stable for him. I'm Cronin's son. McGovern ain't in no condition to drive. You can see yourself how he's been misusing the horse. He puts it up at Bachman's livery stable, and I was just going around there now."

Gallegher's knowledge of the local celebrities of the district confused the zealous officer of the peace. He surveyed the boy with a steady stare that would have distressed a less skillful liar, but

Gallegher shrugged his shoulders slightly, as if from the cold, and waited with apparent indifference to what the officer would say next.

In reality his heart was beating heavily against his side, and he felt that if he was kept on a strain much longer he would give way and break down. A second snow-covered form emerged suddenly from the shadow of the houses.

"What is it, Reeder?" it asked.

"Oh, nothing much," replied the first officer. "This kid hadn't any lamps lit, so I called to him to stop and he didn't do it, so I whistled to you. It's all right, though. He's just taking it round to Bachman's. Go ahead," he added, sulkily.

"Get up!" chirped Gallegher. "Good night," he added, over his shoulder.

Gallegher gave a hysterical little gasp of relief as he trotted away from the two policemen, and poured bitter maledictions on their heads for two meddling fools as he went.

"They might as well kill a man as scare him to death," he said, with an attempt to get back to his customary flippancy. But the effort was somewhat pitiful, and he felt guiltily conscious that a salt, warm tear was creeping slowly down his face, and that a lump that would not keep down was rising in his throat.

" 'Tain't no fair thing for the whole police force to keep worrying at a little boy like me," he said, in shame-faced apology. "I'm not doing nothing wrong, and I'm half froze to death, and yet they keep a-nagging at me."

It was so cold that when the boy stamped his feet against the footboard to keep them warm, sharp pains shot up through his body, and when he beat his arms about his shoulders, as he had seen real cabmen do, the blood in his finger-tips tingled so acutely that he cried aloud with the pain.

He had often been up that late before, but he had never felt so sleepy. It was as if some one was pressing a sponge heavy with chloroform near his face, and he could not fight off the drowsiness that lay hold of him.

He saw, dimly hanging above his head, a round disk of light that seemed like a great moon, and which he finally guessed to be the clockface for which he had been on the lookout. He had passed it before he realized this; but the fact stirred him into wakefulness again, and when his cab's wheels slipped around the City Hall corner, he remembered to look up at the other big clockface that keeps awake over the railroad station and measures out the night.

He gave a gasp of consternation when he saw that it was half-past two, and that there was but ten minutes left to him. This, and the many electric lights and the sight of the familiar pile of buildings, startled him into a semi-consciousness of where he was and how great was the necessity for haste.

He rose in his seat and called on the horse, and urged it into a reckless gallop over the slippery asphalt. He considered nothing else but speed, and looking neither to the left nor right dashed off down Broad Street into Chestnut, where his course lay straight away to the office, now only seven blocks distant.

Gallegher never knew how it began, but he was suddenly assaulted by shouts on either side, his horse was thrown back on its haunches, and he found two men in cabmen's livery hanging at its head, and patting its sides, and calling it by name. And the other cabmen who have their stand at the corner were swarming about the carriage, all of them talking and swearing at once, and gesticulating wildly with their whips.

They said they knew the cab was McGovern's, and they wanted to know where he was, and why he wasn't on it; they wanted to know where Gallegher had stolen it, and why he had been such a fool as to drive it into the arms of its owner's friends; they said that it was about time that a cab-driver could get off his box to take a drink without having his cab run away with, and some of them called loudly for a policeman to take the young thief in charge.

Gallegher felt as if he had been suddenly dragged into consciousness out of a bad dream, and stood for a second like a half-awakened somnambulist.

They had stopped the cab under an electric light, and its glare shone coldly down upon the trampled snow and the faces of the men around him.

Gallegher bent forward, and lashed savagely at the horse with his whip.

"Let me go," he shouted, as he tugged impotently at the reins. "Let me go, I tell you. I have n't stole no cab, and you've got no right to stop me. I only want to take it to the *Press* office," he begged. "They'll send it back to you all right. They'll pay you for the trip. I'm not running away with it. The driver's got the collar—he's 'rested—and I'm only a-going to the *Press* office. Do you hear me?" he cried, his voice rising and breaking in a shriek of passion and disappointment. "I tell you to let go those reins. Let me go, or I'll kill you. Do you hear me? I'll kill you." And leaning forward, the boy struck savagely with his long whip at the faces of the men about the horse's head.

Some one in the crowd reached up and caught him by the ankles, and with a quick jerk pulled him off the box, and threw him on to the street. But he was up on his knees in a moment, and caught at the man's hand.

"Don't let them stop me, mister," he cried, "please let me go. I did n't steal the cab, sir. S'help me, I did n't. I'm telling you the truth. Take me to the *Press* office, and they'll prove it to you. They'll pay you anything you ask 'em. It's only such a little ways now, and I've come so far, sir. Please don't let them stop me," he sobbed, clasping the man about the knees. "For Heaven's sake, mister, let me go!"

• • •

The managing editor of the *Press* took up the india-rubber speaking-tube at his side, and answered, "Not yet," to an inquiry the night editor had already put to him five times within the last twenty minutes.

Then he snapped the metal top of the tube impatiently, and went upstairs. As he passed the door of the local room, he noticed that the reporters had not gone home but were sitting about on the tables and chairs, waiting. They looked up inquiringly as he passed; the city editor asked, "Any news?" and the managing editor shook his head.

The compositors were standing idle in the composing room, and their foreman was talking with the night editor.

"Well," said that gentleman, tentatively.

"Well," returned the managing editor, "I don't think we can wait; do you?"

"It's a half-hour after time now," said the night editor, "and we'll miss the suburban trains if we hold the paper back any longer. We can't afford to wait for a purely hypothetical story. The chances are all against the fight's having taken place or this Hade's having been arrested."

"But if we're beaten on it—" suggested the chief. "But I don't think that is possible. If there were any story to print, Dwyer would have had it here before now."

The managing editor looked steadily down at the floor.

"Very well," he said slowly, "we won't wait any longer. Go

ahead," he added, turning to the foreman with a sigh of reluctance. The foreman whirled himself about, and began to give his orders; but the two editors still looked at each other doubtfully.

As they stood so, there came a sudden shout and the sound of people running to and fro in the reportorial rooms below. There was the tramp of many footsteps on the stairs, and above the confusion they heard the voice of the city editor telling some one to "run to Madden's and get some brandy, quick."

No one in the composing room said anything; but those compositors who had started to go home began slipping off their overcoats, and every one stood with his eyes fixed on the door.

It was kicked open from the outside, and in the doorway stood a cab-driver and the city editor, supporting between them a pitiful little figure of a boy, wet and miserable, and with the snow melting on his clothes and running in little pools to the floor. "Why, it's Gallegher," said the night editor, in a tone of the keenest disappointment.

Gallegher shook himself free from his supporters, and took an unsteady step forward, his fingers fumbling stiffly with the buttons of his waistcoat.

"Mr. Dwyer, sir," he began faintly, with his eyes fixed fearfully on the managing editor, "he got arrested—and I could n't get here no sooner, 'cause they kept a-stopping me, and they took me cab from under me—but—" he pulled the notebook from his breast and held it out with its covers damp and limp from the rain—"but we got Hade, and here's Mr. Dwyer's copy."

And then he asked, with a queer note in his voice, partly of dread and partly of hope, "Am I in time, sir?"

The managing editor took the book, and tossed it to the foreman, who ripped out its leaves and dealt them out to his men as rapidly as a gambler deals out cards.

Then the managing editor stooped and picked Gallegher up in his arms, and, sitting down, began to unlace his wet and muddy shoes.

Gallegher made a faint effort to resist this degradation of the managerial dignity; but the protest was a very feeble one, and his head fell back heavily on the managing editor's shoulder.

To Gallegher the incandescent lights began to whirl about in circles, and to burn in different colors; the faces of the reporters kneeling before him and chafing his hands and feet grew dim and unfamiliar, and the roar and rumble of the great presses in the basement sounded far away, like the murmur of the sea.

And then the place and the circumstances of it came back to him again sharply and with sudden vividness.

Gallegher looked up, with a faint smile, into the managing editor's face. "You won't turn me off for running away, will you?" he whispered.

The managing editor did not answer immediately. His head was bent, and he was thinking, for some reason or other, of a little boy of his own, at home in bed. Then he said quietly, "Not this time, Gallegher."

Gallegher's head sank back comfortably on the older man's shoulder, and he smiled comprehensively at the faces of the young men crowded around him. "You hadn't ought to," he said, with a touch of his old impudence, " 'cause—I beat the town."

A MISERABLE, MERRY CHRISTMAS

By *LINCOLN STEFFENS*

Illustration by THOMAS VICTOR HALL

MY father's business seems to have been one of slow but steady growth. He and his local partner, Llewelen Tozer, had no vices. They were devoted to their families and to "the store," which grew with the town, which, in turn, grew and changed with the State from a gambling, mining, and ranching community to one of farming, fruit-raising, and building. Immigration poured in, not gold-seekers now, but farmers, business men and home-builders, who settled, planted, reaped, and traded in the natural riches of the State, which prospered greatly, "making" the people who will tell you that they "made the State."

As the store made money and I was getting through the primary school, my father bought a lot uptown, at Sixteenth and K Streets, and built us a "big" house. It was off the line of the city's growth, but it was near a new grammar school for me and my sisters, who were coming along fast after me. This interested the family, not me. They were always talking about school; they had not had much of it themselves, and they thought they had missed something. My father used to write speeches, my mother verses, and their theory seems to have been that they had talents which a school would have brought to flower. They agreed, therefore, that their children's gifts should have all the schooling there was. My view, then, was that I had had a good deal of it already, and I was not interested at all. It interfered with my own business, with my own education.

And indeed I remember very little of the primary school. I learned to read, write, spell, and count, and reading was all right. I had a practical use for books, which I searched for ideas and parts to play with, characters to be, lives to live. The primary school was probably a good one, but I cannot remember learning anything except to read aloud "perfectly" from a teacher whom I adored and who was fond of me. She used to embrace me before the whole class and she favored me openly to the scandal of the other pupils, who called me "teacher's pet." Their scorn did not trouble me; I saw and I said that they envied me. I paid for her favor, however. When she married I had queer, unhappy feelings of resentment; I didn't want to meet her husband, and when I had to I wouldn't speak to him. He laughed, and she kissed me—happily for her, to me offensively. I never would see her again. Through with her, I fell in love immediately with Miss Kay, another grown young woman who wore glasses and had a fine, clear skin.

I did not know her, I only saw her in the street, but once I followed her, found out where she lived, and used to pass her house, hoping to see her, and yet choking with embarrassment if I did. This fascination lasted for years; it was still a sort of super-romance to me when later I was "going with" another girl nearer by own age.

What interested me in our new neighborhood was not the school, nor the room I was to have in the house all to myself, but the stable which was built back of the house. My father let me direct the making of a stall, a little smaller than the other stalls, for my pony, and I prayed and hoped and my sister Lou believed that meant that I would get the pony, perhaps for Christmas. I pointed out to her that there were three other stalls and no horses at all. This I said in order that she should answer it. She could not. My father, sounded, said that some day we might have horses and a cow; meanwhile a stable added to the value of a house. "Some day" is a pain to a boy who lives and knows only "now." My good little sisters, to comfort me, remarked that Christmas was coming, but Christmas was always coming and grown-ups were always talking about it, asking you what you wanted and then giving you what they wanted you to have. Though everybody knew what I wanted, I told them all again. My mother knew that I told God, too, every night. I wanted a pony, and to make sure that they understood, I declared that I wanted nothing else.

"Nothing but a pony?" my father asked.

"Nothing," I said.

"Not even a pair of high boots?"

That was hard, I did want boots, but I stuck to the pony.

"No, not even boots."

"Nor candy? There ought to be something to fill your stocking with, and Santa Claus can't put a pony into a stocking."

That was true, and he couldn't lead a pony down the chimney either. But no. "All I want is a pony," I said. "If I can't have a pony, give me nothing, nothing."

Now I had been looking myself for the pony I wanted, going to sales stables, inquiring of horsemen, and I had seen several that would do. My father let me "try" them. I tried so many ponies that I was learning fast to sit a horse. I chose several, but my father always found some fault with them. I was in despair. When Christmas was at hand I had given up all hope of a pony, and on Christmas Eve I hung up my stocking along with my sisters', of whom, by the way, I now had three. I haven't mentioned them or their coming because, you understand, they were girls, and girls, young girls, counted for nothing in my manly life. They did not mind me either; they were so happy that Christmas Eve that I caught some of their merriment. I speculated on what I'd get; I hung up the biggest stocking I had, and we all went reluctantly to bed to wait till morning. Not to sleep; not right away. We were told that we must not only sleep promptly, we must not wake up till seven-thirty the next morning—or if we did, we must not go to the fireplace for our Christmas. Impossible.

We did sleep that night, but we woke up at six A.M. We lay in our beds and debated through the open doors whether to obey till, say, half-past six. Then we bolted. I don't know who started it, but there was a rush. We all disobeyed; we raced to disobey and get first to the fireplace in the front room downstairs. And there they were, the gifts, all sorts of wonderful things, mixed-up piles of presents; only, as I disentangled the mess, I saw that my stocking was empty; it hung limp; not a thing in it; and under and around it—nothing. My sisters had knelt down, each by her pile of gifts; they were squealing with delight, till they looked up and saw me standing there in my nightgown with nothing. They left their piles to come to me and look with me at my empty place. Nothing. They felt my stocking: nothing.

I don't remember whether I cried at that moment, but my sisters did. They ran with me back to my bed, and there we all cried till I became indignant. That helped some. I got up, dressed, and driving my sisters away, I went alone out into the yard, down to the stable, and there, all by myself, I wept. My mother came out to me by and by;

she found me in my pony stall, sobbing on the floor, and she tried to comfort me. But I heard my father outside; he had come part way with her, and she was having some sort of angry quarrel with him. She tried to comfort me; besought me to come to breakfast. I could not; I wanted no comfort and no breakfast. She left me and went on into the house with sharp words for my father.

I don't know what kind of breakfast the family had. My sisters said it was "awful." They were ashamed to enjoy their own toys. They came to me, and I was rude. I ran away from them. I went around to the front of the house, sat down on the steps, and, the crying over, I ached. I was wronged, I was hurt—I can feel now what I felt then, and I am sure that if one could see the wounds upon our hearts, there would be found still upon mine a scar from that terrible Christmas morning. And my father, the practical joker, he must have been hurt, too, a little. I saw him looking out of the window. He was watching me or something for an hour or two, drawing back the curtain never so little lest I catch him, but I saw his face, and I think I can see now the anxiety upon it, the worried impatience.

After—I don't know how long—surely an hour or two—I was brought to the climax of my agony by the sight of a man riding a pony down the street, a pony and a brand-new saddle; the most beautiful saddle I ever saw, and it was a boy's saddle; the man's feet were not in the stirrups; his legs were too long. The outfit was perfect; it was the realization of all my dreams, the answer to all my prayers. A fine new bridle, with a light curb bit. And the pony! As he drew near, I saw that the pony was really a small horse, what we called an Indian pony, a bay, with black mane and tail, and one white foot and a white star on his forehead. For such a horse as that I would have given, I could have forgiven, anything.

But the man, a disheveled fellow with a blackened eye and a fresh-cut face; came along, reading the numbers on the houses, and, as my hopes—my impossible hopes—rose, he looked at our door and passed by, he and the pony, and the saddle and the bridle. Too much. I fell upon the steps, and having wept before, I broke now into such a flood of tears that I was a floating wreck when I heard a voice.

"Say, kid," it said, "do you know a boy named Lennie Steffens?"

I looked up. It was the man on the pony, back again, at our horse block. "Yes," I spluttered through my tears. "That's me."

"Well," he said, "then this is your horse. I've been looking all over for you and your house. Why don't you put your number where it can be seen?"

"Get down," I said, running out to him.

He went on saying something about "ought to have got here at seven o'clock; told me to bring the nag here and tie him to your post and leave him for you. But I got into a drunk—and a fight—and a hospital, and—"

"Get down," I said.

He got down, and he boosted me up to the saddle. He offered to fit the stirrups to me, but I didn't want him to. I wanted to ride.

"What's the matter with you?" he said, angrily. "What you crying for? Don't you like the horse? He's a dandy, this horse. I know him of old. He's fine at cattle; he'll drive 'em alone."

I hardly heard, I could scarcely wait, but he persisted. He adjusted the stirrups, and then, finally, off I rode, slowly, at a walk, so happy, so thrilled, that I did not know what I was doing. I did not look back at the house or the man. I rode off up the street, taking note of everything—of the reins, of the pony's long mane, of the carved leather saddle. I had never seen anything so beautiful. And mine! I was going to ride up past Miss Kay's house. But I noticed on the horn of the saddle some stains like rain-drops, so I turned and trotted home, not to the house but to the stable. There was the family, father, mother, sisters, all working for me, all happy. They had been putting in place the tools of my new business: blankets, currycomb, brush, pitchfork—everything, and there was hay in the loft.

"What did you come back so soon for?" somebody asked. "Why didn't you go on riding?"

I pointed to the stains. "I wasn't going to get my new saddle rained on," I said. And my father laughed. "It isn't raining," he said. "Those are not rain-drops."

"They are tears," my mother gasped, and she gave my father a look which sent him off to the house. Worse still, my mother offered to wipe away the tears still running out of my eyes. I gave her such a look as she had given him, and she went off after my father, drying her own tears. My sisters remained and we all unsaddled the pony, put on his halter, led him to his stall, tied and fed him. It began really to rain; so all the rest of that memorable day we curried and combed that pony. The girls plaited his mane, forelock, and tail, while I pitchforked hay to him and curried and brushed. For a change we brought him out to drink; we led him up and down, blanketed like a racehorse; we took turns at that. But the best, the most inexhaustible fun, was to clean him. When we went reluctantly to our midday Christmas dinner, we all smelt of horse, and my sisters had to wash their faces and hands. I was asked to, but I wouldn't, till my mother bade me look in the mirror. Then I washed up—quick. My face was caked with the muddy lines of tears that had coursed over my cheeks to my mouth. Having washed away that shame, I ate my dinner, and as I ate I grew hungrier and hungrier. It was my first meal that day, and as I filled up on the turkey and the stuffing, the cranberries and the pies, the fruit and the nuts—as I swelled, I could laugh. My mother said I still choked and sobbed now and then, but I laughed, too; I saw and enjoyed my sisters' presents till—I had to go out and attend to my pony, who was there, really and truly there, the promise, the beginning, of a happy double life. And—I went and looked to make sure—there was the saddle, too, and the bridle.

But that Christmas, which my father had planned so carefully, was it the best or the worst I ever knew? He often asked me that; I never could answer as a boy. I think now that it was both. It covered the whole distance from broken-hearted misery to bursting happiness—too fast. A grown-up could hardly have stood it.

MAMA AND THE OCCASION

By KATHRYN FORBES

Illustrations by THOMAS VICTOR HALL

THERE was excitement at school.

Winford, it was whispered, was to have an exceedingly distinguished visitor.

Miss Grimes, our Principal, called a special assembly to confirm the news. "We are to be honored," she announced, "by a visit from Mrs. Reed Winford, that gr-eat lady." Miss Grimes rolled her words like our minister did when he preached Damnation.

"Mrs. Winford is," she continued, "the widow of that gr-eat and no-ble educator for whom our school is named. She will be with us on Chuesday week."

Mrs. Reed Winford, we learned, was famous as an educator in her own right, and had been Dean of Women these many years in an important Eastern university.

Now, since Mrs. Winford intended to spend her sabbatical year in the Far East, she would stop over in San Francisco just long enough to greet the upper-grade pupils and the teaching staff of the school that was a monument to her husband.

Genteel excitement ran high among the teachers, but our eighth grade was not particularly interested until Miss Grimes gave us complete charge of the refreshments for the reception.

Miss Scanlon twittered with delight and appointed Hester Prinn the chairman. Hester took elocution lessons and knew how to speak pieces. She never blushed nor seemed ill at ease when she had to stand up in front of the class.

Now she said: "Let us all work together, girls, to make this a never-to-be-forgotten *Occasion*. Wouldn't it be nice if several of us brought some special little tidbit from home? Made this a real fancy tea?"

Miss Scanlon smiled and nodded. Hester nodded back graciously and held her hands together, very ladylike. "I," she said condescendingly, "shall be glad to bring our Silver Tea Service and our Sterling Silver Cake Plate from home for the Occasion. And the tea."

The girls clapped politely. And for one awful moment I hated Hester Prinn more than anything else in the world. I envied her her assurance and aplomb; I had never in my life seen a Silver Tea Service, much less owned one—and I hadn't the slightest idea what a "tidbit" was.

"Now won't someone else," Hester begged prettily, "also volunteer?"

"My mother makes lovely currant cake," Madeline said.

"Splendid."

"And *mine* makes fancy little cucumber sandwiches when *she* has a tea. I know she will let me bring some." Thyra Marin smiled primly at the rest of us.

"Fine!" Hester said heartily. "Someone else?"

"Cookies?" Mary Weston offered shyly.

"Are they—fancy cookies?"

"Oh, yes. Frosted, and all in different shapes."

"Then by all means, cookies."

Carmelita raised her hand. "I'll bring something, I don't know what. I'll have to ask my mother."

Now I loved Carmelita dearly, but it was unthinkable that she be allowed to get ahead of me.

"I, too, will bring something," I announced loudly. I had no idea what it would be, and to forestall questions, I added hastily, "a tidbit—a special tidbit."

"Thank you all so very much," Hester said. "I appoint the girls who are contributing to be the serving committee."

Before school was dismissed that afternoon, I sneaked a glance in the big dictionary on Miss Scanlon's desk. "Tidbit," it said, "a choice morsel of food."

I breathed a sigh of relief.

When I got home from school, I found Aunt Jenny in the kitchen, visiting with Mama. I told them about the distinguished visitor that was coming to Winford and bragged about being appointed to the serving committee.

"Mama," I asked, "what do you cook specially well? A-a choice morsel?"

"I just cook plain," Mama said.

Aunt Jenny snorted. "You are too modest," she said. "I just wish I had your knack with pastry, with *lutefisk*." She closed her eyes. "And your *kjödboller*," she said dreamily, "in the cream sauce. Why, they melt in a person's mouth."

Mama blushed at Aunt Jenny's praise. "Perhaps," she conceded, "perhaps I do make the good *kjödboller*—the meat balls."

"Oh, Mama," I begged, "would you make some for me to take to the reception for Mrs. Winford?"

Mama did not think that meat balls were quite the appropriate dish for an Occasion. "Why not a cake?" she suggested.

"One of the girls already offered to bring a cake."

"Cookies, then? I will make *kringler*."

"No. Mary Weston's bringing cookies. And Thyra's mother is going to make cucumber sandwiches."

Aunt Jenny was shocked. Cucumbers? Didn't people know that fresh cucumbers were poisonous? Sandwiches, to her way of thinking, were a waste of time. "Give them something to eat," she said heartily, "something they can smack their lips over."

Mama looked uncertain. Had we forgotten that *kjödboller* must be served hot?

But Aunt Jenny and I disposed of Mama's gentle arguments, one after the other. I was obsessed with the idea of showing the "clique" what a wonderful cook my mother was; of bringing some "tidbit" that would so outshine the other contributions that the Occasion would stand out in their memories forever. The girls could not *help* liking me—wanting to be my friends—if I made the Occasion a big success.

And Aunt Jenny was determined that the poor teachers, "thin as sticks, every one of them," should, for once in their lives, taste real food.

Keeping the meat balls hot? Easy. One of Aunt Jenny's neighbors had a contraption called a chafing dish that was guaranteed to keep food hot. And if Katrin would promise to be very careful of it—

"Oh, I *will,* Aunt Jenny."

Aunt Jenny planned it all out, very capably. The meat balls must be prepared in the morning, and I could come home for lunch on the day of the reception and take them back to school with me. Aunt Jenny would instruct me how to light the alcohol lamp under the contraption, and there you were. What was wrong with that idea? Mama had to admit that it sounded all right.

Since Carmelita hadn't told the girls what she was going to bring, I decided not to tell about my wonderful contribution either.

"Wait and see," I told Hester when she asked me. "And will you be surprised!"

Hester and Madeline and Thyra were almost nice to me during the days we waited for the Occasion. Once they let me play in their jacks game, and twice they walked clear across the schoolyard with me during recess.

I was quite happy. After the reception, I dreamed, after the teachers and Mrs. Reed Winford had smacked their lips over Mama's delicious meat balls, the girls would notice me even more.

"I simply *must* have the recipe," I could hear Miss Grimes say.

And Mrs. Winford would ask to meet the girl whose mother cooked so wonderfully. "Quite the nicest tibdit," she would say, "of this whole reception."

And the girls would smile and nod at me. They might even clap. And I wouldn't blush a bit.

"Chuesday week" finally arrived, and I rushed home at lunch time to get the Tidbit.

Mama was flushed, but happy. "Never," she told me, "have I had such good luck with *kjödboller*. Just taste."

I tasted, and assured her that she had indeed outdone herself. Flaky, tender, swimming in the creamy sauce, the meat balls looked like a picture out of a magazine.

Carefully, we transferred them to the chafing dish. And with warnings, Mama gave me the tiny bottle of alcohol and a block of matches. Mama had a great fear of things blowing up.

It started to rain when I got to the corner, but I was too excited to go back home for my raincoat and umbrella. Shielding the precious burden as best I could, I raced the two blocks to school.

When I got there, Miss Scanlon sent me down to the furnace room to dry my shoes. On my way, I tiptoed into the auditorium and deposited the chafing dish on the long, white-clothed table that held Hester's gleaming Silver Tea Service. I wasn't even jealous; the chafing dish looked every bit as nice.

When I got to the furnace room, the janitress was sitting on an upturned soap box, talking to herself.

"Reception," she was muttering. *"Reception."*

She looked at me sternly. "Don't I always keep this school clean?"

I nodded timidly and moved closer to the furnace.

"Better," she declared, "than any janitress ever did. Ask anyone. Ask the Board of Education. They'll tell you that Mrs. Kronever, she takes pride in her work.

"Ha!" she continued. "Ha! Reception!" She rocked back and forth and glared at me.

"Who," she demanded, "who works hardest at this Winford school? Tell me that."

"I guess you do, Mrs. Kronever."

She made her eyes small. "Then why am I not asked to the Reception, too?"

"I—I don't know."

"Ha!" she said again. "All right, all right. Let them have their old Reception. Without me!"

I stood up. Wet shoes or not, I'd better get back to the classroom. This, I decided, was what Miss Scanlon meant when she said that Mrs. Kronever was temperamental. I made my escape, leaving the janitress to her dark mutterings.

The afternoon session dragged by. A cold and driving rain had darkened the day, and we shivered. Three times Miss Scanlon had to send girls down to Mrs. Kronever with requests for more heat, without tangible results.

Dismissal bell finally rang, and the lower grades were sent home. We favored ones in the eighth congregated in the hall outside the auditorium, waiting with the teachers for Miss Grimes and the Distinguished Visitor.

For the first time, I noticed that Carmelita held a long, paper-wrapped package.

"What did you bring?" I whispered, hoping anxiously that it would not be something to compete with the delectable meat balls.

"A bottle of fine wine," she whispered back, and tore off a piece of the paper to show me the bottle, cased in straw.

I shuddered. A faint doubt entered by mind. Were we doing the right thing, Carmelita and I? Of course, meat balls were different from *wine*—but—

"What will Miss Grimes say?" I asked anxiously.

Carmelita shrugged. "The wine," she said, "is very good for the stommack."

I remembered the lecture Miss Grimes had given us on the evils of rum. Had she mentioned wine? I was torn between two loyalties; I did not want to hurt my friend's feelings, nor did I want her held up to the ridicule of the school.

"Wrap it up again," I implored her. "Let me think."

"Is good for the stommack," Carmelita persisted, and tore off the rest of the wrapping.

Miss Grimes came bustling down the hall then, followed by a tall gray-haired lady in a black fitted suit. We stood back bashfully and Miss Grimes opened the auditorium door with a flourish, and bade our Distinguished Visitor enter.

We trooped after her, I to my chosen place by the chafing dish, along with the other members of the serving committee; the rest of the class and the teachers to chairs placed in front of the platform.

The pungent odor of meat balls greeted us, and I sniffed appreciatively as I lighted the lamp under the chafing dish. Miss Grimes looked uncomfortable and wrinkled her nose a little, but she gave a wonderful introduction to the Distinguished Visitor.

Mrs. Winford was a beautiful lady. She stood up and told us how happy she was to be with us; how she had looked forward to meeting us all—I lost the rest of the speech because Hester was motioning to Miss Scanlon from the doorway, and I was curious.

I began to notice how cold it was in the auditorium and wondered why someone didn't turn on the heat. Then Miss Scanlon rushed in and whispered something to Miss Grimes and Miss Grimes rushed out the door.

Mrs. Winford finished talking and we clapped politely. She stood there on the platform until Miss Grimes came rushing back again. Miss Grimes' face had turned awful red.

"*Most* unfortunate," she announced, "but we are unable to find our janitress. She—she forgot to turn on the heat. And, stupidly enough, she has also gone off with the key to the domestic science room and the girls cannot get in to use the stove to boil the water for tea.

"But if you will just be patient," she promised, "we will have everything under way very shortly. I know we are all anxious for our tea."

Mrs. Winford looked as if she could do with a cup of hot tea. But she just smiled graciously and held her coat more tightly around herself. Miss Scanlon sneezed, twice, and Miss Grimes glared at her. The teachers went on vain expeditions for the missing janitress.

Miss Grimes and the teachers sat in a group by the platform and made valiant conversation with our shivering guest, while the nerves of the serving committee became increasingly edgy. We watched the dainty little cucumber sandwiches become soggy and limp. Madeline tried to cut the currant cake with the cake server, and it fell into crumbs. Hester made futile little dashes from the tea table to the hall.

"It's getting late," Hester fretted, "and colder. Miss Lyons thinks she may have a key to the domestic science room at her home. She's gone to see. If we stand around much longer, we'll freeze." She noticed Carmelita. "What in the world," Hester asked crossly, "are you holding?"

"Wine."

"Wine? *Wine?* Don't you know that all teachers are W.C.T.U?"

I didn't know what W.C.T.U. was, but Carmelita was my Best Friend. "It is good," I parroted, "for the stommack."

"They'll probably *expel* you!" Hester hissed.

Carmelita gulped, but held tightly to the wine.

"And what are *you* being so mysterious about?" Hester asked me impatiently. "What have you got in that old chafing dish?"

Reverently, I lifted the cover. "Meat balls," I breathed. "In cream sauce."

It was the signal for laughter. Harsh and high-pitched laughter, vainly smothered by crammed handkerchiefs. Hester and Madeline and Thyra giggled and sputtered; then held tightly to one another and kept repeating "Meat balls!" "To a fancy tea she brings *meat balls!*"

From her seat by the platform, Miss Grimes frowned at the unseemly noise and signaled us to be quiet.

The girls wiped streaming eyes—looked at me—and collapsed into one another's arms again.

"Meat balls!" Hester grimaced. *"Poor* people eat meat balls."

"For *dinner,* if ever," Madeline hiccuped, "not at a tea."

My cheeks burned. My eyes smarted. But I dared not let the tears fall. Nobody liked my lovely, lovely surprise. Soon, now, Miss Grimes and Mrs. Winford would discover my stupidity. And the teachers. And everyone would laugh and laugh. And never, now, would my classmates be friendly.

Through the haze of unshed tears I saw my sister Christine.

She was standing by the tea table, holding out my raincoat and rubbers. "Mama sent me back with them," she said matter-of-factly. "It's pouring out."

"Go home!" I whispered faintly. "Go home!"

Her calm gaze went to the table—to the girls. "I heard—" she began.

"Go home!" I clutched her arm, pulled her out of earshot of the still giggling girls. "If you dare tell Mama—"

Christine shook off my hand. "You and Carmelita should have known better," she said reasonably. "Mama should have known better."

"But her feelings will be hurt, Christine," I pleaded. "Please don't ever tell." Quickly I explained about the janitress. Christine shrugged, and with a cool look at the girls standing by the table, she moved away.

And I watched her go—envying her from the bottom of my aching heart. Christine *would* have known better. Christine had been born knowing the proper things. She was never impulsive, headstrong. Never did foolish, stupid things. Christine moved calmly and clearly through life, serene and—invulnerable.

Miss Grimes mounted the platform to announce that since it was getting late, and stormier, all but the girls on the serving committee would be dismissed.

Those of us left stood awkwardly about the tea table. Madeline and

And Mama came in!

Hester would look at the chafing dish and then make silly faces at each other. I examined the tips of my shoes with infinite care. Carmelita moved closer to me, as if for comfort.

It got darker and colder.

One by one, the teachers made their excuses and escaped.

At last, only the serving committee, the Distinguished Visitor, and Miss Grimes were left.

"Miss Lyons should certainly be here with the key soon," Miss Grimes fretted. "Hark! I hear someone coming along the hall."

We watched the doorway hopefully.

And Mama came in!

In her arms she carried two bulky newspaper-wrapped packages.

I rushed over to her, words tumbling from my lips.

"Christine already brought my rain things, Mama."

Silently, desperately, I prayed: Please, oh, please, let Mama go back home before she finds out. If Christine had told! If the girls dared to laugh at my mother—

Mama smiled at me and walked right over to Miss Grimes and Mrs. Winford.

"You will catch cold," she scolded gently. "You need the good hot coffee to warm you up."

Mrs. Winford laughed ruefully. "What wouldn't I give," she sighed, "for a cup of hot coffee!"

Miss Grimes sneezed violently.

Mama clucked sympathetically. "See now what I have brought. Wrapped in the newspaper to keep the warmth." She herded us down to the tea table, smiled at Hester, Thyra, Mary, Madeline, and Carmelita.

She set her packages down. "In this one—the hot coffee." Mama brought forth our copper pitcher, fragrant steam escaping from it.

"And in this one," she unwrapped the other package, "is the hot chocolate for Katrin's friends."

Within a few minutes, Mama had us all comfortably seated about the tea table. Mrs. Winford and Miss Grimes drank great, loud draughts of the steaming coffee. The girls and I were just as greedy with the blessedly hot chocolate.

Mama was always good at making folks comfortable. Now she passed the fancy cookies and the crumbs of currant cake. She said that Mary's cookies were about the nicest she had ever tasted, and she complimented Madeline on the delicious cake. She also commiserated with Thyra about the collapse of the cucumber sandwiches, and wholeheartedly admired Hester's tea set.

Warm and relaxed, we finally drained the last drop of coffee and of chocolate. Miss Grimes thanked Mama so sincerely that she seemed like a different person from the austere Principal we were so used to. She thanked the serving committee, too, and said she was proud of us. She said that although we had been confronted with a trying situation, the cold—and the long wait—we had acted like Little Ladies throughout.

Mrs. Winford complimented us, too. And when she was leaving, she took Mama's hands in both of hers, and they spoke together for a long time.

After Miss Grimes and the visitor had gone, we began to clear the table. Mama worked with us. Hester started to speak several times. Finally she blurted: "I would—excuse me, but—I would like to taste the—meat balls."

I gulped indignantly and started to say something, but Mama shook her head at me. Serenely, she took a clean saucer, heaped it with *kjödboller,* and passed it to Hester. Hester tasted bravely. "Why," she said wonderingly, "why, they're delicious."

And as the rest of us passed our saucers to Mama for portions, she spoke of other Norwegian dishes. Of *svisker grod,* of the festive *Yule kage,* and *pankaka med lingon.* The girls seemed interested.

"You must bring your friends to our home, Katrin," Mama said to me. "I will make for you the *Norske kroner*—the Norvegian cookies."

I didn't, couldn't, answer.

"Perhaps," Mama continued quietly, "the girls would like to see the baby Kaaren."

Hester's face got pink. "A baby? Have you a baby at your house?"

Mama nodded and smiled.

"We had a baby once," Hester said softly. "My little brother. We—we lost him."

"Kathryn has a big attic, too!" Carmelita bragged loudly.

"An attic all your very own?" Madeline asked.

I looked at the girls. Their faces were friendly.

"Next Wednesday," Mama said. "Come next Wednesday after school. We will make of it a party, yes?"

The girls said they would come. We locked the auditorium door and went out into the schoolyard. Hester, Madeline, Thyra, and Mary not only smiled as they left, but waved, too, and said "Last look!"

Carmelita and I trudged after Mama.

"The wine," I remembered suddenly. "What of the wine?"

"Under the table your Mama put it," Carmelita said succinctly. "For Mrs. Kronever, maybe."

"It will be good," I joked, "for her stommack."

And Carmelita and I giggled happily all the way home.

MY SONG YANKEE DOODLE

By CARL GLICK

Illustration by THOMAS VICTOR HALL

"WHAT is this, my son?" said Fong, viewing with distrust the sealed envelope from the American school which Jin-Wai handed him.

"An invitation to a party," replied Jin-Wai unhappily.

Fong beamed. "Better—much better than a note from your teacher suggesting you go immediately to the doctor and have your tonsils removed, which is painful to you and expensive to me."

"I wrote the invitation myself," said Jin-Wai. "Teacher told me what to say."

"How nice," said Fong, breaking the seal of the letter. He handed it to Mrs. Fong. She couldn't read English, but she looked it over carefully, and echoing the sentiments of her husband, said, "How nice!"

"I shall translate it for you," said Fong. "It says that our honorable presence—yours and mine—is requested at a Pageant of All Nations to be held at two o'clock next Wednesday at the American school three blocks away where our unworthy son sits all day trying to learn the American language, so when he becomes a man he can do much big business with the Americans in their American way."

The letter didn't say exactly that, but Jin-Wai knew his father enjoyed his little joke. Mrs. Fong nodded her head happily. It was the first invitation to attend a party she had received since the Fong family had moved last summer from Chinatown to this "faraway foreign city called the Bronx." She had no intention of attending the party as she never left the house, thus displaying the proper Chinese modesty in a woman. But she had been invited. That was a social triumph. To her there was more pleasure in receiving an invitation than in attending.

"Party—party—party!" cried Hing, the four-year-old baby brother, his little face beaming with delight. But then he was very young and had not yet learned to control his emotions. The invitation, however, neither pleased nor delighted Jin-Wai. The very thought of the party terrified him.

"Tell me more about it," suggested Fong.

This was what Jin-Wai had been expecting and dreading. But his father had instructed him in the ways of truthfulness as explained by the philosophers, and he knew by heart "The Five Principles of Filial Duty." A disobedient son is a disgrace to a Chinese father. It makes him lose "face."

So with eyes downcast and hands folded in his lap, Jin-Wai spoke. "The idea is my teacher's," he said. That completely absolved him from any blame in thinking up such a thoroughly stupid and embarrassing thing. "Wednesday is a day of celebration for my teacher."

"A feast?" asked his mother.

"No, honorable mother. A celebration, but we don't eat."

"The Americans at their celebrations make very long speeches and eat very little," explained Fong. "Why this celebration?"

"Because my teacher says all winter long she's been having us sing songs and do dances, and now she celebrates that we've learned the songs and do the dances. So she says we invite our honorable parents to celebrate with her. She says she is proud of us, and we make our honorable parents proud, too. She says the school does this every year and now the time has come again."

"How nice," murmured Fong.

"She says there is more to it than even that also. She says this is a great big free country but it wasn't once, and now it is. And she says it's a free country because so many different people come here with many different ideas. Many foreigners from many foreign lands, but we all belong to one country now and are all alike, and so we put on costumes of our native country and sing American songs and show we are all one big happy family even though we come from different countries, and it's teacher's idea, but I think it's silly."

Fong scratched his chin and said nothing.

"Teacher says that I—" Jin-Wai paused. How he hated to tell the next. "Teacher says each child should come dressed in costume of his own country, but I don't think it's a good idea."

Fong frowned. "A man should never be ashamed of the proper dress of his own country."

Jin-Wai knew that perfectly. Yet how could he explain how he felt to his father? His father didn't have to go day after day to the American school. He wasn't laughed at and called names. It had been difficult from the very first day. He was the only Chinese boy in the classroom, and he wanted so much to make friends. He wanted to be like the American boys, play the games they did, and understand all the beautiful swear words they used so humorously.

So after school he stepped over to a group of boys and said, "Howdy?"

The boys turned and looked him over critically. "Hi, Chink," said one.

"Likee flied licee?" said another.

Then, "Chink! Chink! Chink!" they all began to yell. Jin-Wai, without another word, turned and fled. It wasn't until he reached the corner, out of hearing distance from the taunts, that he stopped and wiped the tears of shame from his eyes.

After that he made no more attempts to be friendly, but kept to himself. And even though the boys still called him "Chink," he had learned to control his tears and keep his face perfectly expressionless, lest they see how they were hurting him.

And now his father thought it would be nice to wear a Chinese costume at the "Celebration." How could he? The boys would laugh at him more than ever, and yell a lot more, too.

Then to his dismay his father said, "I think it very good if you took your younger brother, Jin-Hing, with you to the party. He has never been, and it will be a new experience for him."

"Party—party—party!" cried Hing.

"He is *only* four years old."

"One is never too young to learn," responded Fong. "He will not disgrace you. When one is the father of two sons, one looks with humble but becoming pride upon their appearance in public correctly dressed in the costume of their native country." Jin-Wai went to bed that night sad at heart.

Had Jin-Wai been an American boy he would have argued with his father, pleaded, made threats, stormed, and done everything possible to keep from being "dressed up." But being Chinese and trained to obedience, had his father told him to cut off his hand—he would probably have hesitated a moment, and then obeyed. Better to lose a hand than to cause your honorable parent to lose face.

His father had spoken, and also Hing was keenly anticipating the party. He would not disappoint either one of them. It was the first burden of manliness placed upon him. And while he tossed all night in restless slumber, he knew he would go through with it and never utter one word of complaint.

But the next day he suffered from self-pity. He was sorry he was Chinese. He wished he could be like other boys, accepted as one of them, and not be looked upon as being different. Didn't he like to go roller skating, too? Didn't he like to play marbles? And didn't he know some fancy swear words he could use on the proper occasions? He could even show the boys some new games, if they'd only let him.

Wednesday came as usual. School was dismissed early after the morning session so the children could go home and dress. Jin-Wai's mother had gotten the clothes from a box where they had been packed away in sweet-smelling herbs. And his father stopped work in the laundry to assist and give instructions. Hing giggled and laughed as he was told how to wear the clothes; and white stockings, the black satin shoes, the silk trousers bound at the ankles, and the beautiful blue blouse.

Jin-Wai closed his eyes tightly as his father put on him the long gown that he said was the proper thing for a scholar to wear. And he squirmed as the round black cap with a button on the top was adjusted on his head.

"Very proud father," said Fong. "Very proud, although I am lacking in modesty to say so. You will do me great honor, my sons. Come home after the celebration is over, and we shall have a feast to celebrate my sons' first appearance in public as becomes Chinese gentlemen."

"Proud?" thought Jin-Wai. His father didn't have to walk through the streets wearing skirts like a girl. He didn't have to have everybody look at him and laugh. And when Hing knew what jibes and jeers were awaiting him he wouldn't be smiling so happily either.

Taking Hing by the hand, Jin-Wai trotted out into the street. His father and mother stood in the doorway and waved their hands. Jin-Wai looked neither to the right nor the left, but trudged manfully forward, pulling Hing along after him.

"Too fast! Too fast!" said Hing, who had short legs and had to give a little jump every now and then to keep up.

But Jin-Wai paid no attention. As he drew nearer the school it wasn't half so bad as he thought it would be. Other boys all dressed up were going into the school, and they were all too busy with their mothers standing about and fussing over details of their attire to pay any attention to him. He found his seat in the classroom and pulled Hing up beside him. As the other boys took their places Jin-Wai looked straight ahead and kept saying to himself, "I am obeying my father. I am obeying my father." The only consoling thought he had.

The exercises were to be held in the assembly hall. It wasn't until they were marching to join the children from the other classrooms that Jin-Wai's teacher saw him. She had been fluttering around trying to calm the excited mothers and keep the boys from mussing up their costumes.

"Why, Jin-Wai!" she said breathlessly. "I didn't know you were planning to come dressed up. How nice you look. And is this your brother? Isn't he cute! Dear, dear—we'll have to think up something for you to do. I wish I'd known." And she dashed ahead to separate two boys who had started a fight.

So she hadn't expected him to come dressed up! In vain had been his suffering of the past few days. He could have stayed away, and he wouldn't have been missed. And now Miss Teacher suggested he do something. He wished the schoolhouse would burn down—right to the ground—this very minute—and everybody in it, too—including himself.

Seats were reserved down front for the children. The proud mothers sat in the back.

The program started with everyone singing "My Country, 'Tis of Thee." Then the school orchestra hesitantly played what was called a medley of popular airs. And as each group went upon the stage to perform, the orchestra sounded forth with a few bars of the national anthem of their country.

Five little Scotch boys in kilts danced to the tune of "The Campbells Are Coming." Jin-Wai felt a little happier when he saw that they, too, were wearing skirts. Thank goodness his bare feet weren't being displayed to the public.

A group of Italian children sang several of their folk songs. Some Finnish boys did a drill. The Spanish boys and girls danced to clicking castanets. And so until all the nationalities had performed. As each group finished they lined up on the stage. Only Jin-Wai and his brother remained in the auditorium.

He heard his teacher say. "But I didn't expect. I didn't rehearse anything."

Then the lady whom he knew to be Number One Teacher replied, "He will be so disappointed if he can't come up with the others. And he looks so sweet."

Jin-Wai shuddered. Disappointed? Not he. He was hoping he wouldn't be noticed.

But his teacher bent over him and whispered. "Wouldn't you like to go up on the platform with the others? Just walk around so everyone can see how nice you look. We don't know what melody to play. We haven't practiced the Chinese national anthem—if there is one."

The pride of centuries of a race of proud ancestors came to Jin-Wai's assistance at this crucial moment. Just because he was a despised Chinese didn't mean that he didn't know the proper thing to do. "Play 'Yankee Doodle,' " he said. "Me take that tune."

A whispered consultation was held with the pianist, and as "Yankee Doodle" was pounded out upon the piano, Jin-Wai, holding Hing by the hand, marched upon the stage. There was a burst of applause. For Jin-Wai carried himself with such dignity, walked so proudly, and had such perfect self-possession that he won the hearts of all the mothers. He faced the audience.

"He's going to do something," whispered the teacher.

Jin-Wai bowed. And Hing, properly trained to do as his elder brother did in public, folded his hands in front of his round little tummy and bowed, too. Suddenly Jin-Wai felt proud and happy. Proud he was wearing his Chinese dress. It was beautiful. Much more beautiful than the homemade costumes the other children were wearing. Silk, his was. Not cheesecloth nor cheap material. He wasn't afraid any longer.

He took one step forward and began to recite in Chinese. The audience listened amused but pleased. When he finished he bowed again. And Hing bowed, too. Then Jin-Wai took Hing by the hand and led him to the place on the stage by the side of the other boys from his classroom. There was a loud burst of applause from the audience.

While the orchestra played another number, there was a hurried consultation among the teachers. Then Jin-Wai saw his teacher come upon the stage.

"The prize this afternoon for the best costume and the nicest performance by unanimous choice goes to Jin-Wai Fong, our Chinese neighbor. Come here, Jin-Wai."

Jin-Wai, still holding Hing by the hand, stepped forward. "What was it you said in Chinese?" asked the teacher.

"I said 'The Five Principles of Filial Duty' by Mr. Confucius. It means you should always obey your parents and do exactly as they tell you to do even though it does not seem to you to be the thing for you to do."

Cheers from the audience at these words so touchingly expressed. The suffering mothers present understood and applauded vigorously. Then the teacher handed Jin-Wai the prize—a nice book full of pictures of the presidents and their wives. Jin-Wai bowed low.

"Present?" asked Hing.

For a moment Jin-Wai paused. He had no right to accept this prize. He had not won it because of anything he had wanted to do. He had made no effort of his own. He was not entitled to it. And if he accepted the prize and ever in his own thought he felt pride, he would to himself forever lose face.

So he turned to Hing and placed the prize in his hands. Let Hing have all the honor. Let him be the one tonight to boast to their honorable father. Then Jin-Wai smiled happily. He had done the proper thing—saved his face.

He took his place again with his classmates. The teacher pulled a rope, and the American flag, concealed in the space above the stage, unfurled and hovered over the children as they all began to sing "The Star-Spangled Banner."

"Hi, kid," said the boy next to Jin-Wai under his breath, and smiled when he said it.

"Hi, yourself," replied Jin-Wai. His heart began to thump happily. The first friendly word he had had. Maybe his father did know what was best. Maybe he should always do things in the approved Chinese way—his way. Maybe that was the right way to understanding and friendliness.